Praise for *Shadows at Dusk*

"The author does a fabulous job of keeping the suspense level high, the danger coming, and readers like me on the edge of our seats!"

Reading Is My Superpower

"Fans of romantic suspense will be truly and rightfully impressed."

Interviews & Reviews

Praise for *Cold Light of Day*

"Goddard weaves a gripping mystery set in Southeast Alaska."

Publishers Weekly

"The first book in Goddard's Missing in Alaska series will keep readers glued to their seats as the tension escalates in this thrilling romance."

Booklist

"Elizabeth Goddard has once again proved she is the queen of romantic suspense thrillers."

Urban Lit Magazine

HIDDEN
IN THE
NIGHT

Books by Elizabeth Goddard

Uncommon Justice Series

Never Let Go
Always Look Twice
Don't Keep Silent

Rocky Mountain Courage Series

Present Danger
Deadly Target
Critical Alliance

Missing in Alaska

Cold Light of Day
Shadows at Dusk
Hidden in the Night

MISSING IN ALASKA • 3

HIDDEN IN THE NIGHT

ELIZABETH GODDARD

Revell

a division of Baker Publishing Group
Grand Rapids, Michigan

Published by Revell
a division of Baker Publishing Group
Grand Rapids, Michigan
RevellBooks.com

Printed in the United States of America

Library of Congress Cataloging-in-Publication Data
Names: Goddard, Elizabeth, author.
Title: Hidden in the night / Elizabeth Goddard.
Description: Grand Rapids, Michigan : Revell, a division of Baker Publishing
    Group, 2024. | Series: Missing in Alaska ; 3
Identifiers: LCCN 2023041573 | ISBN 9780800742065 (paperback) | ISBN
    9780800745882 (casebound) | ISBN 9781493445554 (e-book)
Subjects: LCGFT: Christian fiction. | Novels.
Classification: LCC PS3607.O324 H53 2024 | DDC 813/.6—dc23/eng/20231002
LC record available at https://lccn.loc.gov/2023041573

Scripture used in this book, whether paraphrased or quoted by the characters, is from one of the following:

The Holy Bible, English Standard Version® (ESV®). Copyright © 2001 by Crossway, a publishing ministry of Good News Publishers. Used by permission. All rights reserved. ESV Text Edition: 2016

The Holy Bible, New International Version®, NIV®. Copyright © 1973, 1978, 1984, 2011 by Biblica, Inc.® Used by permission of Zondervan. All rights reserved worldwide. www.zondervan.com. The "NIV" and "New International Version" are trademarks registered in the United States Patent and Trademark Office by Biblica, Inc.®

The New King James Version®. Copyright © 1982 by Thomas Nelson. Used by permission. All rights reserved.

Cover design by Mumtaz Mustafa

24   25   26   27   28   29   30   7   6   5   4   3   2   1

To my brother Jeff—
you're the definition of stalwart.
Stay strong! I love you.

The proper function of man is to live, not to exist. I shall not waste my days in trying to prolong them. I shall use my time.

—*Jack London*

Alaska State Troopers' Creed

From the beginning, society has needed a special few willing to face evil and run towards harm for the sake of others.

I am one of those few. I am an Alaska State Trooper.

My environment is harsh, vast, and unforgiving. I thrive in it.
My state is beautiful, majestic, and the last of its kind. I will protect it.

My integrity is absolute. My loyalty is to what is ethical, right, and true.
My courage will not falter. Fear does not control me.
I am the master of my actions and emotions, regardless of circumstance.

Where action is needed, I will act.
If I fall, I will get back up. If I fail, I will try again.
I will either find a way or make one. I will never give up.

I will be physically superior, mentally tougher, and more tenacious than those determined to bring harm to others.
I will enhance my knowledge and proficiency every day. My training will never cease.

I am a quiet professional. I do not seek recognition for my actions.
I accept and will overcome the mental and physical hazards of my profession.
I will do what is necessary to place the needs of others before my own.
Because I endure this, others won't have to.

Titles will not define me. No man will determine my worth.
I will live my life according to the creed I have written on my heart, regardless of my position, rank, or title.

I stand on the shoulders of those who have gone before me.
I am honor bound to maintain the proud traditions of Alaska's finest.
The fallen are honored by my actions and I commit myself daily to the mighty cause of preserving this honor.

I am an Alaska State Trooper.

ONE

GLACIER BAY, SOUTHEAST ALASKA
FEBRUARY

Get in, get out . . . a blizzard's coming.

A path had been plowed through the snow, guiding Ivy Elliott toward the cabin half buried in the white stuff and surrounded by heavily frosted spruce trees. A photo opportunity if there ever was one, but she wasn't here to take pictures.

And she was running out of time.

Her boots clomped onto the sturdy wood porch. Instinct kicked in and she ducked out of the way when a large clump of snow slid off the roof—a mini avalanche that could have buried her where she stood. She calmed her pounding heart and stepped up to the door. Drawing in a deep breath, she knocked. The door creaked open. It hadn't been latched.

"Hello? Anyone home?"

No one answered.

Prickles crawled up her back. Something wasn't right here, but even so, she was uncomfortable with entering the man's cabin, so she knocked again.

A muted stillness, silence that only a snow-covered land-scape could create, closed in on her. She glanced at the setting, expecting serenity at the sheer beauty to flood her. Instead, the eerie sensation of being watched pinged through her.

Removing her gloves, Ivy reached under her coat, freed her handgun from its holster, and gripped it at her side. She drew in a breath of arctic cold and puffed out white clouds.

One more time she knocked.

No one is home and they left the door open.

Common sense, reason, told her this was a fool's errand. That she should turn around and go. But she wasn't leaving without what she had come for. She eased the door open. "Hello, anyone home? I'm sorry for the intrusion, but I'm only checking on you to make sure you're all right."

Deep shadows obscured the interior of the cabin. Not even a fire in the fireplace to provide warmth or light. She opened the door wider, and the gray of day illuminated the dim space inside, revealing an overturned table and toppled chairs. A familiar coppery scent met her nose. Her breath caught. Pushing the door all the way open, she stepped inside.

A man lay on the floor, pooled in blood. Stunned at the sight, her heart seized. She gasped for breath.

He moved his hand.

Still alive!

She rushed forward and dropped to her knees. "Just hold on. You're going to be okay," she lied. A knife was buried in his chest. "If I pull it out . . ." He could bleed out. Considering the amount of blood on the floor, it might already be too late.

She put her gun away and yanked a blanket from the nearby worn-out couch. She feared pulling out the knife would only create more problems. Still, she pressed the blanket around the knife to try to slow the bleeding. "I'm going to call for help. You must have a radio or a satellite phone. Something." But she already knew from experience not everyone in remote Alaska wanted to be connected or bothered or found.

Taking his shaky, weak hands, she placed them on the blanket. "Here. Press here. Can you keep the pressure on? I don't want you to lose more blood."

Even in the shadowy room she could see his pale-gray skin, and that he was almost gone.

"Stay with me. Stay with me." *God, what do I do? Please don't let this man die.*

When his hands slid away, she pushed harder against the blanket, willing the blood to stop. With her free hand, she fished in her coat pocket for Carrie's two-way radio to call for help.

His mumbled words drew her back to him and she leaned down until her ear was near his lips.

"Find . . . her." He released a long, slow breath as if it was his last.

Her heart seized. She glanced at his eyes and watched the life fade away. Grief constricted her chest.

Find her . . .

Heavy footfalls bounded across the porch and into the cabin, startling Ivy. She looked up to stare point-blank at the muzzle of a gun and lifted her bloody hands in surrender.

I didn't kill him.

TWO

SHADOW GAP, SOUTHEAST ALASKA
TWO DAYS EARLIER

Nothing on earth could have made Ivy Elliott come to Alaska in the dead of winter except the threat to someone she loved and held dear—her mother. Nothing she wanted more than to get this dirty deal done and over with and get home. Impatience would get the best of her if she didn't act right now.

She pushed from the booth where she'd waited for almost an hour and approached the tall, elderly man wiping down the varnished wood countertop—a thing of beauty, like everything in this spacious establishment, complete with animal trophies on the log walls.

His weathered face lit up and his eyes crinkled with his smile. "Ike Lively at your service. You can call me Ike."

Lively? "So, you own this place, the Lively Moose?"

"Sure do. My wife, Birdy, and I started this place decades ago. What can I do for you?"

Ivy didn't want to invite anyone into her private business, but she needed help. "I was supposed to meet someone. Alina Wolf. Do you know her?"

"Lina? Sure do. She works for me. But she's off this week."

"She isn't answering her cell," Ivy said. "And I don't know

where she lives." Ivy hadn't been able to discover that before she got here, unfortunately. Alina—Lina—hadn't been willing to share her address but said to meet her at the Lively Moose.

He nodded with a thoughtful look. "You look like you get a lot of sun. You come a long way just to meet her?"

This guy saw too much. "Yes." She'd leave it at that. Best not to give too much information unless she had to.

His gaze lifted to look at something over her shoulder and his smile brightened. "Hank. I'll have your joe up in a jiff."

Joe up in a jiff. Ivy couldn't help but like Ike Lively.

Then Chewbacca—Hank—slid onto a stool next to her and bobbed a chin hidden by a long, thick beard. "You looking for Lina?"

She took a sip from her mug as she turned to face him, then nodded.

Ike poured coffee into Hank's thermos and looked at Ivy. "Miss . . . I never got your name."

"Ivy."

"Ivy, this is Hank Duncan. He plows the snow off the roads and might be able to help."

"Call me Hank."

How could a road-plow guy help? But if Mr. Nice Guy Ike Lively trusted Hank the Wookiee, Ivy could use the help. "She was supposed to meet me here an hour ago."

"It doesn't sound like Lina to miss an appointment." So, Hank knew Lina that well. His friendly eyes held deep concern and he shared a look with the Lively Moose owner. "I should get out to the cabin and check on her. I plowed out that way two days ago, so it's not like she's stuck." Hank turned his worried eyes on Ivy. "You ready to go?"

Ivy nearly spewed her coffee. *What?* "Now?"

He blinked, then his eyes widened. "Yes. Now. I need to make sure she's okay."

She hadn't expected such a quick response, but she should

have. In her past and current lines of work, she knew to be quick on her feet. She would blame her slowness on the cold.

And just like that, Ivy found herself inside a rumbling, old dump truck that smelled of exhaust and diesel and had a snowplow on the front. On the ride over, she heard all about Hank's quest for Bigfoot and that he was the president of the National Search for Sasquatch Club. He sounded knowledgeable and almost convinced her of the mysterious creature's existence. Hank claimed there was so much out there that humankind still didn't know. New species of creatures were being discovered all the time, and he named a few. That was fair.

Ivy didn't know much about mythical creatures and cryptozoology, but she did know about books. Old books. Valuable books. And she doubted a man who searched the wilds of Alaska for a big, hairy, humanlike creature with enormous feet wanted to hear about old books. Ivy could share a thing or two about her past job with the FBI, but thinking about that only depressed her.

Hank steered off the main road and the big vehicle bounded along another plowed road, and then, up ahead, a small clapboard structure came into view. The path to the house was much too narrow for the truck and Hank hit the brakes and powered down the noisy vehicle that must have announced their arrival.

"I usually shovel the path up to the house for Lina. Looks like she shoveled recently, though." He turned to Ivy while opening his door. "Let's go."

She caught his arm. His impatience to check on Lina might have affected his better judgment. "Hank. You don't even know me. Are you sure Lina wants to see me? To be honest, I half thought she changed her mind about meeting me." More than half.

He took in her face with a thoughtful expression. "She would have called you."

Okay, then.

Ivy climbed out of the big truck, dropping down into the deep snow, glad she'd worn boots. But maybe snowshoes would have been better. Hank was already halfway up the path. Ivy hurried to catch up with him. Big mistake.

Her feet slipped out from under her.

Emptied of air, Ivy's lungs ached. Tall spruce trees weighed down by snow hung over her. The beauty could have taken her breath away—if she had any, that is. She filled her lungs with cold, crisp air. Hank's face, wrinkled with concern, looked down on her.

"You okay?" Hank offered his hand.

Ivy grabbed it and got to her feet. Nothing hurt. "I'm good. Thanks. The snow cushioned my fall."

He looked her over, his gaze lingering on her feet.

"They're Lobbens," she said. "Good in Alaska and Norway, I hear."

"I was gonna say you need better shoes."

"I slipped on a patch of ice, that's all. I'll be more careful."

He turned and continued toward the cabin, once again leaving her behind with his long strides. Despite Hank's assurance Lina wouldn't have stood her up, Ivy had the feeling the woman had changed her mind. Lina hadn't called because she didn't want a confrontation and since she hadn't given Ivy her address, she wouldn't have to worry about facing her. But Lina hadn't considered the Hank factor. And Ivy was probably making this all up in her head.

Hank stomped up onto the porch and knocked on the door. No. He banged. Hank probably wasn't capable of a simple knock. His form was big and intimidating—like the mythical creature he sought—and Ivy took advantage of that and remained behind him. If Lina had been avoiding Ivy, she might not open the door for her. But she'd open for Hank, and Ivy could get a few moments with her, which was all she needed.

Ivy was on a mission.

And she had no intention of leaving empty-handed. She had to convince Lina to honor their agreement.

The door creaked open and the wind chose that moment to shove into Ivy, nearly pushing her into Hank's back.

"What are you doing here?" Lina asked Hank.

Ivy recognized her voice from their phone conversation.

"I'm checking on you, that's what. Seems you missed your appointment." He stepped to the side and exposed Ivy.

Looking into Lina's shocked face, Ivy lost her ability to speak.

"I didn't show up because I didn't want to." Pressing her lips into a thin line, the woman crossed her arms.

See, Hank? Ivy stepped forward. "I came all the way from Florida. Can you at least give me a few moments of your time . . . please?"

Lina's frown deepened and her shoulders dropped. She glanced at Hank with a look of frustration, then opened the door wider, gesturing for both Ivy and Hank to enter. "Coffee's on the woodstove if you want it, Hank."

So, no coffee for Ivy? This didn't seem to be the same woman she'd spoken with on the phone—excited to be rid of what she believed was a curse on her family.

She got the feeling Lina remained standing so that Ivy would state her business and leave.

Ivy gestured at the chairs. "May I?"

Lina nodded, her face scrunched up as if Ivy caused her agony. The woman had changed her mind, and Ivy had to convince her to let go. She couldn't return without it.

Her throat tightened. *God, help me convince her.*

Ivy sat. "I didn't mean to intrude, but I didn't know what to think when you weren't at the Lively Moose. Now that I'm here I'll take a look at it, and then once I determine it's genuine, I'll pay you what we agreed."

Lina's face was pinched. Emotion flashed in her eyes. "Not here."

"Then where? That's why I'm here. That's why . . ." *I came all this way in the middle of winter.*

It was either her or her mother, who was in no condition to make this journey.

"No. I mean, it's not here. It's not in town. It's not at my house. Not here."

Ivy stared at the Alaska Native woman. Alina Wolf was not saying the words Ivy wanted to hear. Ivy pursed her lips and worked hard to compose herself.

Patience.

She could blow this if she wasn't careful. If it wasn't too late. "When we spoke on the phone, you agreed to hand it over, once and for all."

Lines creased the woman's already aged face. "It's my granddaughter, Danna. I sent her to her uncle's before the big storm that's coming. I . . . I didn't know she took it."

Ivy slowed her pounding heart. She could fix this. All she had to do was find the granddaughter. Hank approached and offered Ivy a cup of coffee. She thanked him and took it. The mug would give her a moment to consider her response.

"Well, then I'll go meet her at her uncle's. Let her know I'm coming and that you and I had an agreement. Or do you think she'll give me trouble?" *Oh no. Wrong choice of words.*

"She won't be trouble, but I think she's *in* trouble."

Ivy sat forward. "What do you mean?"

Lina stumbled over and sank onto the sofa. "She finished school and graduated early and wanted to stay with her uncle, my brother, in Dunbar. It's a small town near Glacier Bay and an artist community. She wants to be a writer."

"And that's the reason she took the manuscript. I get it." And that wasn't good news for Ivy.

"No, you don't. When you contacted me, I heard the desperation in your voice. The sister you lost and her love of the famed author's novels. Your mother's cancer returned. I couldn't say no, but I should have."

Lina made Ivy sound like the worst negotiator, but she'd been so desperate, so scared. She wished she hadn't shared so much, but she couldn't risk rejection. Not with that jerk breathing down her neck, threatening her if she didn't secure it. The secret he would reveal would kill her mother faster than the cancer she battled.

Ivy shoved down the frustration. "Tell me why you say Danna is in trouble."

"I haven't been able to reach her or her uncle for two days. She was supposed to call me when she got there. Danna just turned eighteen. Still, I never should have allowed her to go alone." Lina rubbed her arms, her expression wrinkled with concern.

"Did you call the police?"

"Dunbar doesn't have police. I reported my concern to the local PD here, and they referred me to the Alaska State Troopers. I've heard nothing."

"You could have told me when you knew she'd left with the manuscript. Called me before I came all this way."

"I'm worried. Scared for her. It's cursed. You've heard the rumors. I didn't keep it here with us. But I knew where it was. Now she has it. And I have a strong feeling that something has happened to her. I just can't shake it."

And Ivy had a feeling Lina wasn't sharing everything. Ivy glanced around the space trying to think of what to say. How could she help? Photos on the mantel drew her attention. She rose and moved closer to look at the picture of Lina with a young woman. "This is your granddaughter, Danna?"

"Yes." Lina joined her at the mantel.

Ivy took in the big brown eyes, and emotions surged through her. The girl might as well have been Ivy's sister, Grace, staring back at her. Calling out to her. The air whooshed from her lungs, and she fought to keep her composure in front of these complete strangers.

For years, Ivy had prayed for the opportunity. The chance to make right the wrongs. To redeem her biggest mistake, leaving Grace alone for a few minutes only to lose her forever.

She blinked back the sudden onslaught of tears. Held them back. Hadn't she been waiting for the moment when she could find someone else's sister? In this case, a granddaughter? Maybe this wasn't for her, but then again, her search for that blasted manuscript had brought her here.

And she found herself asking, "What can I do to help? I was a federal agent before. And I still investigate. I still track." She might be a rare-book specialist now, but she hadn't forgotten her FBI training and could track people. A person. A young woman.

Danna.

Lina touched Ivy's arm, drawing her gaze.

Ivy studied the older woman.

As if coming to a decision, Lina drew a breath. "I could have called you. But my mind was filled with fear for Danna. I've heard nothing. No one can give me answers. No one cares about us here. And I know you desperately want that manuscript. It belonged to our grandfather . . . so I don't know if you'll get it back even if you find her. Maybe you're here for that reason, but if you find my granddaughter, you'll find the manuscript."

Had Providence brought Ivy to this place, this point in time, for this reason? She didn't need to think about it or pray about it. She *knew* this was meant for her. "I'll find Danna."

Forget the manuscript.

Ivy had a new mission now.

THREE

Sunshine Girl was here.
　　In town.
　　During the winter.
Why?

At 3:30 in the morning, Alaska State Trooper Nolan Long clenched his jaw and concentrated on the circle of light the headlights created as he accelerated faster than was safe along the snow-packed road. The Alaska State Troopers dispatch center had received a report of a woman's scream. Trooper Carl Westfield had been in the area trying to stop poachers, but he was close and decided to answer the callout regarding possible domestic abuse. Carl was with Alaska's Fish and Wildlife Protection Troopers, also known as "Brownshirts," or rather, Alaska Wildlife Troopers, and would soon be transferring to Hoonah, covering the western region of Southeast Alaska, the region he'd wanted to begin with.

Carl had then contacted Nolan. "Nolan. You need to see this. Get here as fast as you can."

He hadn't known that Nolan was on vacation—officially at midnight. But Nolan hadn't left for Florida yet. His flight wasn't until the day after tomorrow. Since Sunshine Girl was here in his state, in his town, he had no reason to visit her home state to surprise her. Vacation or not, he headed out to help Carl. Backup in Alaska could take hours, and regardless, it didn't matter if he was off duty or on vacation, he was going to help. And now he was back on the clock.

The only Alaska State Trooper assigned to this region—well, besides Wildlife Trooper Carl—Nolan had been asleep and having the worst dream. Or the best dream, depending on how he looked at it. But the shrill sound of his cell—loud, meant to wake him from the dead—had pulled him away from that dream about Sunshine Girl.

The one he'd let get away.

He'd seen her here in Shadow Gap.

Yesterday.

What was she doing here in Alaska, and in Shadow Gap of all places? They'd met when he was working out of Fairbanks, eight hundred miles away on mainland Alaska.

The sudden call to action had been like a splash of cold water in the face. He'd scrambled out of bed and into his AST uniform, including bulletproof vest and knit cap, and he'd holstered his Glock 22.

Now he steered down the dark road in his state vehicle, a Dodge Enforcer, facing the cold of an Alaska winter. At least Southeast Alaska wasn't as brutal as the mainland and he had decent light during the daytime. And for this callout, he hadn't needed to use a snowmobile, boat, or plane. The home was several miles outside of Shadow Gap. He passed a vehicle going the opposite direction. The poachers Carl had wanted to catch?

He blinked and, just ahead, spotted a moose standing in the middle of the road.

Great.

He slowed and the vehicle slid, almost slamming into the beast. The huge creature turned its head and stared at him as if ready to engage in a deadly challenge, but suddenly trotted off the road. Nolan released the breath he'd held. Too many moose collisions this time of year. He kept driving until he finally pulled in to park behind Carl's trooper vehicle.

Carl hopped out as Nolan headed toward him.

"The locals are on their way too," Carl said.

Shadow Gap PD. Maybe even the police chief, Nolan's sister.

"What did you find?"

"I'd rather you look yourself. Form your own opinion." Shining his flashlight, Carl headed toward the house, leading Nolan.

Their boots crunched through the frozen snow and then they hiked up the rickety steps. Carl hesitated and gestured for Nolan to open the door and go through first.

"You sure the house is empty?" Nolan asked.

"Yep. I cleared it, but I found something."

Nolan kept his firearm at the ready, all the same. He pushed the door all the way open and led with his flashlight, shining the beam around the small, dirty house. Living room first and then the kitchen. Unwashed dishes in the sink. Frigid temps and no power.

An overturned shelf and broken chair caught his attention. Then the beam of light landed on a large, dried stain on the old brown carpet. Crouching, Nolan examined the stain closely. Looked like the carpet had been saturated with blood. Nolan gritted his teeth. He didn't hold out much hope for whoever had bled here on the carpet.

"Well? What do you think?"

"That's a lot of blood. Can't bleed like that if you accidentally cut yourself while shaving." His gut tightened. Not like the guy would carve up an animal for its meat inside his home when he could do that outside.

"That's what I thought too," Carl said. "The homeowner is Blane Walker. Male in his fifties."

Crouching, Nolan got a closer look. "This was a major, likely life-threatening, wound."

"You're thinking possible homicide then?" Carl asked.

"We'll find out," Nolan said. But they needed to find the guy or his body. "The big question—where is he?" Nolan stood, flashing the light around.

"Like I said. There's no one in the house." Carl cleared his throat. "No . . . body."

"What about in the woods? Maybe he left."

"We'd see a blood trail. But there's just . . . nothing."

"Almost as if someone might have wrapped his body up and carried him out." Nolan shook his head, sick at the sight of blood. This was looking more like foul play every second.

It triggered memories and the reason he'd needed to get away. "Let's collect as much evidence as we can."

Carl rubbed his jaw, then pulled on evidence gloves. "I've already collected some, but I could get more, maybe. MCU will want to as well."

Alaska Bureau of Investigation's major crimes unit would probably take lead in a murder, but they all worked together. "We need more information before sending this over."

"What more do you know about Walker?" Nolan asked. "Was anyone else living here?"

"I don't know much more than the neighbor told me when I got here. I sent him home. Walker lived alone. The neighbor had some concerns. Said he'd planned to report the guy but then it wasn't his business. He didn't want to get involved. But he decided to call tonight."

Nolan shook his head. "What are you talking about?"

"The neighbor—Boyd Victus—heard a woman's screams two nights ago, and then again tonight."

Nolan stiffened. He didn't like the sound of this. A woman's screams. Nobody home. Blood-soaked carpet. "I'll talk to the neighbor."

Maybe he was off duty but now he was on duty for the moment. Time was essential in cases like this, and law enforcement officers were few and far between in this backcountry state. He'd talk to his sergeant out of Juneau, Alton Rogers, who would probably still insist that Nolan take his vacation and get his head straight. He'd been the one to insist Nolan go to begin with.

Emergency vehicle lights flashed through the windows. Shadow Gap PD had arrived. Nolan headed outside to get some fresh, cold air and meet the locals. Shadow Gap Police Department's primary jurisdiction was the city limits, and Alaska State Troopers covered the rural areas.

He couldn't force a smile into his grim expression when his sister, Autumn, stepped out of her official Shadow Gap vehicle, a Ford Interceptor. Nolan opened his mouth—

An explosion rocked through his body, and he turned, stepping back.

"Watch out!" Autumn shoved him aside and they rolled onto the ground.

Chunks rained down on them. He wasn't sure how many seconds—even minutes—passed before he shook off the daze. Ears ringing, he assisted Autumn to her feet. They both stared at what remained of the house, now up in flames.

Carl!

FOUR

In the gray morning light, Nolan stood in the wintry mix of rain and snow, staring at the remnants of the house. The fire chief had been out earlier with his crew and had put out the fire that had resulted from the explosion. The fire chief was now working on his assessment of what had caused the blast.

Flying debris had damaged Carl's vehicle, which had been parked closer to the house. A portion of the front door had gone through the windshield and lodged in the dash. Nolan hiked forward, his boots crunching through the snow that was turning to slush. He opened the door of the damaged vehicle, half-surprised it cooperated.

Nolan slid into the seat, his mind racing to the fact that Carl had sat in this vehicle hours before his death. He'd been staking out the area and planting deer decoys. Poachers would use light to catch glowing eyes in the night, and it was illegal to shoot a deer under those circumstances.

Carl had joined the AST as a wildlife trooper two years ago.

Nolan's whole body was tense with shock and grief. A vacation now was out of the question, but he'd have to wait to hear from Alton on that. In the meantime, he was waiting on MCU out of Juneau to arrive to look at the scene, and together they would work through what happened to find answers. The major crimes division assisted and coordinated with patrol and rural troopers and focused on homicides, suicides, unexplained deaths . . . the list went on. Basically, anything serious.

Nothing more serious than murder with the death of a wildlife trooper involved. ABI units like the MCU all worked together because experience showed a lot of crimes were interconnected across the state. Drug rings. Human trafficking rings. Another list that, unfortunately, went on.

In Carl's vehicle, Nolan thought through the events of the night before—a few hours ago—much of which had been recorded via Nolan's dash cam. Nolan wasn't wearing a body cam, but he wore a personal audio-recording device. He'd turned all his equipment on—force of habit. Carl's dash cam had been taken out with the door through the windshield. Of course.

Why'd you have to come first, Carl? Why did it have to be you?

What had happened here? A propane explosion? Just bad luck and timing? Or something more sinister, considering that it looked like Blane Walker had been murdered? Carl had been inside collecting evidence—now the evidence was destroyed. Nolan couldn't push aside the sense that the explosion had been intentional. But he had no facts. Just conjecture.

But if someone had deliberately triggered that explosion, hoping to bury evidence, they'd only drawn the attention of the state of Alaska. A wildlife trooper had been killed.

Carl . . . Nolan shook his head, bile rising up his throat.

Now and then Nolan would work with Carl and had gotten to know him. Connected. Even if they hadn't, no one ever wanted to see a fellow officer down, killed on the job. Carl had been a friend. They'd gone fishing together. Camping. Enjoyed this great state and shared stories.

Depending on what his sergeant said, Nolan would have to let go and move on when his counterparts arrived, but until then, he would keep working this. Right now he itched to question the neighbor, Boyd Victus. He wasn't getting anywhere sitting in Carl's vehicle. Better head over to talk to the closest neighbor.

He started to get out but noticed the top edge of a file folder sticking up between the passenger seat and door. He reached over and tugged it free, then flipped it open.

A girl's photograph fell out. *What's this?*

Movement outside the window caught his attention. The Shadow Gap police chief.

Nolan grabbed the photo, closed the folder, and tucked it under his arm. He climbed out of the vehicle and faced his sister. Her features grim, Autumn did not look happy. How long had she been standing there?

He offered a smile, though, despite the circumstances. "Nice welcome home after your honeymoon, huh?"

They hadn't gotten any small talk in last night after the explosion. Even now, it seemed inappropriate.

She bobbed her chin slightly. "I would have preferred a nice, quiet return," she said.

"I've got this, Autumn. I'm conducting the preliminary investigation."

"I assume someone from MCU is on the way."

"Yep." He would have been promoted to MCU if he hadn't chosen to remain a rural trooper, but being a patrol guy gave him the freedom to remain close to his family. The only issue was that as a rural trooper he traveled constantly to cover his region, preventing him from being available for his family as much as he'd wanted.

Family . . . was everything. He'd learned that early on, and then was reminded again when Autumn and Dad recently got into trouble. He wouldn't leave them again. Though, really, Autumn was in very good hands now that she was married to Grier. She wouldn't appreciate Nolan's thoughts on the matter, though, because Autumn had taken care of herself and been on her own—was a fantastic police chief—so it wasn't like she needed Grier to take care of her. But Nolan's perspective was that everyone needed others to have their back, whether professionally or personally.

He realized she had been studying him while he'd been lost in thought.

"Even if they're coming to assist, you know you're not one lonely trooper out here. Shadow Gap PD is here to help."

"I know. I'll keep you informed, don't worry. Carl and I had assessed the home and had all but decided Walker had been murdered. If we were right about that, his killer is still out there. Could be anyone. Too many tire tracks back and forth to look at that. I want to take pictures and look for prints coming or going and get what I can before the weather turns. That blizzard is supposed to hit early tomorrow."

She angled her face. "So, what about your vacation? What about Florida? You were supposed to leave tomorrow, right? And surprise her?" Hope surged in her sad expression. Hope for her brother to find someone. Truth was, Autumn had given him the crazy idea to go after the girl. Head to Florida.

"With what's happened here, that could be put on hold. But it's pointless now."

"Nolan. Alton wanted you to take some time—"

"She's here, Autumn."

"What? Sunshine Girl?"

"Yeah." Though he was dressed for the winter weather, the chill was starting to get to him. Maybe they should get back into one of their vehicles to finish this conversation.

"Why is she here?"

"I don't know." But he was itching to find out.

"Well, did she come to see you? To find you? Why don't you know? Why didn't you approach her when you saw her?"

It wasn't as simple as all that. She hadn't come to town to see him, or else he would have heard from her already. "I'm focused on this investigation right now. Carl's death and Walker's probable murder."

Ivy Elliott would have to wait.

Autumn's expression turned serious. "Whatever happened here is in my backyard," she said. "It could affect us all. Like—"

"This isn't anything like what happened before," he said. Criminals descending on their small town hidden in a fjord.

Her eyes narrowed. "You know that how?"

He lifted his hands in surrender. "I don't know anything yet."

She eyed the file he held beneath his arm. Then her gaze shifted to Carl's vehicle.

"Did you happen to notice the door in the windshield?"

He turned to look. "How could I miss it?"

She moved closer to the vehicle and leaned against the front end to peer at the front door now lodged in the windshield. "That looks an awful lot like a bullet hole."

He tugged out his cell and took a few more pictures. He'd gathered as much evidence as he could and shouldn't have missed that. "Could have been there already."

"Or it could explain why blood was all over the floor."

"I hadn't imagined the evidence would be destroyed in an explosion," he said.

"No one was expecting that."

He shook his head and looked at the house. "Especially not Carl."

She frowned and reached over to gently squeeze his shoulder. "You need to get some rest."

"What I need to do is question the neighbor who called. Carl talked to him." And now Carl was dead.

"I'll do it," she said.

"That isn't your call."

"You look too haggard. You haven't slept all night." Autumn was taking that same tone that Alton had taken with him when he urged him to get away.

"I'll be fine." What was with the two of them, anyway?

"You really want to get to the bottom of it, then let me talk to Victus," she said. "Then you can come back with fresh eyes. Bring Grier out with you. He's good at reading between the lines."

They were all trained to do just that, but Autumn especially admired Grier, her new husband. Nolan wouldn't fault her for that.

"I need to be here when someone from MCU gets here," he said.

"Yeah? When will that be?"

She has a point. "I—"

"Go. A few hours of sleep and you'll be as good as new."

Doubtful. But he'd missed the bullet hole. What else had he missed? Alton had wanted Nolan to take a break. He wasn't helping anyone if he couldn't at least do his best.

"I'll look over the scene again," she said. "And talk to Victus. We work together out here." She must have thought he needed more convincing.

"All right. Call me if you learn anything interesting."

"Will do." Autumn had his back. He trudged over to his vehicle and got in.

The explosion, Carl's death, weighed heavily on him as he drove away.

Back at Dad's, where he was house-sitting while his father was gallivanting around the world with the love of his life, Nolan showered and then wrote up his report of the incident. He headed for the bed, still crumpled from the night before. A text dinged. He couldn't shut his phone down to sleep through this. *I shouldn't be sleeping.*

It was Autumn.

I hope you're sleeping and your cell is turned
off. When you wake up, thought you'd want to

know that Victus left town. Caught a ferry down
to Juneau. I'm contacting Juneau PD.

What?

And I need to let AST in Juneau know.

Had Victus already planned a trip? Why was he suddenly leaving? They still had questions. Carl would have told him to stick around.

He sent a text to his sergeant, then there was a knock at the door. Didn't look like he was getting any rest.

Nolan opened the door and couldn't believe his eyes. Maybe he should have expected this.

He opened his mouth but the words wouldn't come.

FIVE

Surprise rocked through her. Warmth surged all the way to her toes and, unfortunately, it had started in her cheeks. She hadn't expected that Nolan Long would be the trooper she would find.

This guy she'd thought about since meeting him last September stood before her looking crumpled and haggard but still good. *Real* good. Before, he'd always been in uniform. Now, in a white T-shirt that stretched tight across his chest, he stared down at her with his ocean-blue eyes, which she remembered were flecked with silver and gray, and his thick, dark hair askew.

Nolan.

Ivy took a step back. Could she be any more obvious? But maybe he hadn't noticed her ridiculous reaction. Still, with that strange look on his face, maybe he had.

Say something!

"I know . . . I'm showing up out of the blue"—*but it's not what you think. I'm not here stalking you.* "I . . . I wouldn't be here unless I was desperate. No. Wait. I shouldn't have come. I didn't know it was you I'd find here." She was making a mess of things.

Turn around. Walk away.

Ivy whirled around.

"Ivy, wait." Nolan's voice was gruff, pained.

The disturbing quality stopped her, pulled her around. He

reached forward, and she let him tug her all the way in. Standing much too close, his hand on her arm, he shut the door. "It's too cold out there. Stay for a while. I'll make you some tea. I think I saw some in the pantry." He started toward the kitchen.

Ivy followed. What did it mean that he remembered she liked tea? Anything?

He glanced over his shoulder. "Who did you think you would find here if not me?"

Ivy shouldn't have said those words. "I . . . uh . . . the lady at the police department told me to come to this address to talk to the Alaska State Trooper." Admittedly, when she found a residence at the address, she thought it kind of strange, but Ivy figured the lone trooper for the region must be working out of his home.

"The lady? The police chief?"

"Huh? Oh, no, the woman at the desk. She apparently works as dispatch too."

"Oh, you mean Tanya. I wasn't sure if you'd meant one of our officers Angie Ledger or my sister, Autumn. She's the police chief."

Nolan had mentioned her to Ivy before. "I didn't get her name. I thought you were working in another part of the state. I . . . that's why I was so surprised." Much more than simply surprised.

Ivy had wanted to follow up on Alina's claims about her granddaughter, especially the mention that no one cared, which basically alluded to the fact that no one was looking into Danna's whereabouts. Before Ivy followed Danna's trail, she'd check with law enforcement. What was being done, if anything?

Since Chief Long was out working an investigation, the woman—Tanya—had sent her to the local trooper. Ivy couldn't forget the strange look Tanya had given her. At the time, Ivy hadn't known the local trooper was Nolan. Now that she thought about it, Tanya acted as if she thought Ivy and Nolan had something going on between them. Which they didn't. One kiss, one long, personal conversation by a fire, didn't make them an actual couple. Even if it had, she'd gone home to Florida and hadn't talked to him since. No Facebook or social media contact—neither of them was on social media. In her former job, Ivy had learned too much about the dangers of the loss of privacy to ever participate.

Nolan found a canister of tea bags. He set a mug in the single-cup maker and turned it on. After hot water poured into the cup, he slid it forward with the tea bags. "Do you take anything with that? Sugar? Milk?"

"No, thanks. This is fine."

"Good, because I'd have to go digging for it. I'm just house-sitting. I hope you like the tea." He glanced at his reflection in a glass cabinet and ran both hands through his hair to brush through the mess.

"I'm sorry I woke you up."

"I wasn't asleep."

"You could have fooled me." She grinned as she steeped the tea bag. She didn't need tea, hadn't wanted the tea, but he'd offered and here they were.

"Nolan . . . I . . ."

How did she explain? "I'm sure you're surprised to see me. I'm here in Shadow Gap on business."

Had he flinched at her words? She must have imagined his re-action, because why else would she be here? Emotion thickened in her throat. Over the last several months, she'd found herself thinking of him often. In their short time together, necessitated by an unexpected storm, she'd connected with Nolan Long.

She'd never met anyone like him.

She'd wanted to see him again, but it had seemed impossible, and really, what was the point? It wasn't like she could stop in and say she was in the neighborhood when he lived in Alaska and she lived in Florida. Theirs was a case of opposites attract, only in geographic terms. They lived at the complete opposite ends of the country, as far as two people could get from each other—well, discounting Hawaii.

Nolan pressed his elbows on the counter and slid forward, his hands clasped a few inches from her teacup. "I know. Why else would you be here?"

A nervous laugh escaped. "Right. I mean, of course I wouldn't fly all the way here for another reason." *Like to see you. Just. Stop. Talking.* Why had she said that? He didn't need to hear an explanation.

If her words had affected him, he appeared to have recovered. What had she expected? That he would miss her after knowing her for just a few days? Well, she certainly had pined away for him—her mother had caught her, and that had been awkward.

She released a heavy exhale. *Focus.* "I'm in the middle of a complicated situation."

"Last time I saw you, you were in the middle then too. Go ahead. What can the Alaska State Troopers do to help you?"

Ah. Now, he'd gone all impersonal on her. Just as well. Nolan still leaned on the counter and his nearness made her uncomfortable. She remembered what it felt like to be in his arms.

No. Don't go there.

Was he off today or something? She sipped her tea rather than reveal where her thoughts had gone with a simple look. At the thought of telling him everything—about Mom and the blackmail—her hands shook, and it was all she could do to set the shaking cup down before spilling all the tea.

Nolan hadn't missed that, and he rushed around the counter. He almost hugged her. Almost. His hands hovered near her arms. "Are you all right? Ivy, what's happened? What's going on?"

And in his voice she heard the tenderness she missed so much. How easy it would be to just slip off the stool and slide forward into his arms. Savor the feel of them around her. And she remembered that one ridiculous but wonderful moment of weakness when they'd shared a tender, meaningful kiss that felt like it could last forever.

When they both knew it couldn't.

She slid off the stool, all right, and moved into the living room, putting distance between them. Now she could breathe.

"It's Mom. The cancer returned." *I want to go home. What am I doing?*

Compassion filled his eyes. "Oh, Ivy. I'm so sorry."

A slight crease grew in his brow. He had to be wondering what any of that had to do with her visit to the police department and getting sent here. But he didn't ask the question. Because he was a gentleman. He was caring and compassionate. She knew that after a very short time with him.

He gestured toward the sofa and chairs. "Have a seat. Make yourself comfortable. Can I get you more tea? Or anything else?"

"No, I'm fine." Ivy moved to sit in the well-worn recliner that reminded her of her father's chair. Mom kept it in the living room, but they never sat in it.

A small fire in the fireplace warmed the room. Nolan grabbed a poker to stoke it. Those memories rushed her again.

Then he turned to stare at her, questions in his eyes.

Why had she come to Alaska when her mother had cancer? Why was she here, asking for his help?

And it hit her—*How is it that I'm sitting here with Nolan by a fire all over again?*

He studied her, waiting for her explanation, and that drew her back to the moment. Where did she even start? She'd come here to tell him about the missing girl, but maybe she owed him an explanation as to why she was here too.

"Just take your time."

Nolan sat across from her on the sofa.

"That's just it. I don't have time. I should be with Mom, but instead I'm here." Ivy lifted her head and sat back. Nolan again waited and listened.

36

"I told you about my sister, how she went missing when I was supposed to be watching her." She'd connected with Nolan that night by the fire. She'd told him—a complete stranger, really—about her responsibility in her sister's death. He had his own story, his own failure. And somehow—she'd finally found someone who understood.

And now, Ivy glanced away from him. The pain of guilt rose in her throat, even after all these years. All she needed to tell him was about Danna. But she found herself blubbering about the past to Nolan. Still, the past had everything to do with today and why she was here.

"Grace had this special room—a small museum, really—she created at Elliotts' Rare Books. Nothing for sale, mind you. It was her special collection of books by her favorite authors, including Jack London. At a young age, she followed in Dad's footsteps. It was a project she and Dad worked on together, and after she died, Dad added to it. First editions. Originals. You name it."

"Interesting."

"You know who Jack London was?"

Nolan scrunched his face and scratched his head. "Not a lot. He wrote *The Call of the Wild*. You mentioned something about it months ago, but didn't share a lot of detail."

No. Because the search for a rare, lost manuscript had been kind of a secret. Mom hadn't wanted her sharing too much with Nolan.

"Before he died, Dad had searched for a lost manuscript that London had written when he'd come back to Alaska for a brief time. For some reason, London rushed back to California and left the manuscript behind. He died and never returned, and it was lost. Or so we thought. Mom and I had come back to Alaska to follow up on some new leads and that's when, well, the weird summer blizzard hit, and you know the rest. You were there to save us. But during that trip, Mom made an interesting contact. Someone who knew a man who might know where the lost manuscript was."

"Does it have a title?"

"*The Cold Pestilence.*"

"And what's the book about?"

She shrugged. "I haven't read it, so I don't know."

His brows furrowed slightly. Ivy might lose him if she didn't get to the point.

"Mom got a call last week. The man had located it. Mom was all set to come here to see it, validate it, and hopefully to procure it. I convinced the person who possessed it to sell it."

Nolan scraped a hand over his jaw. "What's something like that worth?"

"Well, in sentimental value, the fact that Grace wanted it and had longed to find it, it's priceless. Even real manuscripts can sell for as much as tens of thousands of dollars or as little as a few hundred or less. It all depends on the buyer. The lost manuscript could be worth a lot of money through Sotheby's or Christie's—both large auction houses for art and collectibles. I came in Mom's place. I'd prefer to stay with her, but she wants to finish this final piece that Dad had wanted for Grace." Both of them dead now. Ivy shook her head and stared out the bay window at the winter wonderland. The house was near the water, and on the other side, snowcapped mountains filled the view.

Should she tell Nolan about Donovan Treadwell's threat? The real reason she was here? Things could get really complicated. So no, she wouldn't bring that up.

"That's all interesting, Ivy." Nolan lifted his hands. "I still don't get what I can do to help."

Get to the point. "I came here to meet with Alina Wolf, who claims to have had the manuscript. There's a real problem now, a *bigger* issue."

"What's that?"

"Alina's sent her granddaughter, Danna, to see her uncle—Nuna Grainger—ahead of a storm. Apparently, Danna took the manuscript. The story is that it belonged to her great-great-grandfather, who personally knew the famed author and whose cabin London stayed in when he wrote it."

"And?" Nolan read a text that came through on his cell.

She was losing him.

"Alina—Lina—said she spoke to the authorities about her granddaughter. She can't reach her or her uncle. I went to Shadow Gap PD to ask about what's being done to make sure that Danna and her uncle are okay. Tanya explained that they don't have police in Dunbar, but that AST should be able to help. I don't know if Danna made it or what's going on. Lina is worried. She's scared. There's something more behind that, but she didn't tell me."

"Why are you getting involved? Just for the manuscript?" He dipped his chin, his eyes intense. "I have a feeling there's more to your involvement."

How could he understand her so well? "I saw a picture of Danna and I thought of my sister, Grace. Same big brown eyes. That same faraway, lost look. Same mischievous smile. I told Lina I would help find Danna. She kind of tasked me with that because she knows I also want the manuscript. Find Danna and I'll find the manuscript or vice versa. But please understand that making sure Danna is okay is my priority."

And finding Danna could heal her. Maybe she could finally forgive herself.

"I can look into it," he said. "We have protocols in place for this kind of thing."

That was it? Somehow she'd expected more.

"Thank you." *I guess?* Ivy stood. She'd made sure the locals were informed and that law enforcement was indeed looking for Danna. She could check that off her list before searching for Danna herself.

An image of Grace laughing and smiling filled her mind. *Who would Grace have become if she hadn't been abducted and killed?* Ivy forced the image from her thoughts and focused on Nolan.

He stared at her now, his eyes searching hers. "What will you do now?"

He'd said the words to her before, when he'd safely delivered her and Mom back to Fairbanks. She'd wanted a chance to get to know him better, but how and when? She'd gone home to Florida with Mom.

Before she could answer, he continued. "You were a former FBI agent. I don't see you letting this go."

"You're right. I won't let it go. I want to know that Lina's granddaughter is okay." More than that, she wouldn't return without the manuscript until she'd given it her all.

"You could simply go home, back to your mother, and someone will call you. This isn't your investigation."

He wanted her out of Alaska so quickly? "Of course I'd rather be home with Mom. I want to spend time with her. I can't know if she'll survive this time, but I don't want to return until I know Danna is okay." The manuscript in hand would be nice too, or else Donovan was going to tell her mother the truth about her father, or so he threatened Ivy.

"Anything else I should know?" Nolan asked.

There was much more to it, but that was all Nolan needed to know. "There's supposedly a curse surrounding the manuscript. You know how people are about their superstitions."

His brows furrowed. "I do."

"Bad things happen to people who have it. That's what Lina believes, and now her missing granddaughter confirms it—I mean, to her."

His cell rang, and he startled as he glanced at it. To Ivy, he said, "I'll see what I can find out. I'm in the middle of another investigation." Another deep, pain-filled frown. "A trooper was killed last night. A friend."

"Oh, Nolan. I'm sorry." She reached out to touch his arm, steeling herself against the possible surge of electricity. But it didn't happen. He was in pain and she wanted to comfort him. "You should have told me. I wouldn't have taken up so much of your time."

"It's no trouble. It's just a day in the life of a . . ." He stood and scraped a hand through his hair, obviously disturbed. "No, it's not really like this."

How strange she would find herself here in Alaska with Nolan again, a man she hadn't stopped thinking about for months. But everything had changed, and she'd been holding on to something that wasn't real. Anything between them wasn't real. Had never been real. If only the place where he'd touched her heart wasn't longing for that touch again.

Ivy blew out a breath. She shouldn't be thinking about Nolan at a time like this. And clearly, he hadn't given her another thought. He was ready for her to go back to Florida.

"Thanks for listening to my story. It was great to see you." And as weird as meeting him today was, chances were that she would never see him again.

His lips flattened and she could tell his mind was elsewhere—the other investigation?

"I should go."

He walked her to the door, and she exited but turned to say something and found herself mere millimeters from his face. His lips. The smell of him . . . it was all Nolan. Memories rushed through her. The feel of his lips and the roughness of his whiskers against her face. Her breath caught.

She turned and rushed up the shoveled drive.

I'm such a coward.

SIX

S hould he go after her?

No. Definitely not. Why was he even thinking he should? But he wanted to go after Ivy Elliott—the one he let get away.

And here he stood, letting her get away all over again. Funny that only a few months later things were different between them, and he almost felt like he'd only imagined the connection they'd shared.

Cold blasting around him, he stood in the open doorway and watched until she climbed into a blue Ford Focus and drove away. Regret gripped him.

Shutting the door, he cut off the cold and he growled. At himself. At life. At no one in particular.

"I guess I'd better cancel my flight," he mumbled.

After all, tomorrow was the day he was supposed to travel to Florida so he could tell her that he just happened to be in the neighborhood. That had been their running joke and, actually, their last conversation.

"If you're ever in the neighborhood, stop in and say hi."

The way her eyes had shined, he knew that she'd felt the connection between them, and he'd wanted to visit her in Florida to see if that was something to explore. But time and distance and life presented a big fat roadblock.

That was then, and she seemed very different today.

Enough of that. She hadn't come here to see him person-ally. He had a new mission now, and that would help him put romantic thoughts about Ivy Elliott out of his mind.

He hoped Danna Wolf wasn't actually missing and there was a simple explanation. He got the feeling there was much more to Ivy's story about the manuscript, but that wasn't his problem. He really needed to get that rest Autumn suggested if he was going to think through any of this with a clear head. But he couldn't if he tried. He was fully awake now anyway. Seeing Ivy had completely thrown him off.

He called Autumn.

She answered on the first ring. "He slipped through their fingers."

"What? Who?"

"Victus is on a flight to SeaTac."

"And Juneau PD or AST couldn't stop him?" Of course they couldn't. They had nothing on which to hold him, but they could ask him questions. Bring him in for an interview, which would, of course, delay the man's travel plans.

Nolan blew out a hard breath. "He knows something. His leaving is awfully suspicious."

"While I agree, we could still be jumping to conclusions. I need to go. I'll talk to you later."

"Thanks for your help." The call ended and he stared at his phone.

He hadn't asked for her help. In fact, he'd told her that he—as in the troopers—could handle it, but he was one lone trooper in this geographically large region. While Nolan was away for two weeks, another trooper was scheduled to cover his region.

I shouldn't go. This wasn't the time to leave—and besides, he had no idea where he would go now anyway. It seemed counter-intuitive to leave Alaska when the woman he'd planned to see was here. Even though he could tell she wasn't thinking about him in those terms.

Just as well.

His cell buzzed with a call from his sergeant. Finally.

"Alton," Nolan answered.

"MCU is sending Jamison out of Anchorage. He's arriving to look everything over. Mark Peterson will be covering your region while you're gone, but he won't arrive until later today. Pick Jamison up there in Shadow Gap—he's arriving by seaplane—and deliver him to the scene, update him on what you've learned, then you're done for two weeks."

"Sir, I need to postpone my trip." *To nowhere.* "I want to be part of this investigation. I don't have any travel plans." *Now.*

"The reason you're taking time is the exact reason you should not be looking into Walker's or Carl's death."

Somehow Nolan had to get over the past because it was totally affecting his present and probably his future.

"There's also a possible missing woman, Danna Wolf." Nolan explained what he'd learned from Ivy.

Alton cleared his throat. Nolan knew that meant he was thinking on something. "Otto Hanson, our wildlife trooper there, has been contacted to check on Danna and her uncle."

Otto was retiring next month and Carl was slotted to take his region.

"That's good to hear. Any news?"

"That's the problem. We haven't heard from Otto."

Communication could be difficult in parts of Alaska, but they had many ways to stay in touch. The thing about Otto was that he joined the Wildlife Troopers to enjoy the wildlife, and this wouldn't be the first time he'd gone off-grid and into a dead zone, which wasn't hard to do in Alaska. The people in his region loved him and he'd been a trooper for decades, but he frustrated his superiors at times.

"*I'll* check on Danna, then," Nolan said.

"I can't believe I'm saying this but postpone your time off for a week. Since Carl's untimely death, and with Otto missing, we can't afford to be down another trooper. Since you're twisting my arm . . ." Was that a smile he heard in Alton's tone? Likely a pained smile with these new developments. "I'll let HR know that you're postponing for a week. Look into Danna and her uncle's whereabouts and find our Brownshirt over there. A week should be enough time to handle this. How does that sound to you?"

Alton. Always wanting to make sure everyone was on the same page and happy about their plans. It made for a better work environment. "Yes, sir. Thank you."

"You're the only person I know who would thank their boss for postponing time off." He chuckled. "Thank *you*, Nolan, for your service."

"I'll pick Jamison up and bring him up to speed." With only thirteen troopers to cover the entire region of Southeast Alaska, a population of approximately seventy-five thousand living in a region of thirty-six thousand square miles, Nolan would have been surprised if Alton hadn't agreed to keep him working for a few more days, at least.

"I'll update Peterson," Alton said. "We might shift his schedule."

"Keep me informed."

"And Nolan, I'm sorry this happened right before you left, but at the end of this week, for your own sake and the sake of your team here and your family, take this time to get your head straight. To clear your mind and make peace."

Nolan hadn't wanted to take leave so instead had agreed to take a much-needed vacation to keep things low-key. He appreciated that Alton wanted all the troopers under him to be in the best shape not only physically but mentally. They had to look out for each other. "I hear you. Let's hope this gets wrapped up in a week."

"Be careful out there."

He ended the call. Squeezing his eyes shut, he drew in

calming breaths but his gut still churned. Dropping onto the sofa, he pressed his palms against his eyes.

Lord . . .

He didn't have the words. Didn't even know what to pray. But he called Autumn again to catch her up.

"You mentioned that your sergeant doesn't want you working on the Walker case, but I have to bring this up. I noticed the file you took from Carl's vehicle. Care to share about that?"

"I don't know why Carl had created the file, but it was on a missing girl and included a picture. While his primary mission is to protect wildlife, like the rest of us, it's all about enforcing all the laws and investigating major crimes. Maybe he planned to talk to me about the girl. I'll look in the system for anything on the case. It's just strange I wasn't also aware of her. Her name's Candice Claybourn."

"I'll look into it as well," Autumn said. "I'll stop by today and grab it. And when I do, I better hear that you've changed your ticket to a new destination for when you *do* leave. Maybe head to Fiji if Florida has no appeal to you without Ivy Elliott. I want to see your bags packed too."

"That's all I need. A bossy sister."

"Hey. What are sisters for? So, what's Ivy doing in town anyway?"

"Searching for a lost manuscript. Her sick mother wants her to find it."

"I'm so sorry to hear about her mother. I'll be praying for her."

"If I see her again, I'll be sure to tell her. And you're going to love this connection—Danna took the manuscript with her."

"That's interesting."

"Listen, don't stop by. I still need to pick up Jamison and bring him up to speed. I'll be taking him out to the crime scene. I'll bring him by and we'll make copies of Carl's file for you."

"Is there any chance you could just join Ivy on her quest?

You said she was the one who got away, and now as Providence would have it, she's in your backyard. I mean, come on, Nolan."

"What happened to Fiji?"

"I've had a moment to think about it," she said.

Nolan's head was spinning.

A sound came over the cell. Was that— "Listen, Grier's here and I need to go."

Nolan stared at his cell. He couldn't be happier for his sister. As for his own happiness? Right now, he doubted he'd ever find that kind of marital bliss. Look what had already happened to his ridiculous effort to make a fool of himself and drop in on Ivy per her very loosely given invitation months ago.

In the winter, the Alaska Marine Highway ferry only offered service from Juneau to Shadow Gap every other day. So Jamison had taken a seaplane. The temperature was thirty-two with a light freezing drizzle that Nolan barely noticed as he waited at the small building that served as a welcome and information center for visitors. Shadow Gap didn't have an official airport, so no official terminal—just a marina for boats and planes. Easy in and easy out. A landslide had taken out the short airstrip just outside of town, and it still wasn't in use yet. Regardless, at least he didn't have to stand outside in the weather while he waited. The welcome center included a coffee shop with the usual fare of coffee, pastries, and breakfast sandwiches.

While he waited, he contacted Annie McDonald, who ran a big lodge in Dunbar near Glacier Bay National Park and Preserve. She kept it partially open in the winter, as needed, for park or state employees, researchers, and a few winter tourists. If their wildlife trooper Otto wasn't available, Annie could find someone to check in on Nuna Grainger, whose cabin was in Dunbar, not too far from her lodge, and hopefully she would find Danna as well.

"I saw them day before yesterday," she said. "Nuna took the boat up the inlet. I'll give Lina a call myself if you'll pass her number on."

"I'll let her know," he said. "Thank you for the information."

"I could check on them again if you'd like." Annie was a gem. "I'm headed that way this afternoon."

"Better hurry before the storm gets here," he said.

Nolan called Lina, who insisted she still couldn't reach Nuna and Danna, but hearing that Annie had seen them offered her a measure of relief. Nolan assured her that he would visit Nuna and scold him while looking into their unresponsive wildlife trooper, Otto Hanson.

Nolan then reached out to Trevor West, who managed Carrie James's bush pilot schedule. She was booked for the rest of the day, so he'd have to figure out another way to get to Dunbar and Glacier Bay.

He mentally reviewed the facts regarding Walker's probable murder and Carl's death. He'd written up a detailed report and sent that in. Jamison might have already read it, and Nolan was prepared to answer any additional questions he might have before he looked into the incident himself. When he spotted Carrie James's plane landing on the water, Nolan stepped out into the brisk weather. In a few days, he might be trading this for sunshine—somewhere.

Ivy's face crept into his thoughts. He shook his head. Hard to believe what twenty-four hours could do to a person.

Was it just yesterday he couldn't wait to drop in on her and surprise her? He could have ended up with a big fat rejection. Now he saw his crazy plan for the mistake it was and was actually relieved he hadn't gone to Florida only to have her look at him like the pathetic guy he was.

A blue Ford Focus pulled up to marina parking. He knew it to be a common rental car locally, but his heart beat a little faster. Then he spotted the driver. He pressed his lips together. Tried to calm his racing heart at the sight of her. He approached and knocked on the window. She fairly jumped and her eyes widened.

She lowered the window but didn't get out. He didn't blame her.

"Nolan?" The surprise in her voice told him she hadn't come here for him. "Did you learn something about Danna already?"

"They were seen the day before yesterday, but Lina still can't get ahold of them."

At her worried expression, he continued. "I'm going to look into it personally, though. I'm sticking around longer for that express purpose." Why had he said more?

"Sticking around longer?" She angled her head. "I don't understand. Were you going somewhere?"

He eyed the gray skies and watched the plane slowly approach the dock. "I was leaving tomorrow on vacation. But now I'm staying until next week to look into a few things, including Danna and her uncle."

"Well, where are you going?"

He wouldn't say Florida. He shook his head and stared over the top of her car. "Someplace warm."

Her expression dropped. Was it his imagination or was she actually sad to see him go?

"Too bad. I mean, well, I don't know. I'm here so . . ." Her brows slightly furrowed before she gazed off into the distance.

What had she been going to say?

Before he could ask, she said, "Have a nice time on your vacation."

Autumn's words came back to him. *"Is there any chance you could just join Ivy on her quest?"*

Right now, his search was for Danna, who might in fact have the manuscript, and he was also tasked with finding Otto. The noise from the one-engine plane stopped. Carrie expertly maneuvered the floating seaplane toward the dock. Then she climbed out and moored it like one would a boat.

"Thanks." That was it? That was all he could think to say?

He headed toward the dock to wait for Jamison. Ivy got out of the car and followed him but kept her distance. He didn't know what to think. He slowed until she had no choice but to walk beside him.

"I'm meeting someone regarding an investigation," he said. "I promise I'll let you know more when I find out."

"I appreciate your help, Nolan. Really. And it was good to see you again." Ivy remained standing next to him.

Jamison climbed out of the plane and stepped onto the deck. Nolan thrust his hand out. "Good to see you again."

Carrie James acknowledged Nolan, then looked at Ivy. "Are you ready?"

"Yes."

Ivy gave Nolan one last look, handed off a duffel, which Carrie stowed away, then Ivy climbed into the passenger seat of Carrie's plane.

She was on her quest—without him—and he was letting her go. Again.

But he couldn't know if she wanted him along. What had he thought? That he would find the courage to meet her for coffee, take her to lunch, or even spring for dinner, and then kiss her like he'd wanted to kiss her the moment he'd seen her again? Jamison was already heading up the dock, but Nolan remained, watching Ivy.

Maybe she was heading back home to Florida, after all.

"You're leaving already?" he shouted.

"I'm going to Dunbar." She shut the door.

Dunbar? He approached the plane and opened the door. Carrie was preparing to take off.

"What's in Dunbar?"

"I'm looking for Danna, remember?"

"That's not your job, Ivy." But then again, she was here for the manuscript too, and Danna had the manuscript.

"I'm going that way myself this afternoon." He eyed Carrie. Trevor could have told him and arranged for him to go with Carrie, except . . . Jamison. Besides, he hadn't actually mentioned his destination. "Can you wait?"

"Ivy, close the door," Carrie said. "Nolan, we have to beat the weather. Gotta go."

Ivy looked at him and shrugged, her expression filled with regret as she tugged the door shut. The plane powered up and moved away from the dock. This was all wrong. He should be on that plane.

"No, wait!" He held up his arm as if his action would stop the plane. But Carrie had already taxied away from the dock and out onto the water.

Jamison approached. "Listen, I only have a few more hours of daylight. Can we get on with this?"

"Yeah, sure." Nolan walked next to him, planks clomping.

"What was that about?" Jamison asked.

He ignored the question. "I'll take you to the crime scene."

"Actually, could we grab food first?" Jamison said. "I'm starving."

"We can pick something up at the Lively Moose," Nolan said. "Then eat on the way."

"Sure thing."

They got into Nolan's Dodge Enforcer.

"Tell me what happened." Jamison started right in.

Nolan started up the vehicle and turned on the heat, his mind once again whirling. Why couldn't all this have happened after he was long gone? He took Jamison through all the facts. "It's in the report."

"I read it."

"Your turn. Have you learned anything?"

Jamison opened his iPad and pulled up the information. "I've searched on all known connections for both the neighbor, Mr. Victus, and Mr. Walker. And Carl."

Why Carl? Nolan thought of the file he'd taken from Carl's vehicle. "What did you come up with?"

"Carl was looking into a human trafficking case regarding a missing girl, Candice Claybourn. Did you know that?"

"Maybe he found something interesting that could lead us to her whereabouts. I didn't know until I found this." Nolan pulled out the file and handed it over. "It was in his car."

Jamison flipped the file open. "If he found a clue he was following, he didn't update that in any of his reports. Maybe this was in his car because he planned to talk to you about it. On the other hand, maybe he hadn't shared with local law because he thought someone was involved and looking the other way. I see it happen all the time."

And Nolan was related to local law. "Shadow Gap PD wouldn't do that."

"Okay. I hear you. That's your sister's department. But I'm not here about the possible trafficking case of a girl gone missing six months ago. I'm here to look at the explosion site and any evidence to tell us what happened. If this was an accident, or someone was trying to cover their tracks, hide evidence, and Carl was caught in the crossfire. He's dead and if he had new information to help us find Candice, then that's gone now too."

"What about Victus?"

"Victus has a rap sheet back in Nevada. We'll need to question him, and to do that we'll need to find him."

"And Walker?"

"No record. Not even a traffic ticket. Nothing. He appears to be a decent, upstanding citizen, but sometimes those appearances can fool you."

"Send me everything you've got on this," Nolan said, then remembered.

"I'll be working with Peterson when he gets here." Jamison

gave him a look. "Your sergeant doesn't want you working this."

Did he know that Nolan still struggled, though he'd been through the required counseling and approved to return to work?

Fine. "I'll get Chief Long to take you to the crime scene." Nolan didn't have far to drive and parked in front of the small Shadow Gap police station. "The Lively Moose is right across the street."

"What are you doing? I thought you were taking me."

"My boss doesn't want me on this one, remember? Besides, I need to check up on a young woman and find a missing trooper. You could grab a bite before you go to the site, but please be sure to inform Chief Long of everything you shared with me, and give her the file I just handed off to you. She'll have someone take you to the crime scene."

The man pursed his lips and got out, then headed straight into the police station without getting his food. Let MCU figure out Walker's murder. In the meantime, another girl could be missing. If this was about trafficking and Carl had learned new information, it was all time sensitive. Nolan would rather save someone than search for a missing person only to find a body.

And that's what was driving Ivy. Her sister's body had been found months after she'd disappeared. All it had taken was a grandmother's plea and Ivy was taking matters into her own hands.

I don't know if this is what you had in mind for me, God. He spun his tires in the slush and couldn't believe they actually squealed as he sped home to get his gear.

Like it or not, I'm coming, Ivy . . .

SEVEN

T he cabin of the small one-engine plane was warm but the turbulent flight sent Ivy's heart into her throat. She gripped anything she could and silently prayed.

Though I fly through the valley of the shadow of death.

No, wait, not shadow of death.

Though I fly through this turbulent valley, I will fear no evil.

She'd never been afraid of flying, but that didn't mean she enjoyed this kind of ride.

Her conversation with Nolan had only solidified her determination to see this through. Locate Danna and Nuna. She prayed that once she located Nuna's cabin—Lina had given her all the information she needed—she'd find Danna there. How hard could it be to do a welfare check?

At SEA Skies—the small local bush-plane transport company—she'd received a big fat rejection. Initially. She'd even doubled the price when she tried to convince Carrie's manager, Trevor West, that she needed to get to the Glacier Bay area as soon as possible. He hadn't budged, even for the money, but then she'd told him about Danna Wolf and that her grandmother needed someone to find her. Ivy added that she was former FBI, though she hadn't added the art division piece. Let people draw their own conclusions. Trevor had even tried to find a way to take the trip with them, but in the end, he'd needed to stay behind to put out a few metaphorical fires at the hangar.

He'd contacted Carrie on the radio, and it had been agreed that Carrie would pick her up when she was dropping someone else off and then make one village stop on the way to Dunbar to deliver Ivy. He would change Carrie's schedule and make it work, switching out transporting another client south to their other pilot, David.

Most importantly, they had to beat the blizzard coming and going. Had to beat the storm.

She'd been shocked to see Nolan standing there waiting at the seaplane dock, and at first, she'd thought he'd somehow learned about her plans and was there to prevent her from going or even possibly to join her. Maybe he'd learned that Danna was safe and there was no reason for her to make the trip. Except she still had a reason. If Danna was safe, Ivy still wanted that manuscript, and she was prepared to pay for it. But she hadn't bargained for racing a storm system in a small plane.

If it hadn't been for the storm, maybe she would have asked Carrie to wait for Nolan—they could make this trip together. But Carrie's schedule was already tight, and they'd worked to fit Ivy into it.

And Nolan . . . she was disappointed in their exchange. He seemed distant and not at all interested in her. She was happy for him to take some time off. Why wouldn't she be? She would probably be home in Florida before he even left for his vacation, and it felt like the proverbial two ships passing in the night.

Even with the cloudy skies and rain and the beautiful landscape, Alaska felt entirely too big, entirely too lonely, without Nolan. Seeing him again had only made her think of him more. She grimaced inside. Her infatuation with an Alaska State Trooper didn't matter.

What mattered was Danna. The manuscript. And Mom.

As for Nolan's surprise that she was heading to Dunbar in Glacier Bay, she was just saving everyone the trouble by heading there herself to find Danna for Lina.

"No one cares about us here." Ivy wanted to ask Nolan about the woman's comment, but she'd lost her chance.

Carrie banked right, giving Ivy a grand view. The snow-covered landscape below took her breath away. If only the sun didn't dip below the horizon early this time of year, leaving her with only a few hours of daylight in which to work. "How much farther is it?"

"It's just over an hour flight. We have about half of that left," Carrie said. "So you don't get the wrong idea, this storm coming is going to dump a lot of snow and it isn't the usual weather here."

"Even in the winter?" Ivy asked.

"Not even in the winter. Winters are pretty mild. Rarely drops into the single digits."

"This is Alaska."

"Yeah, Southeast Alaska. The winter temperatures can drop below zero on the mainland and especially in the arctic circle, but not here. And you see a lot of rain here, as much rain as snow. Maybe even more rain. At least that's my experience."

Ivy wasn't sure why Carrie was telling her this, but people often talked about the weather to make conversation.

"So . . . um . . . you and Nolan," Carrie said.

Okay. The topic had taken a full one-eighty away from a safe, mundane subject. "Me and Nolan what?"

"Well, for one thing, there was a lot of tension between you two back there," Carrie said. "Rumor has it . . . well, I shouldn't say anything."

"How can there be a rumor? Nolan and I had a brief run-in." That was one way to put it.

"Hello? Small town, USA. It doesn't take much to get a rumor started. Given the interaction I just witnessed, I think there might be something to the rumor."

Ivy could see right through the pilot's tactic. She wanted Ivy to beg for details. "I don't want to hear about the rumor."

"Are you sure?"

"Do you usually dip into your clients' business?" Ivy asked.

"You're not a repeat client, and Nolan, well, he was there for me a few months back." The plane banked left, heading south now, and the wind buffeted the fuselage even more.

"So you feel you have a right to know what's going on?" Ivy was shouting even though she wore a headset. She hadn't meant to shout. But the noise was increasing.

"I didn't say that. But I'll lay it out for you—do you want to hear the rumor or not?"

"I'll make a deal with you. I'll let you tell me the rumor if the conversation can stop there and you'll focus on the worst flight ever."

"At least it's a *free* flight."

"I can pay."

"Trevor used to be a detective. His sister went missing. That's how he came to be in Alaska. So he won't take your money for this. We're here to help you in this endeavor. If it turns out that Danna is actually missing, then we need to get a search and rescue going, but the storm is going to delay things. No way around that."

"Nolan said someone saw Danna and her uncle. It sounded like he would be coming this way too." But she didn't think Carrie heard her.

The plane dropped, and Ivy's stomach rushed to her throat.

"Sorry about that," Carrie said. "The weather almost prevented our trip today."

"I'm the one who should apologize," Ivy said. "You're only trying to help me."

"And I overstepped, trying to find out what you think about Nolan."

"Oh, is that what you want to know? I get it—you care about him."

"I do."

Ivy shouldn't have bristled at Carrie's curiosity. "Well, let's hear the rumor first."

"Nolan came back to the Shadow Gap area when they budgeted for another trooper, but initially he turned down that opportunity. Rumor has it that he'd *found* someone that he was really into. But she broke his heart, and he was quick to accept the offer."

"Well, what can I say? Sometimes rumors are true. But not this time. I didn't break his heart. As far as I know, he moved back for family. I went back to Florida. We knew each other for a week. That's it. So maybe someone else broke his heart. I mean, why would you think it's me?" But Ivy's heart was tripping over itself. What if Nolan had missed her like she'd missed him?

"He let your name slip here and there. Autumn told me about it on a flight."

"You and the police chief are close, I take it."

"Close enough, I guess. So, what happened? Why'd you give him up? Men like Nolan are hard to find."

"Now you really are overstepping." But Ivy laughed, her heart filled with both joy and regret. "I told you that we knew each other for a week. What were we going to do? He had his life here. I had my life in Florida. Not exactly close. So, what about you? Are you married? Have a significant other?" Oh, wait . . . "The former detective, Trevor?"

"And my business partner."

"Are you married?"

"No."

"Engaged?"

"I think, I hope, he might ask me soon. There, now I've given you a small slice of me that no one else knows."

Ivy chuckled. Why would Carrie share that? She liked Carrie, and she might need the camaraderie, especially if she needed to secure more air travel at the worst possible time of year anywhere, but especially in Alaska. "There's nothing more to share about me and Nolan. There really is nothing between us. I mean, how could there be?" But there had been. She'd thought. But what was the point? "Okay, I *wished* there had been something."

"Oh, I'm pretty sure there still is."

Ivy said nothing more as the plane hit even more turbulence, and she prayed they were getting close.

"We're almost there," Carrie said. "Gustavus is considered the official gateway to Glacier Bay National Park and Preserve. Dunbar is a much smaller community, also just outside the park, but Gustavus has the services and gets the title. Dunbar doesn't have an official airport like Gustavus, but it has an airstrip."

"Why are you telling me all this?"

"I want you to be prepared. This plane is amphibious, so I can land on the water or on land. I'll land at the small airstrip near town, and my understanding is that this is a round trip, but depending on how long it takes, we might be grounded by the storm."

Carrie and Trevor had known that going in, and yet they agreed to do this, when Ivy wasn't even sure. At the time, she hadn't known Nolan was making a trip out here either, but then again, he wouldn't have agreed to let her tag along.

"That's not your job, Ivy."

"All I need to do is head to Nuna's cabin, check in on them. If they're there, I might need time to make Danna understand her grandmother agreed to sell me the manuscript."

"And what happens if they aren't there? Then what?"

I don't know what I'm doing here. "I told Lina I would find Danna."

"What does Nolan know about this trip?"

"I already told him everything. It wasn't my intention to step on his toes. I figure, why wait? I want to confirm Danna is okay. This is a time-sensitive issue and I need to do all that I can do for my part."

"And get your manuscript."

"That would be a bonus, yes." She couldn't exactly say she'd still be here without the manuscript because she wouldn't know about Danna without it. Regardless, even with Nolan's information that the two in question had been seen the day before yesterday, she had a bad feeling about this.

And she hated bad feelings.

"As long as this doesn't put you in the middle of an active investigation or put you in danger."

"I guess your detective manager wasn't worried or he wouldn't have reworked your schedule to accommodate me today."

Carrie didn't answer as the plane shook, rattled, and shuddered. Ivy tensed, sensing the aircraft descending. Maybe Carrie hadn't even heard her last statement as she focused on the approach. The plane touched the ground on an unpaved landing strip, and Carrie taxied toward a small building next to a hangar.

Ivy hadn't expected *that* much.

Carrie removed her headset and turned to Ivy. "I held on to the smallest hope we could make it back, but I'm pretty sure we're going to be grounded. The weather is turning faster and nastier than forecasted. Don't worry. This happens all the time. I'll let Trevor know to secure us lodging until we can go back. You just find what or who you need to find. Cell service is spotty out here. Use this." Carrie tossed her a two-way radio. "Call me if you run into trouble or need any help." She grabbed the handgun in her holster. "You packing?"

"Always." Ivy wouldn't try to lift her parka to reveal her subcompact 9mm Glock 43, often referred to as a "baby Glock," which she simply called "Baby."

"Good. Everyone in Alaska does."

Hearing that was somehow less comforting. Danger lurked

around every corner in the form of two-legged and four-legged creatures.

"Even if I wasn't packing"—Ivy lifted her hands—"these are lethal weapons."

Carrie's mouth partially hung open.

"Kidding." She cracked a smile. "I know a few moves. Defensive classes." While a defensive move could kill, it could only go so far against a gun.

Carrie hopped out of the plane and Ivy followed her lead, then waited for Carrie to dig around in the back. Ivy had brought a duffel with her things because Carrie had insisted that was the way things were done—always carry extra with you wherever you go. You never know when you will take a dunk in the water or in the snow and need a fresh change of clothes.

But seriously—*lethal weapons*? Why had she said that? She was well trained in Krav Maga, thanks to her father's insistence after Grace was taken from them. He claimed that Ivy would have been taken too if she'd been with Grace, but he would make sure that Ivy would never be abducted. For that she'd been grateful. After the incident, she carried a healthy dose of fear around with her, or maybe it wasn't so healthy because she was always looking over her shoulder as if someone was following her and tracking her.

Still, in her travels with her antiquarian bookseller parents on their quest for the next priceless manuscript, she'd never once had to defend herself. That was because they never let her out of their sight. After graduating college with a BA in library and information sciences, minoring in fine arts—to please her parents—Ivy found freedom in a mission that energized her when she was accepted into the FBI.

As for self-defense techniques, she'd never had to use them, but she'd had to use her gun to kill someone, and that had left her under investigation and shaken.

And still looking over her shoulder.

No one is out to get you.

"You'll need to go on ahead without me if you're going to make it back before the blizzard starts." Carrie drew her attention back to the moment. "I need to secure the plane. I'll try to catch up with you. Are you good with that?"

"You don't have to come, Carrie. Flying me here was enough. I'll be fine. Lina drew me a simple map."

"If the snow isn't too deep, you'll be fine. I have some snowshoes." Carrie yanked a pair out of the back of her plane. "Here, take these. I also have a raincoat and rain boots—you never know what you're going to get."

"Oh, I hope I don't need those." But she was here. She was doing this. She might be from Florida but she could figure out how to put on snowshoes. "What about you?"

"If I need them, I have another pair. Go before it's too late."

With gloved hands, Ivy tugged her turquoise parka tighter and put the snowshoes over her shoulder. Once again, she was in a race against time. A race against the storm. She entered what went for a terminal out here, a building that was the size of a tiny house, and stared at the big map on the wall that featured the region, including Glacier Bay. Lina had drawn her a map from this town, and by the looks of it, she hadn't been entirely honest about the distance.

Ivy was up for a hike.

Better get going.

I'm doing this for you, Mom.

I'm doing this for you . . . Danna.

EIGHT

Nolan groused that he hadn't gotten to Dunbar sooner. He'd given Trevor a piece of his mind too. Nolan wasn't happy that Ivy was on her way to search for Danna, especially with a storm bearing down on them. There was no arguing with Trevor, though, a man who'd just last year come to Alaska to search for his missing sister.

Nolan had barely caught the ferry across to Haines and then chartered a plane from there. The troopers had commissioned pilots—both state troopers and civilians—working various regions of the state, but until today, Nolan hadn't had trouble getting a flight when he needed one via the local bush pilot service. Maybe he should work on getting his pilot's license and become an authorized commissioned pilot.

He made his way to Nuna's cabin, Carrie hiking behind him. She had been at the hangar securing her plane when his flight arrived. The wind picked up, blasting arctic air down the gap at his neck. He tugged his trooper knit cap down and his collar up, glad he'd paid the pilot extra to deliver his duffel to Annie's Lodge so Nolan could get right to work. He continued following the trail, which had turned to slush and ice thanks to the sporadic rain. Multiple boot prints looked to lead him straight to the place. Once the storm moved in, the tracks would be buried beneath the snow.

He spotted two sets of tracks, which he assumed belonged to Ivy and Danna. One set was fresh—Ivy's?

"It'll be dark soon," Carrie said. "I would have gone with Ivy, but she assured me she didn't need my help. Besides, we were pressed for time with the storm coming in sooner than expected, so she went on ahead of me."

Nolan tried to hide his frustration that he hadn't been on Carrie's plane with Ivy, but he understood Carrie had supplies to deliver, as well as other clients, and the schedule couldn't always accommodate him. "It's fine, Carrie. You don't need to come with me."

"And you didn't have to come all this way," she said. "We could have let you know if there was an issue. It's just a welfare check, right?"

"Our Brownshirt out here isn't responding. I was coming out anyway."

"Oh, you mean Otto? Well, that's not good."

"Wouldn't be the first time." He didn't know if Otto would be keeping his job if he found him, but he was retiring soon anyway.

God, please let this be a false alarm. Plenty of false alarms happened and it was a relief when someone was found safe and sound, but unfortunately, that was also the exception. He slowly approached the cabin, which was surrounded by trees that were burdened with snow. The structure wasn't much better.

He stopped walking. Carrie did the same. Nolan listened.

It was quiet.

Too quiet. The hair on the back of his cold neck stood.

Ivy was inside. She had to be. Was she in danger? What was going on? The thoughts collided in his brain at the same instant he lifted his G22 .40 pistol. He couldn't slow his frantic pace.

"Wait here, but keep an eye out," he said over his shoulder.

He readied his handgun as he approached the log cabin. An

eerie cry from inside the cabin met his ears. Chills raced up his spine as he slowly opened the door.

Ivy looked up at him from where she sat next to a dead man.

Nolan took in the scene. A man lay on the floor with a knife in his chest. Nuna?

Ivy lifted her bloodied hands and the sight left him in shock. "Ivy?" He stared at the scene, glancing from her to the man. What had happened?

"I didn't kill him." Her voice shook, thick with fear.

"Nolan!" Carrie shouted from outside. "He's getting away."

Carrie appeared in the doorway, breathless. "Someone took off. Should I—"

"No. Stay with Ivy. I'll go." Nolan didn't want to leave Ivy covered in the blood of a dead man, but if someone was running from the scene of a crime, he was chasing.

"I spotted him hiding in the trees, watching, then he took off heading west."

Pulse pounding, Nolan raced out the door, off the porch, then spotted the footprints through the trees and followed. He almost slid flat on his face as he continued tracking the trail in the snow, grateful he had something to follow. Getting anywhere this time of year wasn't easy, and the fugitive's disadvantage would be Nolan's advantage. The trail he followed shifted away from the bay and was only taking him away from civilization. If someone thought they could lose him in the snow-covered landscape, they were wrong.

He hiked into deeper snow, and the cold and wet were slipping into his layers. But he had a trail and wasn't going to give up the chase after the person who might have killed Nuna or had at least witnessed something. His hands were gloved, but his fingers were free to pull the trigger. Prickles of cold stabbed at the tips and they would soon grow numb.

As for the rest of him, right now he wished he was wearing ski pants and a fur hat.

"Alaska State Troopers. Step out where I can see you!"

Come on. Show yourself. I don't have all day, and neither do you.

Movement in his peripheral vision drew him around. Not fast enough. A body knocked him to the ground, into the deep snow. He rolled and slipped free. He'd lost his gun in the surprise attack, but no matter.

He pinned the attacker in the cold slush, white clouds puffing from them both as they battled, snow spilling over and covering the man he tried to subdue. Before the guy suffocated beneath the snow, Nolan pulled him up and took in a kid's face. What was he—seventeen? Still a minor. But big and strong.

"Who are you? Why did you run from the scene of a crime?" Nolan used his best intimidating but professional tone, and he also grabbed his G22 from the snow.

"I . . . I don't know what you're talking about," the kid huffed, his eyes wide with fear.

"Why did you attack me?" Nolan released him for the moment. The guy wasn't going anywhere.

"You were chasing me," the kid said. "I was scared."

"I'm law enforcement! You don't run from law enforcement, nor do you attack an Alaska State Trooper."

"I didn't know that."

"You didn't know not to run from law enforcement?"

"Look, I'm sorry."

The kid was scared, that was clear enough. People did stupid things sometimes. "What's your name, son?" Nolan asked.

"Craig Marney."

Nolan handcuffed the kid.

"Look, man. I haven't done anything wrong."

"You attacked me. You were at the scene of a crime and ran. You'll have a chance to answer questions and explain yourself. Right now, we need to get back to the cabin."

Nolan took in the surroundings. Did Craig have accomplices?

Someone to take Nolan or both of them out? He ushered the younger man forward, his gun ready in case he tried anything.

"Am I under arrest?"

"What do you think?" Nolan held on to him as they hiked back to the cabin. Dogs barked in the distance, the sound growing louder.

The moment Nolan stepped onto the path and the cabin came into view, a woman emerged from the trees, holding a couple of snarling dogs on leashes. "Craig?" The woman skewered Nolan. "You handcuffed him?"

"Yes, ma'am, and for good reason."

"That's my son." She glared at Craig too. "There's a storm coming. I was looking for you. I told you to get home."

Oh. Boy.

The wind picked up. The storm was coming in fast. Nolan looked at Craig. "Answer me now and tell me the truth. I know where you live, and I'll come back for you if you lie to me. Why did you run?" Had this kid murdered Nuna? Nolan's gut told him no.

"I was scared."

His story wasn't changing on that part. "Before I got here, what did you see?"

"Can we talk about this later?" his mother shouted.

Nolan fought for patience and gave her a look. "We will talk about it later too. Please, call off your dogs."

The two huskies were barking savagely, taking their cue from Craig's mother's agitation. She gave them a command and they whined but stopped snarling.

"I was scared. I wasn't thinking. I shouldn't have attacked you. I thought you were . . ."

"Were who?" He wanted to grip the boy's shoulders and shake him. "Who did you see go into that cabin?"

Carrie stepped out with Ivy wrapped in a blanket. She must have been in shock after what she'd found. Bad timing, though.

"Her. I saw her go inside."

"Before her, who did you see?"

"No one."

He was lying. Nolan could see it in the kid's eyes. Why was he too scared to tell the truth? This information didn't look good for Ivy on the surface, but someone had committed murder before she got there, of that Nolan was sure. She hadn't come all the way to Alaska to kill a man she didn't know.

"Look, kid. I can see in your eyes that you're lying. You realize who you're talking to? I'm the only person you need to be scared of."

Craig looked at his mother then back to Nolan and gave a subtle shake of his head. "I didn't see anyone, but I heard an argument. It was bad and I was scared to go inside. I don't know, man, I just . . . I was frozen. And then that lady shows up."

"You saw no one leave?"

He shook his head and glanced away.

Why wasn't he telling everything?

"A girl's missing. What do you know about that?"

"My boy told you what he knows!" Craig's mother shouted, and her dogs started up again. "Please uncuff him. He didn't know you were law enforcement."

"I was supposed to meet Danna," Craig said. "But she didn't show up. So I came here. I was in the woods when I heard the argument."

"Did you hear Danna? Who was arguing?"

"Two men."

The other man could have left out the back if what Craig said was true, and he saw no one leave. Nolan would need to get on that before the snow covered the tracks. He uncuffed the kid, deciding to accept his story that he was scared that someone was chasing him.

He got contact information from Craig and his mother. "Don't go anywhere. I might have more questions."

"We're not going anywhere in this storm, and neither are you. You'd better take shelter." She grabbed her son by the collar, and judiciously herded him and her dogs up the path back to town.

He looked at Carrie. "Where are you staying?"

"Trevor got us a room at Annie's. Where else?"

Nolan nodded. "Get Ivy there. Keep her safe. I need to gather evidence and secure this scene. The body isn't going anywhere until the storm is over."

"No need to talk about me like I'm not here." Ivy's voice remained strong, but he didn't miss the tremble she tried to hide.

"But what if you get trapped here?" Carrie asked.

"I'll be fine," Nolan said. "Please, you two get to safety."

"I'm not an invalid." Ivy shrugged off the blanket. "I didn't kill Danna's uncle, Nolan. He's dead now, so what happened to Danna? We need to look for her. Those were his words to me. Before he died, he said to find her."

Nolan had his work cut out for him tonight. "We will. You and Carrie look after each other."

"What about you?"

"Don't worry about me." He watched Carrie and Ivy hike back toward town.

Flashlight out, he made his way around the cabin, taking pictures of the outside. The ground near the cabin and the woods. Nolan spotted half a footprint outside the open back window. A clump of snow had fallen from the roof or a tree and buried the rest.

Had the killer spotted Ivy heading toward the cabin and then fled out the back?

Nolan took as many pictures as he could, but he wouldn't have time to get a footprint cast. Then on the inside of the home, he continued taking pictures. He tried to take his time and take care. Using his satellite phone, he attempted to contact his sergeant but the call wouldn't go through. He used his inReach satellite text-messaging device to send a message to Alton about the body. Once he got back to town and got a good signal, he could make a decent call and talk details.

He opened the door to look outside, then closed it again. Everyone was stuck in Dunbar, including the killer. Nolan didn't want to mess with a crime scene, but the wind howled and heavy snow made it hard to see.

Looked like Nolan was spending the night with a dead body.

NINE

Wrapped in a fleece blanket, Ivy huddled in the corner of the room at Annie's Lodge, which was situated close to the water just outside the small community of Dunbar. The room was bigger than a regular hotel room but had two twin beds and a sofa. Oh, and a fireplace. But no matter how many logs Carrie put on the fire, Ivy couldn't get warm. She might never be able to chase away the chill in her bones.

Carrie was talking on her radio, and Ivy guessed it was Nolan on the other end, but his voice sounded weird and there was too much background noise. How did Carrie even understand him? Ivy didn't like that Carrie's expression had paled considerably. What had Nolan learned? When the call ended, Carrie blew out a breath, moved to the door, and checked the locks.

"Nolan said to be careful," Carrie said. "The killer is still out there."

Ivy took that in. She figured as much. "If he's not a local, then he can't just go home. He has to stay somewhere. What if he's staying here?"

"Annie has very few tourists this time of year, so he would stand out. The lodge is open for those on official business in the area—in case of inclement weather. There's Bartlett's Cove across the bay, but I think it's closed in the winter too. But he would need a boat or a plane to get to either place. I don't think he could have gotten out before the storm." Carrie paced. "We just need to keep our wits about us, that's all."

Carrie went through her big pack filled with not only extra clothes but what looked like survival equipment.

"What are you doing?"

"I figure since I'm stuck here, now's a good time to look at my stuff. See what I have and what I've used and need to replace. Reorganize."

"You need to carry that with you all the time?"

"It's a good idea for anyone who lives in Alaska, and state law says that I need this on my plane with me."

Ivy pulled the blanket tighter around her body, as if that along with her weaponized hands would protect her from a killer. Only two months out of the FBI, and she might just be out of practice. She went to the shooting range regularly but hadn't practiced defense moves, and this scenario confirmed she needed to remedy that. Did Danna know self-defense? How to protect herself?

Ivy closed her eyes. *Lord, please let Danna be somewhere safe.*

As she prayed silently, she tried not to think about what had happened to her sister, Grace. She couldn't stand for that same kind of fate to happen to Danna too. *If there's a way for me to help, to find Danna, please make that clear.*

Otherwise, she truly was just getting in the way of finding Danna when she could go home to her mother. And if she returned without the manuscript, she'd have to face Donovan Treadwell.

Ivy was drawn back to the moment when Carrie pulled her pistol apart, then quickly put it back together again. *Impressive.*

Plopping on the edge of a squeaky twin bed, Carrie studied Ivy. "Are you okay?"

No. I'm not! "I will be when we find Danna. How am I going to tell Lina that her brother, Nuna, is gone and that her granddaughter is missing?"

"You're not. Leave this to the Alaska State Troopers or even Shadow Gap PD."

Carrie was right. But . . . "What would have happened if I hadn't found him? No one was even looking into it."

Carrie flattened her lips. "Eventually someone in town would have found him. AST had already been notified too."

They were spread thin. She got it. "Why don't they have police in town?"

"The residents voted against it."

"They might wish they hadn't now," Ivy said. Still, law enforcement presence in town didn't stop crime. Her personal situation was a testament to that, and the thought reminded her that she needed to call home.

She'd been given a short leash and a time frame, and these unexpected events were proving to be a problem, maybe even impossible obstacles. First she'd check on Mom, then find a way to communicate with Donovan that she needed more time. She didn't want to think about what would happen if she returned empty-handed.

Carrie moved to stoke the fire, her demeanor tense. Ivy was comfortable but she was starting to get cold, even with a fire going.

"Are you worried about Nolan?" Ivy asked.

"Yes," Carrie said.

"I am too." Ivy glanced out the window but saw nothing. It was pitch black. "Maybe we should have insisted he come with us."

"He's an experienced trooper with a job to do."

The wind howled outside, adding the creep factor to their predicament. Carrie continued poking at the logs as Ivy approached to get warmer.

"Did you see anything?" Carrie asked. "Anyone at all when you hiked to the cabin?"

"No." Ivy thought back to when she first arrived at the

cabin. "I would have said something if I had. It was eerily quiet, though."

"How so?"

"Unnaturally," she said. "You know, like even the animals sensed something was wrong and they were quiet. The silence can be beautiful or terrifying depending on the situation." Like the one she encountered today.

"That kid claimed he saw you go in. But he didn't see anyone else."

Ivy shrugged. "I guess it depends on at what point he got there and how long he was standing there, but he heard arguing. I only heard the quiet."

Ivy narrowed her eyes and stared at Carrie. "Wait. You don't think I killed him, do you?"

"No. Of course not. I'm sure it had to be whoever was already inside and argued with him."

"But you don't really know me, so how can you be sure?" Ivy held her breath.

"Nolan trusts you, so I do too."

Ivy released her breath. "Thanks." *I think.* "I need to make a call." At least cell service was available here in the lodge.

"At this hour?"

"Yeah, it's late, but better late than never." *Mom always says.* Ivy called Mom's cell. The connection crackled and it went to voice mail. She should hang up, but she wouldn't waste this chance to update her mother. "I know it's late there, but I needed to let you know that things have gone south here. I'm stuck at a lodge during a blizzard. Lina doesn't have the manuscript. It's complicated. I'll explain later." Probably a good thing her mother hadn't answered because she would insist that Ivy come home after the blizzard was over. Admittedly she might have taken on too much. This was Alaska, after all. A beautiful but harsh landscape with brutal weather. But she wasn't going back on her word to Lina to find Danna.

She ended the call and set her cell on the desk—a simple wood plank propped up on blocks—then moved closer to the fire next to Carrie again.

She was glad that Carrie didn't think she was standing next to a killer. The idea creeped Ivy out. Unfortunately, even if she decided to give up this hunt, she might not be allowed to go home until authorities released her to leave. She'd been found next to a man with a knife in his chest. With the storm moving in, Nolan hadn't taken her statement. Questions would be asked.

"I'm going to bed." Carrie lay down on one of the twin beds and pulled up the covers.

Ivy stared at the fire. How could Carrie sleep knowing that a killer was still out there, likely trapped the same as they were? Maybe even trapped inside this same lodge, the closest one to Nuna's cabin.

Lina had asked her to help with Danna. Now Nuna had done the same thing, telling Ivy to . . .

Find her.

Before the killer did.

TEN

Adrenaline had fueled Nolan through the last step. That, and the fact that he had to make it before the wind gusts picked up again and buried him forever. Or at least until next spring. At the main entrance, he yanked off the snowshoes he'd taken from Nuna's cabin. At two thirty in the morning, the northwest side of Annie's Lodge was half buried in snow. He waded through the nearly knee-deep snow of the porch and clomped up to the door. Tried to open it.

It didn't budge.

That was good and bad.

Good that the staff had locked up to protect those inside. He appreciated the staff's diligence, especially under the circumstances. But bad in that he now had to pound on the door and hope that someone would be awake to let him in or else he was going to freeze to death outside.

He wore layers and a coat. Gloves, hat, and boots. But the cold and wet slowly seeped through to his skin. Maybe even his bones. He'd give one more pound before he tried calling Carrie to see if she could stir someone.

One of the tall double doors opened only a crack, pushing snow aside. Someone would need to shovel this tonight before the snow got even deeper and became a bigger problem, making it hard to open the door at all.

Bruce, a hotel staffer, recognized him and let him in. Once

inside, Nolan dusted the snow off his shoulders and stomped his boots on the big mat placed to catch the effects of winter. Nolan didn't even have to approach the counter.

Bruce handed over his duffel, which the pilot had dropped off earlier, and a keycard. "This is for your room, but . . ."

Nolan took it. "But what?"

"Not sure what's going on but the room isn't warmed much beyond freezing."

"You don't have another one?"

"We don't open the whole lodge in winter. Our available winter rooms are all taken. Just let me know if it isn't warm enough, and I'll see what else we can do."

That made no sense to Nolan but he was too tired to argue.

"Thanks, Bruce. Let's hope this storm passes sooner rather than later."

"I hear that." Bruce moved around the big wooden counter to a back office.

Carrie had informed Nolan of their room number. Maybe he should let them sleep, but he wanted to check on them. He could have texted either one of them, but this had been a harrowing night—actually, two harrowing nights in a row. So what if he wanted to see for himself they were both okay? The killer might think Ivy had witnessed something. Seen him. She could be in danger.

On the second floor, he stood at the door and knocked softly. Let a few seconds pass. What was he even doing here waking them up? They were probably just fine. If they'd been able to fall asleep, he would ruin their night.

He should give up and just head to his own room, which was on the first floor. He turned but then heard shuffling behind the door.

"Who's there?" Carrie asked.

"Nolan," he answered softly, so he wouldn't wake the rest of the hall. This had been a bad idea.

He waited, listening to the scuffling sounds on the other side of the door. The dead bolt unlocked and the door swung open wide, then Carrie waved him in without a word.

Stepping inside the room lit only by a dying fire, he shut the door behind him. "I'm so sorry," he whispered. "I shouldn't have woken you."

The two women stared at him, eyes wide. He dropped the duffel and thrust the snowshoes against the wall, then shrugged out of his winter jacket. What he really wanted was to change out of his wet uniform and vest.

"Nolan . . ."

Hearing his whispered name on Ivy's lips warmed his insides all the way to his frozen toes. She rushed to him, and without a second thought, he grabbed her up in his arms. He was well aware that Carrie watched them, and he closed his eyes so he wouldn't have to endure her scrutiny. She was onto him. He breathed in the smell of Ivy. More than anything, he was glad she was okay.

She eased away, then rubbed her eyes. "I was worried. We"— she glanced at Carrie then back at him—"we worried about you."

He eyed the fireplace. "Nice. You got a room with a fire." He moved to the fire and stoked it. "Normally someone would stay with a body. I thought I'd have to stay the rest of the night, but I couldn't keep the cabin warm." He'd secured the cabin as best he could in case the killer tried to come back, which he very much doubted. "When there was a lull, I took a risk, a chance that I could make it before the wind and snow picked back up again. I was finally able to contact my sergeant. Once the storm passes, troopers and investigators are coming in."

"What about the body?" Ivy asked.

"Not going anywhere until the plane gets here. The state contracts with a service that transports bodies to Anchorage."

Until someone else arrived, Nolan was responsible. But with the blizzard . . . "I know it's early, or late. I should go."

"Go?" Ivy asked. "Back to the cabin?"

"No, my room." It was on the first floor, and he hated being that far away from them, especially if Ivy was in danger. If the killer was in the lodge.

"Stay here, Nolan. You can sleep on the sofa." Carrie gestured to the sofa big enough to sleep on.

He scratched the back of his head. "Bruce said my room wasn't warming up." He shouldn't have added that, but staying close, sticking together, felt right to him, at least for tonight.

"I know how this works," Carrie said. "Been through this before. If the room isn't warm by now, it's not gonna be."

"Okay. I'll just crash on the couch. You go back to sleep. No telling what trouble daylight will bring."

A dead trooper, a missing girl, and a murdered man—maybe two, if Walker was found murdered—were enough already. Why had this happened the day before he was set to leave? In the bathroom, he changed into dry clothes—sweats and a T-shirt—then quietly slipped out and onto the sofa. Keeping his handgun within easy reach, he lay down and rested his arm over his eyes. His mind was so wound up, he didn't think he could sleep. But he'd rest. Catnap.

———

Nolan startled awake, surprised he'd fallen asleep. Grabbing his gun, he sat up and spotted Ivy sitting in front of the fire.

"What is it?" he asked.

She turned to look at him. "Nothing. I didn't mean to wake you up."

He glanced at his watch. Seven thirty? He'd overslept, but it was still dark outside, and he'd bet the storm still raged. Nolan swiped his hand down his face and stifled a yawn. He hated the thoughts that rushed at him about yesterday. Especially hated that all the bad had to overshadow the good—Ivy Elliott in his life again. She was almost a silhouette in the fire, but her long auburn hair was a brighter red around the edges.

Beautiful.

He shouldn't let her affect him like this.

"I keep worrying about Danna," she said. "Where is she? What is she doing? Is she waiting for someone to find her? Is she . . ."

"Oh, honey." He moved to sit on the raised hearth next to her. Why did she have to be involved at all? "I let the authorities know she's missing. A search and rescue team will start searching as soon as possible."

"That's all we can do." She stared at the fire, then glanced his way, sending him a soft smile. "I bet you wish you were on your vacation and someplace warm right now."

He studied her, wishing he was brave enough to just tell her what he'd planned. *I was heading to Florida to see you. See if there was a chance.* But that idea had been ridiculous. "I'll get there at some point."

Carrie stirred on her bed. "What is it? What's going on?" She glanced over to the fireplace. "Oh, I'm going back to sleep."

"It's after seven thirty, Carrie," Ivy added. "We can at least get some food."

"Thirty more minutes," Carrie mumbled.

Nolan never took his eyes off Ivy. A simple, unbidden thought drifted through him. He wanted to reach out and touch her cheek. Run his hand through her hair. He'd been thinking about her for so long after they'd met. The fire reflected and danced in her big chestnut eyes, melting his heart a little. Every bit of this seemed surreal. Nolan had to get his head on straight and rein his heart in. They were both caught up in the middle of a murder investigation and the search for a missing girl.

And right now, that's what was important. What mattered.

Even though she was here for Danna, she must still be holding on to hope that she could return to her mother with the manuscript.

He exhaled. "You know everything will go into evidence."

"You're talking about the manuscript, aren't you?"

He nodded.

She chewed her lip and looked away as if she hadn't considered that, even though she was former law enforcement. "Of course it will. For all we know, it might have something to do with this murder."

Really. *He* hadn't considered *that* aspect. "Even so, it'll be released as soon as possible."

"While I'm glad to hear that, I'm more concerned about Danna. We have to find her."

"Not *we*, Ivy. After you're cleared, you should go home."

"I'm not going anywhere until Danna is safe."

"We'll take it from here." But he could see in her eyes that she'd made up her mind.

What happened to her sister had forever changed her life and still held something over her, but as to why she was no longer a special agent, he didn't know. Nolan was entirely too tired to be thinking about and analyzing someone else's life. Nor was it his business, but he pressed her on one thing, her one true possible connection to this investigation and Danna.

"Tell me more about this manuscript."

"If the manuscript—*The Cold Pestilence*—is destroyed or not intact, it will be worth far less. But I can't go home without it."

Nolan sat up. He didn't like the sound of that. "What do you mean you *can't*? What happens if you don't get it?"

She rubbed her arms. "Right now, the manuscript doesn't matter. The only thing that matters is finding Danna alive. So I'm not going anywhere."

There was more to the manuscript story, but Ivy wasn't sharing. Not yet.

Even if she stayed, he didn't have time to care. But he couldn't help it. *"I'm not going anywhere"*—he wished those words were for him, personally. They weren't and they never would be.

The wind picked up, howling again. Like the raging storm outside that gripped the region, turmoil seized his heart.

ELEVEN

Her hands wrapped around a steaming mug, Ivy crossed the main dining hall that looked like it could hold maybe a hundred people. Most of the tables and chairs were empty. As she made her way to sit with Carrie near the window, her gaze raked over the long table with six men and two women. The group talked quietly among themselves and looked at their phones. Nothing out of the ordinary there.

But she couldn't help but wonder if one of them was the killer who'd run from Nuna's cabin and landed here. A shudder crawled over her. The group appeared to know each other, and the idea that one of them had left their group to commit murder hours before a storm seemed unlikely.

But really, Ivy didn't know enough to form a theory at this point regarding an investigation that wasn't hers and didn't concern her.

Except on one point. Nuna's murder precipitated Danna's disappearance.

Ivy slid into the seat across from Carrie and watched the storm through the enormous windows. They'd left Nolan back in the room to make the necessary communications regarding transporting a body and the search for a missing woman. Before Ivy had escaped the room, he'd taken her statement about finding Nuna moments—seconds, even—before he'd died.

83

Other than the group at the long table, her, and Carrie, the spacious dining hall was largely empty.

"I know it's their offseason," Ivy said. "Normally I might say it's nice to have it mostly to ourselves, but it feels eerie to me."

"I've been here a few times during offseason, and it never felt eerie, like you say. But it does now. I think that's because of the murder."

"And the killer. Any idea who they are?" Ivy gestured over her shoulder.

Carrie had gone down ahead of Ivy while she gave her statement to Nolan. Carrie finished chewing a bite of bacon. "Researchers."

"Researchers?"

"Yeah, you know. Scientists."

"Here?"

"Yep."

Ivy risked a glance at the group and locked gazes with one of the men. She quickly returned her attention to her coffee.

"I talked to them while I was getting breakfast," Carrie said. "It's just us and them and Annie's small staff." Carrie lowered her voice. "Whoever killed Nuna isn't here, so you can relax, at least a little."

Even so, Ivy didn't think she would. "What are they researching?"

"There are several different scientists in the group. The captain told me, but I don't remember the details. Maybe you should ask them. They opted to stay at the lodge rather than ride it out on their research vessel, the R/V *Nautilus*. Captain Norbin was more than obliging with the information. Very friendly."

"So, they're trapped here like us." Ivy refrained from glancing over at the group again, in case she accidentally caught that same man watching.

"They planned for this," Carrie said. "The weather is always changing, and you have to be prepared for anything."

Ivy hadn't exactly planned for this. She was more than ready to get out of here. "I'm sure you regret bringing me. You could be hanging out with your boyfriend."

"This isn't the first time I've been grounded. It won't be the last," Carrie said. "But I don't regret this trip because, as devastating as it is, we learned the truth and found Nuna dead and Danna missing."

"Nolan would have discovered the same thing. He was only moments behind me."

"But he wouldn't have heard Nuna's instructions to find her. Those two words are important."

Ivy wasn't entirely sure about that because, regardless of the words, they would still need to find Danna.

"So, what did you and Nolan talk about this morning by the fire?"

"You weren't listening?"

"I needed another hour of sleep, so no." Carrie grinned.

"Nothing you don't already know. Danna, Nuna, search and rescue, and the manuscript. He said if it's found, it could go into evidence and then I won't be able to take it back with me anyway. I think that was his way of trying to persuade me to go back to my mother."

"But he didn't convince you."

"I'm not in it now for the manuscript," Ivy said.

"Did you happen to notice the cabin seemed empty?" Carrie asked. "Like no one lived there. More like it was a rental."

"No. I guess I was in shock at finding Nuna." Ivy wanted to get the image, the experience, out of her head. "I barely looked at the cabin. But bring that up to Nolan."

"He probably noticed. After all, he was there. Took pictures. Made notes."

"Yeah, when he was supposed to be on his way to someplace warm," Ivy said.

"Florida." Carrie blinked.

She had the look of a woman who had said something wrong. Ivy had seen that look before.

"Wait. What? Florida? He was going to Florida?" Ivy's heart might have jumped. But that was ridiculous. Why hadn't he said something?

"I don't know why I said that."

"Yes, you do." Which made this conversation even weirder. Ivy would stay calm and cool. "Why was he going to Florida?"

"I don't know," Carrie said.

"I thought we were friends who shared secrets. At least a few on the flight over here." Ivy arched a brow.

"I misspoke, that's all. You said warm, and I thought of Florida because you're from Florida, aren't you?"

Carrie was covering up her mistake. Ivy wouldn't get a real answer out of her. She blew out a heavy breath. Her heart might even hurt at this moment, thinking of Nolan in Florida—*Florida*—while Ivy was here. They really couldn't get a break. Then again, he hadn't gone, and Ivy was here at the same time—for at least a few short days.

Whatever. Ivy didn't need the added concern of wondering why Nolan had planned to vacation in Florida. Millions of people visited the state every year, and she shouldn't think his plans had a thing to do with her.

She really needed to think about something else. "So, do you believe that Danna could have gotten away from here before the storm? You doubted the killer had gotten far." Ivy's chest tightened. Honestly, she was hoping the girl was even still alive. "What could have happened to her?"

Carrie pushed her empty plate forward. "You found her uncle murdered. It doesn't look good for her. She's missing and could be in danger. Or she could be the reason he's dead."

Ivy gasped. "You can't be serious. She wouldn't kill him."

"How do you know?" Nolan's familiar voice drew her attention around.

He tugged off his thick coat and positioned it on the chair next to Ivy. Set the satellite phone on the table.

"You were out in that storm?"

"Not for long." He didn't elaborate.

Had he been checking the perimeter? Looking for clues? She wouldn't press him.

"Let me grab coffee," he said. "You want some?"

"Please." She slid her mug over.

Carrie stood and grabbed the dishes. "I'm going to walk around and stretch my legs."

Ivy was onto her. She'd done that to give Ivy and Nolan time to talk. She wanted to ask him about Florida but now wasn't the time. Instead, she stared out the window and listened to the eerie howls. In all her travels, she'd never been trapped in a lonely lodge with a few people and a murderer on the loose. It felt like a mystery novel—one in which she didn't want to be included. Maybe she could contact Donovan and explain the danger factor. Then again, she wasn't a coward, and it was better to face this danger head-on.

A few moments passed, then Nolan returned with two mugs. He slid hers over. "Nice weather we're having."

"It's ridiculous." His sarcasm had pulled a smile from her. She took a sip of the hot coffee, then set the mug on the table. "When will the storm be over?"

"It's forecasted to keep on through the day. Should clear out by late tonight, early tomorrow."

"That long, huh?" *Where are you, Danna?*

Nolan stared at the window, his blue eyes sharp. He didn't miss a thing.

Except right now he appeared lost in thought. Solving the mystery? And being here with him was déjà vu. She and Mom had been on a research trip to find this blasted manuscript when they'd gotten caught in a random summer blizzard. Nolan had been in the region on a training exercise and answered the call for help. She'd gotten to know him while they waited out the storm. And here they were again. At another time, it might have been fun to be stuck in a lodge with a big fire blazing during a blizzard, and with Nolan Long. Did he have those kinds of thoughts about her too?

Thinking about that was so wrong. After all, she'd tried to save a dying man yesterday. And his niece was still missing.

When she looked at Nolan again, she caught him staring, making her nervous under his gaze, but nervous in a good way.

What was he thinking? *Why were you going to Florida?*

"What next? When are you leaving on your vacation?"

His brows slightly furrowed, then relaxed. "I'm holding down the fort, so to speak, until I'm relieved. I need to talk to each of the researchers while they're here."

"What is your working theory?" she asked.

Her question drew a pained look. "My working theory? I don't have enough information. How about you?"

"Me? Why would you think I have one?"

"You're a former FBI agent. You asked the question. So?"

"I haven't put one together yet either. But do you think Danna got out of Dunbar before the storm?"

"There are only a few ways out of here, which narrows things down. I'll question the ferry crews and bush pilots." His eyes flashed to the researcher group then back to the window. "But I don't know where she'd go from here."

The big satellite phone on the table buzzed. "I need to take this."

He started to get up, but she pressed her hand over the phone. "You stay. I'll go find Carrie."

She got up from the table and returned the coffee mug, then headed out of the dining hall. At least half of the researchers were gone, and the few who remained hunkered around the fire on their computers.

Maybe after this was all over, during the tourist season, the summer, she could come back and enjoy Glacier Bay National Park and Preserve. Look at the glaciers. Mom would love that.

Lord, I need to be at home with her. If only she could have come three days ago, before Danna left, and gotten her hands on the manuscript. Paid Lina well for the document and gone home. She wouldn't hand it over to Donovan free of charge, and it would be interesting to see how that played out if she got home with it.

But why had everything unfolded this way? Asking that question was like asking God why anything happened. Life was filled with the unexpected.

Like the larger-than-life Scripture painted on the corridor.

> I lift up my eyes to the mountains—
>   where does my help come from?
> My help comes from the LORD,
>   the Maker of heaven and earth.
>   Psalm 121:1–2

Yeah, she would have to bring Mom right here to this place. She would absolutely love this.

But in the meantime, she could send her a picture. Ivy lifted her cell to capture the image, then texted it to Mom. Her mother wasn't diligent about checking texts, especially if she was busy at the shop curating rare first editions—researching, coordinating binderies, representing clients at auction. She chuckled to herself at what felt like a whole different world. Occasionally Dad had even secured an incunable—a book from before the year 1500, basically when printing first began.

Donovan had taken on the role of representing clients at auction lately.

At the thought of him, she gritted her teeth. Ivy continued down the hall and then up the stairs to their room and found it empty. Carrie must still be walking the halls to get her exercise, so Ivy would too, though now that she thought about it, they should probably stick together. One could never be too careful.

She palmed her handgun—Baby—in the holster at her hip, well hidden under her fleece hoodie. After searching the second floor for Carrie, she went downstairs again. The walk felt good but she didn't especially like walking the hall alone, though everyone had been accounted for. And besides Ivy, Carrie, and Nolan, only the researchers remained—and Annie's staff. But she hoped to find Carrie soon.

Another Scripture filled the wall at the end of the hall, this one from Proverbs.

> The name of the LORD is a strong tower;
> The righteous run to it and are safe.
>
> Proverbs 18:10

Another one to encourage her mother, so again she took a picture, then felt kind of silly. Still, she'd use this image at some other time when she felt it was needed.

The lights flickered. The storm must be causing trouble. In fact, how did they get their electricity? Hydroelectric? She hadn't thought about it nor asked. But the last thing she needed was to get lost in the dark. She turned around and headed back the way she'd come. She should have found the dining room. This place was bigger than she'd realized and seemed like it had been renovated with portions added on, making it a bit of a maze. She must have missed a turn.

The creak of a footstep sounded behind her, and she glanced over her shoulder, hoping to see Nolan or Carrie. But she saw nothing and her imagination was getting the best of her. She grabbed her Glock and held it down at her side, stood taller, and walked backwards to make sure it was her imagination playing tricks on her. Nobody was following her.

She turned around. A man stepped from the side hall and startled her. The same man who'd been watching her in the dining hall. Heart pounding, she held up the gun, aiming it dead ahead, hoping she was just overreacting. And then hating that she was overreacting. Her hands shook slightly. She'd been right to leave the feds. Never aim a gun you don't intend to use. Well, she intended to use it if facing off with a killer, but this guy was a researcher, not Nuna's killer.

He had his hands up. "Whoa . . . whoa. Why are you pointing a gun at me? Oh, wait. Are you a cop?"

He stiffened and looked up and down the hallway. "It's about the missing girl, isn't it? The dead guy. Everyone's talking about it."

"What are they saying?"

He eyed the gun then looked up at her again. "My name's Gene, by the way. Mind putting that down?"

"I'm Ivy." She lowered the gun but kept it at her side while she also kept her distance, as much as was possible in the corridor. Even though he'd come with the scientists on the ship, she wouldn't relax. "What is everyone saying?"

"Not a lot is known, so it's all speculation, really." The lights flickered again. "I'll walk back with you," he said. "I can't wait for this storm to be over."

Relief filled her that she didn't have to walk back alone. "I was an idiot to get turned around in this place to begin with."

"What else do we have to do in this storm except explore?"

"Do you get stuck here a lot?" she asked.

He slowed as if her question had puzzled him.

"I mean, you come here for research in the winter. Does this kind of thing happen a lot?"

Gene gave her a blank look.

"Oh, I'm assuming you've been here before. Is this your first time, then?"

Her cell rang. She glanced at the screen. Carrie.

Ivy answered. "Where are you?"

"I called to ask you the same thing. Where are *you*?" Carrie asked.

"I went for a walk to explore this old lodge and to look for you. It's kind of creepy if you're wandering around alone, but the Scriptures here and there offset that. What's up?"

"Come back to the room. The researchers have left. If they can leave, maybe we can too. The storm is passing earlier than forecasted."

Her skin prickled. Was she being paranoid? Gene was a research scientist, wasn't he? Then why wasn't he with his group? A bead of sweat formed on his temple.

"Ivy? Ivy . . ."

She sensed the moment his demeanor shifted. He took a step in her direction. Ivy dropped her cell and lifted her gun, aiming with both hands, but she'd been standing too close.

TWELVE

Nolan worked at a table in the dining hall. With the storm pushing through the region faster than predicted, the timeline of planned action had to be moved up. He finished typing a message to Alton on his phone, updating him on the situation in Dunbar. An investigator out of Anchorage would join him here within the hour and he would share the evidence he'd gathered. Nolan also communicated with Autumn to see if she'd learned anything more on the Walker murder and Carl's death. He wasn't supposed to work that investigation, per his sergeant, but Autumn wouldn't prevent him from keeping his finger on the pulse of the case. With what happened at Dunbar, he didn't have as much time to think about his friend's death.

Carrie rushed into the dining hall, gasping. Her gaze searched, and when it landed on him, she hurried forward. "Something's wrong. Ivy's in trouble."

More details would be good but he had no time to waste. He bolted from his seat and headed for the corridor. "Where is she?"

"She went for a walk to explore the lodge."

"Do you happen to know where?" He passed Carrie, pulling his gun out. "Ivy!"

"No. I was talking to her when she must have dropped the cell. I heard . . . sounds I didn't like."

"Sounds?"

"Like a scuffle. I'm trying her on the cell again but it just rings straight through to voice mail."

He raced down one hall and then another. A noise drew him farther down a side hall. Gasping, grunting—sounds of a violent scuffle that did nothing to reassure him—echoed down that hallway.

"Ivy. Where are you?" His handgun at the ready, Nolan raced down yet another corridor, pleading with God to keep her safe. A gunshot rang out.

His gut tightened, fear twisting inside. Nolan raced toward the sound, but no one was in the hallway. "Ivy!"

A gust of cold arctic air blew snowflakes past him from the hallway to the right, and he followed the "Exit" sign. He burst through the exit to see Ivy pushing forward through knee-deep snow without a coat. Relieved to see her alive and well, he tried to catch up to her. She chased someone, following the path already carved through the white stuff.

"Ivy, what are you doing out here? Get back inside." He caught up to her and pulled her around to face him, gently gripping her arms. "What's going on?"

"He's here. I mean, someone who wasn't supposed to be here. He pretended to be part of the research crew. It could be the killer. Let's get him."

"How do you know?"

"I don't. But he attacked me."

Nolan let his gaze scan the area. "You get back inside, I'll go. You're going to freeze out here."

"You're not wearing a coat either." Her hair was askew and her cheeks and nose were red.

"Go back inside." His tone was brusque. He didn't have time to argue. Fortunately, she turned back. Every second counted if they were going to catch this guy.

He pushed through the snow and followed the tracks. The

blizzard had passed but it was still snowing, and those tracks would be covered sooner than Nolan would like.

Though, like Ivy pointed out, he wasn't wearing his coat either, he had on layers under his uniform and could last out here for a bit. In the thicker woods, the snow wasn't as deep, and he continued following the tracks. He finally exited the wooded area near the bay and, in the distance, spotted a man climbing onto a small trawler. Nolan started forward but the man had a good head start, and the trawler quickly pulled away from the rickety pier and chugged away.

He fished out his cell, zoomed in, and took a picture. The tracks led to the pier, so Ivy's attacker was on that boat. Why had he attacked Ivy? Even with the attack, they still couldn't know if the escaping man was Nuna's killer, but he could be, and he was suspect until they ruled him out.

And if he was, that meant they had spent the night in the lodge with the killer. He'd been sitting with the researchers. Nolan had interviewed everyone from the research vessel, except this man. He just hadn't gotten to him yet. But it definitely made sense that the killer would have to wait until the blizzard had slowed to make an escape from Dunbar. At least Nolan had taken a few pictures, though with the snow and the distance, he wasn't sure if they would provide the needed details. He could view security footage from Annie's Lodge to get images, though.

By the time he hiked back to the lodge and trudged toward the back exit, he was wet and chilled to the bone. The door remained open wide, letting all the heat out, but he was glad to see Ivy and Carrie waiting for him.

He stepped past them into the warm hallway.

"He got away?" Ivy asked.

"On a trawler that appeared to be powered up and waiting for him. I'll ask for him to be detained for questioning, if possible, but there's no way to know where he's going to land. My guess is he'll get dropped off at another remote location where he can slip away. Slip through our hands." Anger burned through him. If this was Nuna's killer, Nolan should have caught him.

He could only berate himself so much. He started for the dining room to retrieve his coat and phone but paused when he got a closer look at Ivy. He lifted his hand to her cheek, her eye, but didn't touch her face.

"You've got a shiner." Bile rose in his throat. "Ivy . . . that could have been so much worse. You could have been killed."

"I've had to fight worse. He surprised me, or else we'd be questioning him now. I shouldn't have let him get the advantage. I should know better." She shook her head and looked away.

He wanted to remind her that she wasn't part of an investigation. "Why did he attack you?"

"First, I had already pulled my gun out in the hallway. I heard footsteps, I thought, behind me, and so when he came out from another hall . . . let's just say I overreacted. I lowered my gun but kept it to my side and kept my distance. He identified himself as Gene, but I didn't get his last name. He asked if I was a cop and then started asking what was known about the missing girl and the killer, stating that everyone is talking about it. He joined me heading back to the dining hall. I assumed he was a researcher. After all, he sat with them and talked to them like he knew them. So I started asking questions and he gave me a funny look. Then Carrie called and said the researchers were leaving. Either he heard her talking or I telegraphed my suspicions, because he stepped forward and tried to take my gun. I defended myself." Ivy's face twisted up but she stood tall. "I'm out of practice, definitely out of practice, but I gave as good as I got." Then she smiled even as she rubbed her shoulder. "He couldn't win so he had to run away."

An entire lecture formed in his mind but he refrained from giving it to her. Instead, he dialed down the tension and his frustration and said, "You and Carrie can leave today now that the storm is moving out."

"And Danna?" She had that look in her eyes. She wasn't going to let this go and walk away. "The more people you have looking for her, the better. I'm sticking around."

"A search party is preparing to look for her in this area," he said. "But I'm afraid if she tried to weather the storm out in the elements, with this blizzard . . ." He let the words trail off.

"You don't hold out much hope for finding her alive, that is, if she got lost out there."

"I hope for the best and prepare for the worst." He stepped closer, wanting to say so much more to Ivy. Wishing for a different situation entirely, but life's journey was filled with mountains and valleys.

He flicked his gaze to Carrie, hoping she would understand his silent plea.

"I need to get my plane ready," Carrie said. "We should be headed out within the next couple of hours, Ivy."

Nolan had the feeling Ivy was making her own plans. That was her call. He had work to do. They headed up to the room where they'd lodged, and he gathered the rest of his gear.

He opened the door to leave, then turned and said, "Thanks for letting me crash here."

Ivy stepped forward. "Will I see you again?"

That question was filled with so many nuances, at least from his perspective, but she probably hadn't meant it in a complicated way.

"You never know."

THIRTEEN

S o strange to think of the blustery, howling winds and near whiteout conditions yesterday and last night, and now today the clouds broke open here and there to offer a glimpse of the brilliant blue sky hiding behind them. "I see the sun peeking out," Ivy said.

"Don't get used to it," Carrie said. "It doesn't happen often."

"My point is that the day is looking much better. Stir-crazy people will come out. Even if they don't, I can knock on doors. I'm going to show Danna's picture around and see what comes up."

The duffel bag strap slid off Carrie's shoulder and she adjusted it. "How will you get back?"

"I'll figure it out." The words made her sound more confident than she felt. She was definitely out of her element in this cold world as far as she could get from home.

"Maybe you can hitch a ride back with Nolan. Worst case, give me a call and I'll come back to pick you up." Carrie smiled. "After all, we're friends now. We shared a few secrets between us."

"Thanks. I'll be fine."

"Remember, that killer is still out there."

"I'll be careful."

Carrie left Ivy alone in the spacious room. A nice getaway during tourist season. To think, a few hours ago she was in this room with Nolan, talking to him by the fire. A reminder of their brief time before. She kept finding herself in front of fireplaces with Nolan, and it was hard not to see the pattern and think it could mean something. Her mother would say that it was a sign. She hadn't heard back from her mother on the text she'd sent before she fought with Gene, who might be a killer. While working in the FBI art division, she hadn't faced killers, but as it turned out, the last criminal she faced had been a murderer who would have ended her.

But she'd taken the kill shot.

She needed to shake that memory. But it reminded her that she'd looked a killer in the eyes, and Gene hadn't seemed like a killer to her. But if killers could be identified by the look in their eyes, a lot of people would already be incarcerated, and fewer people would be murdered.

Why was she thinking about this? The cold must be getting to her brain, making her nonsensical. Time to get out on the streets and do old-fashioned police work. Talk to people.

She needed to clean up first and, looking in the mirror, she got a glimpse of the shiner, which could be off-putting to people. She gently touched it. Now that she was looking at it and thinking about it, she felt the pain of the bruise. Ivy dug through her duffel, found some NSAIDs, and popped them to ward off the pain and inflammation.

The shiner made her think back to that moment Nolan had seen her face. Tenderness and worry and fury all mixed up together had poured from him. Emotion thickened in her throat. They'd said their goodbyes, which had seemed rather anticlimactic. Obviously, the feelings were only on *her* part. She had no idea why Providence had thrown them together again under similar and yet different circumstances.

The initial circumstances under which she'd met him involved the manuscript, and oddly, meeting him again now also involved the manuscript. But what difference did it make why she had run into him again?

Ivy grabbed her bag and pulled on her coat. She timed her exit just right as she approached the hotel entrance. A van was parked out front. One of the hotel staffers named Bruce was loading the back.

Annie's Lodge provided a wilderness experience close to the bay, so it sat not quite a mile from Dunbar. She'd much rather ride than hike her way to town.

Bruce parked next to a snow berm in town, and they both hopped out. "I'll only be half an hour. Call me if you need a ride. I'll come pick you up." He gave her his cell number.

"That's kind of you. If I don't feel like making the walk, I'll call."

Ivy breathed in the air. So this was what it smelled like after a blizzard. She glanced at her cell to get the temperature. Just hovering at thirty-five, with temps expected in the mid-forties later in the week. If it weren't for the snow and the lack of palm trees, she could even be in Florida. They were having a pretty cold winter in Orlando.

In town, people shoveled sidewalks and plowed roads, giving Ivy access as she took the paths of least resistance. She trudged along the snow-packed path in a small town—more like a village—in Alaska, sticking her nose into someone else's investigation. But the search for a missing woman belonged to everyone here.

Including Ivy.

She stopped to talk to everyone she saw, asking if they'd seen Danna. So far no one knew her or had ever seen her. A gust of wind whipped over her, stabbing her cheeks like tiny knives and reminding her that she was in Alaska and winter wasn't behind them just because the snowstorm had passed.

Her cell dinged with a text from her mother.

Love the Scripture! Doing well here. Got your
message about the manuscript. Praying for you.
On hold with a client.

An outsider would never know her mother was fighting a serious battle for her life. A lump swelled in her throat, and she swallowed the emotion building there, hating the predicament she found herself in.

Focus on finding Danna. And get home.

Although Mom hadn't sent her here to find Danna, nor had Donovan.

One thing at a time. One day at a time. Danna had come to Dunbar supposedly because it was an artist community. Artists and writers. Where were the artists? Were they only here during the summer? Would Danna have stopped somewhere before heading to her uncle's? Had Nuna met her at the dock?

What are you doing, Ivy Elliott?

The sense of time slipping through her fingers gripped her and squeezed. Time was slipping away for two women. Danna and Ivy's mother.

A fifty-something woman carrying a bag of groceries walked in Ivy's direction, and Ivy stopped her.

"Excuse me. I'm looking for this girl." She held up her phone with a picture of Danna. "She's missing. Can you help me?"

The woman's face crinkled, and her eyes filled with a deep sadness. "My husband's on the search team. I was horrified to hear what happened to Nuna. I can't believe it. No one here would have done such a thing."

No one ever wanted to believe a neighbor, friend, or even family member could commit a crime, much less a murder. "And the girl? Nuna's niece? Did you see her in the last few days *before* the blizzard?"

"No." She pushed past Ivy as she said, "I have to get back to watch my grandson."

"Thanks for your help," Ivy called after her.

The woman hurried away. Ivy spent the next hour approaching anyone she found and receiving the same answer. No one had seen Danna. With a population that hovered at two hundred, the community was tight-knit. If Danna had come to town once, someone would have seen her. If she'd escaped Nuna's cabin *and* the killer, would she have come here? Would someone have hidden her to protect her? Was someone *still* protecting her?

A helicopter flew overhead—one of the searchers? Whatever the answers to those questions, Ivy couldn't stand outside any longer. Her bones ached from the cold. She started the hike back to Annie's Lodge. She would love to compare notes with Nolan. Working alone like this in a state that wasn't her own made her feel even more isolated.

Maybe I'm in over my head.

But really, had that ever stopped her before?

She called Bruce, but got no answer, so she left a voice mail. When he didn't return her call, she continued walking. It wasn't that far. As she headed back to the lodge, hoping to get a cup of hot coffee and maybe a bowl of steaming soup, she noted the research vessel wasn't anchored just off the shore. Nor was there a ferry at the dock. Taking the ferry all the way back might give her a chance to talk to the crew, though Nolan and the troopers would question everyone and anyone who could have transported Danna to or from the small town. From experience, Ivy knew that going over the same information, asking the same questions repeatedly, could still yield answers. But it took so long.

And Danna didn't have time—that is, if she was still alive.

In the distance, Ivy finally spotted the R/V *Nautilus* making its way north into Glacier Bay. Even though Nolan had questioned some of the scientists, that had been before the incident with Gene in the hallway, and she wanted to talk to them about any conversations they'd had with the man. But that wasn't happening without some outside help.

She followed the cleared path back to Annie's Lodge along a tree-lined road that seemed to frame the mountains.

Just breathtaking.

Instead of going to the lodge, she continued along the path that led to the water. Stopping at the small dock, she peered at the heavily frosted mountains reflected in the icy cold, clear water. A thin layer of ice crept out onto the water from the edges of the shore. The water wasn't frozen like one might expect in Alaska in the winter, but she'd read in a brochure that this region didn't get the kinds of temps to freeze large bodies of water—which seemed strange considering even a portion of the Great Lakes froze in the winter. Nearby, a family of otters played in the water, taking advantage of this beautiful break in the weather after the passing storm.

But inside Ivy, another storm brewed, and she feared what came next. Scratch that. She feared the unknown. She had no idea what would come of this. She had no control over any of it. And she hated not having control. But even when she had control over something, or the illusion of control, people died.

One small mistake had cost her sister's life. By now she thought she should have gotten over it, forgiven herself. But she held on to that day, and maybe that was to punish herself. At the very least, she would never forget her mistake. Footfalls crunched on the ground behind her, and given the recent events, she palmed her weapon and turned, prepared to face danger if the mysterious Gene returned. But why would he?

Nolan.

The tension eased and she breathed in the cold air. His expression was serious, and his eyes narrowed. Uh-oh. Maybe she should be worried. Even so, she couldn't help but notice that he still looked good. Too good.

And she couldn't help but be glad to see him. "Hi."

"You shouldn't be here." His tone was gruff. "Why didn't you leave with Carrie?"

Hadn't he paid attention? She'd already told him she would stay. "I'm just another searcher here to help." She turned back to the water. He wanted her gone, but she knew he only wanted her safe. "Any news on the pretend researcher that got away?"

"Nothing yet." He stood next to her, looking out over the majestic scenery.

The otters continued to play as if they didn't have a care in the world. They certainly didn't care that humans stood by watching. If only her life could be so carefree.

Needing his reassurance, she glanced up at him. Did she read regret in his eyes? "You don't think you're going to find him, do you?"

"I didn't say that."

"And Danna?" Ivy held her breath as she waited for his answer.

"Alaska's a big state. Some people actually come here to disappear, especially those who *need* to fall off the face of the earth."

"Considering the size of the state and the limited number of troopers, how can you cover all of it?"

"We'll do our best."

He stepped closer. His blue eyes had shifted to a dark, stormy ocean. Her heart pounded at his intensity, and, if she took one more step, she'd walk right into his arms.

What are you doing? Just stay calm. Do not move.

He worked his jaw as if trying to decide what to say. Maybe he argued with himself—oh, she got that. Sometimes what you wanted to do and what you should do were at complete odds.

"Go back to Florida, Ivy." He turned and started hiking away, his footsteps heavy.

Oh no you don't. He wasn't going to just tell her to go away. She followed him. "Just let me help. You need all the help you can get. You know it and I know it."

He stopped then. Hands on his hips, he turned to look at her. "Maybe so, but Alaska requires a different kind of policing. A different way of investigating. You don't know your way around. It's dangerous and I don't have time to watch out for one more person."

"I'm not asking you to. I wouldn't want you to. You focus on your job and forget about me. I'll find my own way."

By the way he pursed his lips and sucked in air through his nostrils, she could tell he didn't like her answer. But she was her own person and didn't need his permission.

And I'm plowing ahead . . . "Or you could use me as a consultant. You troopers work with all agencies, don't you? Well, here I am. I mean, I'm no longer with the FBI but I have the training." She'd even discussed with Mom getting her private investigator's licensing to focus on helping their current clientele track down missing antique books or works of art.

Nolan said nothing, which meant that he was thinking about it or not thinking about it. Her *critical thinking* was getting her nowhere.

She kept walking next to him. "I should go back to talk to Lina. There could be something that was missed that could help us find Danna." Except there was still the issue of a ride out of here. "When are you heading back? Maybe I can hitch a ride with you."

An image of Carrie's smirk slipped across her mind. Ivy hadn't stayed so that she could get more time with Nolan. That had not factored into her decision in any way.

Had it?

"I'm not heading back to Shadow Gap. I have other business south of here. A wildlife trooper hasn't checked in and I'm going to find him."

"But what about Danna? What about Nuna's murder?"

"I'm working with MCU, but they're taking lead on the murder and will be sending another trooper. A warrant was granted so that I could at least get started and search Gene's room at the lodge."

"So, he's really a suspect," Ivy said.

"His actions are suspect. I secured his laptop and it's on the way to the state lab. But as for Danna . . ." He hung his head, then angled it as he looked at her.

Her gut tightened. She suspected she knew what he would say.

"Danna could not have survived if she didn't find shelter," he said. "With what little we know, we think she fled mere moments before you found Nuna, and you know the storm was bearing down on us. Searchers have already located all potential shelter points in the area."

"So they're calling it off?"

"After today, yes, this will be a recovery operation, unless they find some other evidence to indicate they should continue. Even so, the locals will continue searching for months."

"The locals? Everyone I asked said they hadn't seen her in town. She isn't one of them."

"And those you couldn't ask were out searching as volunteers. They care. She was Nuna's niece. But they would search regardless."

Ivy appreciated hearing that, but she wouldn't accept defeat, or Danna's death.

"There are still a lot of unknowns," he said. "She could have been killed, taken, or both. She could have been the one to . . ."

"We don't know that. You don't believe that. And you . . . just like that . . . you're moving on to the next thing? Or are you taking your vacation now?"

He stopped walking and turned to her, and she could tell she'd angered him. "Things happen differently here. I don't have time to explain all the intricacies. But you can be assured we're all working together. I'm still looking for answers on all fronts, including Danna. With the storm"—he shook his head—"we couldn't conduct a search in a timely manner. It takes time to bring in the resources. The dogs are out today and if she's here on this side of the mountain range, we'll find her."

Dogs. "What kind of dogs?"

"ASARD—Alaska Search and Rescue Dogs. They'll find her."

She read in his expression what he didn't say. *Dead or alive.*

"Fine, Nolan. You can rest assured that I'll be here looking for answers too. In case you change your mind and think you can use my help, you know how to reach me." She held up her cell phone, though it was useless here half the time, and then stashed it in her pocket as she walked back to the lodge.

FOURTEEN

Nolan continued back to town.

Before he left the area, he needed to make sure she was all right, at the very least. He couldn't leave without knowing. After what he'd been through early in life—losing his mother and almost losing his sister—Nolan always went the extra ten miles. So he'd left a message with Alton and was waiting on a return call.

The MCU investigator flew back to Anchorage with Nuna's body, and now Nolan waited on the pilot, who would take him south to Hoonah where he could start looking for Otto. The storm had slowed down all his efforts. He held on to hope that Otto would be found holed up in a village somewhere, developing relationships with the locals.

Which brought his thoughts back to Ivy, also developing relationships with the locals—in Shadow Gap, at least, where she planned to talk to Lina again. Even with plenty to keep his attention, Nolan couldn't get over the confrontation with Ivy. He hadn't meant for their conversation to turn south. He'd only meant to steer her away from danger. But he had a feeling his words had the opposite effect, especially since she stated she would continue her search for Danna. She was like a bulldog that got ahold of something and wouldn't let go. Of course, he realized too late he should just bring her in and work closely with her.

Chris Thibault, Nolan's pilot, was leaving in an hour, which wasn't nearly soon enough for Nolan given the limited daylight. But he had time to make calls and get updates and talk to Alton about consulting with a former FBI agent who was also here to look for Danna. He'd leave off the part about the manuscript unless pressed, of course.

He'd spoken with the incident commander and learned that the searchers had come up with nothing, and time was running out. No one expected to find Danna alive in such a harsh environment, but they had given the search their all. Still, they hadn't been able to confirm that Danna had not made it out of the Dunbar region. A ferry had left right before the storm, but according to the captain, Danna was not on it. Gustavus had been part of the search as well, though the focus remained across the bay in Dunbar.

He felt the crush of the town's pain at the loss of Nuna's niece, and also at his murder. The small community had been gutted by all of it. Alaska had issues unique to its geography and demographic, but the last frontier shared with the lower forty-eight states crime statistics involving human trafficking and drug cartels and a growing homeless population. Those statistics had to be factored in as they searched for answers.

He continued to think on everything he knew, which wasn't much. Supposedly, Nuna was a longtime resident. But the cabin where Nuna lived seemed more like a rental cabin to Nolan. Instead of being filled with personal items, pictures, stuff people collected, and too many kitchen utensils, either the cabin belonged to a minimalist or Nuna didn't live there. At least all year long. And that was entirely possible too. He could live somewhere else during the winter season like most snowbirds, except he was here *this* winter.

His cell rang. His sergeant calling him back. "Thanks for getting back to me," Nolan said.

"I'm calling to let you know that Otto is in the hospital, so you don't need to go to Hoonah."

"What happened?"

"Someone found him unconscious and took care of him through the storm until a helicopter could get him to the hospital in Juneau."

"Do we know what happened?"

"He remains unconscious, so we don't have his story. He could have fallen and hit his head. If there's something to investigate, you can look into it, but right now work with MCU on learning more about Nuna's murder."

"Sir, the search for his niece has been called off. Even though ferry crews were consulted, additional charter boats and pilots too, we can't confirm for certain that Danna didn't make her way out of Dunbar to a safe place where she could survive the storm."

"It sounds like you're holding on to hope, Nolan, when you know the chances are slim to none. But I can't fault you for that."

Should he ask? Or would that be pushing things too far? "Anything on Walker's death?" *And Carl's?*

"I haven't read the report from Jamison, but last I heard, nothing yet. As I've already told you, I don't want you to even think about that investigation."

"Yes, sir. One more thing, and the reason for my call. I have a request. There's a former FBI agent here searching for Danna. She had other business with Danna's grandmother, Alina Wolf, who requested that she search for her granddaughter. I'd like your permission to work closely with her, read her in, so we can gain more ground."

"That's a yes. If she's already here working it. You said she's a former agent, so I'm assuming she's a private investigator. We want to work closely with all agencies, including private agencies."

Nolan could neither deny nor confirm his statement, so he said nothing. "I'll keep you updated."

He ended the call. Ivy would probably freak out when he told her the news. With so much on his shoulders, the last thing he needed was to worry about her. If she wasn't headed home and was staying here, she could just work with him. This was no-man's-land to someone from Florida, especially if she was going to explore off the beaten path without a trained guide, if she was going to dig into a murder investigation and search for a missing woman, who could also have been murdered.

Nolan called her cell but he got no response. Still, he left her a message to contact him and sent her a text. Then he berated himself as he left the hangar and hiked toward the town, away from the airstrip. On his way he contacted Chris and asked him to wait, explaining the change of plans and that they were probably headed to Shadow Gap and leaving later than planned. Chris would let Nolan know if his schedule would allow it.

If Nolan found Ivy, he would invite her to go along. Her idea to speak to Lina was a good one, and he could go with her.

Back at the lodge, he was breathless after his rushed hike. Ivy wasn't in the room. At the counter, he asked, "Where'd she go?"

"I drove her into Dunbar," Bruce said. "She was trying to make travel arrangements. All I know is the ferry will be back tomorrow, but maybe she found a bush pilot. But she didn't check out and I assume left her bag in the room because it wasn't with her. What's going on?"

"I'm not sure." Nolan growled under his breath, then hurried back to town. He called Chris, who reassured him that he would wait and also confirmed he hadn't booked another passenger, but another plane had arrived, so maybe Ivy had booked with the other pilot. Chris told Nolan that no woman matching Ivy's description had come to the hangar and no one had contacted him.

Nolan searched for her in Dunbar as he made his way back

111

to the hangar. He stopped in at Glacial Coffee, the only place serving up *hot* coffee, despite the name. He got a cup to chase away the chill.

"I'm looking for a woman with auburn hair and big brown eyes and she wears a turquoise parka."

Charlotte the barista smiled. "And doesn't look like she belongs here. You left off the best descriptor—she has a tan. A *tan*. She's very exotic looking." Her eyes sparkled with amusement. "I saw her earlier."

"Did she happen to mention where she was headed?"

"I overheard her. She met Amos here and agreed to pay him top dollar to take her out to the *Nautilus*."

It took a few seconds for those words to sink in. "The *Nautilus*?"

"You know. The research boat."

"What? When did she leave?"

"I don't know." Charlotte lifted a shoulder. "Fifteen minutes ago?"

How had he missed her? He chugged the hot coffee and cringed as it burned, but it would keep him warm.

Then he stepped outside.

Nobody hurried through the snow and ice, even after it had been plowed, but he had to try. He lumbered along the path, walking next to the berms created by the plow, and tried to reach her on her cell again. He texted again as well, expressing his urgent need to talk to her.

Wait. For. Me.

He might not make it to the dock in time to stop her. What did she think she was doing? Passing several clapboard buildings, he paused when bright turquoise flashed in his peripheral vision, catching his attention. The flash had been between two of those buildings. Ivy? That had to be her.

He stepped back to have another look. Nothing to see now.

He spotted footprints in the snow, though, so he hadn't imagined it. He hadn't seen anyone else around here with that parka. He hurried to follow the footprints and then slowed at the corner when prickles crawled over his skin. He readied his handgun, then peered around the corner.

A man stood over Ivy and held a knife to her throat. "Stop the search for—"

"Freeze! Step away from her." Nolan aimed his weapon at the assailant.

Ivy twisted away and the man dashed between the buildings. Nolan wanted to go after him, but Ivy still lay in the snow, and he assisted her out of it.

"Are you okay?" He looked her up and down. What had happened?

"What do you think?" She dusted the snow off. "My gun is buried somewhere in there. I shouldn't have let him get the best of me. That's twice now. What is wrong with me?"

She searched for her gun and found it. She wiped off the snow and frowned.

"If you're okay, I'll go after him." Nolan took off.

He followed the tracks between the buildings.

"Nolan, wait."

He slowed and let her catch up. "You want to tell me what's going on?"

"I don't know exactly, but I'm going with you. I was on my way to the dock and I can't miss my ride."

He knew about the ride but he could get the details later. "Let's go then!"

Nolan followed the footprints, rushing behind buildings, then through the back door of the small grocer, and out the front again. The trail was lost in snow-machine tracks, but Nolan stayed focused on the large boot prints and he found them again. He moved as fast as he could and yet slower than he would have liked to make sure Ivy could keep up, but then she surged ahead of him. She must be a jogger. He pictured her jogging the beach in the sunshine, waves lapping the shores. Scratch that. He wiped that image from his mind.

She slowed at the corner of a building, where the tracks clearly led, and held her gun up and at the ready.

"Hold on," he whispered. "This is my state. You aren't law enforcement."

She glared. "I don't care. He attacked me and threatened me, in so many words."

Nolan wanted to know the whole story. Rage on her behalf built in his chest. "Move aside," he said.

He slowly peered down the alley where a snow machine plowed between the buildings, covering tracks. "He's gone."

"Let's go." She started for the alley. "I'm not giving up."

"We don't need to follow him. I can guess where he's going. It's worth checking out."

"Where's that?"

"The airstrip. And he'd better not be taking my ride out of here."

Nolan raced toward the hangar that sat two hundred yards from town. He ran around the building and spotted Chris running toward his plane, which had powered up. The Cessna was already speeding down the runway.

"Hey! Come back here!" Chris shouted, then he stopped and bent over his thighs.

Breathing hard, Nolan caught up to him.

Chris pointed. "That jerk just stole my plane."

Nolan ground his teeth and watched the Cessna lift off the short airstrip and fly away.

"I'm sorry, Chris. But we'll get him." Nolan called the Alaska State Troopers and reported the stolen plane and the registration number.

If the man piloting the plane knew his way around Alaska,

he could easily land at a remote location and find his way home and no one would catch him. He caught his breath, then turned to see Ivy standing a few yards away. He closed the distance.

"I need a statement from you," he said. "I need to know what's going on. This is the second time you've been attacked. Is there something you're not telling me?"

"Later. I need to catch the boat I chartered." She turned and hurried back to town.

"Not so fast." He caught up with her.

"I paid this guy three times the going rate to get me on the research boat," she said. "You coming or what?"

"I'm coming. Give me a second." He walked back to Chris. "I need to head out. Are you going to be all right?"

Chris waved him off. "You go. I'll find a ride home. What do you want me to do with your gear? I could make sure it gets delivered to the lodge again for now."

Nolan eyed Ivy. He'd lug it around with him, but he didn't know what the rest of this day was going to look like. "Thanks, Chris. I'd appreciate it."

Chris shook his head and stared up into the sky. "It's not every day someone steals your plane. It's just another story to tell the grandkids."

"Glad you can find something positive about it. Call me if there's anything more I can do to help."

FIFTEEN

Amos better not leave without me.

Pressed for time, Ivy hurried toward the dock where the *Great Lady* was waiting. Though she had paid him a lot of money, he indicated he wanted to get home by dark and he didn't have all day. She didn't want to press her luck and risk him taking off without her. She was an outsider here and someone could take advantage of her if she was too trusting.

As she hurried toward the dock, she thought back to the last few moments. She hadn't had a chance to comprehend the violent way the man had given her a message he could have sent in a text.

But no, he'd followed Ivy here—the middle of nowhere, planet Earth. How?

And why?

See? There was a reason she was always looking over her shoulder. Even though she'd left the FBI, trouble somehow followed her and was closing in around her in Alaska.

"Stop the search for—"

"Freeze . . ."

What else had the man been going to say before Nolan interfered? *Interfered* was a harsh word. Nolan had wanted to defend her and take down her attacker. He was a protector. She wouldn't hold that against him. But the timing had left her with questions.

Had the attacker meant for her to stop searching for the manuscript? Or stop searching for Danna?

Adrenaline kept her going as she hurried across the shoveled and snow-plowed paths. Nolan kept pace with her, asking questions for which she had no answers. She'd prefer to think and process before she told him everything. Or rather . . . anything.

The small, rusty trawler—ironically named the *Great Lady*—waited along the dock, and fortunately Amos stood on the deck, pacing and throwing his hands up in a show of impatience.

I got it. I got it.

She'd paid him enough that he could wipe that scowl off his face, though he'd explained that he had a schedule to keep and he could do it on one condition. That she could leave in fifteen minutes—from the time they had met at Glacial Coffee. He'd left her at the café to take care of a few things, then would meet her at the dock.

"I'm coming!" she called, though he could clearly see.

She almost slipped on a slick patch of ice but righted herself, then hiked toward the trawler. She slowed as she walked along the deck so she wouldn't slip right into the water. Nolan caught her arm and turned her to face him in a manner she wouldn't have associated with an Alaska State Trooper.

"Before we get on that boat," he said, "I need to know what you're thinking. I need to know everything."

Now that Amos could see she was with Nolan and that she was on her way, she wouldn't expect him to leave without her, even if he had a schedule to keep. Then again, she wouldn't risk it.

"I don't know who the man was who attacked me."

"I heard what he said to you. 'Stop the search.' What's going on?"

Sucking in the cold arctic air, she blinked back tears of fury. "I'll tell you on the boat."

"No. I don't want this getting out. I don't want anyone overhearing." Nolan waved at Amos. "Be right with you. Please wait," he shouted. "There. He won't leave without us."

"I came here to find the Jack London manuscript because my family was threatened. I stayed to help find Danna. That man back there, he told me to stop the search in a visibly threatening way. But I have no idea which search he meant. Danna? Or the manuscript?"

He glanced off into the distance, clearly processing the information. "How much could it be worth?"

"Are you asking why would someone go to the trouble to threaten me? I don't think it's worth that much."

"And why are you going to the *Nautilus*?"

"I'll answer your question if you answer mine. What have you learned about Gene, the man in the lodge who pretended to be a researcher?"

"His name is Gene Whitlock. The search is still on, and I should be receiving a report on his background soon."

"Well, I did my own research." She started walking toward the *Great Lady* and her captain, Amos. "While he's in the wheelhouse, we'll talk on the deck."

He took her cue and followed. "What did you learn, Ivy?"

"We thought he had been pretending to be one of the researchers and that he was hiding at the lodge. Maybe he was the one who killed Nuna."

Nolan stopped to answer a call, and she continued forward. Low-hanging clouds had moved in and now hugged the mountains, blocking the view, which made this next adventure seem ominous, but she couldn't get to the R/V *Nautilus* without a ride.

She climbed aboard the trawler. "Thanks for waiting."

Amos's features appeared tight. Ivy hadn't informed him that her need to get to the research boat had anything to do with a law enforcement issue, but then he hadn't asked, nor was it his business. "Not going to leave you when you're the one paying for the ride. Thing is, I'm not so sure they'll let you aboard."

"That's why I'm here." Nolan stepped onto the deck, an

authoritative force to be reckoned with. "This is part of an investigation."

Amos's eyes widened. "This part of the search for Nuna's killer?"

"I can't say."

Amos didn't ask another question, and after giving them a quick tour of his vessel, he headed to the helm and steered away from the dock. Ivy and Nolan remained above deck.

"Let's stay back at the stern while we talk," Nolan said. "What have you learned about Whitlock?"

She removed a glove, then fished her cell out of her pocket and pulled up an image she'd downloaded from social media—the group of researchers were boarding. "That's him. He *is* a researcher. He was on the *Nautilus* legitimately."

Nolan appeared as stunned as she'd been. "I don't understand. Why did he react the way he did? Why attack you?"

"Guilt? Why else? Just because he's a researcher doesn't mean he didn't kill Nuna. When I heard the crew had left and he was standing next to me, I became suspicious, and he saw that in my eyes. He reacted. That was his mistake. He'd been talking to me about the murder. Maybe trying to learn what I knew. He could know something or even be the killer. But if so, why?" Ivy tugged her glove back on and stuffed the cell back in her pocket.

"I interviewed everyone from the research vessel who was staying at the lodge. Everyone except for Whitlock." Nolan frowned. "I hadn't gotten to him yet but had planned to."

"They left without him, I mean, before he attacked me," she said. "We need to know why. We need to know more."

Nolan's expression had remained serious throughout, but a slight smile edged his lips.

"What?"

"You're a good investigator, Ivy. I'm not sure why you left your career as an FBI agent."

The way he looked at her, she knew he wanted to understand.

"Mom got sick. End of story." He didn't need to know the rest. But maybe he suspected there was more, and at some point, he might look into her past and learn the truth for himself if she never told him.

Time to redirect. "I should thank you for what you did back in the alley, but honestly, I would know more—like what he wanted me to stop searching for—if you hadn't interfered."

"Oh, is that how you see it?"

"Yes."

"The guy was holding a knife to your throat."

True, but she'd been about to employ her best defensive move. The guy had left himself wide open for a kick where he was most vulnerable. Kick and twist from the knife. She'd envisioned it in her mind, and then—Nolan. But yeah, even though she wasn't a damsel in distress, she could appreciate a hero when she saw one, or in this case, when that hero was focused on protecting *her*. She wanted to hold his hand, lean against his shoulder, and look out over the beauty that was Alaska.

The fog hovered eerily over the water and the chill was getting to her, even though she was dressed for the cold. "Can we go below deck now?"

He nodded and led her down to the galley, where he made instant coffee and poured her a mug. She pulled off her gloves and wrapped her hands around the warmth.

"Listen," he said. "I've talked to my superior and confirmed that you can be read into my investigation so we can work more closely together. Join forces." His grin broadened. "Since you're not going to stop."

That surprised her. In his eyes, she saw respect. Admiration. "Thank you," she said. "I think working together is a good idea. We can find Danna faster, if possible. I can't help but believe she's still alive out there." Nolan would have told her if the SAR team had found her—dead or alive.

120

"I'm with you in hanging on to hope." He appeared relieved that they would work together. "What more can you tell me about what's going on—the threat, the reason you're here?"

"I want to talk to the scientists about Gene Whitlock as part of my search for Danna. If he's connected to Nuna, then he's connected to Danna. Someone could know something."

"I agree. And one of the scientists could lead us to Gene. At the same time, if we find the other man who attacked you, we could also get answers. Maybe he's even connected to what happened to Danna. After all, she supposedly had the manuscript."

And that thought chilled her to the bone more than an Alaskan winter. Now it was even more imperative that she find Danna. Except she'd been warned away from that search while at the same time blackmailed to complete the search.

"Ivy, what aren't you telling me?"

Nolan was too sharp for his own good, or rather hers.

Amos clunked down the steps.

"Maybe later." She wouldn't talk in front of the *Great Lady* captain.

The man peered into the galley. "The *Nautilus* is roughly two nautical miles away. We'll catch up to them in short order."

"Thank you," Nolan said. He and Amos started talking winter weather and travel, and Ivy let her thoughts return to her predicament.

Nolan already knew too much, and frankly, she didn't want him involved more than he already was. She didn't want anyone involved, but especially not law enforcement. After all, she had plenty of resources she could turn to if she needed help, but any outside help would work against her, possibly exposing the very thing she was trying to keep hidden. As to what the man might have said if Nolan hadn't interfered, she was sure he would have told her to stop searching for the manuscript. She was the only one—that she knew about—in Alaska on that particular search, whereas many were searching for Danna.

But would he also have included a threat to her mother? To her family?

"I need to call my mother," she said, interrupting their conversation. "Can I use your satellite phone? I've got no bars on my cell here."

Nolan handed her the phone. "I'll give you some privacy."

He looked at Amos, who nodded and gestured for Nolan to follow him above deck.

Honestly, that Nolan had joined her surprised her. That he'd invited her to work with him was even more surprising. Nolan was in his official role today, and nothing like the man by the fire—was that only last night? She brushed away thoughts of his more tender side.

I just need to call my mother! Make sure she's all right.

Mom was bravely getting treatments when Ivy should be there. And it irked her that Donovan—of all people—was there to help her. While Ivy was in Alaska, she couldn't extricate Mom from the man who'd posed as a family friend for far too long, nor could she protect her mother from her father's past if she didn't give Donovan what he wanted. And she wasn't even really searching for that now.

She was looking for Danna, who may or may not possess the manuscript.

But those lost pages had value. Maybe she could simply pay him off.

She rubbed her eyes. *What am I thinking? Paying off a blackmailer?* She'd been an FBI agent, for crying out loud. How had it come to this?

With the door to the deck closed, the drone of the engine and the hull slicing through the water prevented her from hearing Nolan's conversation with Amos. Good. If she couldn't hear him, he couldn't hear her either.

Palms sweating, she called her mother and waited an eternity while the phone rang without going to voice mail. Then she tried again. No answer. No way for her to leave a voice mail. Her hands shook as she dialed the business number, expecting the after-hours voice mail service. Donovan answered quickly.

Her skin crawled at the sound of his voice. She could hang up. He didn't know this number, except that it was an Alaska prefix, and that would clue him in that Ivy was the one calling.

"Where's Mom? Is she okay? I couldn't get ahold of her."

He chuckled. She'd never hear that laugh the same again. He hid a sinister side with ulterior motives behind it. "She's right here. We're talking shop and books. You know how that can go."

In the background, Mom's voice sounded happy and energized as she conversed with a female customer. Where did she get her energy? She was so full of life and light, but there was an edge to the sound. An exhaustion she hid, and maybe only Ivy noticed. Though relief washed through her, Ivy worried for Mom. Would she survive and beat cancer again? Closing her eyes, she leaned back against the booth.

"Let me put you on hold—"

"No. Don't put me on hold." But he'd already done it. At least Mom was all right and nothing had happened to her. Nothing other than a disease ravaging her body.

The call dropped. Just as she feared it would. At least Mom would know that she'd called, unless Donovan didn't tell her. She'd try again later.

God, how do I keep her safe? How do I find the stupid manuscript when I'm not even looking for it now? Instead, I'm searching for a young woman who I can't even be sure is still alive. Who I hope beyond hope that I can find alive.

Ivy held out her hands and watched them shake. No matter. She was strong enough to make it through. She had before, time and time again. Investigating multiple tangled mysteries felt all too familiar from her time in the complicated world of museums and black-market art dealers. She hadn't wanted to leave that job or end her career, but when Mom got sick, she knew she had to resign and join her. Help her through the battle.

Ivy had barely survived, barely recovered from her own battle, the details of which she would never share with her mother. She tried Mom's cell again and she finally answered. "Ivy? Ivy, is that you? I don't recognize the number."

"Yes, Mom. It's me. How are you feeling?"

"I'm doing well, Ivy. Please don't worry about me."

Any news on your prognosis? Please tell me the cancer is gone. She fisted her free hand and shoved back the emotion.

"Of course I'm worried about you," Ivy said. "I should be there with you, not chasing after a manuscript. In the grand scheme of life, this doesn't matter. Grace is gone. Dad is gone. Why do you care so much about this that you would deprive me?" *Of time with you—what could be your last weeks and days here?* She wished she hadn't said the words, but her mother already knew how she felt. She should have refused to go. Didn't Mom want to spend time with her? But this wasn't about Ivy. She couldn't make it about herself. And Mom had no idea of Donovan's blackmail, so she would go along with every conversation in such a way that her mother would know how much she loved her and would rather be there with her.

"I will not have you wasting your time ushering me to doctor appointments. Sitting here holding my hand like I'm an invalid. If I accomplish one last thing in this life, finding *The Cold Pestilence* manuscript for your father and for Grace is what I want. That you're doing this for me, going in my place, means the world to me."

Her mother could be so convincing. Would Ivy even be here now without Donovan's extreme coercion? What if . . . was it possible that Donovan had used some sort of blackmail on her mother so that she would persuade Ivy? Using them against each other, as it were? She wouldn't put it past him.

"There's more to this, Mom. A girl is missing. She had the manuscript when she went missing. I've shifted my focus on finding her. She . . ." Ivy choked back the tears. "She has the biggest brown eyes. She reminds me of Grace, Mom."

"Oh, dear. You must stop blaming yourself. If this is some kind of effort to redeem—"

"It's not." Yes, it was. "It's not. I assured Danna's grandmother I would find her."

"And what if you don't?" Mom asked. "Alaska's a big state, honey."

"I have to try."

Mom sighed, and Ivy could hear her true exhaustion coming through.

"Yes. Do what you have to do. I love you and I support you. And if you don't find Danna or the manuscript, come back to me . . . soon."

Oh, Mom. Her insides twisted up into terrible, agonizing knots. Ivy wanted to scream.

God, what am I even doing here?

Her mother's last words seemed to confirm that she didn't know about the blackmail. She wasn't also being blackmailed by Donovan. Ivy wiped away the tears and cleared her throat. "What more can you tell me about the manuscript? What is the *real* value, beyond the sentimental value we hold?" Ivy had been authorized to pay Lina fifteen thousand dollars and a percentage of the sale if it were sold at auction within the next three years. Ivy should know more about the lost manuscript that her father had wanted. Grace and Dad had dreamed about obtaining it for her small museum of classic authors that they'd worked on together. But in truth, Ivy knew few details about the literary work she'd been tasked to retrieve, which she aimed to correct.

Her mother might know something she hadn't shared, and as if to confirm Ivy's thoughts, Mom hesitated. "I'm sure I don't know. I'd have to look at my notes."

"This has been your business for a long time. According to Danna's grandmother, the manuscript is cursed. What can you tell me?"

"Oh, it's not the manuscript itself that's cursed. The manuscript tells of the location of hidden gold, and it's the gold that's cursed."

"Gold, Mom?" Ivy gasped. "You're kidding."

Mom chuckled. "Have you ever known me to kid about something like this?"

"Well then, you mean a fictional location for fictional cursed, hidden gold," Ivy said.

"Probably. But remember," Mom said. "London came to Alaska during the Klondike Gold Rush in search of riches."

"But he left Alaska," Ivy said, "and returned to California without gold. He was completely broke." Ivy could imagine her mother smiling as she sat in her chair in the office she'd once shared with Dad, probably holding a cup of tea as well. This discussion was part of what it was all about to love old books and to discover their history and provenance, the meaning the authors had intended within the pages of their stories.

Mom cleared her throat. "He turned his experiences in Alaska, his travels—the story fodder—into his own gold, becoming the first millionaire writer. Too bad he died so young. More than that, I believe that though *The Cold Pestilence* is based on true events, the location of the gold and the attached curse are complete fiction. A myth. The stuff of legends."

Obviously, not everyone believed that.

SIXTEEN

As the *Great Lady* pushed forward, nearing the glaciers, ice chunks floated in the water around them. They closed in on the R/V *Nautilus*. A hundred and fifteen feet of steel, it looked like an old commercial king crab fishing boat that would be better suited on the Bering Sea. Still, Nolan could see how it could easily be configured for research, especially with multiple winches, a capstan, and a huge crane often used in oceanographic research. A large banner with the words "Research Vessel" was displayed along the side.

Nolan stood on the bow of the trawler as it crept closer. He glanced down at the water to watch small chunks—broken off from the glaciers—hit the hull and float away.

Ice.

A sweat broke out.

His hands shook. Good thing he wore gloves as he gripped the railing. Exhaustion from the last many hours weighed on him, and the images once again hit him. He couldn't stop them now.

Heart pounding, he let them flood him. Just get it over with.

Memories rushed at him.

A woman—Hilary Morgan—stood in the middle of the frozen pond. A man, human-trafficking scum, held a knife to her throat and used her as a hostage. Nolan stood at the edge of the pond trying to talk him down. To negotiate. He'd come to arrest the man on multiple charges.

The sound of cracking ice split the air. The man lowered the knife and looked at his feet, but it was too late. Both of them dropped into the cold arctic water. Nolan tried to save them.

The last thing he remembered was looking at her face as she reached for him from beneath the ice. He hadn't been able to shake her face, or the fact that he'd failed her.

And when he'd woken up in the hospital . . . he'd learned he'd almost died too. He'd drowned but was revived and treated for severe hypothermia.

He'd gone to counseling, but he hadn't been able to get her out of his head. And his own near-death experience ate away at him every day. Was he doing anything meaningful with his life?

The trawler shuddered, pulling his thoughts back. Or had that been him shuddering? As they approached the *Nautilus*, Nolan communicated to Captain Norbin his intent to board. Best to rule them all out now, while he and Ivy discovered what they could about their fellow researcher Gene Whitlock. Though he doubted the scientists on this vessel were involved, he'd been surprised before.

Like when he'd heard Ivy utter the words, "Gold, Mom?"

He'd come down to check on her and, since she was still talking, he'd paused, not wanting to interrupt. He hadn't meant to eavesdrop, and she'd ended the call soon enough after those words.

What was the conversation about? That would drive him crazy.

Next to him, she watched their approach to the research boat. With a beanie pulled over her long auburn hair, Ivy hugged herself in her turquoise parka. Her cloudy breaths puffing out next to him and mingling with his own—hot air hanging in the cold. He wanted to wrap his arms around her and warm her up. Sunshine Girl wasn't accustomed to the cold, and she probably never would grow accustomed to it.

The big reason why they couldn't be together—and the other? The dreams, or rather nightmares, that kept him awake at night. Hilary had been alive, clinging to life, trusting him with hers, and then she was gone from this world, and Nolan had been there, watching and helpless to save her. If he was helpless, what was the point? But he was letting it all come back and get to him at the worst possible time. He had a job to do.

Alton had called right before Nolan and Ivy boarded the trawler, and Nolan had updated him and asked him to facilitate a search warrant for Gene Whitlock's cabin on the research vessel.

"If there's nothing to follow up on when we're done here," he said to Ivy, "then do you still think that heading to Shadow Gap is the next step?"

"Yes. I want to talk to Lina again." Ivy studied him, her gaze taking in his face before stopping at his eyes. "Are you all right?"

"Yes." Alton had been right to urge him to take a break, but then with so much at stake, those plans went out the window, at least for the next few days. Nolan was glad to stay and do his part.

But had he lost his edge? His ability to get the job done? *God, please let me make a difference.*

"I'm not sure I believe you," she said.

Oh, now Ivy was onto him. He wasn't doing a good job of hiding his demons. He wouldn't let himself look at her again and take in her big brown eyes with gold flecks. Ivy might just be able to search his soul, and he was afraid she might have seen too much already. Why had he thought he could leave behind what haunted him, flee to Florida, seek her out, and see what happened? Had he believed the sunshine would wash away the wrong in his life?

"I'm not sure how I can convince you."

She shook her head and looked at the bigger vessel they approached.

"Remember," he said. "Lina is grieving the loss of Nuna and Danna. She might hold on to hope that her granddaughter is still alive since her body hasn't been found, but be prepared. She might not want to talk to you."

"She didn't want to talk to me before, but I found a way in. I keep thinking that someone must have helped Danna. They could be hiding and protecting her, and she could have contacted her grandmother. Or she might have been too scared to even do that much. She could have witnessed Nuna's murder and be traumatized but also terrified, believing that she's in danger."

I hope you're right and Danna is still alive but hiding somewhere.

The *Great Lady* maneuvered into position near the research vessel to allow Ivy and Nolan to board. To Amos, he said, "Don't go anywhere. We'll need a ride back."

"Are you commandeering?" Amos asked with a smile.

"I paid you for a round trip," Ivy said. "You can wait."

"I told you I wanted to get back before dark." Amos grumbled to himself as he moved back to the helm.

Nolan and Ivy boarded the larger boat, and Nolan once again shook hands with Captain Norbin, whom he'd met at Annie's Lodge.

"I admit I'm confused about this visit. We've already answered your questions." Captain Norbin wasn't part of the research scientists' crew but worked for Alaska Marine Vessel Support—AMVS—providing both the working vessel and crew required to operate the ship for a variety of clients. In this case, the scientists who had leased time aboard.

"After you left, we had a run-in with one of the researchers— Gene Whitlock. He was sitting with your group in the dining hall at Annie's and we assumed he had come in from the *Nau-*

tilus." Nolan waited for the captain to either deny or confirm Gene Whitlock's presence on this vessel before he fled.

"I'm not sure I understand."

An image of Whitlock was now circulating through law enforcement channels for detainment. He showed the image to the captain. "This man was sitting with your group. But he wasn't with your group when you left. What can you tell me about him?"

"In my limited understanding of the research groups, Whitlock wasn't affiliated with the National Ocean Observation Research Initiative. NOORI. He'd been granted access to join the *Nautilus* for his own research."

"And what was that?"

The captain shrugged. "I'm not a scientist, and I don't speak their language. My job is to get them in and out safely."

"Do you have any idea why he didn't join you after the storm moved through? As the captain, you must have known."

"Yes. All he said was that he had a sudden change of plans and informed me that he wouldn't be traveling with us."

"When did he inform you?"

Captain Norbin looked from Ivy to Nolan, then gestured for them to follow. "I can give you the exact time. It's on my log in my stateroom."

As he led them along the deck and then belowdecks, the captain explained the various features of the vessel, sounding proud to captain the R/V *Nautilus*. Then belowdecks, he continued as they passed rooms set aside for the science crew. "What research vessel would be worth anything without labs? The *Nautilus* includes a standard hydrographic lab, chemical and wet labs, a gravimeter, computer lab, library, and of course, a gym." Captain Norbin seemed to fight a grin, which would be wholly inappropriate under the circumstances.

Nolan wouldn't ask him about the details of the various labs. Still, he offered the man a compliment. "Impressive."

The captain smiled, obviously pleased with Nolan's comment, and finally they arrived at his stateroom. They entered his quarters where he sat down at a small desk, then opened his computer and searched until he found the record he needed. "I've logged that passenger Gene Whitlock contacted me today at eleven forty-eight. Right before noon."

Nolan and Ivy shared a look. He contacted the captain after he fled. But if he'd been planning to return to the vessel with the other researchers, why had he stayed behind when they left?

"What do you know about him?"

"He's an ecologist. That's the extent of my knowledge." Captain Norbin frowned. "What's this about, really? I've heard about a murder, and I know about the search for the missing girl. My crew and I, the clients, are just passing through."

Ivy stepped forward. "Can you show us Dr. Whitlock's quarters?"

Captain Norbin eyed her. "Are you an Alaska State Trooper too?"

"She's working with the troopers, Captain," Nolan said.

The captain led them into the bowels of the vessel. He stopped outside a cabin. "Per our contract with the scientists, I have the right to search the cabin for any reason at any time, and I'm going to open this for you. But—"

"I have an electronic warrant to prevent any problems and cover all the bases." Nolan flashed the captain the image that had thankfully just appeared via a text on his satellite phone. Gene Whitlock had basically abandoned his cabin, and Nolan would search it on that basis if nothing else.

Using the master key, the captain unlocked the door and opened it. Nolan stepped through first and stood at the entrance, looking around. Whitlock had left clothes, a stack of books, and other personal items behind. This environment and these circumstances didn't lend themselves to waiting for a team of evidence collectors, especially when he was trained to do it.

Using his cell, he started taking pictures of every inch of the cabin, capturing everything Whitlock had left behind. Then he approached the desk and found a journal with notes. "He left this important item behind."

"Then he planned to return," Ivy said. "But he didn't."

When he found you. Nolan needed time to think this through—it seemed the man hadn't thought he would be leaving, but something happened, some new information that kept him from returning to his research. Nolan tugged on latex gloves. Or could it be that with the approaching storm, he simply hadn't been able to make it back, and then when he feared Ivy was onto him, he had no choice but to escape? But . . . the boat he'd taken had appeared to be running and waiting for him. Nolan flipped through the journal and read entries about the environment around them. Simple handwritten scientific notes.

"I need you to keep this room secured for now in case someone from our major crimes unit wants to look at it." Nolan doubted anything in this room could give them answers.

Captain Norbin nodded. "I understand. No one would be getting into his quarters anyway. Not a problem."

The captain frowned, dipped his chin, and averted his gaze.

"Don't hold back on me," Nolan said. "You know something. What is it?"

Captain Norbin cleared his throat, clearly uncomfortable. "He requested we mail the journal to him."

Really. Nolan arched a brow. "I'll need that address." Had Whitlock given his actual home address or simply a post office box? He suspected the guy would not be returning home, at least if he had anything to hide and feared being detained.

Once again the captain frowned. "So, you really think he's a criminal?"

"We'll know soon enough." Nolan wouldn't comment on the investigation.

The man shook his head. "In my limited view, it's hard to imagine him committing a violent crime. I'll leave you to finish up here. Let me know when you're done." Captain Norbin left them alone.

Ivy stepped out as if to follow him, then turned back. "While you gather evidence, I'll go ask around. Talk to the crew."

"No," he said. "Stay here and wait for me. We can do that together."

"Nolan, no offense but you're a bit intimidating. Let me do this. It'll save us time, and I think my approach might gain us more information. Remember, if Danna is on the run, she's in trouble. We can't waste time."

She once again turned her back to walk away.

"No, we can't waste time."

She turned to look at him. "I'm glad you agree."

He held her gaze. "That's why you need to tell me about the gold."

Her brows furrowed. "The gold? You were listening?"

"Not on purpose. I came down to check on you. I heard the word *gold*. If it pertains to this, I need to know." He'd hoped she would tell him on her own—that is, if it was relevant. "Is it relevant?"

"I don't know."

"Then what *do* you know?"

A clink came from the hall, signaling someone making their way through.

She shook her head. "Not here," she mouthed.

Great. Gold could somehow be related.

"I'm going to chat with the crew," she said, and disappeared.

If Whitlock had murdered Nuna, then he most likely knew what happened to Danna. The idea that hidden gold might be related soured in his gut.

SEVENTEEN

Ivy wasn't a treasure hunter.

Her job with the FBI had been to find and return stolen artifacts, a.k.a. treasures, and arrest those responsible for dealing in stolen art in all its various forms. The irony wasn't lost on her that even though she'd left that world behind, she could again be working in that same capacity—only this time while also trying to find a missing young woman who carried an old manuscript around with her while oblivious to its true value as a treasure map to hidden gold.

Or . . . had Danna known?

For that matter, had Nuna?

She was grappling with far too many assumptions. If only she could find Danna safe and sound and purchase the manuscript like she'd planned when she'd come to Alaska.

If only . . . if only she and Nolan . . .

Don't go there.

She focused on asking questions of the crew and research scientists. She hadn't questioned them before—Nolan had—and she hoped to learn something useful. After making her way around, she ended up belowdecks again and found a woman in her late twenties standing in front of a monitor in the computer lab.

Ivy knocked on the glass door. The woman saw her and smiled, then opened the door. "I saw you at the lodge."

"Yes. I'm Ivy Elliott." Ivy thrust out her hand. "One of the investigators."

The woman's smile faltered. "I guess that makes sense. I was about to ask what you're doing here. I'm Cindy Mitchell. I talked to the trooper while I was at the lodge."

Ivy gestured at the wall covered in computer monitors. "What is all this for?"

Cindy huffed a chuckle. "Where do I even start? I won't bore you with the details about the computer systems—we'd be here all day. But there are multiple computer systems running to archive all the data we collect, saving at fifteen-minute intervals, collecting data from ocean surveyors' software, hydrographic Doppler sonar systems, bathymetric mapping, our echo sounder, and—"

"Okay, okay. You lost me at ocean surveyors' software."

Cindy smiled again. "Yeah, I figured I'd lose you. It's boring stuff unless you're an ocean science nerd."

"What do *you* do here?"

"I monitor data and make sure everything is running smoothly. I have an IT background, which I'm sure you figured out." Cindy angled her head. "So, you're here to ask more questions?"

"Yes."

"I don't know what I can tell you. I didn't see the missing girl. I'm so sorry. I hope they find her soon. You can't think that she's somehow hiding on the *Nautilus*."

Interesting that she didn't mention Nuna. Then again, the woman was stuck down here alone in what Ivy would consider a computer dungeon. She was absorbed in her work and that meant she might not be able to tell Ivy anything new. Ivy had learned nothing from the others because Gene Whitlock had kept to himself.

Funny, because at first, he seemed pretty friendly, outgoing even—at least before he attacked her. "What can you tell me about Gene Whitlock?"

Cindy's brows furrowed slightly and she blinked. "Gene? Why . . . why would you ask about him?"

"Cindy, please just answer the question."

"I don't know, really. There's nothing to tell."

"Back at Annie's Lodge, he attacked me. You were on this boat with a dangerous man, Cindy."

Cindy gasped. "What do you mean?"

"Just what I said." Maybe Ivy shouldn't have shared so much, but she needed to rattle this woman and get something out of her.

"Now, in light of that, what can you tell me?"

"I'm sorry you were attacked. You seem . . . okay. He didn't—"

"No."

"I can tell you that he doesn't seem like the kind of man to . . . well . . . attack someone."

"How did he seem, then?"

"He seemed kind of . . . I don't know . . . soft? He had a gentle handshake. So I just can't picture him attacking anyone, especially you. You look like you can hold your own."

Ivy had that same impression of Gene running around in the back of her mind. Gene was definitely a man she should have bested or at least prevented from getting away. But it felt like he'd been fighting for his life, running on pure adrenaline, which could be like a powerful drug to a frantic man. He'd hidden that well until he attacked her. Then Gene had been desperate to escape.

"Anything else you can tell me?" Ivy asked.

"Look. I didn't know him at all. We were all on the same boat doing our own work and research."

"When you were at the lodge, were you all together the whole time, or at least most of the day?"

"No." Cindy moved to an emerging printout to watch.

Ivy followed. "When you left for the lodge, did you go as a group? Was he with you then?"

137

"I . . . yes, we were together, only— Wait . . . he left the boat earlier. Before the rest of us."

Interesting. "How much earlier did he leave?"

"I was taking a break to get fresh air. I saw a crew member taking the tender and Gene was in it. The rest of us didn't start disembarking until much later that afternoon. As for me, I wanted to get as much work in as I could before leaving—shut down certain systems. I could have stayed, but the lodge seemed a nice change."

"Was Gene at the lodge when you arrived?"

"I have no way of knowing," Cindy said. "I didn't see him, but that doesn't mean he wasn't there."

Someone knocked, and Ivy and Cindy both glanced at the glass door. Cindy let Nolan inside, but he said nothing.

"Thank you, Cindy," Ivy said. "Can you contact me if you think of anything else that could help?" Ivy handed over her card, bracing herself for Cindy's reaction.

"Sure." Cindy looked at the card. "Elliotts' Rare Books. I don't understand. Aren't you . . . ?" Cindy looked from Ivy to Nolan, who stood next to her.

"Yes," Ivy said. "I'm investigating."

"Thank you for your help," Nolan said. "If you have any additional information to share, please contact Ivy, or you can call me." He took Ivy's card and wrote his number on it, then handed it back. "That's my direct line."

"I'll be in touch." Cindy stared at the card. "Wait. There was one thing—I don't know if it means anything. But I had the distinct impression that he was on edge."

"On edge?" Ivy asked. "Can you be more specific?"

"He seemed jumpy. Maybe even scared. I know that sounds ridiculous, so that's why I didn't say anything at first."

"If you think of more, please get in touch with us."

"I will."

Ivy followed Nolan out of the computer room and into the passageway.

When they stopped, he looked at Ivy. "Scared? What do you make of that?"

"He didn't appear scared when I met him in the hallway, but now that I think about it, he was definitely on edge. Then, when he tried to take my gun, he was desperate. So this guy was edgy, scared, desperate. Why would he murder Nuna? Or maybe he didn't, but he was already edgy, according to Cindy, before he left the R/V *Nautilus*."

"Probably because he was afraid of getting caught, and while on the boat, he was on edge because he knew what he was about to do. That information doesn't get us anywhere."

"Well, you got an address where he intended to send his journal," she said.

"Someone will be following up to locate and bring him in, but the address is in Northern California, so it won't be me. Did you learn anything else from the other crew members?"

"I talked to everyone. For researchers, they sure aren't very observant. I think they're just very focused on their work and not that into other people. Cindy gave me the most information."

They made their way above deck and prepared to head back. The *Great Lady* sat next to the R/V *Nautilus*.

"I'll let the captain know we're done here and thank him for his help." Nolan left her side for a few moments, then returned.

They once again boarded the trawler and Ivy made her way down to the galley, which felt tiny and suffocating after being on the *Nautilus*. Exhaustion flooded her and she pressed her head against her arms on the table.

Lord, I feel like I'm getting nowhere.

Where is Danna? What can I do to find her? Please keep her safe!

When Nolan sat at the table, she didn't lift her head to acknowledge him. She didn't care what he thought. She was definitely losing her professional edge. Maybe pretending to be a professional investigator—someone who was paid to do a job—was too draining on her.

"Tell me about the gold," he said in a low voice that only she could hear.

Unless Amos had very good ears.

That got her attention. *Oh God, please let Nolan not be someone who would go for the gold.*

After all, she didn't truly know him that well.

She lifted her head. Narrowed her eyes. "Why do you want to know about it, really?"

"I only want to know if it's relevant to Nuna's murder and Danna's disappearance, and if so, then how. I'm reading you into this investigation, and I expect you to share everything you know. Everything matters."

"You overheard me here talking to Mom. No way will I make that mistake again. When I tell you, we'll be completely alone."

"I expect full disclosure. But honestly, I had hoped you would tell me. That I wouldn't have to ask you to begin with, so please don't make me drag it out of you."

"There wasn't time to tell you, okay? Not when I had just found out myself. Besides, Mom says it's fiction anyway. I'll tell you everything, but later." She said the words but wasn't entirely sure she would have mentioned this to Nolan. Not until she got a handle on what was happening here.

He looked at her long and hard, then nodded. "Fair enough."

By the time they made it back to Dunbar, a frigid, eerie darkness had long fallen.

"Amos, I'm sorry that you're getting back after dark. Let me tip you."

He shook his head. "Solve Nuna's murder. That's what matters. Take care of yourselves."

They left him behind and hiked toward Annie's Lodge. Fortunately, the dock was lit, but on the tree-lined road, Nolan had to use his flashlight and Ivy tried not to think about bears and killers hiding in the woods. Though the temperature hovered just below freezing, the cold felt unbearable on the walk back to the lodge. Nolan stayed close as if to protect her—either that or he thought their combined body heat would chase away sudden death by cold. But the whole time, he talked on his satellite phone, trying to arrange a flight back to Shadow Gap in the morning.

At the welcoming door to Annie's Lodge—where the lights burned bright—Nolan finally ended the call and huffed out a breath.

"That didn't sound like it went so well." She opened the door and entered the lodge. No sense in standing out in the cold one second longer. The big fire blazed and drew her over, where she removed her gloves and held her hands to the flames while Nolan approached the front desk to retrieve his duffel and secure another room.

When he joined her, he slid out of his jacket, and for the first time today she smiled. She must be ridiculously exhausted to smile, but . . .

"What?" he asked. "What's so funny?"

"Nothing's funny."

"Why'd you smile then?" The sudden husky tone in his voice drew her eyes to him.

Was he reading her mind?

Just . . . "I admire a man in a uniform, that's all. That's a brownie point for the Alaska State Troopers and a loss for the FBI, where agents don't wear uniforms." Had she really just said that out loud?

She palmed her eyes and winced at the pain from touching her face. She wished she was in her room where she could curl up and pretend this was just a dream. She took off her parka. "Can we just go to sleep now?"

"Sure. That's where I was headed, but you came to the fire

so I followed you. Come on. I'll walk you to your room. My room is just down the hall, and I've been assured that it's warm this time."

Together they walked down the long hallway to the stairwell. Ivy thought back to the incident with Gene and shuddered.

They hiked up the stairs.

Nolan angled his head. "What did you do exactly, with the FBI? What division?"

"Art division."

"Well, that makes sense. Why didn't you tell me?"

"It never came up." Ivy unlocked the door, then entered the expansive room she'd shared with Carrie and Nolan the night before and found the contents of her duffel tossed about. She gasped. "Oh no!"

She and Nolan both pulled out their guns to clear the rest of the apartment. Then Ivy found her laptop, but it didn't look like it had been tampered with. What had they been looking for?

"Is anything missing?" he asked.

"No. There was nothing for them to find." Ivy was so exhausted, and really, she just wanted to cry, but nope. She wouldn't do it in front of Nolan. "Who could have done this?"

"We'll know after I take a look at the security footage."

"Maybe it was Gene," she said. "Maybe he came back."

"Or the man in the back alley who warned you to stop the search. He could have done this *before* he attacked you in the alley."

Ivy sank onto the bed and pressed her face into her hands. She was really tired of this.

"Well, that settles it," Nolan said. "We're staying in my room tonight."

"No. That's not necessary. I'm capable of taking care of myself." But two heads were better than one. They could protect each other.

He arched a brow.

142

Right. She could hold her own in her past job, but she was zero for two here in Alaska. Still, she'd given as good as she'd gotten with Gene, but maybe that was only because he was "soft," as Cindy had put it. Ivy was losing her touch. Whenever she got back to Florida, it would be the gym every day, fighting classes, kickboxing, and the shooting range. But only after Mom recovered fully.

"Okay. Whatever."

Nolan put his hand on the doorknob. "Let's head downstairs to look at the footage, and then you tell me everything later."

Everything? Okay, sure, she'd tell him what she could. But she wouldn't tell him how she'd thought about him constantly since the week they'd spent together in that weird, precarious situation. Now she was in another weird and precarious situation. With the man she hadn't stopped thinking about.

Just how exactly was she supposed to concentrate on finding Danna or the manuscript with Nolan so near?

EIGHTEEN

In the great room, Nolan's gaze traveled over the huge windows, which reflected the inside of the lodge. All he could see beyond that reflection was pitch black. Was someone braving the cold to watch them? At this juncture, he wouldn't discount anything. After all, someone had broken into Ivy's room. Ivy stayed close behind him. In the reflection, he could see her gaze also remained on the panoramic view of the darkness.

Reflexively, he pressed his hand against his gun as he made his way through the spacious room to the dining hall and then the kitchen, following Jasper, the night manager. No hotel security was in place. There hadn't been a need. Until now. Annie might well close down her lodge completely for the winter after this.

Get a grip. This was Alaska. It was winter. No one was hiding in the cold and dark. No one was after *him.* But Ivy had been targeted and he had no idea exactly what was going on or how much danger she was in. She'd yet to tell him everything he wanted to know.

But first things first. Jasper led them through the kitchen where two of the staff were putting away what was left of the clam chowder. His stomach rumbled.

"Mind saving two bowls of that for us?" he asked with half a smile. "We'll clean up the mess."

"Sure thing." The older woman nodded and returned his smile.

They continued through until they came to an alcove. Jasper pointed at the equipment. "I trust you know how to find what you're looking for."

"I do, thanks."

"Good, because I've never used this equipment," Jasper said. "I wouldn't want to lose anything or mess anything up."

"I'm good." Nolan pulled out the chair to sit in it.

"I'll leave you to it, then," he said.

"No, wait. You should see this." Nolan wanted Jasper to know the potential threat and that a security guard was probably needed for the foreseeable future.

He and Ivy should leave as soon as possible to remove any remaining threats and simply take the threat, if it continued, with them. Nolan worked through the security footage, examining the entire day since he'd left this morning.

"There," Ivy said at the very moment he slowed the footage. "That's him. That's the man who warned me in the alley."

They watched a man use a keycard to open the door, breaking into the room. Nolan flicked his gaze to Jasper to see his reaction. Obviously, the criminal had gotten his hand on a master keycard—which wasn't that hard to do.

Jasper pursed his lips and shook his head. "I'm so sorry about this. We need to revamp our protocols. Be more diligent. But to be fair . . . we haven't had an incident here as long as I've been here"—he smiled—"or at least that I can remember. This place has been in my family for several generations. Annie's my grandmother."

"Then you can pass this news on to her for me. She can call me to talk to me anytime. Right now I need to make a copy of this footage," Nolan said. "Got anything I can use?"

"Sure." Jasper picked through a drawer and pulled out a USB drive. "Here you go."

"Thanks. One more thing. That room is off limits to housekeeping or guests for now. Understood?"

"Sure. You want to look for evidence you can use to identify this guy. Easy enough this time of year."

Nolan nodded. He'd inform the MCU trooper to also look at Ivy's old room when he arrived. "We'll get out of your hair as soon as we can get a ride out tomorrow."

"The ferry will be here in the morning," Jasper said.

Nolan glanced at Ivy. "I secured a plane for us. The pilot's coming from Haines."

After making a copy, Nolan stuck the USB drive in his pocket. "Thanks for your help."

"No problem." Jasper left to tend to his night-shift work.

Nolan stood and looked at Ivy. "You hungry?"

"I'm mostly tired, but I wouldn't say no to clam chowder."

They grabbed the bowls left out for them in the kitchen, along with water. At the table, she glanced up from the chowder and smiled. "This is good. Probably the highlight of my day."

"I'm glad you're eating. No telling what tomorrow has in store."

"Tell me about law enforcement in Alaska. What's it like? Do you usually have so much going on?"

"Me, personally? I cover a large rural area, which is how I prefer to work. That keeps me near my family, but the job is busy. I find a way to check on a problem in a village only to be called out to a domestic disturbance on the other side of my region. I'm always on the move."

"Never a dull day, then." She took another spoonful of clam chowder.

"Sometimes I'll do what we call 'RONs'—remain overnights. Some rural communities or villages have VPSOs—village public safety officers—but others don't. So we try to spend extra time in the rural communities. I try to stay over at least once a week in a village. One in particular, I sleep at the village school, where they usually keep mats or a sleeping room for visitors. I always bring my own sheets and pillowcases so no one has to fuss with that."

"Really? That's a different kind of law enforcement duty altogether."

"I'm sure other agencies do what they can, but yeah, we're different here. We have to be. Then, after spending the night in the village school, I'll eat breakfast with the schoolkids and even visit their classes. I hang out with the tribal councils or work on a case and write my reports at the library. Or play ball with the kids. It's important to get to know the people I protect and build trust."

Ivy put down her spoon, angled her head, and looked at him long and hard. Her deep-brown, gold-flecked eyes were filled with so much emotion, so much respect, he couldn't breathe.

"You're wrong about one thing, Nolan. No other agencies do this. That's not what law enforcement is like anywhere else in the US." She reached across the table and pressed her hand over his.

He held her gaze, unsure what to say. Unsure he *could* say it even if he knew, because he couldn't speak. Then she had mercy on him and pulled her hand back but replaced the warmth with her beautiful smile. "I didn't mean to interrupt. Go on. Tell me more."

He cleared his throat. Turned his thoughts to the more serious part of his job. "Investigating multiple homicides isn't common." Except for the surge in crime in Shadow Gap a couple years ago. But his Chief of Police sister knew how to handle herself. He wouldn't worry about her, at least not like he used to. She had her husband, Grier, to do that now, and Grier didn't need Nolan hovering over Autumn, protecting her. He'd moved away to give her space to be the police chief she needed to be without her Alaska State Trooper brother stifling her, but then he'd come back. Everything had changed. He shouldn't have expected things to stay the same. They never did. Just like this moment with Ivy was about to change.

"The sooner we can solve this, the better." He looked down at his soup, then up at her.

"Oh. You mean when we get back to the room, you want to know everything."

"Please."

They finished up their chowder in silence. Maybe he was taking on too much to think he should bring Ivy along and keep her close. He was exhausted but far more curious about the woman who sat across from him. He would get answers soon enough.

She seemed distracted, and why wouldn't she be? Finally she stood and grabbed his bowl to go with hers. "Let's wash these and then get this over with."

"Get what over with?" he asked.

"Your interrogation," she said.

"You make me sound harsh."

She shrugged. After cleaning up their dishes, they headed back to the room. Nolan had already taken pictures of the mess, and they gathered her things and headed to *his* room. He had the culprit on camera breaking into Ivy's room, and fingerprints would help them possibly identify him. He'd gathered what he could, but the footage revealed the guy had been wearing gloves. The state lab could possibly pull prints with the latex gloves if they were found.

Back in his new room—one that actually had a fireplace—he got the fire going quickly, while Ivy got ready for bed in the bathroom. He couldn't wait to get out of his gear, honestly. She came out in sweats and an oversized Alaska State T-shirt. She glanced down at it.

"Got it at the airport." She pulled her gun out from her back and lifted it. "Just because I'm comfortable, doesn't mean I'm not still dangerous."

"Oh, I have no doubt." And he meant that she was danger-ously attractive, but he wasn't in the mood for a broken heart.

In the bathroom, Nolan splashed water on his face and cleaned up.

Lord, if Danna is out there and still alive, please keep her safe. Help the right people find her, and . . . keep Ivy safe too. She could defend herself, and maybe the incident in the alley was nothing more than an anomaly, but in the end, they both had to watch each other's back.

On his laptop, Nolan transferred the security footage of the man who'd broken into Ivy's room to his sergeant and wrote up a detailed report.

He shut the laptop and moved to the sofa, where Ivy sat by the fire. He suspected she was waiting for the "interrogation."

He sat at the opposite end, not too close. "We're making some progress. We have the name and face of one suspect, and the face of another. What I don't know is if any of this is connected. So tell me everything. Please."

She hung her head. "I hadn't wanted anyone involved because it was just too risky."

"But I'm in this now. And not just because of proximity. Danna could be in it too. Nuna could have died because of it."

"Or another reason we haven't uncovered yet. I'll tell you, but please keep it between us. Although, I realize that if my search for *The Cold Pestilence* has truly intersected with Nuna and Danna's lives and caused harm, you won't be able to keep it between us."

"Understood. It feels kind of like you're stalling."

"Not stalling. Merely trying to get ahold of my thoughts. Donovan Treadwell is . . . or rather, he was . . . one of Dad's close friends. Retired now but decided to fill his days helping Mom in the rare book business. He knows a lot and seemed to enjoy talking with customers. Wanted to keep his fingers on the pulse. Mom jumped on that, and for a while, the way they flirted, I thought maybe there was a blooming romance. But it comforted me to know that someone was there to help her with the store while I worked with the FBI."

Ivy stopped and pursed her lips. He had a feeling she was trying to figure out how to hold out on him. He understood. He had his own demons to overcome, and he didn't like talking about that time, or thinking about it, but apparently he wasn't able to forget.

"Mom's cancer returned, and I resigned from my job to come back and be with her and help. Not two months into that, she wanted me to come to Alaska to look at what Alina had in her possession. Validate that it was, in fact, Jack London's lost manuscript, *The Cold Pestilence*, and purchase it. Again, I said no, but then Donovan approached me and tried to talk me into it. When I continued to refuse, that's when he revealed his true self. He's only a treasure hunter. He threatened to expose a secret he knew about my father that would devastate my mother. When he shared that secret with me, I was shocked. Horrified. I didn't believe it."

She looked at Nolan. "And I'm not sharing this with you here, because it doesn't matter. But I came to Alaska because of that threat. And . . . now, here we are."

He roughed his hand down his face. He'd really like to know what her father had been accused of doing that was so bad. Telling him the truth might be better than leaving him to his imagination, but as she'd said, that was her business, not his. At least at the moment.

"So, he wants you to get the manuscript and bring it back."

"To him, of course," she said. "I have no doubt that he won't let us keep it for Grace. He'll abscond with it."

"Because of the gold."

"Probably."

"So, about the gold . . ."

A pained expression crossed her face. "Lina had mentioned the manuscript was cursed. So when I asked Mom about it, she said that though *The Cold Pestilence* is based on true events, the location of the gold as well as the supposed curse are complete fiction. She called it 'the stuff of legends.' So, there you have it. You know as much as I do about the gold."

Interesting. Could someone still believe the gold detailed in the book really exists? "There's the matter of the man who doesn't want you to keep up your search."

She cracked a smile. "Apparently, he believes enough in my skills that he thinks that if he doesn't warn me away, I will actually find it."

"I have no doubt that you're good at what you do. What you did before." His opening into letting her tell him why she resigned—the real reason. He sensed there was more. "You mentioned the attacker must have thought your skills were good, and that's why he threatened you to stop. He somehow knows you. Could he know you from your time at the FBI? Could your job in the art division be related?"

"I don't think so, but anything's possible."

She wasn't going to tell him what happened at the FBI directly, but he would get her to talk. "Tell me *your* story."

Her scrunched face was a mixture of incredulity and amusement. "You know my story."

"I don't know what happened. Why'd you really resign, Ivy? People don't usually resign from a job like that without a lot of thought." He suspected Ivy's reasons went beyond her mother's illness.

"Do we really have to do this?" Her tone challenged him.

He'd much rather get to know her for personal reasons, and maybe his questions were a little of that too. Honestly, more along those lines. He held his breath as he waited for her response.

"We don't have to get to know each other," she continued. "We can work together . . . without getting close." She subtly flinched as if she wished she could take back the words.

Ouch. And he released that breath. More like it was punched from him. But he had his answer. He'd admit, that kind of hurt.

It helped when people shared everything. As former law enforcement, Ivy knew that. But people rarely offered up everything. If necessary, he'd have to keep digging and chipping away. He wasn't sure why he'd expected a different response from Ivy.

"I want to introduce another possible thread," she said. "Danna was trafficked before. I went back to see Lina after I met with you at your home office that day. Lina said that she brought Danna to Shadow Gap because this trafficking guy—who hasn't been arrested, by the way—really wants Danna. Her father, Lina's son, is not around, and her mother was an alcoholic, and Danna was basically all alone, so vulnerable. When Danna returned from her stay with Nuna, Lina was going to use the money from the manuscript to move them to the lower forty-eight, far from the trafficker who is fixated on Danna. She could go to college and make something of herself."

Ivy snagged her cell and scrolled through, searching for something. "The trafficker's name is Wayne Novak. Though someone is after the manuscript, and she was the last one to have it in her possession, her disappearance could be a simple matter of Novak getting his hands on her. Lina said that he'd come down to Shadow Gap to find her, and that was part of the reason she sent her to Nuna's." Ivy looked at Nolan. "How often does a trafficker chase after someone? I don't understand why he hasn't been arrested."

"Stalking tactics are often used to coerce people into trafficking, but I admit that does sound extreme. I'll look into what's going on. Why didn't you bring this up sooner?"

"I'm bringing it up now. From what I gathered, Danna has lived in Shadow Gap with her grandmother for a year, basically hiding so the guy wouldn't find them and follow. But somehow he did. Maybe Danna contacted him."

"I don't know why she would do that," he said.

"What if she contacted a friend, and he found her that way?" she asked.

"It's possible."

"Another thing. I think Lina was eager to accept the help I offered because of something she said."

"Oh yeah, what's that?"

"Lina said, 'No one cares about us here.' Mind telling me what she meant by that?"

Those words slammed into him. He hung his head, feeling the weight of her accusation on his shoulders. "I don't think it's a secret that trafficking is a huge problem—everywhere—but yes, definitely and especially in Alaska. A huge chunk of it is underreported. Victims go through intense trauma, and they're afraid to come forward and ask for help. Young women are especially targeted in the villages, the outskirts, then brought to the city. Sadly, compared to other cities, including New York and Oakland, Anchorage has the highest trafficking. Danna is fortunate to have escaped."

"And considering the vast difference in populations . . . how is this happening?"

The thought gutted him. They were failing. "The state has already put measures into place to fund training and investigations into missing and murdered Indigenous people. But honestly, the biggest issue is the lack of law enforcement in rural Alaska. So it's really more that the violence and trafficking is an epidemic in a huge state." He inched forward on the sofa and leaned in close. *Please . . . hear me, Ivy.* "I promise you, Ivy . . . I care. I'm doing my best to catch the bad guys."

And to keep vulnerable populations safe. But was it enough? *Oh God . . . it's not enough . . .*

He squeezed his eyes shut and pushed the images away—Hilary's eyes stared at him from beneath the ice. Not now.

"You know, it's not all that promising to hear you're searching for bad guys and a missing girl in a place that has the Alaska Triangle."

He opened his eyes to see a soft smile, which added some levity to their heavy conversation. Both of them were exhausted.

Neither of them could sleep.

"We're not in the Alaska Triangle."

"We might as well be."

"You really don't like Alaska, do you?" If only he could show her all the beautiful places, she'd change her mind.

Ivy rubbed her eyes, then dropped her hands to stare at the fire. "It's beautiful. But I don't have a lot of good memories here." She flicked her gaze to him. "Except for you, Nolan. The way you were there to help us when we got lost and stuck in that weird summer blizzard, you were my hero that day. That entire week. When I think of Alaska, I think of you." Her smile was pretty and sincere.

But she didn't like Alaska, so he didn't find those words encouraging.

"Maybe you should come to Florida sometime." She shook her head and then stood to leave. "But it's too far and too sunny for you, I'm sure."

Really, Sunshine Girl? Before she could escape, he gently grabbed her hand and pure attraction rushed through him. He should let go. He really should. But he held on. He'd wanted more with her before, though with her living in Florida and him in Alaska, that had been impossible.

She'd already laid down the ground rules with her proclamation that they didn't need to get close to work together. And they shouldn't. But letting go of the thread of connection between them was proving to be impossible.

And his next word proved that. "Stay."

NINETEEN

She stared down at him. He'd gently grabbed her wrist and held on. Nolan Long had all the charm and the looks, and everything about him made her insides turn to Jell-O. The look he gave her now nearly melted her completely.

She'd tried to ignore the tenderness coming off him as they talked about the case. He'd been authoritative and distant all day, but now, here alone by the fire, he was Nolan again. The man she'd met last summer in the middle of a weird blizzard. The man she might fall for, given the chance, but she couldn't see how that chance would ever happen.

"*Stay.*"

That word from him had definitely held her in place.

He was patiently chipping away at her walls. He wanted to know what happened, why she'd resigned. Telling him what she didn't want to think about could do no good. No good at all. And would definitely drive a new wedge between them. After all, Nolan was well-respected in the law enforcement community and came from a law enforcement family.

"What . . . what more is there to talk about?"

Yeah, he had a deep, dark secret too. Something happened . . . before. She knew that look. She shared that sentiment. And that's what he was really asking of her—to share her secrets.

"Please," he said. "I need to tell you something."

155

She sat again, decidedly too close to him. But he stood, for which she was grateful.

I can breathe now.

He scraped both hands down his face—he'd been doing that a lot lately—and paced in front of the fire.

"Nolan. What is it?"

"A few months ago, I joined a task force focusing on human trafficking, investigating missing and exploited women."

More pacing. Huffing and sighing.

"We were closing in on a ring that targeted a village. I tracked the ringleader. He took one of the trafficked women as a hostage out onto the middle of a frozen pond. Held a knife to her throat. They both went through the ice. I tried to save them. Save her. I can't get the images out of my head. She stared up at me from under the ice, then she disappeared."

Ivy's insides tangled into a knot. Emotion thickened in her throat, but even if she could speak, what could she say? He was clearly tormented, and she wouldn't pretend to have the power to comfort him.

But when he said nothing more, she sat forward. "I'm sorry, so sorry."

"I woke up in the hospital. I'd fallen through the ice too, but I don't remember that. I only remember seeing her staring up at me. She'd been taken. Had counted on me and I failed."

He moved to the fireplace and leaned an arm against the hearth. Stared down at it.

"Why did you share that with me?"

"Because I care, Ivy. I've been one of those working on this exact problem. But I understand why Lina feels like the authorities have failed her."

She got it. Nolan felt like he had personally failed. She also got something else.

He'd shared this gut-wrenching story with her that was probably the stuff of his nightmares. And he wanted something from her—he wanted to know why she had resigned from the FBI. That he'd figured out it was more than her mother's cancer returning told her that she hadn't hidden her emotions well enough from him. Regardless, she wasn't ready to tell him tonight and wasn't sure she ever would be.

Then he angled his head toward her, his intense gaze landing on hers and searching. His need to know what happened before, his need to know *her* . . . sent a palpable ache through her core.

And just like that, she felt their deep connection—like Ivy, Nolan had struggled in his career trying to help people. He'd fought and lost. He willed her to understand, and she did. Oh . . . she did. But how did he know she could? Surely he didn't already know what she'd been through. That wasn't possible.

But somehow, he'd sensed it.

She could see it in his eyes.

"Tell me," he whispered.

I can't . . .

But then again, she couldn't deny him. And sharing this much with him would make her even more vulnerable. She stood and moved to stand with him by the fire. He leaned over to stoke it.

It was getting late and they both needed to sleep, but she knew she wouldn't be able to. Not yet. Putting the poker away, he stood to his full height and looked down at her.

Why did I move to stand so close to him? After the story he'd shared, she wanted to comfort him, but she didn't know how. And with her own baggage and current predicament, she probably wasn't the one to help him.

But then again, she could offer the one thing he was asking and share her story. That could help. Maybe.

"You can trust me, Ivy. I told you what happened so that you would know that I understand." He touched her chin and gently lifted it so she'd have to look into his eyes again. "I understand *you*."

She'd been drawn to this man the first moment she'd met him, and then the week she'd spent with him had anchored her thoughts, her heart, and nothing had changed after months apart. She wanted to press into him. But he was asking . . .

She closed her eyes. "It's part of a past I want to forget."

"Is it something you can't share? Part of an ongoing investigation?"

She opened her eyes. "I suspect they're still investigating the terrorist group because of a suspected planned domestic terror attack. I was undercover as an art buyer. The group was trying to fund terrorist activities and selling stolen art to a very specialized group of collectors. It was my job to infiltrate and find those collectors at an auction, and I'd worked for two years to establish myself as one of them and learn their identities."

He took her hand and led her back to the sofa. "Sounds dangerous."

"No more dangerous than fighting crime in this rugged terrain while facing a potentially lethal environment and dangerous weather." She gave him a tenuous, nervous smile. "I got tasked with working undercover to search for evidence or intel about a suspected terrorist named Danny Hinckle. He caught me searching his office and aimed his gun at me. I knew he was going to kill me, and I fired my weapon at the same time he did."

"Were you hit?"

"Grazed, but I killed him. In front of his daughter, Natalie. That tore me up—the look of horror on her face. I mean, I'd taken this girl to the museum, even. I . . . I got too close. During the investigation, she claimed that I was the one to threaten him. She lied, but for a while there, I wasn't sure if I would be found innocent."

Nolan studied her for a few moments, then hung his head. Finally, he lifted his face to look at her. "What a nightmare. I'm sorry you had to go through that."

"Not everyone believes I'm innocent. I think Natalie convinced herself of what she saw. Thought she saw. Had me even doubting myself."

"You had the right to defend yourself."

She nodded. Pulled in a breath. "When Mom's cancer returned, she didn't ask me, but I knew it was time to resign and go be with her. Work at the store. Return to that life."

"Why'd you leave that life for the FBI?"

"After getting my degree, I just decided that I needed to do something. Do more. I still blamed myself for what happened to Grace. I decided to join the FBI. I wanted to be part of the CARD unit—Child Abduction Rapid Deployment—but with my degree and background, they wanted me in the art division. I wanted to save children. Somehow make up for my biggest mistake. A mistake that cost a life. And instead, I shot and killed a man in front of his daughter. How was I supposed to recover from that, even with therapy?"

Nolan gently pulled her to him and she went willingly, held on tightly as she leaned against his sturdy chest. She felt the strong, steady beat of his heart, maybe beating faster than normal. She felt the rush of emotion, the reassurance he tried to pour into her. Maybe sharing her story with him hadn't been such a bad idea because he seemed to know exactly what she needed. He was the one to help *her*.

"So, you resigned. And then Donovan blackmailed you to find the manuscript."

"Yes."

"Why not get help from the FBI?"

"Donovan knows I won't do that because I risk exposing my father's past and hurting my mother. If she died because of the devastating news when she needs to remain optimistic for her health, especially during her treatments, then that would be on me. It's not worth the risk to Mom's life. A blow like that when she's trying to beat this illness, that alone could kill her."

"And she needs you back with her."

"I wish it was that simple. And now someone shows up to warn me away from searching for the manuscript."

What am I supposed to do, Lord?

"But since I'm not looking for the manuscript now, not really, I don't know what to do with that. All I know is that when I saw Danna's picture, she reminded me of Grace and my heart nearly cracked wide open."

"And you made it your mission to find her."

"Yes." Ivy pushed away from him, suddenly feeling awkward at their proximity. She shook her head and looked away, then stood and moved to the fireplace and rested her hand on the hearth. She was sharing far more than she would have imagined with Nolan Long.

A stranger.

Why would she trust him with what happened when *she* hadn't fully processed it yet?

"We should really get some sleep," he said.

Of course.

Honestly, she felt lighter having told him. Aside from her debriefing by the FBI and, of course, processing the fact that she'd killed a man, working through that with their on-staff therapist, she hadn't talked to anyone else.

She headed toward the bed, knowing he would take the sofa again like he had last night, knowing both would remain on alert. Nolan said nothing, but he was listening. From their brief time together before, she knew this about him. He listened to people. He listened . . . to her.

In the bed, she wrapped the blankets around her and prayed for sleep, even though her brain was too wired after revisiting, reliving, what had happened in the past, what could happen in the future, and what could happen in the present with Nolan Long.

TWENTY

The next morning, Ivy's soft snores woke Nolan long before sunrise, which didn't mean much since the sun didn't grace them with daylight until after 8:00 a.m. in February. Still, he hadn't actually been completely dead to the world. He'd slept with one eye open, as the saying went, and he would have suspected the same of her, but for the snores. The sound made him happy—because it meant she could relax with him. Trust him so completely she could fall asleep, even though she was concerned about the many layers of danger twisting around them. Worry that Danna remained missing weighed on them both.

They held on to hope that she was alive and had escaped both the storm and the killer. Maybe they were two people leaning too hard on what would ultimately prove to be false hope.

He was eager to get back to Shadow Gap to talk to Lina and find out more details that could help them in their search for Danna. And though he wasn't supposed to be working the investigation, he wanted to find out more information about Walker's murder because Carl had died in the man's house. He hadn't been informed about the cause of the explosion that took out the house with Carl inside. The thoughts and questions swirled in his mind. Pressure built in his chest. He wanted answers *now*.

Remaining as quiet as possible, he rose from the sofa and

stirred the fire again to chase away the chill. Last night, in addition to locking the door, he'd shoved a chair up under it for good measure, considering a man had gotten into their other room with a stolen keycard. It could happen again with them inside this time.

Her arm covering her face, Ivy hadn't moved and seemed to be in a deep sleep. He wouldn't wake her just yet. To think, he was with Ivy Elliott and not because he'd gone to Florida to connect with her again. It was surreal. He was grateful he'd been given permission to bring her in close and work with her.

Nolan had chosen a rural area to serve, knowing that the troopers wanted someone in this region who could think outside the box, be creative and innovative. And that's what he was doing. Nolan had little backup but he was well aware others had far less support—especially those troopers in the rural mainland of Alaska. Still, when minutes counted, it didn't matter if help was fifty or a thousand miles away. That's why AST were encouraged to work with what they had, and keeping Ivy close was his way of being creative. They were on the same team and might as well work together, and at the same time, he could protect her.

Sure, Ivy was trim and fit and trained and fully capable, but when he'd seen the second attacker standing over her—his heart had stuttered and might have completely stopped if the man hadn't fled. Ivy claimed she could have handled it, and while he hoped that was true, he was glad he didn't have to find out.

Nolan had already been involved in too much trauma involving people he cared about. He quietly moved to the window and glanced outside, unsure of what he thought he might see in the utter darkness of a cold winter. Reassured that no one was going to come barging into their room in the next ten minutes, he headed for the shower.

Nearly seven in the morning and the sky was slate gray.

He left the bathroom door cracked—just in case—and

hoped to be finished showering before she woke up. He didn't bother shaving. That would take too much time. Sweats on, he wrapped the towel around his neck.

Hearing a noise, he grabbed his gun and stepped out of the bathroom.

Ivy sat on the edge of her bed. Her hair was askew and her eyes looked sleepy. But she blinked the sleep away and then far too slowly lifted her gaze to his face. Her eyes slightly widened—some feral emotion flashed in them—then she looked away.

"Mind putting a shirt on?"

"Not at all." The spark of appreciation in her eyes had his heart pounding erratically.

He snatched the T-shirt off the back of the door, then pulled it on before stepping out again. "I thought I heard something. I wanted to make sure we're safe. If you're going to shower, do it now. We need to get going."

She stretched, her long auburn hair tumbling over her shoulders, and he averted his gaze and made a beeline for his pack on the sofa before she caught him staring. He should be glad they were heading out of such close quarters because Ivy Elliott could drive him crazy. He needed to get through the next few days, find the answers, during which time he couldn't let the beautiful, intriguing woman distract him.

He needed to let go of the one who got away.

With the bathroom door shut and the shower running, he finished dressing, then checked his phone after a text notification.

He read the text and his spirits sank.

"Are you kidding me?" he grumbled at the news.

The plane had mechanical issues and could be delayed for hours. Nolan rubbed his forehead, pushing against the deep frown. They might take the ferry after all.

Of course, one of the many calls he'd been waiting for was returned while he'd been in the shower.

While searchers had come to the region, Nolan had put in

calls to all possible transports out during the specific window of time in which Danna had gone missing. Her name hadn't appeared on any manifests. She could have taken a private boat or plane, but everyone knew she'd gone missing and should have reported that information.

He returned the call, and fortunately the man answered. "Captain Seymour."

Seymour captained the M/V *Brady*, a smaller day vessel named after a glacier in Glacier Bay.

"Nolan Long here. Thanks for returning my call. You have information for me?"

"As mentioned, Danna Wolf didn't make a reservation and wasn't on the passenger manifest. You suggested we look through security footage. Our security officer discovered that she'd clearly been on the M/V *Brady*, getting a ride out on our last transport before the storm."

"Do you have the name she was traveling under?" Nolan asked.

"We're working on learning that information."

"Was she traveling alone?" he asked.

"As far as we can tell."

"And where did she disembark?" Nolan had so many more questions.

"We're still reviewing footage but haven't confirmed where she got off. After Dunbar, we stopped in Juneau, Mountain Cove, Shadow Gap, and then remained in Haines yesterday until the storm cleared. We're back in Dunbar this morning, of course."

"I need a favor." Nolan took a long breath. "Please don't broadcast the news that Danna is alive or share this information with anyone."

"I don't understand," Captain Seymour said. "People want to know that she's alive and well."

"The situation is complicated, and she could be in danger.

For the moment, let's hold the information close. I'll need to speak with her relatives as well, and, if anything, they should hear this news first."

"I'll instruct my security personnel that reviewed the footage."

"Thank you. I'll be booking a ride for two this morning."

"I look forward to seeing you," he said, and ended the call.

Nolan quickly called the ferry reservation number rather than fumbling around online and made the reservations. He wouldn't take advantage of the Alaska State Trooper program allowing him to ride the ferry system for free as long as he served as security while on board. Of course, he would be available, but he and Ivy needed to work on their investigation. The M/V *Brady* only carried 125 people, small for a ferry, and he was relieved to learn he and Ivy were among 50 people leaving Dunbar. Of course, they would pick up more people at other stops. What he needed to know was where they should get off.

Where did you go, Danna?

Until he learned otherwise, Shadow Gap would remain their destination. He put a call in to Lina Wolf, but the call disconnected before he could leave a voice mail. He sent her an urgent text to call him.

Danna had been seen alive before the storm. Relief filled his heart. Now, to keep her that way.

Nolan hoped that information hadn't already been leaked. Someone was after her. If nothing else, she'd witnessed a murder, and she was on the run from the killer and possibly even from Novak, the trafficker that had held her captive before. Nolan didn't believe she'd killed her uncle, but then again, he couldn't completely rule that out, even with Craig's statement—the kid could have gotten his facts wrong. Happened all the time.

As he considered the possibility that Danna was responsible for her uncle's death, Nolan didn't like the scenario under which that could have happened—an uncle trying to harm his niece, maybe even for the manuscript and the *cursed* gold. Though she'd taken the ferry, he still had no information on where she'd gotten off or her destination or where she was now. The bathroom door opened and steam escaped, along with the scent of honey and vanilla. Ivy stepped out wearing a T-shirt and ski pants, her hair in a towel.

"Change of plans." He zipped up his duffel.

"What's that?"

"We're taking the ferry."

"What? Why? Won't that take longer?"

"Considering our plane has mechanical issues, no. But I have news. Danna made it out of here."

Ivy's relieved smile hit him across the room. "Oh, Nolan. I'm so happy to hear it. I kept hoping and praying she had."

She dropped to her bed and pressed her hands over her face. Hiding tears of joy? Then he knew he'd guessed right when she dropped her hands and looked at him.

"She took the ferry," he said. "We're taking that same ferry and we'll ask questions of the crew on the ride. So, it's all working out. By the time we arrive in Shadow Gap, we'll know more."

"Like where Danna headed?"

"And why she's running."

"You don't think she was the one who killed Nuna, do you? I can't believe she would."

"You don't know her."

"But I do know what I saw and heard from Nuna. The look in his eyes when he said to find her. It was one of love and fear—for *her*. She's on the run. Someone is chasing her, and it could be Novak."

"He could even have killed Nuna. We have too many questions and not enough answers. But don't forget, someone could be watching you too, Ivy. The man who warned you away from searching might still be watching somehow. Tracking you. Give me your phone. Let's get rid of it now."

"What? No."

"If he's tracking you, and you don't go back to Florida, he might suspect you're still searching and that puts you at risk."

And Nolan was just now thinking of it. He wanted to kick something. Kick *himself*.

"Good. Let him." She stood in defiance.

"He might come after you."

"I'm counting on it." Anger flashed in her eyes as she pulled on a fleece top and then her turquoise parka. Then she held up her small Glock with confidence, flashing it at him, before tucking it away in a holster at her side. "I'll be ready."

Fine. "I'll keep your gun with me. You're not allowed to keep it with you on the Alaska Marine Highway Ferry but have to hand it over to the custody officer for the ride."

She frowned and gave him her pistol. He was bending the rules here, but under the circumstances, he wouldn't completely relieve her of her ability to protect herself.

He'd face the threat with Ivy and, this time, capture the man and get answers. He was almost with her in wanting the attacker to return with another warning. Almost.

TWENTY-ONE

vy was quick to decide she preferred the ferry to a bush plane. She wasn't gripping the rails on the boat, holding on through turbulence, fearing that any moment they would crash. This experience, so far, was much calmer. Still, while the day after the storm—yesterday—had been glorious, today was cold and gray and rainy and nasty.

Not that she'd had much time to enjoy the view until now. She and Nolan had taken a tour of the ferry, reviewed the footage of Danna, who'd been wrapped up tightly in her coat and topped with a fur cap. Her face had been covered with a scarf, but they'd gotten a brief glimpse when she rewrapped her scarf. That was her, all right.

Then Ivy and Nolan had conducted interviews with the crew, some of whom had been on the ferry with Danna, and so Ivy needed this break on the deck to get fresh, cold air along with a view. She enjoyed the brief reprieve and stood alone on the top deck out in the elements, enduring the blustery wind to take in this magical land.

The air was thick with fog, and clouds hung so low over the water she could almost reach out and touch them, and beyond the low-hanging marine fog she could still see the top of the snowcapped mountains on either side of her—coming and going. In all directions, really. A gust of cold air swirled around her and she tugged the hood of her parka over her black knit beanie.

This place was the definition of a winter wonderland. Honestly, she'd never seen anything more beautiful, even compared to Florida with its white beaches and warm sunshine. Except she wasn't here to sightsee but to keep up the search for Danna.

Thank you, Lord, for protecting her. Please help us find her before it's too late.

After talking to the crew members that had been present on the ride with Danna, she and Nolan learned that two of them remembered Danna, but she'd registered as Lila White. Knowing the alias she was using could help them in their search. She'd obviously had another ID on hand and, under that name, had booked a ride to Haines, but the ferry had made stops in Juneau, Mountain Cove, and then Shadow Gap before moving on to Haines. Danna could have gotten off at any of those stops and not returned to the ferry. They couldn't confirm where she'd landed.

Ivy and Nolan held on to the hope and their theory that Danna was heading home to her grandmother, Lina, who had rescued her from trafficking in the northern part of the state. Nolan had left a text message with Lina to call him. Then he tried again to call her, but failing to get through, he'd left another text message asking her to stay home and wait for her granddaughter, who was very much alive. Then Ivy had listened in on the call he'd had with his sister, Shadow Gap Police Chief Autumn Long. The town was on the lookout for Danna and on alert to protect her from anyone who was waiting for her return with malicious intent.

They needed to protect Danna, but also, she had answers to their biggest question—Who had murdered her uncle, Nuna Grainger? But if they found Danna at home with her grandmother, then Ivy's mission would be complete, and she would

no longer be needed. Maybe Danna also still had the manuscript, in which case Ivy would validate it as best she could,
then transfer funds to Lina, who could then continue with her
plans to move them far away from Novak's reach. Danna could
go to school to become an artist or a writer or whatever she
wanted to be.

Ivy wholeheartedly wished that would be the case when they
arrived in Shadow Gap. But her gut told her that it wasn't going
to be so easy. Things usually didn't unfold for her or naturally
wrap up in a tidy bow so she could go home unscathed.

She just wanted to be in Shadow Gap right now. Find Danna
right now.

Because time was ticking.

And this ferry moved. So. Slowly. As it sliced through the
cold, dark waters that carved through this land known as the
last frontier.

Again, she took to heart the beauty before her. A stunning
wilderness she could never imagine and—she chuckled inside—
made more gorgeous since Nolan Long was here. She could
not escape the image of shirtless Nolan standing in the doorway as he exited the bathroom. With that physique, the cut
of his muscles, he had to work out all the time. He had to eat
just right. And yet she'd seen none of that on this investigation, which he'd insisted they work together. He wasn't fooling
her. He wanted to work together so he could keep an eye out
for her.

Nolan was a protector. Fine by her. She just had to be sure to
keep her distance—personally, that is. But that was proving to
be harder than she thought. The wind gusts picked up, biting
into her skin, buffeting her body.

She sensed when someone stood behind her, then Nolan
stepped up to the rail right next to her, his arm bumping hers,
and leaned against the rail to look out over the water at the
view.

"Why don't you come inside and get warm?" he asked. "A Florida girl like you must be freezing out here. You're not accustomed to the cold."

She chuckled. "You *live* here and you're not accustomed to it."

"Touché," he said.

She turned and caught the concerned look on his face. "What happened?"

"I'd prefer that we talked inside. Besides, another weather system is coming in. Might as well get warm and get ready for a potentially rough ride. We can head to the observation lounge. You can still see the view but you're out of the elements."

She wished he would tell her now what he'd learned. The wind picked up as she trailed Nolan.

Inside the observation lounge, they found seating near the window, where she viewed the fast-moving gray clouds. The marine fog had been blown away, making for a clearer view. The water started churning, becoming rougher, angrier, as the wind increased.

She might have decided on ferries over planes too early. There were pros and cons for each.

"What's going on? One look at your face . . ." and she knew the news wasn't good.

"Autumn got ahold of Alina. Danna isn't there. If that's where she was headed, she had plenty of time to find her way home."

"What do you think could have happened?"

"I don't know." Nolan took her hands in his and rubbed them. "You're so cold. You should put your gloves back on."

And miss the warm tingles you're giving me? No, thank you. "No, please keep rubbing them. You're warming them up." Warming her whole body up, but she kept that to herself.

Though he continued to rub her hands, she could tell his mind was a million miles away. She pulled her hands from him, then jammed them in her coat pocket. The inside of the lounge was much warmer than outside, but still chilly to her way of thinking.

"Something else is bothering you. What is it? What have you learned?"

He pursed his lips. Worked his jaw.

"Nuna was a retired research scientist, though he'd been working as a consultant at Pacific Northwest Lab."

"A scientist—like Gene Whitlock."

"Right. That's a possible link, so we're getting somewhere, but I'm surprised to learn of Nuna's background."

"This surprises you, why?"

"Well, for one thing I want to understand the family dynamics. How does he work as a research scientist while his niece becomes vulnerable and then is trafficked? I don't get that part. I don't understand it."

"But you know it happens. People get busy with their careers and lose track of what happens to others, especially if they aren't talking to them or seeing them daily."

He removed his knit cap and scraped a hand through his hair.

"What else?" she asked. "What *kind* of scientist?"

"Multiple specialties. I'm still trying to unpack it. Chemistry."

"And what else?"

"Autumn was going to send me all the information she could pull up. But one of the items that stands out is his certificate in international security, and that he spent twenty years at Los Alamos National Laboratory."

"You mean *the* Los Alamos National Laboratory of the Manhattan Project fame?"

"Yep. That's the one. Despite the nasty nuclear weapons business, LANL is still considered the Department of Energy's premier science institution."

This news left her reeling. She couldn't have imagined it, but still, what did it mean for the murder investigation? She was only here to find Danna. "Can you send me the information when you get it?"

"Yeah. We can pore over it together."

Ivy studied Nolan. His scruffy face. Dark-blue eyes, almost gray today, as if reflecting his mood, or the environment in which he lived. The intensity she saw in his eyes—his whole face, really—scared her.

As if reading her mind, he looked away. Measuring his next words?

"Are you thinking what I'm thinking?" she asked.

"Maybe." He shifted toward her again, that look in his eyes saying he hoped that she was thinking something else entirely. "What are you thinking?"

"Nuna's murder could be about something much bigger, something other than a treasure-map manuscript with cursed gold or a crazed trafficker. Danna could have been at the wrong place at the wrong time. And the stupid manuscript is a subplot, a side story."

"Yep. My thinking, exactly."

"If that's the case, this takes everything to a whole new level." She almost said "*threat* level" but held back.

"Autumn and Grier are digging deeper, but carefully. This is more Grier's field of expertise, so we're in good hands."

"I'm surprised that Nuna's information was so easily accessed."

"I didn't say it was easy," Nolan said. "But it could simply be the tip of the iceberg, and we won't see more than that. He's one scientist among thousands of scientists."

"And murder makes him stand out among his peers, which is an interesting thought." One Ivy didn't like one bit. "What about your trooper buddies? The MCU? Don't you need to talk to them about the discovery?"

Leaning over his thighs, he clasped his hands. "I'll put it in my report, but I have no idea if they'll do anything with it. Or if they'll even inform me of what they've learned, though we're supposed to work together. And I'm worried this investigation, working with you, will also get sidetracked with all my other responsibilities. I wouldn't be able to focus in on finding Danna. I'm sure when I get back to Shadow Gap I'll have to answer callouts in the region, and my role in this investigation could take a back seat. It's a juggling act and the nature of the beast, that's all."

"You wish you'd taken your vacation, don't you?"

The hint of a smile cracked his lips. "No. I wouldn't want to miss this."

Had she imagined that look that told her he was glad to be here . . . with *her*? That he wouldn't miss this because she was here? She gave a semi-incredulous smile and shake of her head.

"If I end up getting pulled in a thousand directions, if it comes to that, then maybe I'll insist on taking the vacation."

"But then you wouldn't be part of the investigation, so how would that help?"

"Not officially. But you and I are working together pretty well. Maybe because we're working together, we'll find Danna before it's too late. And find Nuna's killer. I'm saying I want to focus on this. I'm already distracted enough." He glanced at her again, then looked away.

Oh yeah. He was a distraction to her too.

Then he sat up tall. "Something feels off."

"What exactly?"

"I'm talking about the ferry." He stared intently out the windows. "We're off course." He started to stand.

A loud boom resounded as the boat shook and rocked, jarring her insides. The lights flickered, then shut off.

TWENTY-TWO

He was knocked back to the seat.

His whole body tensed as he gripped the seat with one hand and held on to Ivy with the other. He waited for his eyes to adjust to the much darker room. He'd never been on a ferry when the power had failed. He glanced around at the panicked passengers.

Ivy's wide-eyed gaze landed on him. "What's happening?"

"I have no idea, but I intend to find out." He released her and stood.

Before Nolan got far, Captain Seymour entered the deck. As soon as they saw him, the few people huddled together on the far side rushed forward and bombarded him with questions. He held his hands up. "Just calm down. It's going to be okay."

"What happened?"

"Just remain calm. Everything is under control. Please remain seated and wait for instructions."

"Where are we? What's going on?"

"We've had some engine trouble and are docking until we can get it fixed. We're at Four Bears Island. Again, please remain seated and I will keep you informed."

He looked at Nolan and lowered his voice. "Can we talk?"

Nolan followed him to a private alcove, tugging Ivy along behind him. When Captain Seymour gave him a questioning look, he said, "She's with me. Now talk."

"As I shared with the passengers, we started having engine trouble. A generator failed and so we limped along to the nearest place we could hope to dock—Four Bears Island, where there's a small village, Bolgar—which isn't on our route, but it's close. Unfortunately, the rough water pushed us into the pilings."

"The dock pilings? Is the structure unstable now?"

"My crew is looking into all issues. In the meantime, Jared, the one man on security, was injured and he's down for the moment. I need your help in keeping everyone calm. The crew is ushering the rest of the passengers up and onto this level. We're fortunate that we were only carrying half our capacity."

"And why is that?" Ivy asked.

"The less disgruntled passengers we have."

Nolan suspected the captain wasn't sharing everything, but that was his prerogative. "Back to what you said about a failed generator. I know the ferry system has had some troubles in the past"—even to the point that only one working ferry was available because the rest were getting repairs or waiting for repairs due to lack of maintenance funds—"but is this common?"

"You know about the M/V *Matanuska*, right? A three-day trip turned into three weeks. And that was due to a new piece of equipment that broke down. I hope that's not the case here. The mechanic will let us know if this can be fixed or if we're going to wait on a part or another ferry for transport. Depending on what I find out, we'll be offering the passengers refunds, but in the meantime, we can offer free accommodations and food for any additional time they're stranded." He shrugged, a painful expression on his face, then he smiled. "It's all in a day's work here in Alaska, eh?"

"Yes, it is." Nolan loathed this delay, and it interfered with a time-sensitive investigation and the search for a young woman in danger. "I'll stand with you as you explain what's happening, and let's hope my presence will help keep them calm."

"I appreciate your help. Another aspect here is the weather. It's turning nasty again. High winds are expected and rough waters. I've been in touch with the Ruckus Inn over on the island, letting them know they may get an influx of people who don't want to remain on the ferry. In fact, I'm going to suggest everyone head for the inn because the power keeps flicking on and off and it might be too cold to stay."

"The *Ruckus* Inn doesn't sound family-friendly," Ivy said.

Nolan was glad she'd mentioned it. This wasn't part of his region, so he wasn't familiar with it.

"Named for the sound the gap winds make," the captain said. "And guess what? This is the time of the year when they hit the hardest. I'd prefer that anyone who plans to stay at the inn until we know our estimated time of departure get there before the winds hit."

Great. "Thanks for the heads-up."

Nolan gestured for the captain to lead him out and face the crowd of fifty people gathered and waiting. Captain Seymour stepped out with a half smile—obviously not too pleased but needing to project confidence. He was good at this. Passengers closed in, gathering around him, then shouted and made demands. Nolan was surprised at how much outrage a small group of people could produce, but Captain Seymour answered their questions and provided instructions.

"Once power is fully restored," the captain said, "then you're welcome to board again and stay until we've either completed repairs and are on our way or other transportation is arranged."

"How long will that take?" one passenger asked.

"I can't say just yet, but I'll keep you informed as I learn new information." Captain Seymour was slowly backing away, ready to make his exit. Two crew members stepped forward. Getting ready to usher people across the dock with the damaged piling?

Nolan understood the passengers' anger and frustration at this turn of events.

Bottom line, it could get too cold to stay aboard, so most passengers and probably crew would leave, except those who were trying to fix the generator. The crew members working to resolve this were under a lot of pressure. Nolan knew little about the ferry lines. Even one ferry out of service put a strain on a system already old and struggling, and as far as he and Ivy were concerned, this turn of events definitely put them in a bind.

After the passengers settled down and accepted their fate, he got on his satellite phone to contact Autumn. The sooner he arranged for another mode of transportation for him and Ivy, the better. The next step would include helping the crew usher passengers to the island and the Ruckus Inn. The passengers would then be responsible for re-embarking when the time came.

Autumn answered the call. "Nolan, where are you?"

The connection crackled. He might not have long before the call dropped, so he quickly explained their predicament.

"See if you can get me a bush pilot with a floatplane to fly down to get us. We can't waste time sitting here while we wait for another boat or this one to be fixed. I just learned that not that long ago, a ferry was stranded for three weeks. Not saying I think that's going to happen here, but please, just get us out of here."

"I'll see what I can find you. Worst case, I'll use the *Long Gone*."

Dad had renovated the old boat years ago, and Autumn used it for police business when necessary if the Shadow Gap PD's patrol boat wasn't available.

"I appreciate the help."

Nolan walked close to Ivy as they fought the wind and icy rain along the slippery dock, then hiked the barely paved path toward the Ruckus Inn with the group of grumbling passengers whose vehicles remained on the disabled vessel. If the ferry couldn't be fixed, then all those vehicles would have to be transferred to the new vessel or remain on the old one and be towed. What a time-consuming mess.

Frigid rain poured down on them as they rushed forward and finally into the Ruckus Inn, a two-story clapboard structure. The light-blue paint needed another coat or two or three, especially since it was the first stop welcoming visitors to the small community. Nolan opened the door and held it for the passengers, who would probably fill the place to capacity.

Ivy came up last and rushed inside. He closed the door and leaned in so she could hear him above the noise. "The good news is that there's a warm place to hang out for the next few hours."

"What are we going to do, Nolan? We don't have time for this."

"I'm hoping Autumn will send us a ride."

Ivy eyed him in surprise. "It's that bad, huh?"

"No point in waiting to see how long it will take."

"Why is everything so hard in Alaska?"

"It's just a way of life here. I'm sure Florida has its issues. Like traffic. Overpopulation. Overcrowded beaches. Sinkholes." Oh, he could keep going, but at that warning look in her eyes, he would stop now.

Nolan led them through the dimly lit pub-like restaurant to find a corner where two chairs sat against the wall near the stairwell. The tables were all filled up—local patrons and ferry passengers too. "Sit here while I talk to the manager."

At the counter he talked to a flustered waiter stunned to have to deal with so many unhappy customers, though Captain Seymour had already had a conversation with the manager to expect a rush on the place.

"They need to buy something to sit at the tables," he told Nolan.

"I believe arrangements have already been made with you. I need to talk to the manager."

"He's just there. Stepping out of his office."

Nolan approached the short, round, balding man and leaned in. "I want to secure adjoining rooms for the night."

"What? For just you and who else? What about all the others?"

The door opened, letting in a gust of cold, and another crew member entered. "I was told arrangements have already been made, but if not, I suspect the man approaching will take care of the situation and compensate you for your trouble."

"We don't have rooms for this many people."

"That's why I'm trying to secure two connected rooms right now." He couldn't stay in the same room with Ivy again.

The guy nodded and urged Nolan into his office. "No. Right here, right now."

He wouldn't leave Ivy unprotected. Ever since the lights flickered on the ferry, he'd worried this whole scenario had been a deliberate attempt to slow their efforts, because this was just too much bad luck in one day. Mechanical failure on the plane he'd chartered and now this. He might be overreacting, overthinking. Then again, no point in taking any risks.

The manager moved behind the counter and Nolan gave him his name, then handed over the appropriate cash to receive old-fashioned keys for two connected rooms. "These are my only rooms that connect. Smart thinking."

Before he headed back to Ivy, he received a call and answered it quickly. Captain Seymour relayed additional information that was disturbing, to be sure.

After ending the call, Nolan weaved through the packed tables to get back to Ivy. They were all stuck here until they weren't. He suspected others were trying to secure transportation on their own but were falling short. There were only so many ways around this state without a road system to connect everything.

He considered taking additional passengers when Autumn arrived—as many as the *Long Gone* could reasonably hold.

But they were heading back to Shadow Gap and not making stops elsewhere. He would see what was happening when she arrived and make a decision then.

"Uh oh." Ivy stared at her cell, then looked up at him. "I wouldn't have thought I'd have cell coverage here of all places. I got a text from Donovan."

He leaned closer as she read the text but couldn't see the words. "Well?"

"She fired him! What is going on? As far as Mom knew, he was there just to help. He was good to her and took her to her infusions." She turned her back on him to make a call, then growled. She turned back around. "The call dropped."

"Here." He handed over his phone.

"Thanks, Nolan. I don't know what I'd do without you."

The words were innocent enough, and she hadn't meant them the way he found himself wanting her to mean them. She made the call and put some distance between them. Just as well. He could barely hear her over the hum of voices.

He settled into the uncomfortable chair, waiting for the moment when they could discreetly lug their duffels up the stairs to the rooms he'd secured. The manager might have thought him selfish to secure a room before others tried, but he was thinking of Ivy and her safety. Autumn was working to get them out of here, but he was planning for a scenario in which it could take hours for help to arrive just for Nolan and Ivy. He couldn't count on the ferry's power or generator being restored anytime soon.

That's right. Justify your actions to yourself.

Ivy turned to him, the phone to her ear, then lowered it. "I can't get ahold of him. I don't know what this means."

She handed the phone back, and he took it but grabbed her hand and held it.

She freed her hand to press it over her eyes. He hated seeing her so tormented.

He wished he could do more. When he'd first seen her in town, the thought that Providence had brought them together again flitted through his mind. After all, she was just the woman he'd been looking for.

But he was beginning to accept what he'd really known all along—the girl he'd let get away . . . could never live in his world. He had no idea what he'd been thinking to surprise her in Florida. Autumn had nudged him to take the risk, and he'd seen how happy she was with Grier. Still, Autumn and Grier were an unlikely couple. But he shouldn't have listened to his sister because, in taking that next step, booking the flight, he'd let himself hope. Weird to think that Ivy was here in his part of the world and his hopes were dying in the midst of a murder investigation.

She finally sat up and tried to appear composed. "Let me try again."

He handed over the phone. She stood and moved toward the front of the lodge, weaving through the tables. Nolan would give her space, privacy, except his Spidey senses buzzed, telling him that danger was closing in.

His mind slowly recognized the threat hurling forward. A mass shattered the window and flew toward them.

He didn't think.

He acted.

TWENTY-THREE

Stunned, Ivy blinked up at the ceiling and pushed against the hulking form on top of her.

I can't breathe . . .

The breath had been knocked from her, but now she could barely suck in air with the heaviness pressing against her body, her chest, squeezing her lungs.

"Are you all right?" Nolan's voice was in her ear.

"I . . ." she croaked out.

Nolan shifted away and she sucked in a breath. Icy rain or snow or sleet—she wasn't sure—lashed at them from the hole that used to be a window. "Is this another blizzard?"

"It's just the gap wind." The manager assisted both Nolan and Ivy to their feet. "Are you okay?" he asked.

"Gap wind. Captain Seymour told us about it." But she hadn't realized the harm it could cause. Ivy glanced from Nolan to the manager, then realized that others from the ferry stood around them, watching. The floor was covered in shattered glass and the chunk of driftwood that had flown through the window.

"The island sits in the inlet but near the mouth of a river. The wind blows down from the mountains."

"Like a wind tunnel?"

"Yep. We were working to shutter the windows, expecting the weather system moving in." His face twisted as he looked between them. Was he afraid she would try to sue him for the accident?

And Nolan looked seriously worried. He pulled her aside and gripped her arms. Looked her over from top to bottom.

Suddenly the wind stopped, and the large room darkened—the window had quickly been boarded up. Hammers continued nailing the board to secure the window. Ivy swiped at the cold moisture turning her face numb.

"Are you hurt anywhere?" Nolan asked.

"I'm fine. I'm good."

"Let's step completely away from the glass." Nolan urged her over to the wall. Two burly men carried the driftwood out the back and returned to clean up the shards. They continued with such expertise, they had to be practiced. The Ruckus Inn's name was beginning to make a lot of sense.

"Now that I can breathe," she said, "I think I need to sit down."

They returned to their chairs and their bags that had fortunately remained untouched where they'd left them. Her legs shook and she was glad to finally sit.

"You acted so fast. I didn't even see it coming. Thank you for pushing me out of the way. That could have been bad." Lethal even. She didn't want to think about what might have happened if the driftwood had hit her. "It's surprising that no one was hurt."

"You had moved toward the window and were the only one directly in the path of destruction."

Her cheeks warmed at the memory of him covering her with his body to protect her, the feeling of Nolan so close. So protective. "You could have been hurt."

"Everyone is all right. That's what matters."

Oh no. "I was trying to make a call when—"

She followed Nolan's searching gaze to the floor. One of the men cleaning the shattered glass lifted the smashed satellite phone and examined it, then turned to Nolan and Ivy with a deep frown. He held it up. "This yours?"

"Yep." Nolan got up and skirted the glass as he made his way over, then took it from him. He returned, holding the phone, and frowned.

She slowly shook her head. "I want to ask if this could get any worse, but looking at the glass on the floor, the chunk of driftwood they removed, I know it could have been worse. But it could still *get* worse, couldn't it? This certainly isn't over yet."

"No, it's not. And the problem is, we don't know from which of many directions trouble can come next."

"The driftwood coming through the window due to the 'gap wind' had nothing at all to do with bad guys," she said. "I'm getting the idea that in Alaska, the terrain and the weather are a constant factor that you have to fight if you want to survive."

"Or work with. But yes, more than you know."

Or even want to know. But Nolan didn't need her bashing his home state. For all the calamity here, it was absolutely the most beautiful place she'd seen. And she had to admit she could get used to the quiet, the emptiness, the lack of crowds. Being here in the Ruckus Inn, packed with the group from the ferry, was an anomaly and not the norm. A person could get out here and find a place to be alone if they chose.

Her thoughts went to the call she couldn't make now. She glanced at her own cell phone again and the zero bars. Even so, she composed a text to Mom, as well as a woman from church with whom Mom had lunch on Tuesdays. Maybe she could check on her and take her to her treatments.

Ivy had made the decision to find Danna and see this through. But still . . .

"I feel like I'm worthless. I've done nothing to help Lina. Nothing to find the manuscript for my mother." And at this juncture, she almost couldn't care less if Donovan were to share with Mom everything her father had done. A thick knot grew in her throat. That wasn't true. She didn't want her mother to spend the rest of her life in anguish about her husband. Ivy hated hearing those secrets from Donovan, and though her father's image had been tarnished in her mind and heart, she'd had to forgive him and think of her mother. She refused to let a person's past ruin the present or the future.

"I wish it was summer," she mumbled to herself, half wishing she hadn't said anything at all. Nolan might have heard.

In fact, he had. He studied her with that intensity that washed over her in waves. He seemed to push the clutter out of the way to try to see Ivy for who she really was underneath the tough former agent determined to save her mother, Danna, and her father's legacy.

If she didn't know better, she might think that Nolan Long was interested in her. They'd had a short, sweet, gentle romance, and maybe it was just a lot of flirting and nothing deeper. And when she'd gone back to Florida with Mom, she'd tried to push thoughts of Nolan out of her head, but he'd stayed in her head and in Alaska.

It was that north and south thing, and they couldn't even meet halfway. She felt at home near the Tropic of Cancer and he was an Arctic Circle guy. His expression softened. "There's nothing we can do except wait this out. Wait for help to come."

"If we can get internet, we can do our own research while we wait."

"I'm not sure that will be available to us. The weather can affect everything. But I'll try to arrange that." He leaned closer and spoke in a low tone. "In the meantime, why don't you get some rest. You have your own room. I wasn't sure how long it would be before we got out of here, so I got two connected rooms before there were none left. Let's go. Grab your bag and try to be discreet."

Like no one was going to see them go upstairs.

He went with her up the creaking, rickety steps. The paneling was dark, and with the howling wind, the entire building seemed to shudder under the force of nature called the gap wind. Why would anyone build a community or anything at all in the path of this wind? Key in hand, he opened the door and let her go in ahead of him.

Nolan shut the door behind him, then handed her the key. "Let's stick together."

"In other words, don't go anywhere."

She dropped her bag to the floor. He moved to the door between the rooms and unlocked it, tossing his bag into that room.

"Have you heard anything from Autumn about our transportation?"

"No."

"And now you can't contact her, though you could use my phone when it's working." Ivy moved to a small window that wasn't boarded. But it wasn't in the path of the gap wind, she supposed. Either that or they hadn't finished covering all the windows. What a chore to be out in this cold, brutal environment.

"I haven't had a chance to tell you everything," Nolan said.

"Everything?"

"I'm not entirely sure the boat wasn't sabotaged."

She whirled around to face him. "What are you talking about?"

"The plane we were supposed to take out this morning had mechanical failure after arriving. The ferry we took has a generator failure. What are the chances?"

"You can't seriously believe someone would go to the trouble to sabotage us. That's reaching."

"Is it?"

She stepped forward. "What proof do you have?"

"Before the driftwood incident took out my phone, Captain Seymour called. One of his crew members had been found tied up in a utility closet. Someone had stolen his uniform."

"What? Did they catch the fake crew member?"

"No. They found the uniform later. The captain said they've reviewed camera footage, but the man knew how to avoid the cameras, so we don't have an image."

"Why would someone fake their way as a crew member when they could just pay for a ride?"

"Why do you think?"

"Okay, okay. To get where only the crew can go." She didn't like where this had already headed in her mind. She understood what Nolan was getting at. "This is just hard to believe. Hard to swallow that someone would sabotage the ferry."

"Why is it hard to believe after someone held a knife to your throat and warned you to stop searching?"

"For what? I don't know because you chased him away."

"Well, either way—the manuscript that supposedly tells where to find hidden gold, or Danna, who witnessed a murder. Whatever this is about, these people—person, whoever is behind it—are serious."

"The imposter obviously escaped the ferry and that means they could be here in this lodge." She rubbed her arms. What were the chances the ferry had been sabotaged for some other reason that had nothing to do with her and Nolan's search for Danna?

"And like I said earlier, maybe going back to Florida is the best thing for you."

"Well, it's not like I can go anywhere right now, is it?" Exhaustion fueled her frustration. She shook her head and plopped in the chair. "I'm sorry. I shouldn't have snapped at you."

He blew out a long breath, then retrieved her Glock and handed it over.

She gladly took it. "Baby," she whispered as she grabbed it.

"What?"

Her cheeks warmed. "Oh, I call it my baby Glock, or just 'Baby.' It's not that creative. I mean, that's what they're called."

He half smiled, then turned serious again. "Stay here. Stay alert. I'll be back soon. I need to see if I can get another phone. Talk to some people and find out more."

"I could use the downtime anyway to see if I can get a connection and do some research."

After he left, she wished she had talked him into staying. But she was a big girl, and monsters weren't lurking in the shadows in the small room.

She tugged out the small laptop and booted up, knowing she probably couldn't get a connection—though she'd happily discovered the "Free Wi-Fi" sign on the wall downstairs. But nope. Nothing was connecting. No surprise. The gap wind probably interfered with everything around here.

Despite the wind siren, it was quiet and she was alone, and she needed a few moments to regroup. She was grateful for what she had. Shelter from the storm.

Ivy plopped onto the squeaky bed and stared at the ceiling. That's what Nolan felt like to her.

Shelter from the storm.

And now that she thought about it, when that driftwood had flown through the window like a battering ram, the man had put himself in harm's way, risked his own life for hers, without a thought. If he had stopped to think, she would have been battered to death, or at least left bruised and unconscious. But yeah, probably dead.

The window rattled and walls shook as the wind gusted. Goose bumps crawled over her, and she rubbed her arms.

Closing her eyes, she imagined herself on a warm beach. The sun shining. Mom smiling next to her as they drank alcohol-free piña coladas. Surfers sluicing through the waves. And warmth.

Glorious heat.

And all those thoughts almost felt like a betrayal because she was here now . . . with Nolan. He loved it here. At times, she was drawn to Nolan emotionally, and she couldn't deny she was also drawn to him physically. She wanted to be in his arms. But she had to stop thinking about him in those terms. She was working with him, and her time here was supposed to be about the search for Danna. And the secondary quest to find the manuscript.

Ivy curled the blanket around her and tried to rest. She couldn't stop thinking about Danna's big brown eyes in the photograph. Grace's big brown eyes.

Ivy let herself think back to that day when she left Grace and never saw her again. Grace was eleven and Ivy was fourteen, barely babysitting age. They had all traveled to Boston for an auction. Mom and Dad were with a client across the street and down the block and had left Ivy to watch Grace in a small mom-and-pop bookstore. Safe enough.

"Let's head across the street, Grace." Ivy had spotted a guy from their hotel. They'd shared a few smiles and waves, and he was about her age. "I want to grab some coffee."

"You don't drink coffee. Besides, they have it here in the bookstore."

Ivy needed to convince Grace, who was wasting her time. "I prefer the coffee across the street. Come on."

"I know what you prefer." Grace gave her a knowing look. Ivy was fourteen going on twenty-five, and Grace puckered her lips and batted her eyelashes.

Ivy wasn't going to fool her sister. "Are you coming?"

"Nah. I want to look at books. I love the smell of bookstores."

"We *own* a bookstore."

"Old books. Antique books. Sometimes it's wonderful to spend time in a place with new books."

"Dad told us to stick together, and I'm babysitting, so you're coming with me."

"I don't need a babysitter, but if I did, then you need to stay here with me. Give me five more minutes." Grace pulled a book from the shelf and opened it.

Ivy rushed to the front window and spotted the boy pointing at his wristwatch. He was leaving soon, and Ivy was running out of time. Back at the hotel, with Mom and Dad hovering, she probably wouldn't get a chance to talk to him.

She rushed back to Grace. "Okay. I'll be back after grabbing the coffee."

Grace giggled. "Take your time enjoying your *coffee*."

Ivy crossed the street but didn't see the cute guy anywhere in the coffee shop. Grace had caused her to miss this chance to talk to him. Frustrated, she stood in line to order coffee so she could show her sister that she had in fact gone for the disgusting stuff. Now and then she glanced through the window across the street at the bookstore and could just see Grace in the aisle browsing. Just before she was up to purchase the coffee, she looked again and Grace was talking to a boy—well, a man, really, but late teens? No, wait. Early twenties. She hurried to pay for her coffee, then rushed back to the bookstore. Pushed through the door, then headed for the aisle where Grace had been, but she wasn't there.

She must have gone down another aisle in search of more books. Ivy made her way around the bookstore but couldn't find Grace. She checked the restroom. Nothing. Ivy headed across the street. Maybe Grace had gone to the coffee shop to search for Ivy and Ivy had missed her crossing the street. Her heart rate sped up. She had to find Grace.

But her sister wasn't in the coffee shop. Ivy pushed back the growing panic. Maybe Grace had gone next door to that gadget shop. Ivy made her way through the nearby stores and then ended up back in the bookstore, searching every aisle again, coming up empty.

Heart pounding, Ivy paced in front of the store, then Mom and Dad returned from their meeting. Ivy tried to hide her panic.

"What's wrong?" Dad asked. "Where's Grace?"

Ivy burst into tears.

Even now, in bed in the coldest place on earth, the tears surged. She hadn't meant to lose Grace, but of course she blamed herself for not staying with her and watching out for her. She'd deprived her parents of their daughter. Her family of their Grace.

She closed her eyes, then drifted in and out of a fitful sleep.

Ivy held a gun on the suspect—Danny Hinckle.

In her peripheral vision, his daughter, Natalie, watched her from the corner. Whimpered and asked them both to please stop.

Ivy fired her gun at the same time as Danny. Ivy hadn't missed. Natalie screamed and rushed to her father.

She glared up at Ivy. "You killed him. You shot my father!"

Her brown eyes morphed with Grace's. Ivy's heart pounded as the images ran together. Grace and Natalie.

She'd taken her father's daughter, and she'd taken a daughter's father.

And Danna. She had to find Danna. *God, please help me find Danna.*

She tossed and turned and twisted in the blanket.

And realized someone was in the room. She quickly grabbed Baby—a round already chambered—but she couldn't see a thing. Huh? Hadn't she left the bathroom light on and the door cracked to give her some illumination?

"Don't shoot."

TWENTY-FOUR

t's me," Nolan whispered, then turned on the small flashlight so she could see his face. He needed to see hers, too, to make sure she was all right.

"What time is it?" She squinted up at him. "Why is it dark already?"

"It's ten thirty," he whispered.

"What? You let me sleep? Why didn't you wake me up?"

"I'm waking you now. You were having a bad dream."

"Is that why you're here?" she whispered, following his lead, and pulled the covers up tight around her shoulders.

"No. The power's out."

"Not surprising. The wind is crazy. Wait. What's that sound?" she asked.

"The sound of silence. The wind died down."

"Why are you here? Why—"

"The power is out and I can't be sure that it's not deliberate."

"Just like on the—"

"Ferry. I talked to a crew member downstairs tonight, after I left you. The power was cut. The generator was sabotaged."

"By the imposter," she said.

He gave her a few moments to process while he figured out their next steps. He gripped his gun. At any moment someone could try to break into his adjoining room or her room. He hoped not.

"Well, we knew that whoever sabotaged the ferry must be staying in the Ruckus Inn or in the village."

"The crewman who'd been tied up was here and tried to find the man, to identify him, but couldn't. But that doesn't mean he wasn't hiding out or biding his time," he said.

"To what end?" she asked. "To simply slow us down?"

That disturbed him too. And if he couldn't slow them down, then he might even take it a step further, which worried Nolan the most. So far, the saboteur had been successful at slowing Nolan and Ivy down, but he and Ivy weren't giving up. Ivy wasn't stopping her search. How far could she push the person behind the warning?

"They've definitely slowed us down, but not for long."

Ivy threw off the covers and stood. She was still in her jeans and fleece top. "You're in this with me. So if I'm in danger, you're in danger. I didn't mean to cause trouble. I hope the manuscript isn't the cause of Danna's and Nuna's problems."

"If it is, then they had trouble before you came along."

"Did they? Because we—Mom and I, Dad before us—stirred up the questions, the search for it."

"No point in blaming anyone when we don't know what's going on. Four days into this and we don't know. All we know is that we have to get out of here."

"What? How? I mean, if we could, we would already be gone." She arched a brow.

"Our ride is here," he said. "Get ready to go."

"Our ride?"

"Autumn and Grier. They brought the *Long Gone* and are at the dock. With the break in the wind and storm, we have a short window in which we can safely get out of here, so we need to go."

Ivy tossed her bag onto the bed and stuffed her laptop into it, then holstered her Glock. "What about the others? Are we going to take any of the passengers with us?"

"Everyone is asleep except the lodge owner, who showed up to assist the manager. We can't risk any of them coming—any of the passengers could be the person who sabotaged the boat. Coming with us could also put innocent people in danger."

"But they could be in danger here."

"Ivy. What do you want to do? You want to stay?"

"I mean, no. I just want to do the right thing." She rubbed her eyes.

"They're going to get off this island safe and sound at some point. They aren't your responsibility. I thought we could take a few, depending on the situation. Things have changed."

She nodded. "Okay. I'm getting ready."

She weaved her hands through her thick hair, then pulled on the beanie and her parka.

"Granted, there are both pros and cons to leaving, but getting away from here is best for everyone involved. We can get back on track with the investigation and find Danna, keep you away from whoever is trying to stop you, and draw the danger away from anyone else trapped at the lodge until the ferry is repaired."

She zipped up her bag. Nolan set his on the bed next to hers and pulled on his coat.

"How do we escape without alerting everyone?" she asked. "Every move we make, the floors creak."

"We're going out the window."

"From the second floor?" Her beautiful eyes grew wide again. "When am I going to stop being surprised by you?"

If the situation wasn't so precarious, he might have smiled at that. He hoped . . . never. *Never stop being surprised by me.*

From his room, he hefted up a thick-roped fishing net and carried it into Ivy's room.

"Where did you get that?"

"I did some exploring earlier and snagged it from a storage closet. Thought it would come in handy if we needed to make a quick escape. And now we do, so hurry. You guard the door while I get the window open. We need to be quick."

Ivy retrieved the gun she called Baby, then stood with her back to Nolan.

God, please help us get to the Long Gone *safely.*

That's all he wanted. To get Ivy to safety and find Danna alive and well, but both women were in danger. He needed to figure out what was going on in order to adequately protect. Under different circumstances he'd hang around to see if he could root out the saboteur, if he was still here. But he was at a great disadvantage. Others could be taken hostage if the saboteur felt trapped.

At the moment, Nolan was the one to feel trapped because the window wasn't budging.

It was stuck. After he applied enough pressure, it finally opened with a resounding *thunk*. Then he had to kick the heavy shutter open. Great. He was making more noise than he intended, and possibly giving away his escape plans. He tied a part of the fisherman's drift net to the bed and rolled it out the window. "It's the best I can do unless you want to hang out and drop into the snow. It's been shoveled, so it isn't going to soften the fall as much."

She didn't argue and handed him her bag.

He tossed both bags to the ground while trying to decide if he should go first. Either way, danger lurked. If she went first she could be in danger, if she stayed behind she could be in danger. Their best chance was the element of surprise. Going out the window into the dark, frigid night had better be the right move.

He slid out the window and picked his way down the net and then dropped to the ground. He glanced up at Ivy and waited. Leaving the window open would allow heat to escape the inn. Nothing he could do about that, except contact the owner and explain once they were well on their way.

Hesitating, Ivy remained in the window.

"Come on," he whispered.

Ivy slid out the window awkwardly, and he feared she might fall. He was prepared to catch her if she did. But she grabbed onto the net with her feet and her hands and maneuvered down like she'd done it a thousand times. On the ground, they grabbed their gear, and he led the way, shining the flashlight. Unfortunately, the light could draw attention, but it was too dark to go without. Hurrying through the heavy slush after the freezing rain, they tried to move soundlessly, but in the quiet night they were like a couple of bears knocking over trees. Ivy slipped and he caught and steadied her. Then he slipped and she returned the favor, and they shared a smile in the middle of this ridiculous escape in the night.

Only a little farther.

Autumn had been instructed to keep the boat lights to a minimum so they would not signal their arrival, which made maneuvering to the dock dangerous. He flicked his flashlight, letting her know they were nearing the dock. The *Long Gone*'s lights came on. He wanted to feel relief, but they weren't out of this until they were on that boat, steering well away from danger.

TWENTY-FIVE

Inside the galley of the boat, Ivy shivered and wished she hadn't relinquished her coat. Nolan had tossed their coats into one of the staterooms, but then when she was still shivering as she sat tucked into the booth, he draped a blanket around her. He sat next to her, and across from them sat Nolan's sister, Autumn, the Shadow Gap police chief, along with her husband Grier, who worked with her. One of Autumn's police officers was at the helm.

The old, refurbished boat rocked and rolled on the rough water.

Since Nolan sat so close, his body heat went a long way to chase the chill away. The galley wasn't that cold, but her teeth chattered. Nerves. Had to be nerves. She'd worked undercover and shouldn't let the situation get to her. But admittedly, she felt completely out of her element. And scared. Ivy . . . Ivy didn't get scared. Not like this. She wasn't only scared for herself, but for her mother and for Danna. That stupid manuscript. But clearly this was much bigger than cursed gold.

Lord, please let us make it to safety.

She thought back to the Psalm 121 passage at Annie's Lodge. *"I lift up my eyes to the mountains—where does my help come from? My help comes from the LORD, the Maker of heaven and earth."* How she appreciated those words on the wall. After this was over, she might send the owner a message and let her know to keep up the good work.

She recalled more of that passage from memory. *"Indeed, the sun will not harm you by day, nor the moon by night."*

Nor the ocean when racing away from danger on a boat in a storm. So she'd added that part, but she held on to the thought. Exhaustion weighed on her. From the moment she'd found Nuna dying in that cabin, she had been on the run, it seemed, even while being snowed in by a blizzard. They had been racing against the clock while running from an unseen force. She stifled a yawn and wished that she could just climb into bed. She could have slept in the Ruckus Inn, despite the howling wind, for the rest of the winter, except Nolan claimed someone was closing in on them.

Had gotten too close. Sabotaging an entire ferry? Whoever was behind this had wanted Nolan and Ivy to be trapped on that island. Had that really been to slow them down? Or to kill them, make them disappear, never to be found?

She shuddered again. She couldn't wrap her mind around any of it, but she could wrap her hands around the warm mug while she stared at the hot cocoa inside, trying to ignore the fact that Autumn was studying her long and hard. Did the chief suspect Ivy of some wrongdoing? Was it just part of her law enforcement process to memorize the appearance of everyone new to her?

Enough already. She lifted her gaze to meet Autumn's and took in the strangely colored irises. She found Autumn's eyes disturbing and preferred Nolan's dark-blue eyes just fine. She wouldn't change them. What *was* she thinking? She was in no position to think about Nolan's appearance and what she loved or didn't love about him.

Love.

Right. She did . . . *enjoy* his appearance. His heart. His need to be a hero. But Ivy was too exhausted, too scared, and, frankly, too cold to care much about any of that at the moment. She just wanted to get warm. That, and she wanted to calm her pounding heart.

The boat tilted and she fell into Nolan. She gripped his arms to steady herself. The strength, the build of his muscles, was impressive, and she lingered maybe a few moments too long. And honestly, she just wanted to stay right here with him. Then she lifted her eyes to his. He was looking at her and she thought maybe he'd like to stay here too.

But Autumn was watching.

"Oops. I'm sorry."

"Are you okay?" He hadn't budged an inch but instead was like granite.

She finally moved away. "I'm fine."

Except that nausea threatened.

Autumn must have read her expression. "I'll take you to a cabin."

She led Ivy through the small galley to a bedroom at the front of the boat. "The head is just there. I'll shut the door. Shout if you need anything."

Ivy thanked Autumn and swallowed the bile rising in her throat.

Autumn paused before shutting the door and stared at her. "Are you going to be okay?"

Ivy couldn't answer in her rush to the bathroom where she lost what little she'd eaten.

TWENTY-SIX

Nolan almost regretted that he'd called for assistance from Autumn.

But really, who else could he call under the circumstances? She wouldn't let him down, even in the worst weather. No one else had his back like his sister, his family. Dad would help if he wasn't traveling.

The *Long Gone* was a tough old boat and weathered the storm, rolled with the waves, as they maneuvered along the waterways in the Inside Passage toward Shadow Gap.

Gripping the counter at times, Nolan washed out all the mugs and secured them in the cabinet.

"I'll see if I need to relieve Ross at the helm," Grier said.

Nolan wanted to ask if he knew anything about the Walker investigation—like had they found the homeowner's body, or had they discovered the reason for the explosion that killed Carl, or had they located and talked to Victus?—but he'd wait for the right moment.

Autumn emerged from the cabin at the bow, shutting the door behind her. She steadied herself as she made her way to the booth and slid in behind the table, her face pale.

"This rough ride is getting to you too, huh?" he asked.

"Not just me. Ivy isn't holding up so well. Poor girl."

Nolan whirled from the counter. "Is she okay?"

"She will be."

"I'll check on her." He started for the room.

Autumn held up a hand. "Down, boy."

He hesitated. "I don't think she should be alone."

"It's just motion sickness. She'll be fine," Autumn said. "I gave her some Dramamine."

He puffed his cheeks, then blew out the breath. Ivy . . .

He wanted to check on her for himself, and then again, he didn't want to be overly concerned in front of Autumn. He didn't need her reading too much into his relationship with Ivy.

He slid into the booth next to Autumn. Elbows on the table, he shoved his face into his hands and grumbled under his breath. He wanted to find out more about what was going on with the Walker investigation, and knowing more would help him, prepare him, before he found Jamison. The man had left him the message that he had new details, but he hadn't left those details, nor had he called Nolan back or responded to his calls. Granted, Nolan didn't have a phone now. Maybe Jamison had misspoken and remembered too late that Nolan wasn't supposed to work on that investigation. Whatever—his message left Nolan wanting to know more.

"What do you know about the Walker investigation?" he asked.

"I thought you weren't working on that one."

"I'm not, so that's why I'm asking—because I'm not investigating, and therefore, I don't know what's going on. That said, Jamison left a message he'd learned something, but he didn't give me the details."

"Honestly, I've been a little frustrated with him," Autumn said. "He warned my department away from the crime scene. I'll dig into this and see what I can learn for you, and for the rest of us. People in town don't like to think there's a killer wandering around out there. Whatever happened to Carl is one thing, but we've been looking for Walker's body, and you can't keep that a secret."

"What about the trafficked girl Carl was looking into? Ivy mentioned a trafficker by the name of Novak had been seen in Shadow Gap. He was stalking Danna, whom he had trafficked up north. What do you know about that?"

"I know the story but not because Lina told me. But Hank told Grandpa Ike who told me. I dug into Novak's background. I don't know why he's not behind bars. If I see him, I'll put him there, but I haven't seen him in town, Nolan. Do you think he's involved with this? Wrapped up in Nuna's murder and the reason Danna is in hiding?"

"I'm not sure, given what we've learned about Nuna."

"It makes you wonder, doesn't it?" she asked.

"I need to map it all out," he said. "There are too many moving pieces right now."

"I bet you wish you were on vacation, don't you? You could miss all the fun."

"Nah. But Alton insisted I was heading out next week. He might have spoken too soon. I guess we'll see."

"Well, I'm just sorry you didn't get to go to Florida." Autumn stared at him.

"What?"

"I see why you like her. She's sharp and beautiful, especially with that tan. Maybe you can just go to Florida with her when she goes home." Autumn shrugged with a grin. "I mean, of course, for a visit. I want you to come back to Alaska."

"Keep your voice down, will you?" He hissed a whisper. Hissed or snapped. Either way. "Not here. Not now."

He wished he hadn't listened to Autumn's urging to "follow his heart," as she'd put it. That was a romantic dream and he'd never been a romantic.

Autumn smiled and leaned forward. "She had no clue you were coming to Florida, did she?"

If Nolan could get up and walk away, he would. Oh, wait. He could. He grabbed his coat and tugged it on as he headed to the steps and clomped up. Before opening the hatch, he pulled on his cap and gloves, then he moved to the barely enclosed pilothouse and found Ross, a Shadow Gap officer, at the helm along with Grier.

The cold gusts and frigid spray were brutal, and he had to shout. "Head down and get warm. I'll take it from here."

"I've got this," Grier said.

"No, let me do it," Nolan said. "I need to clear my head and this will do it."

Grier smirked. Did he have a clue that Nolan wanted space from his sister?

"Go on, Ross," Grier said.

"You sure?"

Grier nodded. "The water's getting rougher and you need a break."

When Ross released the wheel, Nolan took his place, and Grier simply nodded. Nolan glanced at the navigation system. Still another hour or more to go and all of it in the dark.

"You can go back, Grier," he said. "I've got this."

"I enjoy the challenge, but I could use a cup of coffee. I'll be back in a few minutes to check on you," Grier said.

"No rush."

A few moments later, Autumn was the one to stand next to him. "You didn't have to leave, you know. I didn't mean to push."

"And you didn't have to travel all this way in bad weather to get us." He turned to look at her, hoping she could see he really meant his next words. "I can't thank you enough, Autumn."

"You don't have to thank me. We're family. You'd do the same for me."

He kept the boat going at a slow pace and steered at an angle to reduce the impact from the waves, wishing he could trust autopilot—but not on a night like this. Why couldn't this have been a nice winter night with the stars shining bright and a smooth ride? That would have been so much easier. He could deny it all he wanted to everyone else, and even to himself, but deep inside, he really wanted Ivy to love Alaska as much as he did.

"When we get somewhere quiet and safe," Autumn said, "we need to talk about what's going on. I don't want to distract you. Our lives are in your hands."

"Way to put on the pressure." He sent her a wry grin along with a look of appreciation. Regarding the talk, did she mean concerning the crime spree, or did she want to know about what was going on between him and Ivy?

"We should be out of this storm system soon," she said, "or else I'd suggest just using the storm anchors and riding it out."

No waiting this out. "We need to get to Shadow Gap as soon as possible."

"Agreed."

"How is she?" he asked.

"She's still sick." Autumn squeezed his shoulder. "You have it bad for her, Nolan. Everyone can see that."

Everyone except Ivy.

Nolan didn't bother responding. Autumn wasn't expecting a response, and he didn't want to admit she was right because then he would be admitting it to himself. Saying something out loud, even on a stormy, windy, impossible night, made it painfully real.

TWENTY-SEVEN

'm in a nightmare.

Ivy lay in the bed, glad the motion sickness medication was finally taking effect. A cross-stitched Scripture verse hung on the wall.

> Do not be afraid of sudden terror,
> Nor of trouble from the wicked when it comes;
> For the LORD will be your confidence,
> And will keep your foot from being caught.
>
> Proverbs 3:25–26

The verses reminded her of the Scriptures in Annie's Lodge, only they were different, and almost felt like a warning, so in that way they were less comforting.

". . . trouble from the wicked when it comes . . ."

Yeah. A warning. Trouble from bad guys was coming, no doubt about it.

But why had someone thought to put *that* Scripture on the wall? Still, that she was once again staring at Scripture on a wall felt like God was reaching out to remind her of his constant presence in her life, even when she didn't feel like he was near. But he was here in the middle of this literal storm. And like Jesus walked on water and calmed the storm, she wished she could do the same, but more so for the storm brewing in her heart and mind. She couldn't think clearly about the current dilemmas involving her mother, the manuscript, and Danna, so she closed her eyes and tried to sleep it off and escape that she was miserable. When would the wind and waves stop rocking the boat?

What am I doing out here in the middle of the Pacific Ocean—well, a waterway, but still the Pacific—on a cold, stormy winter night?

She had the constant sense that she was in the wrong place. And there was no wrong time to add to it. There was never a good time for her to be here. Except, she couldn't ignore the fact she'd been blown away by the magnificence of God's creation when she'd been here before with Mom. And this time too. Even now, during the winter, the sheer beauty took her breath away.

At least at the moments when she could find time away from the danger and fear of her dire circumstances to catch her breath in the first place. Maybe it would have been better to stay in the village and face off with whoever Nolan believed had gotten too close.

Seriously, now that she thought about it, they should have stayed. What did it matter? Hindsight was always twenty-twenty, as the saying went. They also needed to get to Shadow Gap and talk to Lina and find Danna.

God, please let me sleep and wake up when this is over. Or at least when we get to Shadow Gap.

An image of Danna came to mind, and then Ivy's sister, Grace. The set of big brown eyes so similar. *I made a mistake before.* A huge mistake that had cost her sister her life. She'd never been able to live that down, at least in her own heart. She hadn't been able to move past it to prove herself, even working as an FBI special agent.

Why can't I forgive myself?

Another set of eyes drifted across her groggy mind. Nolan's

blues. He was so serious and caring. Rugged and tough and handsome. And he listened.

She wanted him.

Yeah, but you can't have him. He was an Alaskan, through and through.

And she was not. She felt a presence in the room and slowly opened her eyes. There he was.

"My mountain man," she whispered.

But she was dreaming. She had to be dreaming. *Please, let me be dreaming.*

Mountain Man took her hand in his and squeezed. His hand was much bigger than hers, and kind of rough, but it was a nice rough. Protective. Ivy smiled because she was finally having a nice dream and could forget about the winter weather and the terrifying storm and arctic cold water and floating ice they'd seen near the glaciers.

Ivy blinked in the gray light of morning and yawned, taking in her surroundings. The night before came rushing back. The storm had passed and the boat gently rocked. She turned and found Nolan asleep in the chair next to the bed.

How long had he been there?

She didn't want to get up and disturb him, so for a few moments she took in his scruffy jaw and thick, dark hair. If she ran her fingers through his hair, would she wake him up? Would it be wrong if she stole a kiss from him, just one kiss, before she returned to Florida?

No. You cannot kiss Nolan.

Yes. Absolutely it would be wrong. She needed to clear her head and think straight before she did one thing. Said one word.

Nolan's lids fluttered and then he opened his eyes—dark, stormy eyes—that peered at her as he slowly woke up. A deep ache throbbed in her chest. There could be something between them. She'd been ignoring it, and she had a feeling that, at first, he'd been trying to kindle it, but she'd snuffed it out.

Like this was any kind of time to think of a relationship with him. Kissing him. Loving him.

But there it was.

He leaned forward. "Ivy . . ." Exhaustion clung to his voice and deep concern to his eyes. "How are you?"

"I'm good." *Not true. I'm miserable. I don't want to leave you.*

TWENTY-EIGHT

At Dad's house, where Nolan was house-sitting while he was in town, he showered, then infused himself with caffeine, but . . . *please, keep it coming, thank you very much.*

Nolan wiped off the whiteboard in Dad's office. He didn't think Dad would mind. After all, months'-old grocery lists, to-do lists, and travel plans didn't exactly constitute a murder board, though Nolan usually called it a crime board, but this time, yeah, murder board would work. What you called it depended on who you talked to and, of course, if murder was involved.

Years ago, when Dad had taken the job as Shadow Gap police chief, he had planned to use the board to figure things out in his at-home office, but it turned out that Shadow Gap didn't have the kind of crime that required a board like Dad had used in Kansas. That was a big reason why Dad had moved here, or at least that's what he'd told Nolan and Autumn most of their lives.

Of course, Grandpa Ike and Grandma Birdy were the biggest reasons Dad had moved his family from the heartland of America closer to the Arctic Circle. Southeast Alaska wasn't actually close to the Arctic Circle, but all things being relative, it was much closer than Kansas, and their grandparents in Shadow Gap could help Dad raise Nolan and Autumn after their mother's death.

As for less crime, that had been true for most of Nolan's life growing up in this house, or at least through his teenage years, before he took his own path with the Alaska State Troopers.

But lately, criminal activity had shifted. Gotten complicated. Nolan would step up to meet the challenge. After finally arriving and docking at the Shadow Gap Marina well after the break of day, he'd picked up a new satellite phone, which was charging on the desk. But the regular cell he used when remaining local kept buzzing and driving him nuts.

Nolan finally learned the information that Jamison had wanted to share. He'd given Nolan a heads-up that Alton was going to release Nolan to leave on that vacation he'd been planning. Peterson had finally arrived to cover him, residing in Haines for now, and the Alaska State Troopers had a handle on the current caseload.

Not on your life.

He'd thought it, but he wouldn't say it. He was still in uniform today. And worst case, he'd go on vacation, but he would stay and finish this with Ivy. No way was he leaving until, well . . . she did. He wanted to find Danna too. Nuna's murder case could take a while to solve and, depending on whether the scientist's intriguing background had anything to do with his murder, the investigation could be removed from the state's law enforcement jurisdiction entirely.

A door opened and shut somewhere in the house. Cold air whooshed through before Autumn stepped into the room and frowned, or was that a smile? "What are you doing?"

"What does it look like?" He set the whiteboard eraser down. "I'm creating a murder board."

"Grier will be here soon. I just texted him. He has information we're going to want to hear."

Upon arriving in Shadow Gap this morning, they'd taken

Autumn's Interceptor to Lina's and, like her granddaughter, the woman had disappeared. She wasn't in town, and there was no sign of Danna either. In a small town like Shadow Gap, people talked. Strangers were noticed. And a person couldn't just go missing without at least one person seeing something. After a night on the water fighting the storm to get here, Autumn and Grier had gone home to clean up, and Nolan had brought Ivy to the house. Still not feeling one hundred percent, she'd taken a nap in the guest room. They'd all agreed to meet up again in a couple of hours.

And now it was showtime.

Ivy dragged through the door and yawned. She rubbed her face, then seemed to suddenly realize Nolan and Autumn were in the room and watching her. She straightened her shoulders. "I need coffee." Then she headed for the desk where he'd placed a carafe.

"Should Ivy be here?" Autumn asked. "She isn't part of the official investigation."

"I beg your pardon," she said. "Lina is the one who invited me when she asked me to find her granddaughter, so I'm in this and I'm staying."

"Alton approved her being read in and knows she's working with me." Nolan turned his back to the board to face them. "She's involved in this whether she's in here with us or not. Might as well keep her close."

"Good enough for me," Autumn said. "Honestly, Ivy, I just wanted to hear you say it. This is a strange team we've cobbled together, but if it gets the job done, that's all that matters."

Yep. Dad had taught them to serve justice with love and kindness and mercy while walking with God. That Micah Scripture, whatever it was.

But to serve justice, one had to solve the crime. While all of it was still in his head, Nolan needed to create this murder board, writing and drawing and connecting all the clues. He'd turned down an offer to join the major crimes unit so he could remain a rural trooper and close to family, but that didn't mean he wasn't fully capable of working like he was in that unit. He accepted the challenge.

"Everything is going on this board," he said, "and I do mean everything. I'm going to follow the timeline as best as I can." He started writing, the black marker squeaking as he moved across the board, listing everything starting with Carl's response to the report of a scream at Walker's house, then Danna leaving with the manuscript, Ivy and Nolan finding Nuna murdered, and the attacks on Ivy, including Gene Whitlock's attack. And then, finally, their sabotaged travel plans.

"Dr. Nuna Grainger is retired from Pacific Northwest Lab," Autumn read from the board. "Before that, he worked at Los Alamos National Lab and has a background in multiple specialties and . . . I mean, a *certificate* in *international security*? Who knew that was even a thing?" Autumn sounded incredulous.

Nolan continued writing on the board, his arm aching by the time he was done. He turned to face the unofficial task force.

"Is it necessary to put all these facts on the board?" Autumn asked. "There appear to be multiple cases here."

He capped the marker. "Are they?"

"Yes. They can't all be related. Certainly not the manuscript piece."

"Oh. I almost forgot." He turned and added the words *cursed gold* next to the manuscript.

"Cursed gold?"

"Ivy, you want to share what you know?"

"At this point, I don't know more than you. Lina had complained that the manuscript was cursed and she didn't want it, and that was one of many reasons she wanted to get rid of it. When I asked my mother about the curse, she said the manuscript wasn't cursed, but the gold was cursed. The story is supposedly based on true events, but again, it's a novel, so it's fiction. But it feels like someone thinks there is truth to the location of the gold described in the story."

Autumn crossed her arms. "You're saying this could be about hunting for treasure?"

"Unclear," Nolan said. "But it needs to be on the board."

"I'd still suggest keeping the cases separate," Autumn said. "Divide the board into thirds, and then if we need to connect them, we can."

He drew two lines to divide the board so that the Walker/Carl investigation was separate from Danna and the manuscript, and Danna and Nuna's murder.

"Oh." Autumn shrugged with a grin. "I got it. You were already doing that."

Grier stepped through the door. "I thought I heard voices." He entered with a box of donuts and set them on the desk. "Autumn texted me to bring donuts. Said you already had coffee brewing."

Ivy snatched a donut and poured coffee from the carafe. She handed Nolan his refilled mug, surprising him. He took it and smiled.

Holding her coffee, Autumn took a seat and propped her boot up on a box of files. "Grier, tell them what you learned."

"Nuna Grainger was a retired chemical engineer, but he still worked as a consultant with a team focused on chemical and biological detection forensics."

"What does that even mean?" Ivy asked.

"Good question. From what I gathered, it has to do with identifying threats, or rather, detecting the signature of a threat either by natural-born pathogens or deadly toxins, anything that can be used in an act of terror. That sort of thing."

Nolan could hear his heart beating in his ears as the room fell silent. Everyone turning to their own thoughts about what this could mean. He wanted to completely erase the words *manuscript* and *gold* from the board.

But . . . not yet.

"I think we're all pondering the same question. Does his murder have to do with his consulting, and is it connected to national security?" Nolan said.

"And if so, where are the feds?" Autumn said.

"Already here." Grier's tone was matter-of-fact.

Everyone looked at him. Stared.

He shrugged. "If it's related, they're here, just not making themselves known yet. National security, like you said."

"Whatever the federal government's role in this, whatever the motivation behind Nuna's murder, we can't forget our role in this—Danna is witness to that murder," Autumn said. "And, if this is linked to national security, she's in more danger than we imagined."

"I agree," Nolan said. "As a witness, she's in serious danger."

"I'm starting to wish this was all about the manuscript and a pot of gold at the end." Grier rubbed his temple.

They'd known much of what he'd shared, but their information meant nothing until the detail gave context. Grier's information could change everything, ramp up the danger level. And that obviously weighed on him.

Nolan dropped into one of the chairs. "All the more reason we find Danna before it's too late. Anyone connected to her is in lethal danger. That includes her grandmother." He held Ivy's gaze. "That includes you, Ivy."

"And you, Nolan," Autumn added.

Nah, he wasn't a target, but he wouldn't argue with her.

"You can go ahead and just erase the word *manuscript* off the board," Grier said. "That has no relevance. No importance. No bearing in any of this."

Nolan rubbed his hand over his jaw, glad he'd shaved. "Nuna's murder could be part of a larger picture. But then again, not necessarily, so it stays on the board for now."

Ivy slowly lifted her hand like she was in school.

"You don't have to ask permission to talk." He smiled.

He couldn't help it. In the middle of this dilemma, she made him smile. Still, he remained disturbed that she was here and in the crosshairs.

"I think I might know where we could look for Danna and her grandmother."

TWENTY-NINE

W hy hadn't she thought of this sooner? The thought had come to her so suddenly, so ridiculously, that she felt childish even suggesting it. All eyes were on her now, and they might want to know how she got the idea. That, she would never tell them.

Nolan angled his head just so, then glanced back at Ivy. He'd cleaned up and even shaved, and she thought of how he'd held her hand last night when she was on the boat. Sick. Thinking she might actually be dying but believing that she was dreaming.

And she thought of the snowplow guy—how he'd offered a helping hand to her when she'd landed in the snow on her backside, and then . . .

"The snowplow guy has a thing for Lina."

"The snowplow guy?" Nolan asked.

"You mean Hank?" Autumn stared.

"Yes. That's his name. He took me to Lina's on the day she was supposed to meet me. He talked about her and was worried about her. They seemed close . . . really close. Their hands brushed, intentionally." Her cheeks grew hot. She sounded like she had watched them much too closely. "I notice things, okay? So I had a feeling they were into each other."

"And you think that she's with Hank?" Grier asked.

"Why not? If they're scared, and Hank knows about it . . ."

Her gaze flicked to Nolan's and held on. "He's going to protect her with everything in him. He's a big, intimidating guy, but a softy. A fierce softy." And that's what he believed about the Bigfoot creatures—they were big and fierce, but also protective and gentle.

Autumn and Grier stood at the same time and headed for the door.

"Wait," Ivy called. "I'm going too."

She caught up and Autumn turned to face her as if to stop her.

Ivy spoke first. "Lina asked *me* to find Danna. No offense, but I'm not entirely sure she trusts you. I need to see this through, even if I didn't find her."

"If she's with Lina and we find them, then in a sense you did. This was your idea. Let's go."

Ivy followed Autumn out, and Nolan joined her.

If they finally found Danna, then Ivy could go home—with or without the manuscript—but definitely without Nolan, who belonged here with all things Alaska. Big skies and aurora borealis and mountains and glaciers and waterfalls. Ivy would love to see the northern lights just once before she left.

Grabbing her laptop, she rushed after the two Shadow Gap police officers and hopped into the back seat of Autumn's Interceptor. Grier got in his own vehicle. Nolan climbed into the back seat next to Ivy. Before Ivy got her seat belt on, Autumn peeled out of the slushy drive. A hard, cold rain was turning the snow into a mess.

Nolan grabbed her hand and held it as if it was the most natural thing to do, and as if they always held hands. At his touch, his reaching out, her heart pounded. Her emotions were kind of like the slippery, muddy mess Autumn was navigating. Ivy wanted to free her hand, but she couldn't move. His grip felt right and good, and she would hold on to that for as long as she could.

While Grier and Autumn talked over the radio, driving their separate police vehicles, Nolan leaned in.

"I hope you're right about this," he whispered.

"Me too. We all want this to be over and Danna to be found safe." Ivy hadn't whispered, and Autumn glanced at her in the rearview mirror.

"Even if we find her," Autumn said, "she's a witness to a murder with dangerous people after her. She's still in trouble."

"We could be going about this all wrong. What if we shouldn't find her?" Ivy said. "Maybe she's better off if we leave her in hiding."

"You have a point, Ivy," Autumn said, "but she will eventually be found, and it's important that we find her first and learn the truth before it's too late. And we also can put measures in place to protect her."

"The degree of danger will depend on who killed Nuna," Nolan said. "It's likely that she doesn't know who killed him, but we hope she saw a face and can describe the murderer."

God, please let us find her safe.

Autumn steered her Interceptor to the side of the plowed two-lane road, gesturing toward a steep snow berm. "Well, we're not getting in there with my Ford. Hank hasn't plowed the road."

Autumn called Hank with her cell. "He isn't answering."

She left a voice mail for him to call her, then texted as well. "He's not good at checking his voice mail."

"So, we take snow machines as far as we can get and snow-shoe in the rest of the way to his cabin," Nolan said. "Whatever we need to get there."

"Right," Autumn said. "I was expecting the plow guy to have plowed his own drive." She turned the Interceptor around. "We have three machines at the house. I should have thought to bring them."

Autumn steered back the way they'd come.

"What could it mean that he hasn't plowed?" Ivy asked. "I mean, is he even there? Maybe he left with the two of them. Maybe they aren't even with him." She hated for them to go to all this trouble only to come up empty-handed.

"All good points," Autumn said.

"You want me to call Grandpa?" Nolan asked.

"I'll do it." The Interceptor slid and Autumn corrected, then said, "Okay, you do it."

Ivy had met Autumn's grandfather at the Lively Moose that first day here.

Ike's voice came over Nolan's cell. "Nolan, what's up?"

"Have you seen or heard from Hank?"

"Not since he took that outsider over to Lina's. Have you found her granddaughter yet?"

"Still searching."

"The whole town can search for her if we need to."

"No, that won't be necessary." Nolan eyed Ivy. He didn't want the wrong people finding her if she was here. "But if you see him, Alina, or Danna, call me immediately."

"I might not see him for a few days. He trades out with Sandford to plow, and with the rain instead of the snow, Sandford might not have much to do until the next storm."

"Thanks, Grandpa. Talk to you soon." Nolan ended the call. "What do you think?"

"I think that Ivy was right," Autumn said. "Hank is hiding with Lina and Danna, or they have all skipped town together."

"If Sandford hasn't plowed Hank's drive," Nolan said, "then *Sandford* could know something."

"He could, indeed." Autumn steered up to the house. "To me, this could mean that Hank didn't want anyone finding their way to his cabin, or at least he could deter them if they happened to know where he lives. The snow would slow their approach."

"If he's even there," Ivy added.

"We have to find out," Nolan said.

THIRTY

Fire burned through Nolan's gut as he squeezed the handles and accelerated the snow machine, riding atop the deep snow dumped by the blizzard. He carefully weaved between the thick trees of the Tongass Forest toward Hank's cabin. Branches hung heavy with the white frosting, which slid off at times, leaving mounds of snow and adding to their obstacle course. The frigid rain beat down on them and turned the landscape icy. Not the best scenario for crossing the snow on a machine.

Inexperienced on a snow machine, Ivy rode double with him, her arms wrapped around his thick coat. Since that covered his bulletproof vest, he was surprised he could even feel her, but she was strong, and probably a little afraid of falling off.

In the distance, he finally spotted the half-buried cabin, and with that, his hopes sunk that they would find Hank. The man wouldn't let so much snow gather and cover the place, even if he was trying to hide his presence.

Smoke spiraled from the chimney, and Nolan's fears they were at a dead end skittered away.

On a hunch, he steered the snow machine around to get a view of the back. The snow had been shoveled and the roof cleaned off. Autumn and Grier steered up behind him, and they parked where the machines wouldn't get stuck. He was glad they hadn't had to hike in on snowshoes.

Hank had to be here. Given Hank's strange behavior—not plowing his road—Nolan bet Lina and Danna were here too, and that Ivy had been right.

Autumn hopped off and removed her helmet, then stared toward the cabin. Grier joined her. She called over her shoulder. "I need Hank to know it's me so he doesn't come out armed and loaded for bear."

Nolan and Ivy slid off their snow machine and followed Autumn and Grier to the cabin. "Let's hang back, just a bit." He waited near the edge of the trees, looking on. A burly man stepped out of the cabin holding a long rifle and aiming at them, peering through the scope.

Wait. Hank wasn't the man standing at the door aiming at the local police.

Sandford stepped out into the open where Nolan could see him better, holding a rifle like he was prepared to defend Hank's place from a deadly threat. His gray-haired buddy Otis stood behind him, looking at them.

"Lower your weapon, Sandford," Autumn said.

"Autumn? Grier?"

Bear, Hank's dog, raced out of the cabin and barked a greeting at Autumn and Grier, then raced over to Nolan, who crouched to pet him. Then the dog made a beeline to Ivy, whom he hadn't met. She gave Nolan a wide-eyed look, then removed her glove and held her hand out for the dog to sniff until he was satisfied that she posed no threat.

Sandford finally lowered the rifle. "Sorry, Chief," he said.

Ivy and Nolan continued forward to join the group. Nolan glanced around them. Snow had a way of quieting the world, and at moments like this, Nolan found the sound of silence unnerving.

"Can we take this inside?" he asked.

Sandford lifted the rifle again to peer through the scope all around them and even up into the mountain peak, visible over the treetops. The guy was edgy and with good reason. Nolan would be interested to hear what he had to say. Like they had suspected—Sandford knew something.

Once inside the cozy cabin, Nolan had to remove his coat, as did Autumn, Grier, and Ivy. The space was much too hot after coming in from the cold. Nolan crouched to give Bear the rub he expected, while pushing down his own disappointment.

He'd held on to the smallest of hopes that Hank would be inside along with the two women.

"Mind explaining what you're doing here?" Autumn asked.

Not "Where's Hank?" but her question would get the answers they wanted. Nolan liked her tactics. She wasn't giving anything away without hearing from these men first.

Sandford and Otis shared a look. "We can trust you. But we don't know *her*."

"I'm Ivy Elliott. Alina—Lina—asked me to find Danna. She's in danger. Do you know where she is?"

Sandford narrowed his eyes. "Lina said nothing about you."

"Enough," Autumn said. "Danna is involved in a murder and we need to find her."

"Someone's trying to kill her," Otis blurted out. "Nuna was murdered, and Danna's scared to death and came back to her grandmother so that they could both hide. Alina came to Hank. Said he's the only person she can trust. She said nothing about you, Miss Elliott. Sorry."

"And where did he take them?" Grier asked.

"We're here to see who comes for them." Sandford rubbed his jaw. "Buy them some time."

"And taking the law into your own hands?" Autumn fisted her hands on her hips.

"There's not enough law to go around at times," Otis said. "You know that. So what do you want us to do? Stand around and watch someone get hurt?"

"You should have talked to me about this," Autumn said. "The last thing I need is for one of *you* to get hurt."

"How long have they been gone?" Grier asked.

Again, the shared look.

Sandford set the rifle against the wall and stoked the fire. "You won't find them, so it doesn't matter. You can't protect that girl better than Hank."

"We're here to protect Danna. You don't understand who and what you're up against. In addition to her current location, tell us what else you know." Nolan stood in the middle of the room in his most intimidating demeanor. These guys needed to take law enforcement seriously. He gentled his voice with his next words, though. "What did Danna see? Who killed her uncle?"

"She didn't see the man's face." Sandford pursed his lips as if measuring his next words. He hung his head, then looked at Nolan. "She said he was an Alaska State Trooper."

The words punched through Nolan's chest.

No . . . that couldn't be true.

All eyes shifted to Nolan.

He took a moment to compose himself, gather the words. "We'll get to the bottom of this."

Otto had been found unconscious. Someone must have stolen his uniform to commit murder. Whoever got to him had done this. That had to be it.

"How do you know that Hank made it to his destination?" Autumn asked.

When he didn't answer, she narrowed her eyes.

"I radioed him, what do you think?"

"So, you're in contact?"

Otis stepped up. "Look, Chief, Hank is trusting us to keep his secret. The truth is, we don't know *where* he took them."

"If you radioed them, he's close enough." Autumn turned and scraped her hand through her thick, curly hair.

"In the mountains," Otis said. "He's still impossible to find."

Nolan gauged Grier's reaction, and he appeared subdued. He was pretty good friends with these guys, but they'd cut him out of this particular loop because of his connection to the chief, and of course, he was law enforcement. They were law-abiding citizens, but with this new development, news from Danna that someone in the Alaska State Troopers had murdered Nuna, they were wary of trusting law enforcement. He didn't blame them.

While Autumn talked to Hank's loyal friends and tried to learn his location, Nolan had some unfinished business with Ivy. "Can I talk to you outside?"

They put their coats back on and then he opened the door for her. Ivy stepped out in front of him. At least the rain had stopped. She continued walking toward the edge of the groomed area until she stood close to the tree line near the snow machines.

She blew out a breath that formed a white cloud around her head. "I needed some fresh air anyway."

"Cold, but fresh." He offered a grin but could tell by the look on her face that she hadn't enjoyed his humor.

"What's on your mind?" She angled her head.

"Danna is with Alina. That's all you promised you'd do. Find her granddaughter. Danna is with her grandmother. And for the time being, safe with Hank." *That we know of.*

"Well, it wasn't because of me that she was found."

"It doesn't matter," he said. "So it's time for you to go home. Go back to your mother and be with her." *While you still can.*

She gave him an incredulous smirk. "Are you kicking me out of your state, Trooper?"

"Of course not. But your self-imposed task here is complete."

"You forgot one thing. The manuscript. You're right about all of it, of course. I want to be back home with Mom. But

. . . I feel like we're so close. We've almost found them, Nolan, and I need to see this through. If I can come home with that blasted manuscript, all the better. I can sidestep what's being held over me. Let me at least see Danna and talk to her and ask her about the manuscript."

Her eyes shimmered and she glanced away. He could tell she was anxious to get home but also determined to finish what she'd started, and he admired her. He took a step closer and wanted to touch her cheek, like he'd done before, and feel the soft skin. Connect with her.

Instead, he gently touched her arm. "I promise, Ivy, if I find the manuscript and it isn't held as evidence, I will send it to you." *I might even hand deliver it.*

Ivy looked away from him and stared into the woods as if there was a decision to make.

But there wasn't. This wasn't her investigation.

"Autumn and Grier, along with the troopers, can handle the rest," he continued. "I'll let Autumn know I'm taking you back to Shadow Gap so you can fly back to Florida."

"And what about you? After this is over, are you going to continue your vacation plans to *Florida*?" She gave him a wry grin.

She knew about that? Who had told her? Had to be Autumn. Heart pounding, he didn't know how to answer. He needed time to think and this wasn't it. And that she'd asked him gave him hope, but he quickly doused it as false hope. Nothing lasting could happen between Sunshine Girl and Mountain Man, as she'd called him when she'd been mumbling in her Dramamine-laced sleep on the boat. He doubted she even remembered.

She suddenly angled her head. "Do you hear that?"

A snow machine. Wait . . .

More than one.

THIRTY-ONE

Her pulse skyrocketed as she shared a look with Nolan because she saw the raw fear in his eyes. "What if we led them here?" she asked.

Nolan turned and hiked toward the cabin.

"It might be someone out having fun," he said.

"I hope that's all it is," she called after him.

He picked up his pace. "Except nobody comes out here to have fun. The snow machine trails are on the other side of town."

She followed. "I hear more than one, Nolan. We need to get out of here."

Getting trapped in the cabin was the last thing any of them needed. She stepped inside and found Grier putting out the fire, but it was probably too late. Plus, their snow machines gave their presence away.

Everyone in the room gathered weapons. Ivy admired these fierce men and women who knew how to handle guns, ride snow machines, steer a boat through a stormy night. All of it. They had to in order to live in this harsh land. The room shifted around her, and her mind went right back to the standoff with Danny, the man she'd killed in front of his daughter. Her heart was in her throat. She'd made the right decision to resign because she was in no mental condition to function as a special agent anymore.

But here and now, she had no choice but to push aside the insecurities dogging her and stand her ground like everyone here. She gripped her Glock—truly a baby compared to the other firearms around her.

"If they're coming for Danna," Autumn said, "then we'll make our stand here. Take them down and find out who they are before they find Danna."

Nolan took Sandford's rifle with the high-powered scope and headed for the door. "I'll get in position."

"Wait, what are you doing?" Ivy asked. "Where are you going?"

"Let him go." Autumn touched Ivy's arm. "He's a marksman. He can take care of himself, and take care of us, too, while he's at it." She turned to her husband. "Grier, you're with me outside. If this is a dangerous party, then I want someone in custody. Preferably all of them. I'll settle for one. Let's see what we're facing. And Otis?"

"I'll be outside too. That leaves Sandford inside alone, though."

"You good with that, Sandford?" Autumn asked.

"I'm good."

"You can answer the door, but don't open it," she said.

He was loading a handgun. "Yep."

Getting caught here, possibly ambushed, had memories flooding Ivy. Danny finding her searching his desk drawers, discovering she was working undercover, and lifting his gun to kill her. Her palms started sweating. No. Not now! She pushed those images aside and followed Autumn outside, catching up to her.

Ivy gripped her baby Glock. "I'll take up a position outside too."

"You and Otis can stick together in the trees. Follow him."

Autumn and Grier snuck around the cabin to the right, and Ivy took the left, edging into the trees, and caught up with Otis.

"Autumn told me to team up with you."

He nodded and gestured for her to follow him deeper into the trees, but the snow machines had stopped, which meant whoever was coming was now hiking in the rest of the way on snowshoes, following the snow machine tracks Autumn, Grier, and Nolan had left behind that led to Hank's cabin.

Otis gestured for them to hide under the cover of low-hanging branches where they could peer through and spot the approaching danger. She gripped the Glock with her fingerless gloves, a round already chambered.

God, please let no one die today. Let no one get shot and die!

Ivy sank in the snow at the base of a nearby spruce. Otis took the trees near hers and dipped his head. They were ready and waiting. She hunkered down, but not too low or she'd be buried in snow. At least the snow hid her . . . except for tracks, which she couldn't get away from.

Tracks or no tracks, she was ready. Holding Baby, her G43, she made sure she was well hidden. She calmed her pounding heart so she could hear the sounds around her, but that was proving difficult over the pulse roaring in her ears. Now and then she glanced at Otis, and he never moved. He melded into his surroundings.

The muted landscape might have comforted her, except she knew danger was approaching. Soon enough, she heard someone's failed attempt to be stealthy. Ivy focused on the moment.

Though she couldn't see anyone—except Otis—she trusted the others were in place as well on this pseudo-stakeout. Or ambush—she wasn't sure which. Either way, if they could snag these men, they could get answers.

A clump of snow fell on her face, sending icy cold needles into her cheeks. She swiped it away. She squeezed her eyes shut, then blinked a few times to clear her vision.

The snowshoes stopped. She'd known there was more than one person, but how many more? Two or three?

A man in cold-weather tactical gear—body armor, load-bearing vests, utility belts, the works—entered the area cleared of snow, moving from tree to tree for cover. From the trees, he peered through a high-powered scope. All she could do was remain still and pray this ended well.

Seeing this man in his gear, her gut tightened. What was he? A mercenary? Who had hired him? Was he with their own government?

Like Grier had mentioned—*they're already here.*

But this guy was only one. Where was his partner in crime?

He finally stepped from the cover of the trees and approached the cabin. Holding a semiautomatic handgun at his back, he knocked on the door. They were all assuming they'd been followed to the cabin. If that was true, then this guy had seen the Shadow Gap Police Department vehicles and knew local law enforcement was involved.

"Who's there?" Sandford called from inside the cabin.

"I'm lost out here," the mercenary said. "I need some help finding my way."

Don't open the door. Don't open the door.

"I can't help you. Move along."

The man tried the knob, then kicked at the door, then whipped out his gun to shoot the door open, but Autumn appeared from the corner of the cabin, behind a nearby spruce, and Grier from the other side. Both aiming their handguns at this big, intimidating assassin in tactical gear. Nolan had their backs from the high point to prevent someone else from taking them out. Ivy peered around her, but she couldn't see much. She remained aware of her surroundings while she also aimed her gun at the threat in case his next move would not be what they wanted.

Don't do it. Don't do it.

"Drop your weapon and lift your hands in the air where we can see them. You've got no move here, so don't even try. You move, you're dead." Autumn's threatening tone was the voice of authority.

The man whipped his gun around at Autumn. Ivy fired her gun, aware that Otis fired his gun as well. Rifle fire echoed around Ivy as more gunfire cracked the silent, snow-covered land.

The man fell.

Autumn fell.

Heart pounding, adrenaline surging, Ivy glanced around her. She needed to get to Autumn. The cabin door opened, and Sandford rushed out, aiming his gun into the woods, leaving himself dangerously exposed. It was up to Ivy and Otis to stay here and take out whoever else might shoot at them.

Gasping for breath, she tried to pull her eyes from the crimson snow. Her gaze riveted to Grier as he dropped next to Autumn, still protected by the tree. She hadn't intentionally exposed herself, but no one had thought the mercenary would take a shot. Ivy hadn't been fast enough, but neither had Nolan, or someone else remained in the woods and could have shot Autumn.

"Otis?" She glanced to her right.

He was slumped against the tree.

A vise gripped Ivy's arm and flung her away from the tree, tossing her into the deep snow, which toppled down onto her, covering her. But she'd held on to her gun. She tried to roll out of the way, then aim at her attacker. Pain ignited in her head. Darkness would bury her.

THIRTY-TWO

The moments happened in slow motion as if time had almost stopped completely. Nolan searched the woods but saw no one else. Heard the snow machines. Whoever was left was fleeing. He should chase them. Heart jackhammering, he scrambled down the slope through the deep snow, stumbling. Nearly falling onto his face. Rifle still in his grip, he trudged forward, sending a thousand prayers.

God, please don't let my sister die.

Too many trees stood between Nolan and Hank's cabin.

Nolan and Autumn.

Through the trees, he could see Grier next to Autumn. Sandford stood next to the body of the man Nolan had killed. He broke through the deep snow and raced across the small, groomed pocket. Dropping to his knees, he slid forward next to an unconscious Autumn. Her face was pale and slack.

His insides were gutted by the scene.

Grier said nothing as he used gunshot wound powder to stop the woman he loved from bleeding to death. Then Grier briefly glanced at Nolan and filleted him with one look. Grief and shame tormented him.

Sandford squeezed Nolan's shoulder. "We've called emergency services."

"How long?"

"Fifteen, twenty minutes out."

His throat constricted. How had this happened? How had he *let* this happen? Grier was there too. How had either of them let Autumn get shot?

Why hadn't he taken the shot sooner? This had all gone wrong. Very wrong.

Sandford motioned for Nolan to join him, walk with him. Nolan didn't want to leave Autumn, but he saw the severe concern on Sandford's face.

When they reached the corner of the cabin, the man spoke. "I heard other snow machines, so I'm assuming that whoever came with this guy is gone. Someone should go after him."

Otis trudged out from the trees, then stumbled. Sandford rushed to assist him and then Nolan saw that Otis's left eye was completely shut. Someone had hit him. "Ivy? Where's Ivy?" Otis asked.

Ivy!

Nolan stiffened, fear twisting his insides as he glanced around. "Ivy!" he called, but she didn't answer.

His fear ratcheted up.

"I'll go search for her," Sandford said.

"I'll do it." Nolan ground his teeth. "There's nothing I can do for Autumn here, except get whoever's responsible."

"Well, you got one of them. Maybe we can learn his identity, and then we'll know more."

Nolan started off.

"Nolan, wait." Grier glanced up at him, then back at Autumn.

Nolan moved to Autumn's side again. Her eyes blinked open—she was coming out of it—and she looked up at him. He could see the pain and fear in her eyes.

"I'm so sorry, Autumn. You're going to be fine. You're going to be okay." *Please forgive me.*

"Don't blame yourself. Not your fault . . . Nolan." Her words came on a cracked whisper. "Get whoever . . ."

233

Is responsible.

A tear leaked out the corner of her eye. Fury reached inside his chest and fisted his heart. Squeezed hard.

Nolan turned. He couldn't look at her anymore. He had to finish this. Find Ivy and finish this. After slinging the rifle over his shoulder, he gripped his loaded handgun and marched forward into the woods, following Ivy's tracks to the tree where she'd hidden. She was gone.

He spotted signs of a scuffle on the ground and snowshoe tracks. Nolan got back on his snow machine and followed those tracks until they came to snow machine tracks, which he followed through the woods. He'd failed the two most important people in his life. Autumn and Ivy. But he wouldn't let his utter disappointment in himself stop him from fixing this. He had to make it right.

The jerks behind this travesty wouldn't get away. Nolan pressed forward, searching the woods as he traveled deeper and farther away from Hank's cabin. He had no idea where Hank's hiding place was up in the mountains, and that was probably a good thing. Hank was doing what he had to do to protect the two women he cared about the most. So far, Hank had succeeded.

But not Nolan.

Still, all Hank had to do was stay hidden.

Autumn and Ivy had joined Nolan in facing off with the danger. They all knew the risks. But knowing that didn't make what happened to Autumn sit any better in his gut. His shattered heart.

A figure stumbled out in front of him.

Ivy . . .

He stopped the snow machine, then jumped off and ran to catch her up in his arms. She embraced him as if she would never let go. Nolan might hold on to her forever. But . . .

He held her away from him. "Are you hurt?"

She shook her head, and her hair fell forward, revealing the blood caked to her scalp.

He ripped off the cap. "Someone hit you."

"Stunned me. That's how they got me on the snow machine. But I got *his* weapon"—she held up a handgun—"and escaped. I shot him before he could get me again. He got on the snow machine and got away. It was supposed to be a kill shot. At least we have DNA from his blood." She pointed at a few drops in the snow. "You should collect it before it's too late."

He nodded, not caring nearly as much as he should. "I will. And we have his partner." He gently lifted her chin and angled her head so he could get a better look at the wound. "I'm more concerned about you." Yeah, that needed tending.

But she was alive. Ivy hadn't been taken and tortured and killed. Or shot and left holding on to her life like—

"Autumn . . . is she?" Ivy searched his eyes.

The roar of a medical helicopter echoed off the mountains and through the trees. "She's alive. That must be her flight out of here."

He grabbed a bag from a pack secured to the snow machine and got the blood in the ice. Then tucked it away. "Can you hold on? You're not too dizzy or concussed, are you? Please tell me the truth."

"I'm okay. I promise to hold on." Ivy climbed behind him onto the snow machine and wrapped her arms around him, squeezing. Her grip comforted his soul, and he was going to need that. He had to prepare for what came next.

THIRTY-THREE

At Hank's home, where so much had gone wrong, a paramedic examined Ivy's wound, cleaned it, and suggested she get her head checked out. "I never passed out, okay?"

"Fine, but any dizziness, you get it checked." He put his supplies back in his medical pack.

"I promise."

The paramedic headed out the door where everyone else remained outside in the cold. The temperature hovered near freezing. She might never get warm enough, even standing next to the blazing fire someone had resurrected after the chaos.

I'm taking you back to Shadow Gap so you can fly back to Florida.

Not just yet. She needed to see Danna for herself. See that she was safe and with her grandmother. Especially after the tragedy that happened here today, that grieved them all. Too much had gone wrong. And she prayed that somehow, someway, something would finally go right.

Autumn had been transported to a nearby hospital, and Grier had gone with her. Local law enforcement officers Ross Miller and Angie Ledger had arrived, and they had plenty of questions for the two men—Sandford and Otis—who'd been the last to communicate with Hank. And for Nolan, who had killed the man who shot Autumn. Or at least they believed it was that man's shot that had hit the vulnerable spot her vest hadn't protected, but ballistics would tell the story. That man's body would be transported to the state medical examiner in Anchorage and hopefully identified. But the only official law enforcement involved in this incident were Autumn, Grier, and Nolan.

Unfortunately, today's disaster reminded Ivy of her undercover assignment gone terribly wrong. That same nausea roiled inside, leaving her unsteady and feeling disturbed to her core.

She'd found her Glock in the snow but had turned it over to one of the Shadow Gap officers for the investigation into the shooting.

Ivy had no idea what would happen next for Nolan—would he be taken off the case or finally sent on his vacation that had been waylaid? She suspected that he didn't much care at this point. All he cared about was getting answers. Taking down criminals. And Ivy was right there with him and wished she could adequately convey her determination.

The cabin door opened and quickly slammed shut. She turned to see who'd come inside. Nolan's face was carved into a deep, terrifying frown. Her heart kicked around inside at the pain in his eyes.

And the anger.

"Come on. Let me get you out of here." He held out his hand.

She didn't really want to leave the fire and kept her arms folded around her. "What's happening?"

"I need to get you to the clinic so they can check your head."

"One of the paramedics already did." She pointed at her head. "See? I have a bandage. I'm fine. It's a knot. I've had worse."

He surprised her by not arguing and turned to stomp out. She followed him, understanding he needed space to process his part in what had happened. There would be an investigation, no doubt. Maybe he didn't really want the burden of worrying about Ivy added to his concern for Autumn, and perhaps at the bottom of his worries—his job. He didn't need to be concerned for her safety, but that was part of his nature, who he was. A protector.

And failing Autumn had to be eating at his very core. Ivy wanted to comfort him, but she didn't know how.

"Listen, Nolan, I'm sure one of the others can take me somewhere." Where, she didn't have a clue at this juncture. "If you need time alone. But I'm in this with you until the end."

"No, you're not."

"You can't stop me."

He continued toward the snow machine and handed her a helmet. "Go home, Ivy. Go spend what time you have left with your mother. What if she dies while you're here? You'll never forgive yourself."

The words—so hard, so brutal—cut through her. But he wasn't wrong. "And if I don't see this through with you, I won't forgive myself."

"This isn't your fight. Your investigation. You have no stakes." He got on the snow machine and waited for her.

Okay, now he was being downright mean. Hurting her on purpose to get rid of her? She could dig in her heels. "And you've probably been taken off the investigation for the time being." A trooper whose sister had just been shot. A trooper who'd just killed a man. A bad man, but still a kill shot that would require investigating.

She climbed on behind him and held on tight, but she felt like she was clinging to a stranger, and to a lost cause.

Nolan steered through the woods until they arrived at the snow machine trailers. He onboarded his snow machine. The other officers arrived on theirs. Sandford and Otis had taken the ones Autumn and Grier had used. The vehicles loaded up, the two officers agreed to return the snow machines.

Ivy rode with Nolan in Autumn's Interceptor and endured

a long, uncomfortable silence. They finally arrived at the small hospital where Nolan paced back and forth in the waiting area. Grier had come in with Autumn, and he groused in another corner of the small room, neither of them speaking to each other. Too filled with grief and anger for words? Or was Grier really that furious with Nolan? From where Ivy had been sitting, she didn't think he could have acted any faster to take out the threat. Ivy had taken a shot too, and she had also failed to stop the man.

Her gun had been taken as evidence so they could figure out whose shot had actually killed the man. Who *was* the man? Where was Danna? Still, after all of this, none of their questions were answered because the mercenary was dead and his partner on the run.

Autumn had just been doing her job.

And Ivy had taken on a job that wasn't hers.

Ivy's cell phone was charging, and she hoped to talk to Mom to give her an update, and to find out what was going on since Donovan had claimed he'd been fired. Why had Mom fired him?

While she waited, she sat with her laptop open, searching for answers. She'd taken a picture of the crime board that Nolan had created. She tried to eliminate any pieces that appeared disconnected and could be discarded regarding this investigation into who killed Nuna and who was after Danna.

She lifted her gaze from the keyboard and caught Nolan leaning against the wall with both hands, hanging his head. That broke her heart. More than anything, she wanted to set aside the computer and move to stand with him, wrap her arms around him and hug him, infusing him with comfort. But soothing his injured soul would take far more than her arms around him.

If she were Nolan, she would do everything in her power, with or without permission, to find the people responsible. Heavy footfalls resounded in the hallway and Nolan looked up. He stiffened. Two Alaska State Troopers approached him. Their voices remained low and she couldn't make out their terse words.

He walked with them down the hall and disappeared around the corner.

Grier stood and moved to watch Nolan leave. Hands on his hips, he shook his head, then turned in time to talk to a doctor in scrubs who'd exited the operating room. Grier glanced over his shoulder and caught her watching, then gestured for the doctor to speak to him in another room. Great. Nobody trusted her. Nobody wanted her here.

Her cell dinged and she looked at the text from Donovan.

Need update.

She returned the text.

Dangerous.

Then it hit her—had he known? Is that why he hadn't come himself? But he should have warned her.

Did you know?

He responded.

Time is running out.

That wasn't an answer.

Why did my mother fire you?

We're in love. Wants us to take it slow.

"What?" Ivy stood with outrage. Others in the waiting room looked at her. "Sorry . . . sorry." She eased back into the seat.

Ivy grabbed her now fully charged cell and the charger, stuffed everything back into her bag, and headed to a private corner in the hospital, then called Mom.

"Hello?" Another voice. Another woman.

"This is Ivy. Can I please speak to my mother?" Why was someone else answering Mom's cell?

"Oh, hello. This is Myrtle."

The friend from church she had texted before. Ivy's heart dropped. She couldn't breathe. "Myrtle, what's happened? Where's Mom?"

"Sleeping. Not to worry, dear, she's just resting. I thought it might be you, so I answered."

Ivy leaned against the wall. She should have stayed with her. "I'm coming home, Myrtle. On the first flight I can get out of here."

Shuffling and muffled voices sounded over the connection. "Ivy, this is Mom."

Ivy smiled as relief filled her. "I didn't mean to wake you. How are you doing? What's going on? Why did you fire Donovan?"

She wished she had thought of that but keeping their enemies close had seemed like a good idea.

"I miss you, Ivy."

"I miss you too, Mom." She waited a few heartbeats, then, "What about Donovan?"

"The truth is . . . I never liked him, honestly. He was your father's friend, and yes, he was helping in the business, but I don't think I can trust him."

"What? Why?"

"That Bible verse in Jeremiah comes to mind, Ivy. 'The heart is deceitful above all things, and desperately sick; who can understand it?' That is to say that the nature of humans is inherently evil."

"Okay?"

"For all Don's smiles, I have the feeling he has ulterior motives. I'm done with him."

"So, you aren't in love with him?"

"In love with him?" Mom coughed and laughed with incredulity. "Where did you get that idea? Enough about that. Let's talk about you. I've made a decision, Ivy. If you don't get the manuscript by the end of this week, just come home. I don't know how much time is left."

Mom, don't say that! "What did the doctor say?"

"He says God has not put an expiration date on me. He thinks I'm a tough old woman—a sick one, but a tough one."

What did that mean? *Why am I not there?* Ivy wanted to bang her head against the wall. "What do the tests say?"

"I'm getting better, Ivy. The tests say that, but I'm not *feeling* better. I wish I hadn't sent you on that fool's errand. You're a good daughter to do my bidding. The best, but it seems ridiculous now. Life is so short. What do I care about that old manuscript, really? Sure, your father wanted it for Grace, but both of them are gone and it's just you and me now. And honestly . . . well, never mind."

"What, Mom? Don't do that to me. Tell me."

Her mother sighed heavily. "Oh, all right. I'm only running this place because your father loved it so much. I used to dream about doing something else with my life, and—you're going to laugh—I even fantasized about selling the business one day. But when he died . . . I just couldn't sell it. He loved it, and now I can't let go."

Oh, Mom!

"I hope that doesn't upset you," Mom said. "You quit your job with the FBI to come help me. I'm sorry, Ivy. I shouldn't have let you do that. You're the best daughter a mother could ask for, traipsing off to Alaska in the winter to get a piece of Jack London's lost work for me. And look at you—you're still there, searching. Determined. Unwilling to come home without it."

Ivy didn't have the heart to tell her that she wasn't a good daughter at all—at least by her mother's standard of measurement. She had only gone because of Donovan's blackmail. But it was time to come clean.

"Mom, you rest and take care of yourself. I'll be home in

three days with or without that manuscript." Most likely without. "I love you, Mom. And tell Myrtle thank you for me."

"I love you too, Ivy."

Ivy ended the call.

So, Mom didn't trust Donovan. She was onto him. What had he done? Ivy couldn't wait to find out, but she was back on track. Three days. She had three days to make a difference here and then she would be in Florida with Mom, who was recovering. She had to believe her mother was getting better.

Thank you, Lord.

Ivy and Mom had been given a reprieve. Until the next time. It was a battle to stay in remission. Ivy found another seat in the waiting room and yanked out her computer. Time to use what little information she had on hand to find connections if there were any. She researched everything she could find on the internet about Nuna and his past, missing the databases to which she'd have access if she'd remained with the feds. Then she moved from him to Gene Whitlock and found as much as she could about his education on LinkedIn, and his childhood home and school. Then moved to the Alaska State Trooper— Otto Hanson. She found his name on the news report regarding his hospitalization and worked backward from there. Read about his education and his hometown.

Hours slipped by and Nolan still hadn't returned.

Grier paced and spent time on his cell, and then he finally disappeared, she assumed into Autumn's recovery room after surgery. She would survive. Ivy was glad Nolan wasn't here because Grier probably wasn't ready to let him inside her room.

Family feuds.

Back to her laptop. Nothing jumped out at her, so there might not be any connections, but still, Nuna and Gene were both scientists. There had to be. She then started reading anything she could find on Wayne Novak, the man who had trafficked Danna in the past. Nolan had mentioned the trooper who'd died in the explosion was also looking into a trafficking case, so Ivy continued to read about all human trafficking in the Southeast Alaska region.

Her neck ached and she was tired of sitting, so she got up and grabbed coffee and a sandwich from a vending machine. Actually, she might be better off just heading to the motel in town or the Lively Moose to work. Their cobbled-together investigation group had slowly fallen apart with the chief's almost-fatal injury.

That would shake any community.

And as long as Hank, Lina, and Danna were safe at the moment . . .

But how long could they hold out? Ivy needed to find Nolan soon and make a plan. Back at her computer her eyes began to glaze over. What she needed was an energy drink. A case of them.

Skimming the information she'd read about Nuna and then Gene, she finally spotted a connection.

Are you kidding me? Nuna Grainger and Gene Whitlock both attended the University of Michigan in Ann Arbor before heading on to other educational institutions for their multiple degrees and PhDs. Nuna studied chemistry, biochemical engineering, and physics. Ivy couldn't comprehend a brain like that. Gene studied ecology and chemistry. Could they have known each other? Could they have met in the chemistry department? That had to be it.

Thinking about it, she looked up the moment Nolan appeared down the hallway in jeans and an overcoat as well as a ball cap. Not in uniform.

He headed straight for Grier, who also emerged from the corridor on the opposite end.

Showdown.

THIRTY-FOUR

Anguish engulfed Nolan, but he wouldn't let it stop him as he approached Grier, who stood in his path, hands on his hips.

"Are you really going to stop me from seeing her?" Nolan tried to stay strong, but his voice cracked. Just a little. He was broken. Shattered.

Pain filled Grier's eyes and he sagged, blowing out a breath. Hung his head.

"You think I don't blame myself enough?"

"I'm angry, Nolan. I'm furious at how this all unfolded. It's going to take me time not to blame myself. Between the two of us, we should have kept her safe." Grier blew out yet another breath. "Right now, she's resting."

"Let me see her," Nolan said.

"Only one person at a time can go in," Grier said. "I'll wait, but make it fast."

"I will." He had to hurry because he had news, and he and Ivy had to get out of here. No sense in bringing Grier into this. The guy needed to stay in the hospital and focus on his wife.

Nolan slipped into the hospital room, thinking back to not too long ago when they'd almost lost Dad to a criminal element. He moved to her bedside and looked at all the tubes hooked up to her. Grief hammered his chest until it was too painful to bear. "I'm sorry, Autumn. You counted on me."

God, when am I going to stop failing people? He fisted and refisted his hands. He had to make this right.

He'd just spent several hours talking to Alaska State Troopers Peterson and Jamison, as well as his sergeant, Alton. He was officially on his vacation. Alton gave him the option of administrative leave while they investigated what happened or the vacation he was supposed to go on anyway. He'd taken his vacation—not the way he'd wanted—because he wasn't done with this investigation.

He slipped his hand into Autumn's unresponsive one and leaned down to kiss her on the forehead. "I'm going to finish this," he whispered.

He felt the slightest movement in her finger—and his heart warmed. Breathing hitched. He turned and walked out and found Grier staring down the hallway, waiting.

Grier caught him as he passed and gave him a bear hug.

"Hang in there, Grier. Be there for her, no matter what happens."

Grier gave him the briefest look—confusion and then maybe understanding. Nolan wasn't sure. He moved to Ivy, who stood, holding her laptop.

"Let's go." He held her arm at the elbow, ushering her out, and she didn't refuse.

"Where are we going exactly?" she asked.

"To the airport. Time for you to get back to Florida."

"What?" She stopped walking. "No. I figured—"

Leaning in, he whispered, "Just roll with it."

He ushered her to Dad's old Ford pickup. He'd gone back to the house to trade Autumn's Interceptor for the truck and changed out of his uniform for the next phase in this operation.

He opened the door for Ivy and she slid in. Once Nolan was inside, he steered away from the hospital.

"You're out of uniform," she said.

"I'm off the investigation for now. Off . . ."

"Then what are we doing?"

"Finishing this."

He expected Ivy to question him on his decision to move forward. She was quiet for a few moments, so she had to be processing it, thinking it through. He was doing the same, honestly. But he'd been left with no choice in the matter.

"I have three days, Nolan, and then I'm going home."

"We should be done before then."

"Good. I don't know if this means anything, but I learned something. I wonder if I should tell the troopers, or Grier. Someone on the investigation."

"Whatever you think, but first you should know that I have news for you too. Danna is talking, but Lina will only let her talk to *you*. She isn't going to talk to the troopers or anyone else. She's terrified."

"But . . . where? Where are they?"

"We cannot let ourselves be followed, which is a problem in a small town. Dad's truck is old enough it has no tracking system, so this is a start."

"But what does that matter when people are watching and can see the truck, like you said, in this small town?"

"Good point. I'm making this up as I go, okay? Honestly, I'm not worried about the Shadow Gap residents. I'm more worried about the outsiders."

Nolan steered up to the house and parked. They got out and went inside. He put a finger to his lips, hoping she would get on board with the charade.

"Let's get you a flight out for the morning back to Florida. How about I go with you for my vacation?"

"Sure, whatever you say." She scrunched up her face.

He placed his satellite phone on the counter, then retrieved two burner phones that had been charging and handed her one of them, then held out his hand. She took in the situation and understood. Ivy fished her cell from her pocket and set it on the counter next to his phone. Good. They understood each other. He didn't want their phones to be tracked, and maybe he should have done this much sooner. He had an emergency satellite device, untraceable, but he could use it to reach Grier if he couldn't get the cell to work. Then he retrieved a Ruger LCP Max, a .380—a small handgun—along with a holster, from a locked drawer and handed it off to Ivy. The Ruger wasn't her baby Glock, which hadn't been returned to her, but it was small, and it would do. He wouldn't leave her unprotected.

She smiled when she took it from him. He didn't have to communicate his thinking because she seemed to understand what was going on.

"Come on, I want to show you something." He took her hand and led her out the back and into the night. He flipped on the outdoor lights and took her down the steps to the water's edge. He'd cleared the steps of any snow or ice so they wouldn't be slippery or dangerous.

Nolan sat on the steps and Ivy joined him.

"What were you going to show me?"

"You said you always wanted to see the northern lights." He grinned. "When we first met. But it never worked out then. I'm hoping you can see the aurora borealis this trip before you leave."

"But it's cloudy tonight."

"Yes, it is."

"You just wanted to get me outside?"

He nodded and hoped Ivy was tracking with him. The man at the cabin had been military trained. Who was behind sending someone to get Danna? And had they been sent to kill her? Or question her? He didn't know, but he couldn't trust anyone except those closest to him until he knew more. He wouldn't put it past the searchers to bug his home to learn what he knew about Danna's location.

"You think someone could be listening in?" she asked quietly.

"Possibly."

They sat in silence for a few more moments. Nolan hoped this was going to work.

Where are you?

The whir of a small motor echoed in the distance, then suddenly, the sound stopped. Nolan was beginning to second-guess this plan.

"What's going on?" Ivy whispered. "What are we waiting for?"

"Trust me?"

Her nod was tenuous. He saw in her eyes that she *did* trust him. Completely. Emotion thickened in his throat. And with that trust he felt the weight of responsibility. This had to work. *God, please let it work.*

Water sloshed and Nolan held his gun ready. He couldn't be sure who was approaching, and maybe they shouldn't be standing out in the open like this. A skiff came into view, and using oars, the boater maneuvered close to the small dock. Good idea. The oars were silent compared to a boat motor. Nolan stood and led Ivy over to the dock where he stepped into the boat, then turned to assist her, but she gingerly hopped in without his help. The boat rocked slightly as they sat without a word.

And disappeared into the cold, dark night.

THIRTY-FIVE

The darkness, the icy cold, seemed to take on a palpable presence, wrapping around her as the house lights grew distant and finally faded away completely.

Oars lapped the water, occasionally bumping something—she didn't know what, and that creeped her out.

Ivy had never been so cold. Nolan sat behind her to balance out the boat. They said nothing. Her heart remained in her throat, an unnatural fear paralyzing her for no reason. Plenty of reason existed to feel afraid, but at this moment her anxiety was irrational. Fear of the unknown gripped her.

Finally, the boater set aside the oars and started up the small engine but still did not turn on the lights, so they were floating in the dark. His hood and thermal mask had prevented her from making out his face. This was maddening. And how could he see a thing? Was he wearing night-vision goggles? That had to be it. The tension slightly eased out of her shoulders, but she still couldn't breathe easier. Her chest remained tight and her pulse high until the boat approached a barely discernible dock near a floatplane.

The unnamed boater moored the small boat, then stepped onto the dock. He assisted her up and then Nolan joined them. Quietly the man led them around a building that looked like a hangar and then she realized she'd been here before. This was Carrie James's hangar. She desperately wanted to find out what they were doing here, but no one was talking. Quiet was the order of the day. Or rather night.

Nolan gripped her hands, then pressed something into them. "Goggles," he whispered.

Night vision? She slipped them on and then could see. If it had come to using night vision, then she should be terrified out of her mind. Anyone hunting them could do the same as well as use thermal technology. But she wouldn't question or argue in the middle of this. They could only use the tools available to them. She kept close to Nolan, who followed the stranger who'd brought them here, then they entered a cabin deep in the woods.

The windows had all been blocked off with dark shades, and inside, the space was dimly lit. Once inside, they pulled off the night-vision goggles. The boater pulled off his hood.

Trevor West.

Hank rose and approached Nolan to shake his hand. Behind him Ivy saw Lina and Danna. Relief rushed through her. They were safe . . . for now.

Then Hank smiled at Ivy. "It's good to see you, Sunshine Girl."

Sunshine Girl. She glanced at Nolan. He'd called her that once before—the first time she'd been in Alaska. Warmth surged in his gaze, and it flooded through her too.

Shrugging out of her coat and gloves, she approached the fire. "I'm surprised you have a fire going."

"No one can see smoke at night."

"Was this the best idea?" she asked.

"We were up in the mountains," Hank said. "But they were closing in. I spotted them searching as if they knew where to find us."

"None of your friends would give you away," Nolan said.

"You're sure right they wouldn't. I didn't tell them where I was. No one knew."

"It doesn't matter," Trevor said. "Let's get to this."

"Hank contacted Trevor and explained the situation. He got us out and brought us here," Lina said. "But I refused to let Danna speak to anyone. I'm not sure he should be here." She eyed Nolan. "He's one of them."

"No." Ivy said. "He's not. He isn't involved. He was with me when . . ."

"It wasn't him." Danna stood, her voice shaky.

Nolan stepped forward. "I'm glad you know that. We don't have much time. Tell us what happened. What you know."

"No." Lina stood in front of Danna. "She speaks to Ivy alone."

Ivy approached Lina and Danna. "Please, it's all right. Danna, can you tell me your story? You can tell me in front of these others. They're going to help us. Help you."

"We need to get somewhere safe," Hank groused as he paced. "They're going to find us here."

"Then we should hurry," Ivy said. She gently took Danna's hand, led her to the sofa, and sat with her. "Your grandmother told me a lot about you."

"She told me about you too." Danna stared at her with those big brown eyes, reminding her once again of Grace. She would do everything in her power to keep this young woman safe. "Tell me what you know."

Danna glanced at Nolan and then Trevor.

"You can trust everyone in this room with your life," Ivy said. "We're all here to help you."

Ivy looked at Lina and held her gaze, then finally the older woman nodded.

Danna pressed her face into her hands and her shoulders shook. "I don't know where to start. I'm so confused."

"Take a deep breath and start from the beginning."

"Everyone is staring at me. I can't do this." She jumped from the sofa and ran into a room and slammed the door.

Lina started after her. "No, Lina, wait. Make some tea. Something relaxing. And bring it to us. I'll go to her."

"I need to know what's going on too," Nolan said.

"Then you wait outside the door and listen. I'll try to record the conversation as well." She headed down a short hallway and gently knocked on the closed door before opening it and stepping inside to find Danna crying into a pillow.

She'd been traumatized and people were after her. Seemed like a lot of trouble for one small, young woman, even if she was a witness to a murder.

Ivy took the one chair. "When you're ready, Danna, tell me what I can do to help you."

She pressed record on her phone and set it on the bedside table. Lina entered the room with two steaming mugs. "I found just one bag of chamomile tea."

"Good enough," Ivy said. "Thanks."

Danna sat up and took one of the mugs.

"You want me to stay?" Lina asked.

"You can go. I'm okay." Danna looked at Ivy.

Lina had told her enough that the young woman seemed to trust Ivy, though she'd only just met her. But it felt like they shared a connection that Ivy couldn't explain, and for her part, Ivy could not let this young woman down.

"Start from the beginning. Your grandmother sent you to your uncle because she saw the trafficker in town."

Danna sipped from the mug. "No. I *told* her that *I* saw him in Shadow Gap so she would agree to send me to Uncle Nuna's."

"Why did you want to go in the first place?" And take the manuscript. But Ivy wouldn't bring it up. By comparison, the lost manuscript had no value to her now. This was about something much bigger.

"Uncle Nuna contacted me and asked me to come. He'd always talked of the beauty of Glacier Bay during the winter and wanted to show me the glaciers when no tourists were around, and he promised to connect me with a writer, a mentor. Nuna asked me to bring the Jack London manuscript."

Interesting. Ivy kept quiet and sipped the tea, the recording still going. Danna had given a lot of thought to how to tell this story despite her earlier declaration that she didn't know where to start. Ivy resisted the urge to push her to share what she'd seen when Nuna had been killed.

Just let her tell her story.

"When I got to Uncle Nuna's, he was making plans to visit the glacier. He'd had a boat waiting and ready, and we took the boat. He told me we were taking the manuscript to bury it."

"What? Why?" Ivy tried not to express too much interest, but she couldn't hide her surprise.

Tears leaked from Danna's eyes. "Have you read it?"

Ivy shook her head. "No. How could I? It was lost."

"But you came for it. Grandmother told me she was going to sell it to you."

"Danna, I'm not concerned about that anymore. Yes, I came to buy it from her, but I don't care about the manuscript. I care about you and what you saw. I want to help keep you safe. Your uncle's murderer has to be brought to justice. The manuscript doesn't matter anymore."

"What are you talking about?" Danna's eyes grew wide, framed by a deep frown. "All of this is about that stupid manuscript!"

So, this was a hunt for gold after all? "Okay, okay. Just calm down," Ivy said. "I spoke out of turn. Tell me the rest."

"Uncle Nuna told me a story about when he was growing up. He heard the story from his grandfather. About gold diggers and the gold rush. A few gold diggers struck gold, but they got sick and died. And then a local tribe buried them and covered the gold, and they also died."

Ivy sat forward in the chair, listening.

Danna held her gaze. "The lost manuscript talks about this

cursed gold, but it's based on a true story. And the Indigenous people weren't happy with Jack London for telling the story. He ultimately left it behind and in his friend's hands—my great-great-grandfather's hands. But the story got twisted up in the telling. Grandmother only wanted to sell it and secure a future for me. But she didn't know she could be killing a lot of people if anyone finds the location detailed in *The Cold Pestilence*."

The title was starting to make sense. The gold miners uncovered an illness in the ice. A plague, or pestilence.

"Uncle Nuna grew up knowing that story, and he ended up going to school and becoming a scientist to learn more about when this happens. That's what he told me." Danna rubbed her eyes. "His job as some kind of scientist—I can't remember exactly—had to do with tracking dangerous substances or pathogens. He found where the cursed gold was and quietly studied the area to learn more. He called it a 'signature.' I don't know how it works. He said that when questions started coming his way from people outside his lab, government officials he didn't trust, he worried that what was buried under the ice was being sought and could be dangerous if found."

Ivy's stomach tightened and her shoulders tensed. That was his job, after all, to search for those kinds of signatures and locate the dangers.

"Danna, why would he tell *you* all of this? It only puts you in danger."

"Because I was someone who would listen. And if something happened to him, someone had to know why and what was going on. Everything about this, including the exact location of the cursed gold, was in his head. He destroyed all his research. That is, until he died. And now . . . it's in my head. The location and some information, but not the research." She shot a mournful half grin at Ivy. "He worked with someone else on the project, and he promised to destroy his research too."

Ivy couldn't fathom a scientist destroying research. "Do you happen to know the name of his coworker?"

"He didn't say."

Ivy would guess it was Gene Whitlock, and Gene had betrayed Nuna.

Her gut ached, twisting tighter. "What *is* the pathogen?"

THIRTY-SIX

Nolan had heard enough and paced the living room. Carrie had arrived, and she and Trevor spoke in low tones in the corner. Probably trying to come up with an escape plan.

Nolan was officially off duty, but his supervisor had shared that the Alaska State Troopers had been bumped out of the investigation and basically told to stand down, but Alton didn't share by whom. When Nolan had fought to stay in the investigation, Alton had taken him aside and told him that he was officially on vacation. Nolan had explained that as long as Ivy was involved, he couldn't simply walk away. Alton then added a warning.

Just. Stay. Alive.

But that might be hard to do.

Without knowing more, he had no real idea of what they were up against. For one thing, if something dangerous lurked under glacial ice, buried so long humankind had never seen the likes of it, then why hadn't Nuna taken the information to the proper authorities? That was the entire purpose of Nuna's job on a team that focused on chemical and biological detection forensics. Obviously, things had gotten messy.

Ivy stepped out into the room, her face pale. She held up the phone.

257

"I got it. I got everything." She set it on the table and hit play so everyone could listen.

He listened again and heard the last part he'd walked away from.

"The pathogen in the ice is some kind of new microbe. Nuna was able to have it analyzed, and it was deadly, as we already know because of the story Jack London shared, and the local tribes passed down a similar story."

"But scientists are making a lot of these discoveries with the ice melting around the globe," Ivy said. "This is nothing new, necessarily."

"Nuna said it could be used as a weapon. But there's more. Deeper under the glacier is a meteorite that contains an extremely rare . . . some kind of critical element we need for technology and weaponry. Right now, we have to import almost all of it from China. It's worth billions."

"And getting to it means digging down through the ice, which would unleash the pathogen, even if it weren't used or collected for biochemical warfare purposes," Ivy said.

"Yes. Nuna didn't want our people harmed. He was afraid for us. For Alaska and for the world."

Oh. Now Nolan got it. Nuna feared for the Indigenous people and that disturbing what had been safe in the ice for thousands of years would bring harm to them—first. Unfortunately, Nolan couldn't argue with the man's thinking. Maybe he'd tried to process the information through the appropriate channels—he'd done his job and the right thing—but that's when the wrong people approached him asking suspicious questions.

"You've done well, Danna," Ivy said. "To remember all of it. To share the truth with me. I'd like to get justice for your uncle. Now I need some important information. What happened when he was killed?"

"After we got back to the cabin, Uncle Nuna started acting strange—well, stranger than normal. He told me to hide under the bed. He gripped my arms, almost hurting me. His face was fierce and angry. Afraid, even. He said, 'Don't. Come. Out. No matter what.' Then he shoved me toward the room. I ran and hid. But I left the door open.

"Someone banged on the front door. Nuna opened it. Argued with a man. I had to see, had to peek. I saw the moment the man—the Alaska State Trooper in a brown uniform—plunged the knife into Nuna. I screamed." Danna was crying now as she spoke. "I knew I had made a big mistake, and I opened the bedroom window and jumped out. He almost got me. Almost grabbed my hands."

"Wait," Ivy said. "I was told that you didn't see his face."

"I . . ." Danna hung her head. "My grandmother told me to say this. Not seeing his face would mean I didn't know who killed my uncle."

"But even seeing his face, do you know who killed him?"

"I never saw him before, no."

Was she telling the truth? Did she know who killed Nuna? At least she'd seen the murderer. But if this person was from an outside group, an outside agency that was after the information or sent to silence Nuna, he doubted they had mug shots to show her.

"I ran and just kept running," Danna continued. "I hadn't even gotten out of my coat yet."

Ivy hit the stop button and held Nolan's gaze. "Now we have the story," she said.

He couldn't hide his deep anguish, and he saw that same anguish reflected in Ivy's face.

"And we still don't know who's behind this." And responsible for Autumn nearly losing her life.

"I looked into a few things," Ivy said. "Nuna and Gene attended the University of Michigan at the same time, both studying chemistry. I'm guessing that he worked with Nuna but betrayed him."

"No." Danna stepped out from the hall, her dark hair in tangles. Her eyes red. "The man he worked with came to warn him someone was coming. Someone would try to kill him."

Ivy shared a look with Nolan. "When did this happen?" She'd left that out of her story.

"He told me. That's why he was acting strange. He was afraid. He found the note from . . . GW. I didn't remember that part until I heard you."

"Nolan, if that's true, then Gene didn't kill Nuna. He warned him." Ivy held his gaze. "Cindy, who was on the *Nautilus* research crew with him, said he was scared and on edge. Maybe during that time that he'd left the group, that's when he left the note for Nuna. He'd gone to find him to warn him. Maybe that's why he was even on the boat, so he wouldn't draw attention on a research trip, and he'd gone to warn Nuna. He was terrified."

"He thought someone was out there and was going to try to kill him," Nolan said. "Maybe he thought you were part of that plot, Ivy, and that's why he attacked you and ran."

"We need to find him and talk to him," she said. "If he's still alive, he has the answers."

"If he's in hiding, he'd better be hiding good or he's not going to survive," Nolan said.

Nolan glanced at a text on his inReach messaging device. "From Grier."

His heart jumped to his throat. Had something happened to Autumn? He read the text.

Walker's body was found . . . in his house.

Nolan stumbled back. He wanted to ask more questions, but that was likely all Grier knew. He responded and thanked Grier.

Grier texted again.

Autumn says to watch your back out there.

Hank had been quiet through it all, until now. He stepped into the fray. "Enough. We can figure this out later. Where do we go to hide and stay safe?" Hank's voice boomed through the cabin.

"I'll take you at first light," Carrie said. "Fly you all out of the state. I know a place."

"It can't be anyone you know or are connected with," Ivy said. "No family. No friends. No connections whatsoever."

Nolan was surprised they hadn't already been discovered here in the remote cabin. Then again, Alaska was good for hiding people, except when someone was getting too close.

"It's not," Trevor said. "Just a place my sister once mentioned to me. A storm-watching inn. Remote and secluded. Not easy to get to. I'll go and help Hank keep them safe." He nodded to Nolan. "You finish this."

"You know I will." Nolan and Trevor gripped arms.

"Our other pilot, David, is going to manage the clients for a few days," Carrie said. "Get some sleep. We're heading out first light, which in the winter is actually later than I'd like."

Ivy sat back on the sofa and leaned her head back. Closed her eyes.

Nolan eased next to her. "What do you think?"

"I think we need someone in a federal agency that we can trust with what we know. We are in over our heads, Nolan." She opened her eyes to peer at him. Her gaze roamed his face, lingered on his lips, then traced up to his eyes. "Even if we learn everything, discover who killed Nuna, we need the power and authority to take them down."

"I hear you. This is my home. Hank, Danna, and Alina's home. Let me face off with whoever—"

"You tried that at Hank's cabin."

And look what happened.

She didn't say the words. She didn't need to. He still couldn't believe his sister had been shot. He should have acted faster. Pulled the trigger. She'd almost lost her life.

He couldn't let Ivy get hurt. "This time, you really are going back to Florida. I need you to be safe." *And I'll come for you after this is over.* He searched her eyes—would she welcome him if he did?

"No. You and I are going to get the manuscript. Danna told me where it is."

"What? I didn't hear—"

"I didn't record that part. You need me to get you there and we're getting it, and not so I can take it back to my mother. So we can destroy it and make sure that no one finds it."

"Or give it to someone we can trust to handle the rest. Make sure the site is secure if there really are pathogens under the ice."

"But who, Nolan?"

"I don't know." And that terrified him.

THIRTY-SEVEN

Behind her closed lids, hushed voices drew her from a deep sleep. Ivy sensed sudden movement. Shuffling. She'd slept in an uncomfortable position, and she stretched the crick from her neck. She had a vague memory of sleeping against Nolan's chest. His arm around her, keeping her warm.

Was it real or a dream? Not that it mattered at this moment.

Nolan approached and crouched to whisper. "Carrie is taking them out tonight. Grier texted that someone claiming to be with Homeland Security had come to the hospital asking questions."

"And he didn't trust him?"

"He knows enough that something set him off. Said we need to all scramble."

Cold rushed into the cabin. Trevor shut the door quickly. "Let's go. Carrie's at the plane and we're ready."

Hank ushered Lina and Danna forward. Danna glanced over her shoulder and held Ivy's gaze, her eyes full of trust and appreciation.

Ivy nodded. "Stay safe." *I'll make sure your story is only told to the right people.*

She had no idea how to find the right people. Everyone had secrets, it seemed. Even her father, the best man she'd ever known, had a devastating secret. So finding more than just one person to protect this information from those wanting to use it for harm would be a long, hard search after which she feared she would come up empty-handed.

Nolan stood over her, holding his hand out. "Time for us to go too."

"Go where? Trevor brought us here in a boat. How are we going to leave and where do we go?"

"We'll take the *Long Gone* and we'll get lost."

"On our way to find the manuscript?" she asked. "I can't believe that I'm saying this. It seemed so unimportant compared to everything else."

"Now we know differently."

"I don't get it. Why didn't Nuna just destroy it? Burn it?" she asked.

Nolan grabbed his coat and started getting ready to go out into the cold night. "I assume out of respect for his ancestors, elders who held on to it rather than destroying it. The document tells the story of their deaths and serves as a warning."

"Okay," she said. "On the way there, we can figure out what to do next. But I'm not entirely sure I like the idea of holding this manuscript in my hands, finally, even though it's why I came to Alaska."

Ivy pulled on her coat, hat, and gloves, and Nolan led her out of the cabin into utter darkness. Again. He donned his night vision, as did she. Still concerned about drawing attention. If there was attention anywhere near to draw, Carrie would have drawn it when she started up her plane.

At their cloak-and-dagger moves, adrenaline spiked through her, reminding her of the job she'd given up due to unfortunate events. She might actually miss being an agent at some point, but . . . not yet. She started for the hangar and the water.

Nolan whispered. "Where are you going?"

"The boat."

"We're driving." He waved her forward and she caught up with him.

He climbed into a truck and started it up. "Trevor's. He gave me the fob."

"All stealth to get here and now you're just going to drive to your house?"

"No. I'm heading to the marina. The *Long Gone* is in town. And we're still getting you to Florida, in case anyone asks. We're heading to Juneau to catch a flight. I'll let Grier know our plans. I need to update him on everything."

"But we're really going to . . ." She trailed off to let him finish, hoping they remained on the same page.

"To Glacier Bay."

"To the Barrett Glacier, specifically," she said.

Nolan steered through the quiet town of Shadow Gap. She noticed lights on at the Lively Moose, where it had all started for her—this trip, at least. Nolan grabbed her hand and squeezed, and she turned and smiled at him. She had a feeling he wanted to say something, but he never said a word. She kept quiet, too, on the outside. On the inside, her mind whirled a thousand miles an hour with too many thoughts fighting for her attention.

Nolan parked at the marina, and they got out of Trevor's truck. Nolan left the fob under the wheel well.

"Really?" she whispered.

"He's not worried about someone taking it," he said.

Then he led her back to the *Long Gone.*

Ivy slowed her pace, hesitating until she stopped walking.

Nolan turned around. "What is it?"

She stared at the boat, memories of nausea racing through her mind.

"That's right. You had a rough ride last time. The waters are pretty smooth right now. Are you good to do this?"

Smooth waters weren't much consolation considering they could change at any moment, but she wasn't staying behind, so she nodded. She could do this. She had to do it. She'd already gotten a shiner and a knot on the head. What was one more harrowing boat ride? Ivy started forward and Nolan led them to the boat. Ivy waited while Nolan prepared the *Long Gone* to cast off. While the engine warmed up, he led her down into the galley and turned on the lights and heat.

"You might as well get some shut-eye while you can." Then he started to head above deck, but he turned and moved back to her. "It's not too late to go home, Ivy. Go see your mother. I'd prefer you weren't here at all." He frowned. "That didn't come out right." Tenderness surged in his eyes, then concern and . . . fear. He half smiled, then added, "It's not that I don't want you here. I just don't want you to be in danger. To get hurt."

Oh, Nolan. He probably still carried the burden of Autumn's gunshot wound on his shoulders, blaming himself. He was a protector, after all, and to fail to protect could strip a man's confidence. He might even question his ability to protect Ivy, but he was still here, sticking with her and seeing this through, even when he was no longer officially on the investigation. She assumed he could even potentially be reprimanded or fired, but he hadn't said anything about it. Though she hadn't known him long, Ivy *knew* him. Trusted him. He was the one she wanted in this with her.

She lifted her palm and pressed it against his rough cheek, surprising both him and herself. His pupils dilated slightly and heat rushed through her, but she couldn't pull her hand away. Right here. Right now. She savored the connection, both emotionally and, this time, physically. Ivy's pulse raced as her feelings for this man surged through her. She desperately wanted to kiss him.

"We're good together, Nolan," she said. "I wouldn't leave you to do this alone. I would worry about you. And . . . I trust you to protect me. How about we protect each other?" She smiled.

The intensity in his eyes exploded with longing, and her breath hitched. Nolan dipped his head, leaning closer until his lips reached hers. His mouth took hers, and without thinking, only acting, she slipped her hands around his neck. He pulled her in close and deepened the kiss, stirring her heart and her insides. Her soul danced with his as pleasant sensations swirled through her mind and body until she could hardly stand on her own.

Leaving her breathless, he eased from the kiss but held her close. "I've wanted to do that for so long. I—"

She pressed her hand over his mouth. "Shh. Don't apologize." Though they would both regret it when this was over. "None of us knows what tomorrow brings. Or even the next hour."

He kissed her again as if she'd given him permission, and maybe she had.

His burner cell buzzed and buzzed and buzzed. She freed herself and pressed the back of her hand against her raw lips. "Maybe you should get that." Now wasn't the time, but she sensed that Nolan had been fighting, resisting, following through with their mutual attraction since she had arrived.

She felt the same.

But it was for nothing.

He snatched his cell and answered, heading above deck.

This time, she followed. The clouds weren't so thick and heavy that she couldn't see the sunrise. The sky had turned a brilliant gold to the east, reflecting against the cirrus clouds. She didn't want to see another snowflake, much less a blizzard, and please, no icy cold rain. After casting off the lines, Nolan steered from the marina.

"That was Grier," he said. "He's learned a few things."

"I'm listening."

"The man who shot Autumn is part of a black-ops group."

"Makes sense. Paramilitary paid to carry out a covert operation, but by whom? A private party? Or a government? What do we know?"

"Nothing yet. Black ops are hard to pin down, which is the point."

"What was their goal?"

"Grier is very analytical, but with Autumn recovering, I'm not sure he can think clearly at the moment. On the other hand, he is more determined than ever to find who is behind this."

"Like you are, since this is your sister."

"Right. He thinks there's more than one entity at work here." He leveled his gaze. "He learned something else that will interest you. A dash cam caught an image of the man who held a knife to you and warned you away from searching."

"Let me guess. He's an activist of some kind."

"His name is Timothy Treadwell."

Ivy stilled at that news. "Wait. *Treadwell?* Is that a coincidence?" Did she believe in such a thing?

"I told Grier about Donovan, and he confirmed this is Donovan's son."

The son of the man who had blackmailed her to come to Alaska for the manuscript? "Why would his son follow me and threaten me like that with a *knife?*"

"Obviously, he doesn't want you to find the manuscript and give it to his father."

"Donovan wants the manuscript because someone is paying *him* to get it," she said.

Someone with a lot of power. Someone who would stop at nothing.

THIRTY-EIGHT

Nolan didn't want to bring another person into this, but glacier ice cave hiking wasn't something he knew anything about. He wouldn't willingly walk into this unprepared, especially with Ivy.

So Annie had recommended a local guide, Jay Sulllivan, who provided the additional gear they needed—helmets, crampons, and ice axes.

Ice axes?

And he led them now, guiding them toward the Barrett Glacier and the ice cave. But the tour guide was a talker. Someone accustomed to tourists, and during the winter months, he didn't get to chat it up like usual.

Nolan wasn't in the mood for conversation, but he could listen.

"Personally, I'd only go hiking in the winter anyway," Jay said. "People are all over the glaciers and the caves in the warmer months and the summer when they're unstable and the ice is more likely to collapse or present other dangers, and visiting an ice cave in summer is not recommended."

As they carefully entered the open cavity in the glacier, Jay continued talking and shifted to what must be his spiel when he took tourists.

"When you think about it, a glacier is just a big river of ice. It moves slowly, shifting and changing, and sometimes creating what we call ice caves." He continued with how the caves were formed.

But Nolan only half listened as he remained aware of his surroundings, not just the dangers presented by a moving river of ice that was white, sure, but also black and brown and, frankly, looked dirty because of all the debris it picked up on the journey. The ice inside the cave, however, presented as various shades of blue, including vast swathes of brilliant turquoise or cerulean blue. If he was on a different kind of exploration, he'd take a picture of Ivy in her turquoise parka next to the similarly colored ice.

Jay's voice droned on, animated at times, but he clearly loved his job. "The reason the ice is blue is because it's only the short wavelengths, which are blue, that aren't absorbed by the ice and make it through."

Nolan moved ahead of Jay, eager to make it to that fork in the cave Ivy had mentioned. He heard Ivy's small gasp at the beauty before them, and he couldn't help but remember the sound she'd made when he'd kissed her. Like an idiot, like the fool he was, he'd kissed her in the middle of this terror. In the middle of this race against time to save lives, he'd taken the woman he couldn't stop thinking about in his arms like he'd wanted to do if he ever made it to Florida. Like he'd wanted to do in his far-fetched dreams.

Maybe this hadn't happened overnight. This feeling he had for her had been simmering for months now, and here they were in the proverbial crucible. Who was he to resist?

But, Lord, I don't want her in this with me. I want her safe and sound in Florida.

Except there wasn't anything safe in Florida. One of the bad guys involved in this torment was back in Florida and had coerced her under duress to Alaska. The thing was, once they found the manuscript, if they found it in this weird choice of a hiding place—a glacial ice cave, thanks to a deceased scientist— what were they going to do with it?

Ivy had caught up with him, leaving Jay behind a few yards to look at his cell.

Nolan leaned in and whispered. "Why not let it die here, buried in the ice, and keep its secrets?"

"We have to do this, Nolan. Someone is going to find it. It needs to be us. We put it somewhere safe. Put it to rest somewhere, locked in a vault."

"Or we could burn it," he said.

"Yeah, we could."

"What's that you want to burn?" Jay asked.

"Nothing," they said simultaneously.

She glanced at him and then away, but he saw a spark of affection flash in her eyes.

"Danna said she paid attention. Kind of wrote it out in her head like a writer would. Once we take the right fork, then we'd find a patch of stones, rocks on a thin layer of ice where the ground was dug up."

"Hey, Jay," Ivy called over her shoulder. "Up ahead, I see the fork. We want to go right. There should be a patch of rocks."

"I know just the place. Let's go." He hiked forward, passing them, and Nolan followed, making sure that Ivy was okay too. Not that she needed him, but he *wanted* her to need him, at least a little. He watched his step, too, as his crampons sank into the ice.

Ivy standing there with the cold cerulean blue behind her would remain captured in his mind forever.

"Here you are, folks," Jay said. "You've been an easy group."

"Um . . . can you give us some privacy?" Ivy leaned into Nolan.

Jay's brows arched. He cleared his throat. "Well, okay. I suppose so. I'll just be around that corner." He hiked away and talked to himself.

Nolan chuckled, then continued smiling, thinking of that kiss back on the *Long Gone*. He knew she'd only led Jay to believe they would share a private moment, a kiss or a hug, but they had a mission.

She stepped around a pile of rocks, scrutinizing it. "This should be it. Let's find it, Nolan."

"Yeah, let's do." And then what? He really didn't know.

Lord, I'm making this up as I go.

He didn't know if they were doing the right thing. After all, Nuna lost his life protecting a secret they were about to dig up. But then Nuna needed justice for what happened to him. Autumn needed justice, and Danna shouldn't have to look over her shoulder forever. And Ivy should be free to live her life without fear or danger—with or without Jack London's novel detailing a pestilence in the ice.

THIRTY-NINE

I vy hadn't expected her heartbeat to race as she dropped her pack to retrieve the small trowel. But she should have.

Boy, if Mom could see her now. If *Dad* could see her now, though he was gone. Dad probably never had to dig in a glacier ice cave for a rare book, for sheets of loose pages handwritten by a famous author long dead. And she wished she could celebrate this moment, the culmination of her family's long search for something worth so much more than the money the pages would bring at an auction house. Had Dad known the history behind the story?

And Grace . . . what would she think if she had survived to witness and experience what her family had gone through to secure this old document for her because she loved the author's work so much?

Thoughts of this manuscript, the search for it, really, had taken up a good portion of Ivy's life. Her sister, Grace, had longed to secure it to present it to the world in a museum, preferably her museum at the shop. Dad had encouraged her, coming up with the idea to begin with. They'd worked on the project together since Grace had been his protégé. Ivy almost smiled to herself. She'd let herself do this for Grace . . . once she held it in her hands.

But the cost, the price of finding the manuscript, had been much too high.

The ground had been disturbed here, confirming the spot Danna claimed they had buried the manuscript rather than destroying it. Ivy wasn't sure she understood completely, but at the same time, she was glad for the chance to finally get her hands on it.

Nolan gently removed the largest stones. Setting the trowel aside, she helped him move rocks out of the way until she reached dirt.

"Who would have thought a girl from Florida would find herself at the bottom of an ice cave in a glacier?" Nolan whispered.

"Are you reading my mind?"

"Maybe. But we need to hurry."

She picked up the trowel and started to dig, finding the ground not hard or frozen like she would expect with permafrost. Nuna and Danna had already pierced the frozen layer to bury the manuscript, so Ivy was able to reach the softer ground quickly. With her gloved hands, she began gently removing dirt. An old manuscript would be destroyed here, but Danna assured her they had buried it in a protective bag. Ivy thought back to Danna's words.

"Nuna said, 'The ice will eventually bury it forever. I don't have the heart to destroy the history, the story behind it.'"

"Wait," Nolan said. "See . . ."

"Yeah, I see." Something stuck out. She gently removed all the dirt around the object, then hefted out a thick, clear plastic bag. And inside, she saw the pages.

Words scribbled in Jack London's handwriting. She held her breath at the sight as her throat thickened with both painful and joyful emotions. Tears brimmed in her eyes. Dad had wanted to find this. Grace had wanted to see it.

She understood now why Nuna hadn't had the heart to destroy the work of a great and celebrated author—not completely—but instead had returned it to a glacier. Not *the* glacier that contained the toxic pathogen, but there was symmetry in this. Ivy stood, pressed the novel against her chest, and closed her eyes. In their search for this document, they'd never imagined the deadly secrets it held.

"Come on, now," Nolan said. "Stick it in your pack."

She only now noticed he'd shoved the dirt back into place and was replacing the pebbles and rocks.

Jay was no longer talking to himself, which probably meant he was returning to find them. Nolan was hefting the last rock when Ivy heard footfalls rounding the corner. She turned her back to continue tucking the manuscript in her bag. Nolan stood and turned.

Next to her, he stiffened.

"I thought you were dead."

FORTY

"Clearly, you thought wrong."

"Walker's body was found . . . in his house."

Grier's words came rushing back, their meaning clear.

They found Walker's body, not Carl's.

Nolan was stunned to see the man he thought was his friend, Wildlife Trooper Carl Westfield, aiming a handgun at him.

"Remove your guns and set them on the ground. Kick them over."

Ivy and Nolan complied.

"All of them, Nolan. I know about the small extra."

Nolan removed the smaller handgun at his ankle, set it on the ground, and kicked it over too, but Carl didn't pick any of the weapons up.

"You faked your death, Carl." Nolan took a step forward.

"You're stating the obvious and wasting my time."

"What's your role here?" Nolan asked, inching forward just a little.

Carl stiffened and shifted his aim to Ivy. "Not another step."

"Then tell me what you want, Carl." Was that even his real name?

Carl half smiled, half smirked. "I'm here to secure the manuscript. I know you have it. Give it to me."

"What did you do with Jay?" Ivy tried to press past Nolan,

but he thrust his arm out, hoping to keep her behind him to protect her.

"Ivy, don't." Carl would shoot her without another thought. He might have orchestrated Walker's death or taken advantage of the situation.

"He'll be fine."

Nolan was surprised that Carl hadn't killed Jay, but he wouldn't point that out. Still . . . "Did you kill Nuna?"

"The less you know the better."

"I thought we were friends." Nolan hoped so and would play that card as long as he could.

Carl gave an incredulous huff. "You're doing your job. I'm doing mine. Now hand it over. I don't want to hurt you."

The guy wouldn't get away with this. "Who wants it?" Nolan asked. "Who was behind the men who shot my sister?"

"You shouldn't even be here, Nolan. I gave you a trail to follow. Then your department was told to stand down. You were sent away."

"The girl in the folder. The trafficking scheme." Nolan studied Carl, trying to read him.

"Yeah. Victus is guilty. Walker too, but he's gone. They were working with a trafficker named Novak. Victus never called in a woman's screams. I did, to put you onto Victus. You should be on his trail, not in a glacial cave. So . . . I'm telling you now to just walk away. You and your girlfriend, get out of here."

Nolan couldn't do that. He was pressing for as many answers as he could get. Anger burned through his gut now. "Who was behind the ambush at the cabin? Who hired that black-ops team? Was it you?"

Nolan envisioned getting his hands on Carl's throat and squeezing. He wanted justice. Or maybe it was vengeance for his sister. "She almost died." Fisting his gloved hands, Nolan wanted to reach for his gun.

"Don't even think about it," Carl said. "I have the drop on

you. I can put you and the woman down before you reach your gun. Just give me the manuscript now, and I'll disappear, and this will be over."

"Who are you going to give it to?" Ivy asked, her voice shaking. "Why don't we just destroy it here and now, so no one can use whatever information is hidden here to harm others?"

"We already know what we need to know," Carl said. "I can't let the manuscript inform anyone else. I followed you to make sure that it didn't still exist."

"We? Who is *we*? Who are you working for?"

"Remember, the less you know, the better." Carl flattened his lips. He was getting impatient.

"Then let's destroy it," Ivy said again.

"My orders are to take it from you and bring it in."

"And you trust your superiors with this?" Because Nolan certainly didn't trust anyone at this point. Carl had killed Nuna, of that he had no doubt. Carl had been trying to transfer to Otto's region and was about to do just that so he could be close to Nuna, be in position. He was working undercover, but for whom, Nolan couldn't be sure.

"Doesn't matter."

Nolan had to keep the man talking. Keep him distracted and get Ivy out of here. Jay slowly approached from behind. Carl must have used a technique to render him unconscious, or tied him up, but either way, Carl had underestimated Jay. He misstepped, alerting Carl to his presence. Carl turned to shoot and Jay dove behind a chunk of ice as Nolan rushed Carl.

Another man stepped into view. What? One of the mercenaries that had come to the cabin? The man looked at Ivy, who held the manuscript, and started toward her.

"Run, Ivy. Get out of here!" Nolan shouted as he tangled with a man who'd served with him in the troopers but had really been an undercover plant this whole time.

He grappled now, with the gun, with Carl, who tried to aim

it at Nolan. Gritting his teeth, his muscles straining, Nolan pushed the muzzle away from his face. Ivy had taken off, and he was glad. But where was Jay? Had he been shot, after all?

Nolan wrestled with Carl across the cold, frozen ground, rocks and sharp edges of ice digging into his back through his thick coat. He tried to reach for one of the guns he'd set on the ice earlier, while at the same time preventing Carl from shooting him. Carl maneuvered his gun back around between them. It could go off any minute. At point-blank, it could do some catastrophic damage. Nolan worked to keep Carl's hands, his fingers, from reaching the trigger.

"You should have handed it over." Carl grunted and gasped the words out. "I don't want to kill you."

"Then leave," Nolan said. "Tell them you destroyed it."

"You know I can't do that."

The gun went off. Nolan stilled, the breath frozen in his chest. Carl slumped against him. *No . . . no, no, no.*

Heart pounding, he pushed the man off him. If only it could have ended another way. Jay crawled forward. "Sorry I couldn't help you more, man."

"You okay?" Nolan asked. "Are you hurt?"

"In my leg, but it's not bad," Jay said. "I sent out an emergency call for help. You had to do it, Trooper. He was going to kill you."

Nolan removed his glove and pressed a finger against Carl's carotid. His pulse was thready.

A scream echoed, bouncing off the ice walls.

Ivy!

FORTY-ONE

She wasn't a screamer. But he pushed her from behind and she slid down an ice slide . . . that had brought the terror to the surface. He was the black-ops man she'd shot when he'd abducted her on the snow machine. He was back for her. Alive and well. She wished she'd killed him before. Now she didn't even have a gun, thanks to Carl.

Ivy headbutted the man in the face. His nose burst with blood, and she tried to run with her crampons across the glacier ice, away from the cave opening, leaving Nolan to his own fate. She prayed he and Jay would overcome Carl and that somehow, someway, they would make it out of this situation alive.

But no matter what, at all costs, she had to get the manuscript somewhere safe or destroy it. She'd wanted to stick with Nolan and Jay, but she'd acted on instinct when Nolan shouted for her to run, and Jerk Face had singled her out—for the manuscript. Too many people had already died because of it, and she wouldn't be the reason more died when the wrong people found it.

Like Mom had said, the heart was deceitful and the nature of humans was inherently evil. That was playing a role in all this right now.

Since leaving the FBI, she hadn't done enough to keep up her physical strength and practice her skills, so it was better to run than to face off with this big guy. This wasn't the movies, where a woman took out all the bad guys by hitting them with high heels or a well-placed kick or by wrapping her body around their necks to take them down. This was real, and she had to be smart. If she had to fight him, she'd fight dirty—she knew how to do it.

It was better to escape with the sought-after manuscript than risk losing it. But he was gaining on her, and then, of course, her crampon lodged between a rock and chunk of ice.

And would not move.

Are you kidding me?

She tugged on it, and shifted every which way, but no matter how much she kicked and shoved and twisted and moved, she wasn't getting out of it. She slipped her foot out of the boot, and raced away, her socked foot quickly growing cold on the ice. Breathing hard, she risked a glance over her shoulder.

Jerk Face was closing in on her. Fury poured from his gaze. After all, she'd shot him—though it didn't seem to have held him back much—and she'd broken his nose. Too bad she hadn't blinded him in that strike. She wasn't going to move fast enough to keep him away. She was going to have to turn and fight or cross the lake. Ivy had never walked on a frozen lake, but it looked like only a portion of the lake was ice-covered. She could see water out in the middle.

She wouldn't be fleeing across the lake, then, after all. *Okay. I can do this.* She turned and faced the enemy.

He smiled. "I'm going to enjoy this," he said.

"Oh yeah? What movie is that from? Get new material."

He removed his gloves and pounded a fist into his palm.

She tore off her gloves, too, and retrieved a knife from a sheath at her back. Carl hadn't asked for knives, only guns. Sure, she knew self-defense moves, but she could use the knife in all those moves. He punched a fist at her and she parried, praying under her breath, hoping Mom was praying for her now, as she dodged his beefy fists. At least the one crampon kept her from slipping too much.

She knew that he was playing with her. All he had to do was shoot her and take the manuscript. But she was grateful he liked games. Maybe killing her, shooting her, would take all the fun out of it for him. In the meantime, she'd play along with him and try to get as much information out of him as she could.

"Who hired you? Who are you working for? You should be helping your friend Carl back there. He's probably already dead."

"He's not my friend. I don't know who he is."

"Come on. Didn't you ride out here together?"

"No."

That news surprised her. Was this guy representing the group that Carl was trying to prevent from getting the manuscript? She and Nolan had made a big mistake since they'd simply led all parties—bad guys and worse guys—to the manuscript that Nuna had buried but not deep enough.

Danna never should have shared the location with me.

Adrenaline kept Ivy just out of reach of Jerk Face and his fists. He was sweating now, as was she, but once they stopped, they were going to get cold. He pulled out a knife, changing up the game. She would have to work harder now to stay out of reach of his knife, and she was getting tired. Still, she was faster on her feet—one sock and one boot—than he was, and continued to employ a mixture of defense moves. All those years she'd never had to use those techniques, but here in Alaska, she had to fight to live.

Or she would die.

"How many miles do you jog a day?" Breathing in the arctic air was hurting her lungs. She couldn't catch her breath. She gasped for air.

Just keep him talking and engaged. Buy some time to figure out how to outmaneuver him and escape.

He started grinning again like he had the advantage. He was only trying to intimidate her.

Nolan appeared over the rise, followed by Jay. Jerk Face whipped around with his gun and fired, but Nolan was quicker, shooting him.

He dropped to the ground.

Relief flooded her. Part of her wanted to take the guy out on her own, but backup was always welcome.

She took a step and a loud crack resounded, sending a shudder through her core. She glanced down and realized she was out on the ice.

That's why he'd been smiling. The whole time he'd been pushing her away from the shore and onto the ice. She glanced up at Nolan, holding his gaze, seeing his desperation, a millisecond before she dropped into the frigid water.

FORTY-TWO

Noooo!"

This can't be happening! God, no, don't let this happen. Please help me save Ivy.

Not again. Nolan couldn't lose someone again. He couldn't lose Ivy to this frozen world.

"You can't walk out there. You'll go in the drink too. You won't last," Jay called after him.

"You got ropes in your pack. Get them. Secure them. Throw them to me. I'm going in after her." He dropped flat and crawled out to find her. To see her.

She bobbed up once and spurted out water, but she quickly sank, the water pushing her under the ice.

She was directly beneath him, looking up at him. Her big brown eyes shouting her terror, filleting Nolan.

"No. Hold your breath." He moved to the hole . . .

"Wait. Nolan!" Jay tossed him the rope and he gripped it, tied it around himself, then taking a deep breath, he slipped into the forbidding, deadly cold.

He couldn't see Ivy in the darkness, but he continued to swim beneath the ice in the direction he'd seen her. Then the rope stopped.

No. No . . . I need more. He started to untie himself, but his hands were already numb as he fumbled with the knot.

Pounding caught his attention and he glanced. He could see Jay's silhouette. There. He was pointing.

Ivy was floating against the ice. Nolan had enough rope and swam toward her, grabbed her body, and then swam back. Or was Jay tugging on the rope?

Nolan surfaced. Jay was lying flat and pulled them forward.

Nolan's muscles burned with the last ounce of his strength, and he pulled Ivy up and onto a section of ice. Jay backed to the shore and pulled Nolan forward. He dragged Ivy along with him until the ice was thick enough that he could stand. Then he carried her to the shore, where he stumbled forward and fell to his knees with her still in his arms. He laid her on the ground and started chest compressions and CPR.

"Hypothermia . . ."

Before he could snap at Jay, the man tossed a blanket.

Nolan put that over her, frustrated with her lack of response. "Ivy, no. Please . . . you can't die on me."

"The blanket's for you. She's gone."

Nolan continued compressions and mouth-to-mouth against Ivy's frigid body. He would not lose her.

Not to the ice.

Not to geography.

Not to the next life.

She's not gone!

FORTY-THREE

ift your eyes . . .

White light lit up the darkness, the arctic cold.

Help me . . . I'm so cold.

Cold.

Lift up your eyes . . . to the mountains.

The mountains. Alaska.

Awareness, consciousness, returned but her lids felt heavy, as if they were sealed shut. *Why can't I wake up?*

"Ivy? Ivy . . . please . . ."

Ivy reached deep inside, searching for what felt like every ounce of strength she had to simply open her eyes. Her lids fluttered and Nolan's face filled her vision.

Deep frown lines carved into his face, then suddenly relaxed. "Ivy! Thank you, God! Ivy, we're going to move you now to someplace warm."

He lifted her in his arms, and she appreciated the warmth she felt resting against his chest, not the hardness of his usual vest. And this position next to him, hearing his breathing as he rushed her somewhere safe, filled her with a sense of peace. And comfort. Exhaustion, drowsiness, pulled Ivy down.

She woke up in a room with Nolan sitting next to her. "Nolan. What happened?" Memories rushed at her. "The ice. I fell through—"

"Yes." Pain filled his gaze.

Ivy started to sit up.

"No, don't," he said. "You should remain horizontal."

Then she realized she was wearing a warm robe and was inside a sleeping bag. Her cheeks burned. "Who?"

"Jay's sister and daughter were here to get you out of the cold, wet clothes. They had to cut them off, I'm sorry. We had to handle you gently so we didn't cause ventricular fibrillation."

Ivy tried to comprehend how cold she must have gotten, but her brain was still fuzzy.

"Where am I?"

"Jay's place. We revived you but you were still so cold, and you fell asleep again. Had to get you somewhere warm. The medical helicopter is on the way."

"Well, call them and tell them to turn around. I'm going to be fine."

"You need medical attention, Ivy." He pressed his forehead against hers, then sat back. "I'd give you something warm to drink but I'm not sure your core temperature has improved enough."

"But I thought—"

"It depends."

Jay appeared in the doorway, his eyes widening. "You're awake. We were worried about you."

"Thanks for saving me." Ivy looked at Jay.

"Thank him." Jay gestured at Nolan. "He jumped in after you."

That memory suddenly hit her—looking up at him through the ice. "Nolan, you didn't."

"He did."

"You need medical attention too, then," she said.

"I wasn't in as long as you. I didn't . . ."

Drown. He was going to say drown.

"I can hear the chopper," Jay said. "You ready?"

"No. I'm not ready," she said.

"I'll go out and meet them and bring them back." Jay disappeared, and she heard a door open and close.

"Nolan, you're coming too, right?" she asked. "Ride with me. Let them make sure you're okay."

"I'll keep you close as long as I can, but I have to stay."

Ivy couldn't think straight. Why were her thoughts so sluggish? "What happened? Where's Carl? Was he arrested?"

"He's being transported in the same helicopter with you. He was shot. There's a matter of the other guy I shot. Troopers will be arriving soon."

"The other guy . . . he claimed he wasn't working with Carl." At least she remembered that part. Her thoughts would clear up completely at some point and she might remember much more.

"We're still sorting everything out."

"So, Danna is still in danger?"

Jay rushed in, leading a couple of paramedics. "Let's go. The helicopter landed."

She held Nolan's gaze as they gently transferred her onto a gurney, then walked it out. The gurney barely fit through the doors. Nolan walked with her through the house, then out of the house.

Into the night. It was already dark out. Nolan stopped as they loaded her into the helicopter. "This is stupid. I feel fine."

"When your body temperature is back up, then you'll be fine." Nolan leaned in and kissed her on the lips and then the forehead. "I'll catch up to you."

Greens and purples flashed across the sky. "Nolan, look."

"I'm looking."

"No, at the aurora borealis. I've always wanted to see it. Watch it with me." This hadn't been the scenario she'd imagined, but she would take what she could get.

"We need to get going." The paramedic rolled her completely into the helicopter and started an IV.

Nolan remained at the door. She turned her head sideways

to look at him. A paramedic tried to put an oxygen mask on her, but she pushed it away.

"Wait. Where's the manuscript? I had it in my pack."

"I have it. Don't worry, Ivy. I'll keep it safe until we figure out who we can trust with it." Nolan moved back out of the way and the rotors started up. The door closed, blocking her view.

The chopper lifted.

"I'm putting the mask on you now, all right?"

"Okay."

The mask secured, she glanced at her other side and spotted another gurney. Carl. He wasn't conscious, and a paramedic was checking his vitals. It looked like he'd been stabilized for the moment.

Adrenaline rushed out of her. Tears leaked out the corners of her eyes.

They had a few answers but more questions, and that should have taken up her thoughts, but with nearly dying . . . all she could think about was Nolan. And Mom.

Once she was released from the hospital, she would head home with or without the manuscript. Donovan's son had warned her away from finding it. Donovan could know all about what was under the ice and the potential threat. Either he was hired to secure it or he was more intricately involved.

Then it hit her. Why had she so easily taken his word for it that her father had a years-long affair with Donovan's wife? No. She wouldn't believe it. Why hadn't she demanded proof from Donovan? He pretended to be her father's friend. Why would anyone pretend that if what he said were true? With her mother in a delicate way, she hadn't wanted to risk any kind of disturbance.

Maybe she shouldn't have fallen victim to his scheme. Ivy closed her eyes and let exhaustion take her. What felt like a few moments later, the helicopter landed at the hospital in Anchorage. The paramedics quickly carted her into the hospital and headed for the emergency department where they continued assessing and treating. She had no idea the potential threat to her lungs, and honestly, they did hurt. As she was warming up, she could think more clearly, and feel the pain.

She didn't want to die.

Lift up your eyes . . .

God had been with her even in the cold, dark water when she'd drowned. She'd felt his presence. He'd been with her through it all, and he was with her now whether she lived or died. Maybe that's why her mother seemed to be at peace even through her trials and battles with a deadly illness.

Ivy slept again.

The next morning, she was hoping to be released but instead remained in the hospital connected to tubes, and the doctor continued to check her lungs.

Where was Nolan? Though disappointment settled in her chest, exhaustion weighed on her, and she slept on and off throughout the day and the night.

Someone squeezed her hand, and she heard a familiar voice. "Ivy?"

She opened her eyes. "Mom?" Ivy sat up. "What are you doing here?" She glanced around her. Had she been transported to Florida without knowing it? But she spotted the mountains out the window.

"I lift up my eyes to the mountains." Ivy smiled. Yes, she was still in Alaska, and that made her happy.

Mom's chuckle sounded nervous. "I came to make sure you're all right. I never meant for you to come to harm. I should never have asked you."

Ivy wanted the nurse to come in and pull the tubes out. The doctors to clear her. Maybe something had happened that she hadn't been told yet. "I was coming home as soon as they released me, I promise. So, why did you come all this way? You shouldn't be traveling."

"I wore a mask. Myrtle came with me."

"But how—"

"Now, Ivy, calm down."

"I'm glad to see you, Mom." *But you shouldn't have come.* "Who told you?"

"Your Alaska State Trooper friend, Nolan Long. The hospital wanted to contact family and he informed them. They called me. As soon as I heard, I booked a ticket."

It would have taken her a day, at least, to get here.

A new physician entered and introduced himself. "I'm Dr. Tom and I have good news. I'm discharging you today. I'll set the paperwork in motion. Someone will be in for you to sign the documents and you're free to go. You're a very lucky woman, Miss Elliott."

"Oh, we don't believe in luck," Mom said. "God was watching out for her."

He smiled but said nothing when he left.

Mom squeezed her hand again. "I'll make arrangements for us to get home. Unless, of course, you want to stay."

"Why would I want to stay?" But the question didn't feel right, and a deep sadness clung to her. Still, she couldn't deny that she missed her home and the sunshine. But she would miss Nolan even more, now that she just might have fallen completely in love with him. Their ordeal had sealed that for her, but she didn't know how he felt. She couldn't just drop her life in Florida caring for her mother for the cold of Alaska, even for Nolan.

Her mother sighed. "To be honest, I hoped you'd run into the trooper while you were here. I know how much you liked him, and you were thinking about him a lot."

"Wait. Don't tell me that you were playing matchmaker when you sent me here."

Mom shrugged. "That, and the manuscript would have been nice."

Should I tell her the truth about why I came?

"Mom, about Donovan."

Her mother waved her hand. "He is out of his mind. I knew he was only getting close and hanging around to see if he could abscond with some of your father's treasures. He wanted that manuscript too."

Ivy feared he was still hovering out there somewhere, hoping to get his hands on the manuscript. She needed to know what was happening in the investigation. Why hadn't Nolan contacted her? He said that he'd catch up with her.

"Myrtle and I are going to grab some coffee at the vending machine," Mom said. "Do you need anything?"

"I'm good. Thanks."

Mom left and Ivy wished she had asked to use her cell so she could call Nolan, but she didn't know his number.

She stared at the IV, wanting to pull it out herself. Did she even have clothes to wear out of here? She'd been brought in wearing just a robe, and Nolan had mentioned her clothes had been cut off from her.

She could check the closet to see, and if she had nothing, Mom would need to grab her some clothes from a local store. Mom put on a good, strong show, but she had to be exhausted. She shouldn't have come to Anchorage. While Ivy understood the hospital wanted to call someone and Nolan had only been doing what he believed was right, she wasn't happy with this outcome.

Ivy threw her legs over the side.

"What do you think you're doing, young lady?" A nurse came in and shut the door behind him.

The voice sounded familiar. She took in his face. Behind the mask . . . Donovan? A chill crawled over her. He must have followed her mother. "What are you doing here? Get out of my room right now."

She reached for the nurse call button, but he snatched it away.

"Where is the manuscript?" He loomed over her, looking nothing at all like the family friend he'd pretended to be.

"You're not getting your hands on it," she said. "Who are you working for? Who are you selling to?"

"Do you want your mother to find out the truth about your father?"

"I'll tell her myself," Ivy said. "If it's even true!"

He leaned in. "I haven't harmed anyone, Ivy—yet. Your mother is safe if you tell me right now where it is. I'll get it myself, but I need to know where."

"You won't touch her. You'll have to face me first."

"You're going to be out of it forever if I don't get an answer."

He flashed a syringe, the needle oozing something, and prepared to stick Ivy. To kill her. Heart pounding, shock rolled through her. "You'd actually kill me. The daughter of your longtime best friend."

"That cheated with my wife. So maybe I want my revenge. But you're more useful to me alive." In other words, he would keep blackmailing for other purposes.

"I'm making you the deal of a lifetime." He smiled. "Pun intended."

Dizziness still plagued her after her ordeal. Her limbs remained weak. But for her mother's sake, and for her own, she had to pull this off. In one fell swoop, she slid off the bed, and using the pillow to protect her from the deadly stick, knocked the needle away at the same time she threw her leg into his face in a familiar kickboxing move. He stumbled back, stunned, but recovered faster than she had hoped. She yanked the IV from her arm and hit the call button he'd dropped.

He scrambled to his feet and headed for the door.

"You'll be looking over your shoulder for the rest of your life," he said.

Suddenly Nolan appeared in the doorway, blocking his path. "Oh yeah? Why's that?"

He moved completely into the room, his protective form intimidating. Ivy had this. The guy was running, but she was relieved that Nolan had stopped his escape.

Mom and Myrtle rushed in and gasped. "Ivy? What's going on? Donovan? What are you doing here?"

"Threatening me, that's what," Ivy said. "I only came to Alaska to get the manuscript because he threatened to tell you about Dad's affair with his wife."

"What? Oh, Ivy. I'm so sorry you had to learn about that from him."

"Wait. You knew?"

Before Mom could answer, two men in suits stepped into the room. FBI Special Agents Tanner and Rowley introduced themselves, flashing their badges on their lanyards. "Donovan Treadwell? You're under arrest."

"On what charges?" He stood defiant, even as they brought out the handcuffs.

"Multiple charges, including money laundering schemes and funding of terrorist groups . . ."

The agent continued with a list of charges, but Ivy barely heard the rest when dizziness hit. Nolan assisted her into the chair. Donovan was handcuffed and removed from the room.

"Did you know about this?" she asked Nolan.

"I handed all the information that we learned together over to my sergeant, and then Carl did a lot of talking because I saved his life after I shot him in self-defense," Nolan said. "Law enforcement caught up with Gene Whitlock. We were right. He was running for his life, afraid he would be killed, and he'd come to warn Nuna, but he was too late."

"What did Gene say?"

Nolan leaned close and kissed her on the forehead. "You have guests, and I'm not supposed to talk about it. I'll catch you later."

He moved to leave, but she snatched his hand. "Nolan." *What about us?* But she couldn't make a fool of herself in front of Mom and Myrtle. Why couldn't they get a clue and give Ivy some privacy?

Nolan knelt in front of her. He gently pushed a strand of her hair behind her ear. That's when she realized that she must look like an absolute mess. But he still looked at her like . . . like what? He loved her? She pursed her lips tight, trying to stop the unshed tears, but her quivering chin gave her away. "Right now, you need to focus on taking care of yourself and your mother."

He opened his mouth to say more, but an Alaska State Trooper entered the room and looked at him. What was it with everyone just barging into her private room?

"Can I have a word?" the trooper asked.

Regret surged on Nolan's face as he stood. "I'll see you, Ivy."

And he left.

"I brought you some clothes." Mom opened up a bag on the bed and laid out several items for Ivy to choose from. Her mother didn't seem at all fazed by the news of Donovan's crimes, or his attempt to kill Ivy. But if Mom had known about Dad's affair and hidden that fact all along, she was very good at hiding things.

Ivy was stunned by all of it, but more so with Nolan's actions. He just turned around and walked out of her room, leaving her heartbroken. But she'd known whatever was between them would end this way. Maybe Nolan cared about her and felt about her what she felt for him, but they had both known that at the end of this ordeal, she would return to her world and he would stay in his. That was her reality. Her mother was here to usher her back to Florida.

Where she belonged.

FORTY-FOUR

Nolan learned that Ivy had returned to Florida with her mother yesterday, the day after she'd been released from the hospital. He felt hollowed out at the news. He had no idea what to do about her, but he had plenty to keep him busy until he had time to process everything that had happened, including how he felt about Ivy. For one thing, he needed to focus on his sister. He couldn't have been more relieved that Autumn was at the home she shared with Grier and would make a full recovery. But dark circles remained under her eyes and the guilt slammed him all over again.

"Don't look at me like that, Nolan. I'm alive. We all did our best. We know the risks." She smiled when Grier entered the room.

Grier sat on the edge of the sofa. "All right, boys and girls. I've got the goods."

"What?" Autumn asked. "You brought me donuts?"

"No. Only healthy food for you. Doctor's orders." Grier rose and moved to her side and kissed her. "I love you, honey."

"I love you too, but I could really use a cream-cheese Danish." She made a face. "Okay, give us the story."

He sat back on the sofa and Nolan remained standing. He hadn't liked Grier at first and warned Autumn to stay away from him. He'd been completely wrong about the guy.

Grier cleared his throat. "Donovan Treadwell is involved in

all kinds of illicit dealings, including money laundering for terrorist organizations. Apparently, art, antiques, and rare books are used in these schemes. He was the one to hire the mercenaries after he thought that Ivy would fail to get the manuscript. He was running out of time to produce an item he'd promised." Nolan crossed his arms. "His son, Timothy, disguised himself on the ferry to try to stop you and Ivy from leading the mercenaries to Danna, or finding her yourself and getting your hands on the manuscript. Timothy knew about his father's dealings and tried to warn Donovan that the manuscript should not be handed over to a terrorist group known for biowarfare activities. Timothy is a former special forces guy and works in private security. He wanted to scare Ivy into stopping without telling her about the manuscript."

"And when she didn't stop, he sabotaged my plane and the ferry?"

"He claims no lives were threatened. He was afraid your search would end up putting the manuscript in the wrong hands. He has been charged for his crimes, but my guess is that he'll cut a deal, trading information he has on his father."

Nolan blew out a long breath.

Grier grabbed his laptop off the coffee table. "I have a recording of Gene Whitlock's statement. Who wants to watch?"

"I do," said Autumn.

Nolan nodded.

The video showed Gene looking haggard and terrified. He explained that he'd wanted to warn Nuna and had left a message when he found the cabin empty, the door unlocked. He'd wanted to speak with Nuna in person so he'd gone back one more time to make sure he got the message, but before he got to the cabin, he learned from a kid and his mother, along with a couple of angry huskies leaving the area where Nuna's cabin was, that something was wrong. He feared the worst, so he decided to bide his time at the lodge with his coresearchers until he could escape. He'd chartered a boat to take him away and had planned to have his things shipped to him, though he never returned to his home address.

Nolan leaned in closer as Gene was asked about the information he and Nuna were hiding. He licked his lips, clearly debating if he should share everything, but the interviewer prodded him with the fact that the interested party—the Department of Energy—already knew much of it.

Nolan thought about Carl's claim that he had been an undercover agent sent to monitor the situation. But Carl had not been tasked with killing Nuna, or with framing Otto by using his knife, so he would be facing charges. Nolan focused back on the interview.

Gene nodded and spoke in his scientific language about the tens of thousands of previously unknown pathogens—viruses and bacteria—being unleashed in the melting ice. New and never before catalogued microbes.

He continued. "In glacial ice, researchers have discovered smallpox, still intact, and the Spanish flu viruses in frozen tissue. We've learned that pathogens can be preserved in frozen tissue and still cause an outbreak, like what happened in Siberia several years ago." Gene licked his lips again. "Surely you read about the anthrax from a frozen reindeer carcass that had thawed in the melting ice."

"Nuna and I traveled to the"—he glanced up at the camera in the corner—"the location, and we made sure to wear hazard suits as we gathered samples. We discreetly hired a virologist and microbiologist to assist us in determining the pathogen. I hope . . . I hope she's okay. She didn't complete her study—it takes a long time. But we still know it's lethal."

Gene drank from the glass of water offered. "Then Dr. Grainger—Nuna—started getting inquiries about his work. He felt uncomfortable with the line of questioning. In our search for answers and our multiple scientific studies, my emphasis on ecology and the environment, we returned and took glacial ice sample cores and then used ground penetrating radar and discovered the meteorite. We put together a small team that included a geophysicist, and he brought LIDAR and hyperspectral imaging." He sighed. "That was our mistake."

"Why do you say that?" the interviewer asked.

"The government is laser-focused on finding the necessary minerals we need to fuel technology, the military. Our biggest threat is disruptions in the supply chain, and unfriendly countries own the majority of the minerals we need."

"You're saying the meteorite includes needed minerals, and finding those is a mistake?"

"I'm saying that we need to use all precaution." Gene looked away. "We can't afford to unleash a pathogen we know so little about, even to secure the needed minerals. We dispersed as a team, returned home to formulate a plan on how to handle a situation that could get out of hand quickly and maybe already had. Then one by one, each member of the team disappeared or mysteriously died."

"Except for you and the virologist, Dr. Penn."

"Am I going to die now?"

"Of course not, Dr. Whitlock."

Nolan leaned forward. Gene was still terrified, and rightly so. Grier turned off the footage and sighed.

"What does any of that mean?" Autumn asked. "Are we in danger of them exploiting this information, risking more lives?"

"I think—I hope—that we're in a good place. Dr. Whitlock has been offered a position and included in the project to study the pathogen and provide insight into the region as it pertains to his specialties. He has been assured that the Department of Energy will not be excavating the meteorite . . . for now. Their hands are tied at the moment, anyway, considering the local tribe created a sacred burial ground over the area where the excavation would need to happen, as if their ancestors somehow knew that future laws would protect them."

Autumn released a heavy sigh. "Well, that's something. I hear Danna is returning with her grandmother now that she's no longer in danger. But it's sad that they won't get the money for the manuscript."

"Oh. That's what I forgot." Grier moved to a pack and tugged out the big plastic packet. "Copies have been made, just so you know." He handed it over to Nolan.

"It isn't needed for evidence?" he asked.

"Not anymore. Sensitive parts have been removed, so you'll find pages missing."

"Well," Nolan said. "It belongs to Alina."

"And you can deliver it to her. Oh, and on another note, you'll be glad to know that Novak has been arrested in Juneau. Victus, however, is still at large. We'll get him, though."

Nolan was relieved to hear that news. Grier tugged out a small gun that Nolan recognized.

"Baby," Nolan said. "Ivy's baby Glock."

"Nolan." Autumn sat up. "This would be the perfect excuse you need to go to Florida. You need to find Ivy. Do what you were going to do on your vacation before it was ruined."

"I . . . can't go. What would I say?"

"You could tell her that you love her," she said.

"And what would we do next?" Nolan asked.

"Look, Nolan." Grier stood. "I come from a different world than Autumn, a different place, but we figured out a way to make it work. And you will too. You just need to say those three little words. I saw the two of you together. It's apparent the feelings are mutual."

"And what if that means I end up living in Florida?" Could he do it? Could he really give this place up? Give his family up? Yes . . . yes, he could. If that meant being with Ivy. And suddenly his heart was light again . . . but Ivy might feel differently.

"Come on, Nolan," Grier said. "Ivy is worth it, isn't she? You risked your life to pull her from the water. Jay told me all about it."

And Ivy had saved him, too, now that he thought about it. He'd saved the woman this time, pulling her from the ice. That image, that memory, washed away the trauma of his past failure. The realization left him feeling free. The heaviness was gone. Ivy's presence in his life had changed him more than he realized.

FORTY-FIVE

Lying on the chaise lounge on the beach, Ivy kept her eyes closed behind sunglasses and soaked up the sunshine. Since it was only March, she wasn't getting in the water—that would be too cold for her. Especially after her dunk in the frigid lake in Alaska.

Just her and Mom on the beach now drinking their nonalcoholic piña coladas. The shop was closed on Sundays, and she and her mother needed this break, this time to spend doing nothing at all but hanging out. They needed to celebrate that Mom had a clean bill of health.

Ivy imagined Alaska's white-frosted mountains and spruce trees heavy with snow. The place had struck a deep chord in her heart, and she couldn't shake the feeling that was growing inside.

"Tell me about the girl you mentioned," Mom said. "Danna."

Just like her mother to hear something in Ivy's voice as she'd given her the CliffsNotes version of her adventure. "I wanted to find her because she reminded me of Grace."

"And you thought that finding her would redeem you."

"Yes, but in the end, I didn't find her." Then again, maybe she had. She'd been the one to suggest that Danna and Alina were with Hank, so she'd found Danna for the others.

"Did it work?"

"What do you mean?"

"Do you feel redeemed, Ivy? Because you know, in truth, there's only one who can redeem, and he has already paid the price."

She smiled to herself, then sighed with contentment. "Yes, Mother. I've let it go." And she'd made peace with herself and God regarding killing Danny in front of his daughter, Natalie, but she wouldn't share that story with Mom. One sad story was enough.

"Good, because I've let something go too," Mom said.

"Oh? What's that?" But Ivy suspected she knew.

"The shop. I'm putting the place up for sale. Doesn't mean that I can't dabble in searching for rare books or selling them. But that'll be on my own time. You could join me. Maybe you could even be a book detective."

"A *book* detective?" Ivy laughed.

"You're clearly experienced," Mom said. "And we can go back to Alaska and visit your hero. I know you want to, Ivy. I see that dreamy look in your eyes."

Leaning back against the chaise lounge, Ivy closed her eyes and pictured her hero, as Mom had called Nolan. Ivy missed him so much, and she hadn't been able to stop thinking about him.

"Let's say that I love him. Yes, okay, sure, I'll admit that. And let's pretend for a minute that he loves me. How do we make this work?" She frowned, her mother's suggestion disturbing her peace when she thought she'd already made peace with living in Florida, *without* Nolan.

"What if you don't have to pretend anymore?"

The familiar voice shocked her. Sent thrills through her. She was dreaming and had to shake it off. Opening her eyes, she bolted from the chaise lounge, knocking her piña colada all over herself.

And all over . . . "Nolan? What are you doing here?" Sitting in her mother's chaise lounge, no less. Mom waved from a distance where she spoke with Myrtle, who must have been the one to deliver Nolan. How else would he have found them?

Nolan stood and wiped his hands down his shirt, but he couldn't free himself of the sticky, sweet drink. Still, he stepped forward and smiled.

"What are you doing here?" she asked again.

"I . . . I . . . uh . . . I came to tell you that I returned the manuscript to Alina—with a few missing pages, that is."

"Missing pages?"

"The powers that be wanted to keep the entire manuscript but finally settled on simply protecting the location of the site, at least for now, by removing the sensitive pages."

Fair enough. "I'm surprised they agreed to that much. You were right to give it to Alina. She's the rightful owner and might decide to keep it." He could have told her this with a call.

He angled his head and smiled. "She'll sell it to you if you still want it."

"Then we'll keep our commitment to buy. Right, Mom?" Ivy knew Mom was listening to this entire exchange.

"Oh, and I brought Baby," he said. "I left your gun in Myrtle's car, though."

She sucked in a breath. "You did? Oh, thank you!"

She took in Nolan's handsome form. He wore jeans and a T-shirt stretched tight across his chest, looking better than she remembered. How was that possible? More than anything, she wanted to step into his arms and find out if he missed her too. But . . . not yet. "Why are you here, really?" Oh, she could have worded that so much better. "I'm glad to see you, Nolan. But you didn't have to travel all this way just to tell me the news."

A few heartbeats ticked by before he answered. "Earlier you mentioned pretending that I love you. You don't have to pretend, Ivy, because I *do* love you." He stepped closer. "I let you get away from me twice. I'm here to try to convince you we need to be together." He leaned in, hesitantly, as if making sure she wasn't going to push him away or slap him.

Honestly, she was in too much shock to react at all. Except, well, she closed the distance, and grabbed him by the collar, pulling him forward so she could kiss him senseless. The smell of him drove her crazy, and all the visions from their adventures rushed back to her. "I love you too, Nolan Long."

Mom and Myrtle clapped, but Ivy ignored them. Then when she ended the kiss, she stepped back and squinted as she stared up into his cleanly shaved but still rugged face. He wore sunglasses, too, so she couldn't see his eyes or read them.

"I know what you're thinking, Ivy. You want to know how we can make this work. You're worth it to me, and I'll move here to be with you. All you have to do is say one word."

One word? She couldn't breathe.

He got down on one knee in the sand and tugged his sunglasses off. Squinting up at her, he offered up an open bluevelvet box with a beautiful solitaire diamond ring. "Ivy Elliott, will you marry me? If it's too fast, too much for you, I understand. We can have a long engagement while we figure it out. But I didn't want to hold back. I wanted you to know how I feel about you."

She had not been expecting that, and dizziness rushed over her. "I don't know what to say."

The one word . . .

Nolan had taken a big risk coming all this way to tell her that he loved her enough to give up all he knew to be with her in an environment probably hostile to someone from Alaska.

She couldn't help the big smile that spread over her lips. Her heart was bursting with joy. "Jack London once said, 'The proper function of man is to live, not to exist. I shall not waste my days in trying to prolong them. I shall use my time.'" She tried to read his expression. "As for me, I'm not going to waste my days merely existing without you, Nolan. I want to live my life with you. *Yes* is the one word. Yes, I'll marry you, Nolan."

He stood, then removed the ring from the box to slide it on her finger but dropped it in the sand. They both fell to their knees and started searching. Where had it gone? Then they bumped heads.

Ivy started laughing and then Nolan laughed and wrestled her to the ground. Then he revealed that he'd found the ring. He slipped it on her finger and gently kissed her on the beach. "Who would have thought we'd be lying in the warm sand getting engaged? I admit, I kind of dreamed about it on the flight here. I didn't want to waste another minute, or let you get away this time. I want you forever."

"Forever sounds nice. And impulsive." She laughed. "But we'll figure it out, Nolan. Let's start in Alaska, figuring it out there together. Maybe Mom could come, too, on her own adventure. I'm going to be a book detective, so I might need to travel."

So much love filled his blue eyes. "Sounds like you've already given this some thought."

"I have. If you hadn't shown up here today, then I think I would have come to Alaska for you. I couldn't stop thinking about the man I love. You're my hero, Nolan."

"And you're mine, Ivy. You saved me in ways I can't explain. I love you, and I look forward to a lifetime of showing you just how much." His grin sent tingles over her.

Smiling, she pulled him close and shared a kiss with him again as waves rushed around them with the rising tide, leaving them chilled from the cold seawater and laughing with the sheer joy of a future filled with love.

AUTHOR'S NOTE

Alaska is commonly referred to as the land of the lost, and so my Missing in Alaska series has focused on finding lost and missing people. But in this last installment of the series, I wanted to add some*thing* that had been lost—and a Jack London manuscript was the perfect answer! I fell in love with his novel *The Call of the Wild* when we were required to read it in middle school. We were tasked with a creative project that would bring to life a favorite aspect of the story, and I created an oil painting of the main character, Buck, which I gifted to my teacher. Fast-forward several decades—my brainstorming friends (whom I'll acknowledge in the appropriate section) tossed me the idea of a lost Jack London manuscript, and, of course, I was all over that!

As I researched London's story, I was surprised to find myself inspired by his writing journey. London's is the proverbial rags-to-riches story. My tale of the lost manuscript that he wrote when he came back to Alaska is complete fiction. As far as I know, he never returned to Alaska after his time searching for gold.

Here are the facts: At one point, he lived on the streets of San Francisco but eventually joined in the search for gold, traveling across the brutal land of Alaska to the Klondike. But London never made it all the way to Dawson City; instead, he wintered in a cabin where he almost died, and he returned to California as soon as winter gave way to spring. He never found riches in Alaska, but he turned his experiences into gold.

"It was in the Klondike," London said, "that I found myself. There nobody talks. Everybody thinks. There you get your perspective. I got mine."[1]

In California, he tried his hand at writing and became a literal starving artist before his stories about his experiences in life, and especially in Alaska, finally began to provide him a living. When *The Call of the Wild* took off, he became the first writer to become a millionaire and, surprisingly, at the young age of twenty-seven. Setting aside his various questionable ideologies that, like those of many intellectuals of that period, were shaped by the time in which he lived, I was inspired by his work ethic and discipline of writing one thousand words a day until he achieved his goals of success. He received at least six hundred rejections, and yet he never quit. He has inspired generations of writers who credit him for their inspiration and the commitment to continue and answer the call to write. Supposedly, he brought to life the adventure fiction genre. Maybe *The Call of the Wild* is the true inspiration behind my love of writing adventure stories.

He was only forty when he died, and in that way—at least to me—he truly was a shooting star per his statement, considered to be his credo:

> I would rather be ashes than dust. I would rather that my spark should burn out in a brilliant blaze than it should be stifled by dry-rot. I would rather be a superb meteor, every atom of me in magnificent glow, than a sleepy and permanent planet. The

1. Jack London, quoted in Michael Gates, "Jack London Stories Filled with Yukon History," *Yukon News*, June 30, 2016, yukon-news.com/letters-opinions /jack-london-stories-filled-with-yukon-history-6993945#.

proper function of man is to live, not to exist. I shall not waste my days in trying to prolong them. I shall use my time.[2]

All this to say that, as my novel unfolded and took my characters in a surprising direction, I struggled for a way to keep the lost London manuscript as a key element in the story and considered that it might need to simply be a subplot. As most writers I know regularly experience, I was in the middle of a mundane task when—out of nowhere—the answer hit me. I knew exactly how to incorporate my fictional lost Jack London manuscript into a vital part of this adventure story set in Alaska.

I hope you enjoyed the story and that you'll join me in my next romantic suspense series!

Elizabeth Goddard

2. Jack London, *Tales of Adventure*, ed. Irving Shepard (Garden City, NY: Hanover House, 1956), vii.

ACKNOWLEDGMENTS

This last installment of the Missing in Alaska series has been so incredibly fun to write. I greatly appreciate my brainstorming friends who tossed me the idea to use a lost manuscript. My sincere gratitude goes to Chawna, Michelle, Sharon, Lisa, Shannon, Susan, Lynette, and so many more writing friends for your ideas and encouragement and support through these many years. I'm so glad God brought us together on this journey!

My very special thanks to Sergeant Bryce Weight, Alaska Department of Public Safety, for answering my questions regarding the Alaska State Troopers and providing the kinds of details that make stories come alive. Thanks to Commissioner Cockrell for providing permission for my use of the Alaska State Troopers Creed, as well as AST Communications Director, Austin McDaniel, who provided that the creed is also in the public domain. Lieutenant Mike Roberts wrote the creed in early 2014, and the Alaska State Troopers adopted it.

To Wesley Harris—you've been so good to answer my police procedural questions—even if I send them two days before my deadline. Thank you!

To my family—my kids, Rachel (and husband, Patric), Christopher, Jonathan, and Andrew, and my husband, Dan—

thank you for cheering me on and for the joy and laughter you bring to my life. Gabriel and Penn—you make my heart sing!

To my Revell team—I'll say it again—you guys are the absolute best publishing team on the planet, and I'm so blessed to be working with you.

To Steve Laube—dreams really do come true. Thank you for believing in this writer in my very early days.

To Jesus Christ—thank you for being my Lord and Savior and for walking with me, guiding me, being with me every step of the way.

Turn the page for a
sneak peek at the next
thrilling series from
ELIZABETH GODDARD!

Time was short.

And Paco was missing.

The storm system of the decade bore down on the Washington coast, and Remi Grant was right in its path on a beach battered by waves during what was projected to be a king tide.

Oh, she knew better. But . . .

"Paco! Where are you?" She doubted her shouts could be heard over the breakers lashing the shore, crashing into the rocks.

The expected heavy rain hadn't started yet, but the wind remained cold, constant, and strong.

Sea stacks dotted the beach, and a rocky outcropping blocked her path as the tide rushed in, rising too quickly for comfort.

The only way around was to wait for the breakers to subside. Another wave crashed against the formation, then slinked back beneath the next one rolling in, building momentum.

Now!

She rushed around the mass of rocks, her efforts slowed by wet sand packed with rocks, barnacles, and shells. Beach Safety 101—never turn your back on the waves. But Remi did just that as she ran toward the bluff while simultaneously watching her steps along the rock-studded beach. Twisting her ankle or falling could be a death sentence.

Behind her, the roar of the sea resounded in her ears, filling her with fear. The ocean was closing in on her, and the beach would be gone in minutes.

The Pacific wouldn't take her today. Not if she had anything to do with it.

She made it to the dry beach—what was left of it—and that's when she heard the smallest of cries. Given the thunderous waves echoing against the cliff, she was surprised she'd heard anything else. Heavy sea spray doused her, but she'd expect no less from the approaching ferocious monster.

Heart pounding, she moved along the cliff, searching for the small pooch. *He must be frozen in terror.* Remi had to find him in time, for both their sakes.

She always expected the unexpected. And while she waited for the unexpected, she planned everything to the last detail. She'd prepared for the storm system of the decade, but she hadn't expected a guest from Texas to lose their lapdog on a dangerous beach as a storm moved in, eventually bringing mammoth twenty-foot-or-more waves.

"Paco! Come on, boy. Where are you?"

In response, she heard nothing but the angry surf, best enjoyed from a distance during a storm, which was just the setting her lodge on the bluff provided. She couldn't return without the Yorkshire terrier. Remi shouldn't be on the beach now—no one should—but here she was, headed north and away from the safety of the lodge.

Where could he be?

He probably would have hunkered as far away from the encroaching Pacific Ocean as he could get. She hurried along the cliff, looking into the crevices and around small piles of rocks and tumbles of driftwood. In this mess, she might never find him.

"Paco! Where are you?" Could he even hear her? If he did, would he trust a stranger with his fate? "Come on, boy . . ." she mumbled to herself.

Concern for the small creature chased her, but she wouldn't entertain the strong possibility that he might already have been swept out to sea.

And there . . .

Huddled in the smallest of alcoves at the base of the cliff face, Paco shivered. Though time was running out, she approached slowly so he wouldn't feel more threatened. If the dog ran away from her, escaping her efforts, then she wouldn't have enough time to find and save him.

Salt water rushed toward her, reaching farther with each crashing breaker.

God help me. I'm out of time.

Crouching, she continued forward, wishing she'd brought a treat. "I know you're scared. I am too. But let me get us out of this."

Trembling, cold, and wet, he shrank against the porous bedrock, deeper into the small recess. Then Paco sprang from his hiding place and dashed between her and the rocks, his short legs carrying him faster than she would have thought. Except he was in survival mode, adrenaline fueling his doomed getaway.

But it also fueled Remi, and with everything in her, she reached out for Paco.

But he slipped away. "No!" She raced after him as more salty water rushed toward them. "Paco, come back." *You're going to die if you don't!*

He slowed, turning back in fear as the tide chased them.

His hesitation gave her the chance she needed. She sprang forward and snatched him, careful not to crush his small body while still maintaining her grip. Barking and biting, he tried to wriggle free, his sharp little teeth sinking into her thumb, but she ignored the pain and held him against her. "I've got you. It's going to be okay."

Rushing forward out of the water's reach, she gently tucked Paco inside her heavy raincoat to keep him warm. The terrier seemed to finally trust her, or he succumbed to exhaustion, but either way, he settled against her inside the coat. His trembling form reminded her of her own predicament.

Their predicament.

Remi pressed her back against the cliff, then raced toward the rocky outcropping that could trap her and block her escape to the staircase up to the lodge at the top of the bluff. Waves washed back out to the ocean, but she saw now what she'd feared. The tide had already come in, blocking her way to the steps to safety.

So she turned and headed north in search of a place on the cliff where she could find traction and climb higher. Rescue crews would be hard-pressed to reach her in time out here, and she couldn't afford to wait for help.

Her radio squawked. She fished it out of her pocket. "I got him. I just need a way out."

"Use Jo's ladder!" Harmony's voice sounded garbled over the radio.

"Roger that."

Remi had never found a need to use the rope ladder Jo had secured at the end of the campsites in case of an emergency until they could build another set of actual steps. But they'd always been adamant about when the beach was safe and when it was not safe, especially in the winter months during the storms that people came to the lodge to watch. Today, someone had violated those rules.

Paco squirmed inside her jacket, and she continued to speak to him in soothing tones. The cold wind knocked into her, bringing salty, cold spray along with it, as she jogged forward. Polished rocks—large and small—made up most of the beach and were a tripping hazard if she didn't watch where she stepped. Half jogging, half slow-stepping, she made her way to a patch of wet, gray sand.

She should almost be near where the campsite ended on top of the bluff, and she paused to stare up the cliff face. Jagged edges melded with patches of dirt and bedrock, and at the top, loamy earth and thick evergreens. In places along the coast, the cliffs were as high as a hundred and fifty feet. Here, it was half that. Still . . .

Tidewater rushed around her ankles, reminding her that time was slipping away, along with her way out of this.

There . . .

She spotted the marine rope ladder that Jo had secured for the unfortunate scenario of getting trapped by the tide. Her heart jumped with hope.

But to get to the ladder, Remi had to traverse significant piles of driftwood stacked against the cliff. Sighing, she rushed forward, weaving her way around the large, pale tree trunks, some of them massive, which meant she'd have to climb over them. She stepped over one driftwood log after another, slid down between two larger ones, then crawled over the last log.

Once the water started rushing in, she'd have more to worry about than sneaker waves or breakers that could smash her against these rocks. She would be crushed by the driftwood.

She stood at the bottom of the cliff and looked up.

That Jo had assembled a rope ladder to span the distance was impressive, but it didn't hang low enough for Remi to reach.

She peeked inside her coat. "I'm going to need you to stay still, okay?" He wasn't going to like it but she had no choice. She secured him in the inside pocket of her coat, grateful he was small enough, and zipped it closed. Then she tightened the bottom of her jacket, zipped it completely up to her neck, and secured the snap, then pulled her hood tighter—all of this just in case he clawed or chewed his way out of her pocket.

"Hold on, Paco." She jumped for the rope.

Jumped again.

Then she pulled a small chunk of driftwood over and balanced on it. Just one last jump. She reached with both hands and caught the bottom rung. Then pulled on it and walked along the rocks until she could gain traction with one foot, then the other.

Calisthenics. She'd done her share of them in the past, but clearly, she needed to beef up her exercise routine. Muscles straining, she climbed the ladder, which she realized didn't have anchor points. Once she got out of this, she and Jo would have a long talk.

"Hang in there. I'm climbing this ladder, Paco, and before you know it, you'll be safe in your momma's arms."

Despite the cold temps and buffeting winds, sweat trickled down the middle of her back. She was halfway there.

We're going to make it.

The ladder suddenly dropped a few inches. Her heart rate jumped.

Pulse soaring, eyes shut, she held on as the rope swung out and slapped against the bedrock. At least it had held.

Holding on tight, she stared up. What was going on? No time to ponder that question. This thing was slipping for some reason she couldn't fathom. She gripped the rope. Stepped on another rung, pushing through the fear of falling and breaking her body against the rocks or driftwood.

Don't look down. Don't look down.

Remi looked down.

Mistake. Big mistake.

The tide had come in hard and fast, and seawater rushed against the cliff directly below her. Driftwood shifted and moved with the force of nature. Her heart clamored against her ribs. Remi once again squeezed her eyes shut, the sound of her pounding heart overpowering the waves.

You can do this. Just keep going.

One hand on the rope, she reached for the next rung, but it broke in half, leaving her pawing the air. Her palms slicked as she found the rope again and held on for dear life.

Caught her breath.

Paco whined. She could feel his body quivering in her pocket. "It's okay, buddy. I've got you."

The words came out breathy.

And you've got me, God.

She just had to focus and climb. She'd be up on top soon. Otherwise, she'd be swept away, lost forever.

Like the big hole in her life that left her unsure who she could trust, wary of everyone. And beyond this cliff, once she made it—and she would—she knew that time was running out for her. She could feel it.

But she could only worry about one crisis at a time as she continued climbing the failing ladder. She should be nearing the top. Ten feet.

Eight feet.

Five feet.

Four . . .

She looked at the last three rungs. Broken. She saw the crack in each of them. They wouldn't hold her weight. She'd just have to pull from all her past training and climb the rope instead. Hope for the best.

Remi glanced up, focusing on what must be done. She started climbing and realized that the rope had been shredded.

She literally hung by a thread.

Her chest constricted. All the air whooshed out of her.

What am I going to do?

With the next crash of waves, she could have sworn she heard a voice. Had she imagined it? Desperation fooling her mind? But she glanced up again, searching, hoping.

Hands reached for her. A stranger with steel-blue eyes stared down at her.

"Grab my hands now before it's too late."

"What . . . ?" Her throat constricted.

"You're going to die if you don't take my hands now."

Images suddenly crashed into her mind, paralyzing her, blinding her, then she was somewhere . . . hot, dry . . . somewhere else.

A breaker lashed hard against the cliff, bringing her back to the present. The rope thrashed with the impact. The thread broke. Remi reached for his hands and missed. Once again she pawed the air.

Fear paralyzed her.

I'm going to die!

But the man caught her wrist.

Below her, the rope ladder tumbled down the cliff, leaving her feet dangling.

Now a stranger held her life in his hands.

Elizabeth Goddard is the *USA Today* bestselling and award-winning author of more than sixty novels, including *Cold Light of Day* and *Shadows at Dusk*, as well as the Rocky Mountain Courage and Uncommon Justice series. Her books have sold nearly 1.5 million copies. She is a Carol Award and Reader's Choice Award winner and a Daphne du Maurier Award and HOLT Medallion finalist. When she's not writing, she loves spending time with her family, traveling to find inspiration for her next book, and serving with her husband in ministry. Learn more at ElizabethGoddard.com.

Uncover the Secrets of the North in the
MISSING IN ALASKA Series

"A must-read for every romantic suspense reader. Goddard's novels keep getting better and better."—DiAnn Mills, author of *Concrete Evidence*, on *Cold Light of Day*

Check Out Elizabeth Goddard's
Can't-Miss Series
Uncommon Justice

"Unique and intriguing romantic suspense that will have your heart racing. Goddard's fast-paced storytelling combined with emotional depth will keep you guessing until the very end."

—RACHEL DYLAN,
bestselling author of the Atlanta Justice series

a division of Baker Publishing Group
RevellBooks.com

 Available wherever books and ebooks are sold.